The Event

By

I G Lepist

Copyright © 2025 I G Lepist

ISBN: 978-1-917778-34-3

All rights reserved, including the right to reproduce this book, or portions thereof in any form. No part of this text may be reproduced, transmitted, downloaded, decompiled, reverse engineered, or stored, in any form or introduced into any information storage and retrieval system, in any form or by any means, whether electronic or mechanical without the express written permission of the author.

Prikat, Uzbekistan – Central Asia. Some miles out into a mountainous wine region.

Day 1 Friday
10 am (GMT + 5) February 17th, 2023

He sat at the farmhouse table, his back to the window, facing into the gloom. It was poky, he thought, and cluttered. The bookcase next to him was piled high with stuff he couldn't be bothered to deal with – unopened mail, some dirty dishes, and a vase of very dead flowers.

The water had evaporated so long ago it had left a dark green residue and tidemark.

The miniature Ukrainian flag hanging from its stand was faded and dusty alongside the painted wooden lady in national costume. Once significant and precious to him, they now looked tawdry. His guitar was also thick with dust on its shoulders. The idea of playing it, breaking the miserable silence, made him feel squeamish.

It seemed his presence in the house was diminishing. His body was taking up room and there seemed little point in it and his stuff being there. Familiarity had definitely bred contempt. He hated the place.

Caught in limbo, between dead and alive, he was indifferent, feeling nothing about anything. His pulse and heart rate today felt so slow and indeterminable, he hoped it would just stop. Somewhere, he'd read that indigenous people in Australia could switch themselves off by autosuggestion. Sitting there for long enough, without moving, perhaps he could do the same.

His dog Misha, an exceptionally large black and tan, long-haired German Shepherd sauntered over and rested her chin on his thigh and looked up at him appealingly. She wagged her tail which rocked her whole body side to side.

A lump immediately came to his throat as he looked into her hopeful eyes. He couldn't contain it. He broke and started to cry. His big shoulders shook and then he sobbed and sobbed, noisily and unrestrainedly. The pain and sadness ached so much; it was driving him to insanity. He couldn't stand it.

The dog was distressed and he apologised, rubbing her ears as big tears and snot plopped into her fur. Bending down, he buried his face into her neck.

One reason to be alive. He felt bad that he had not considered her.

And then the moment was over. Grabbing a napkin, he blew his nose and stuffed it into the pocket of his fleece jacket. He placed his large brown hands out flat on the table, feeling the surface contact his skin and then pushed himself up, which dragged the chair backwards, grating behind him across the stone floor. He winced. It did it every time. He would have to do something about it.

Misha followed him to the door. She was a former police trainee cadaver dog that had failed her exams and also proved to be an ineffective guard dog – too friendly.

Something compelled him to get out of the house.

He had to duck on the way out (being so tall), but left the door open, despite the freezing cold, to release the misery trapped inside. His and Misha's warm breath formed smoke-like clouds around them in the bitter air. It was minus two degrees.

He strode over to his gateway which was formed by two mounds of stones a few feet high. These were attached to tumbledown stone walls, forming a perimeter of a large, neglected garden and orchard. This hadn't been repaired since the last major earthquake.

The farm was situated on high ground surrounded by hills, with a view of snow-capped mountains in the near distance, so any tremors were rarely felt. The river took snowmelt and rainwater gently down-hill about one hundred meters away. One small but very steep mountain of rock and black leafless trees loomed on the other side of the river, casting a shadow. This would eventually creep around to plunge the farmhouse into darkness and cause it to drop temperature quite dramatically at that time of year.

He heard the truck before Misha did, spying the black Mitsubishi Shogun through the trees down the track two hundred metres away. It was progressing slowly, bouncing up and down because of the potholes and flooding from the previous day's torrential rain. The track was private and led only to him – there was no other reason for them to be there.

By this time he was out in the open. He felt defenceless with no weapon and no cover to speak of, but he didn't run. They'd finally come for him, he thought. Standing with his hands in his pockets he looked up at the sky.

So, today is the day.

He could feel his heart now. It was banging against the inside of his jacket and the din had reached his ears.

The Shogun stopped about twenty metres away from his gateway. No-one materialised for what felt like ten minutes but was probably only two. He was becoming impatient.

Get on with it then.

The door finally opened. He could see a figure's legs behind the door. It stepped back and pushed it shut.

It was a woman.

His shoulders relaxed a bit, but then he chastised himself; a woman is not necessarily any less of a threat than a man.

She turned round to face his direction and walked towards him. Her hair was thick and a cloudlike mass of coppery corkscrew curls, whipping into her face in the wind. He observed she was probably late twenties, early thirties, of average height and build, dressed in a green wax jacket, black walking trousers and boots. Her features came more into view. He narrowed his eyes to get a clearer picture. First impression – she wasn't a local. Curly hair was uncommon.

Misha bounded over to greet her. She was met with equal enthusiasm. The woman went down on her knee to make a fuss. Misha looked back at him with her tongue hanging out, as if grinning with approval.

The woman got back up.

'Good morning. Sorry to trouble you. I wondered if you could help...'

She spoke Russian like a local, so he was confused when she asked equally fluently:
'You don't by any chance speak English?'
'Do you?' he replied puzzled, in the same language.
'Yes...because I am English,' she answered in English, smiling broadly. 'My Russian is pretty rubbish.'
I bet it isn't, he thought. She waved her hands, one of which held a map to make the universal sign for – *I have no idea where I am.*
'I'm lost,' she said.
'That makes two of us.' He took himself by surprise. He hadn't meant to say it out loud.
His English was almost perfect, with a distinct Ukrainian accent.
He noticed her eyes. Very light golden brown. Amber was what came to mind. Unusual, he thought.
Her face appeared concerned, appearing to study him carefully.
'I think perhaps I've come at a bad time...'
He paused. He wasn't sure what she meant. Then, remembering, he very quickly wiped his face, still wet with tears, with his hand. He supposed his eyes would still be red.
She started to walk slowly backwards.
'No – don't go.' *Shit.* That sounded desperate, he thought and exhaled sharply. He reached his hand out and pointed to her map. 'Where do you need to be?'
Her face brightened as she walked back to stand next to him. She smoothed out the map resting it on top of the stones. He tried to get a good look at her, but then she patted her head and pockets, tutted and rolled her eyes.
'I've left my bloody glasses in the car. Sorry. Can you hang on a sec while I go and get them?'
He smiled, feeling his face crease again. It hadn't done it for so long. He shrugged his shoulders a little.
'It's fine...take your time.'
He kept Misha to heel and watched her walk away. Manchester. Definitely Manchester, he thought, but not very strong. When he'd worked in the oil industry, he'd led a team

briefly in Aberdeen. The head of the Project Management Office was from Eccles and this woman sounded just like him. He'd learned that when this guy reported in – 'things weren't going quite according to plan,' or were – 'a bit of a pain', this actually meant; it was a complete and total Clusterfuck.

He'd decided he liked her but then remembered he shouldn't. He had to consider if it really was her glasses she was going back for.

He couldn't tell if she had retrieved what she was looking for, when she stepped back to shut the door. At that same moment, an echoing crack split the air.

He instinctively ducked, diving behind the gate post, remembering he had no weapon to return fire. He peered tentatively round. It took a while for his brain to compute. He stared, having to blink two or three times. A tree was speedily making its way down the mountainside.

Misha barked at it, like she was rabid.

'Run!' he roared toward the woman, but she wouldn't have heard him.

There was an exploding, deep thunderous roar along with a sinister snapping and cracking sound.

From the initial crack it took three seconds for the side of the mountain to slip, crashing into the river below, creating a tsunami of snow, mud and trees, rising up, monstrous and beastlike, with the tail end of it crashing down, hitting the woman and the side of her truck.

She was gone.

He sat back around, leaning against the stones for support, trying to comprehend what had just happened, but there was no time for that.

Default battle mode kicked in. Whether she was an assassin or not, he was driven to get her out.

He scrambled to his feet, leaving the safety of his cover and accepted the fact that a further landslip might mean game over and drowning in mud. A bullet to the head now seemed preferable.

He ran with Misha and began wading and stumbling through the freezing foot-numbing mud, debris and snow, reaching the vehicle. He looked about him, panting and gasping – there was nothing. There were just piles of dirty snow, rocks and tree branches. The truck was now on its side resting on some rocks, still filling up with muddy water.

Misha made high-pitched whining sounds whilst dancing back and forth.

He had a thought. How to set her going? There would be blood and she had been trained to detect homeopathic levels of it. Well-meaning Misha nudged her head under his hand to be petted. He pleaded with her.

'Go find! Fetch. Go on. Please Misha…go!'

She just stood there with her tongue hanging out. He threw his arms in the air.

'Do your fucking job – just this once!'

He bent over to catch his breath, his lungs burning from the cold and observed that the mud had drifted up the underside of the truck, but the trunk was reasonably clear.

His freezing fingers were able to release it and force it open. Just what he was after, a snow shovel. There were also blankets, rope and a jack…she'd come prepared.

Believing that she would most likely have drowned by now, suffocated, or incurred fatal injuries, led him to lose energy suddenly and for the ache of despair to drag him to his knees. People's lives kept slipping through his fingers. He'd be pulling a body, yet again out of the wreckage. Mud, blood. Blood and mud everywhere…

He suddenly snapped out of the desperation that was engulfing him. Misha had given two very loud sharp barks, a tone of bark he'd not heard before. She was ten yards away standing to attention. He grabbed the shovel.

'Are you sure? All the way down here?'

This recovery felt different. He'd made a connection with the woman, albeit briefly, having gained a sense of her energy and life force, he supposed it was. A vision of the copper curls, expressive dark eyebrows and quirky smile came into view.

He'd cast aside the premise that she was an assassin for the moment; too scatty. Or was that misdirection, all part of the honey-trap?

Instead, he toyed with the notion that she had been sent to him – a gift, but God had disallowed it, considering him unworthy, snatching her away. The Rage began to simmer in his stomach over the injustice of it. He would get her back.

***

'I'm not dead then?'

'Not yet,' he replied without thinking, wishing it hadn't come out quite like that.

'My name is Igor,' he announced on hands and knees, attempting to wipe away the mud, bits of foliage and grit from her eyes and mouth with the napkin from his pocket. He had to push Misha out of the way, who was intent on licking the woman's face.

She flickered her eyelids and reached her hands out to touch his face. They were shaking with cold.

'Prince Igor,' she whispered through the shivering.

'No... just Igor.' He pulled her hands away, embarrassed.

'...and so handsome.'

'You must have shit in your eyes,' he snorted. Definitely a bang on the head, he decided.

The words coming out of her mouth now didn't seem to fit with the woman he'd met earlier.

He'd wound up with some sort of Snow-White character. Before, she was... abandoning that thought, Igor moved swiftly to an assessment of the damage and began to check her arms and legs.

'What's your name?' Igor was brusque. Business-like.

'Sophonisba,' she answered, annunciating carefully through the violent shivering.

You're taking the piss, he thought.

'I'm not taking the piss!' Her words were starting to slur. He was pretty sure he hadn't said it out loud. What were her parents thinking?

'Keep talking and do not close your eyes.'

'If you give me a minute...Igor... I'll be on my way.' Her teeth chattered violently as she attempted to hoick herself up on to her elbows. Without success, she slumped back down. He caught the back of her head in his hand.

'Keep still.'

Sophonisba ignored him and tried to bend her knees. On raising her shaking hands, she observed all the mud. Slightly turning her head left and right she looked about her.

'I'm very sorry about the mess… and the inconvenience.'

This made him laugh. A sudden hearty, earthy and infectious laugh which tired him and made his diaphragm hurt. These muscles had not been used for such a long time. It felt good.

'You haven't broken anything, but you're probably concussed and in danger of hypothermia. We must be quick. Do not close your eyes and keep talking,' he scolded. 'I do not want a dead body on my hands,' he muttered.

'You're right,' she said, trying to clear her throat, 'think of the paperwork.'

'I'm going to lift you,' he said, suppressing a smile.

'Please don't. I'm bloody heavy, you'll do your back in.'

He was affronted. Igor was a huge, strong hulk of a man. He would have no problem.

He put one arm under her back and one under her knees and heaved.

'Fucking hell, you're heavy. What is with you?'

'I just am – sorry.' She gave a quiet moan and inhaled through pursed lips, making a hissing sound, and screwed up her eyes.

'I'm sorry, I don't think I can walk it.'

'Will you stop apologising…'

'I'm British…I can't help it – sorry.'

He was partially cross with anxiety but was trying not to laugh.

'I'll have to drag you then.'

The despair began to creep up on him again. He needed to be gentle and avoid jolting her.

She nodded. In the meantime, Misha was agitated, still whining and mithering Igor.

Igor spoke in Ukrainian to Misha, soft reassuring words, stretching one hand out to stroke her under the chin.

He reverted his attention to his patient.

'Right... Sophonisba, are you ready?'

She gave a weak gasping laugh.

'No-one really calls me that. I'm Nisba. Nisba for sh ...' She'd run out of energy.

Igor placed his forearms under her armpits and pulled her around so he could get her up the track. He looked back at his farmhouse. It seemed miles away. Flood water, mud and debris obstructed their path until they reached higher ground where it was clearer. Very gently he placed her back down again and patted her face which was becoming waxy looking. Not a good sign. Igor called out.

'Nisba. Hey...Nisba! Come on.' No response. He had to be able to lift her.

***

That was as far as he could go and, she was right. He'd done his back in and was exhausted and now fearful for her life. He was not looking forward to CPR. He'd done it many times before. There was often the breaking of ribs and chest bones to bring people back. Brutal and ugly; not like in the movies.

Igor dragged Nisba as smoothly as he possibly could the rest of the way and then straight into the house, banging the door back, dragging the rug with them, leaving a trail of mud and lumps of snow along the stone floor. After bumping over the threshold and across the wooden parquet of his bedroom, Igor hauled her up onto the bed. Her clothes were sopping with mud and snow melt.

It was a time when he wished he'd tidied his bedroom. The bed was unmade and he couldn't remember when he'd last changed the sheets. She was creating a wet body shape on his bed.

He pulled back her eyelid and checked her pupils and her pulse. She would be alright but needed warming up, but not too quickly. He patted her cheeks again.

'Can you hear me?'

There was a faint affirmative moan.

'I'm taking your clothes off,' he warned, immediately regretting it, thinking he needed to position this differently.

Misha danced back and forth making deep growling noises.

Igor couldn't pull off her boots. They had been tied properly and went up her ankle. It felt like an eternity getting them unlaced. After peeling off her socks, Igor rubbed each foot hard between his hands. Leaning over to his chest of drawers, he felt around and pulled out a bundle of mountaineering socks. The coat was next. It was difficult to be gentle about this. It felt brutal and dangerous. She didn't complain, which concerned him; less noise usually meant a more serious condition.

There was something in the inside pocket. Maybe some ID. Igor put his hand in and pulled out a plastic zipped-up wallet. Smart he thought. It contained two passports. Raising his eyebrows, he threw them on the bedside cabinet. Maybe he'd rescued his assassin after all. He had checked for a weapon when he first pulled her out of the mud. There was no sign of one in the vehicle either, but he made a mental note to check that properly later.

Igor leaned over her body to unbutton her trousers, needing to move fast. Worryingly, she had stopped shivering.

'I'm taking your trousers off now…alright?' There was no reply. He called out again. Nothing.

Shit. He would just have to get on with it and pulled down the soaked muddy trousers with difficulty, as they were stuck, dragging on her wet, freezing cold skin.

Igor then put her into the socks. They were big and woolly. Kneeling astride her, he attempted to negotiate Nisba's sweater which was plastered to her skin down to the tops of her thighs.

'Nisba...tell me you're still there.' His heart rate was so fast now; it was making him breathless. 'I am going to help you sit up.' He attempted to pull her sweater from the back by the collar but it was stuck to her too much for that. She leaned up against him, her face in his chest.

Misha's anxiety was building. Short sharp barking sounds were hurting Igor's ears. It was distracting.

'Quiet Misha. Please,' he shouted, trying not to sound angry.

'Can you put your arms up?' he asked Nisba. It took quite a while until they were above her head, then she rested her hands on his shoulders to steady herself. He ripped it off up over her muddy head and she fell backwards onto the bed.

Igor wasn't expecting what he saw. He wasn't quite sure what he should have expected, but anyway, this wasn't it. It made his jaw drop.

Satin and lace underwear. Dark bluey green against honey-coloured skin. She was curvy, yet very toned.

Fucking Hell. Maybe he wasn't completely dead after all.

Whilst he was standing there blinking in awe of the view, she suddenly sat up. The panic was almost audible. Her eyes met his. He had seen that look before, finding women after the Russians had been.

The Rage started to stoke again in his chest, followed by a feeling of shame and soon after that – pity.

'I'm not going to hurt you or do anything bad to you,' he urged. 'I don't take advantage of women. Alright? I'm just trying to help you...do you understand?' He floundered around for blankets in the chest of drawers and linen cupboard.

Nisba did not look convinced. She looked about her to pull something up to cover herself, grabbing the muddy coat. Holding it to her chin, she drew up her knees.

By this time, Misha had launched herself onto the bed, squaring up to Igor. He felt under siege. Bewildered, he began to ramble.

'Look...I have a reputation to think about and I don't go around behaving like a fucking animal. You need to get dry and warm so you can recover....and then you can get away.'

He grabbed a towel from the en-suite bathroom radiator and draped it around her shoulders.

It was nice and warm.

'It's nothing I haven't seen before,' he continued. 'I've seen plenty of wounded bodies in my time. Men, women and...he rubbed his head with his hand. 'I'm just going to do what's necessary...do you see?' He paused, out of breath from the adrenaline.

'I can let someone know you're here...if you're worried that I'm some sort of psycho that's going to...'

Igor trailed off and sat on the bed and looked down and around at her. His shoulders sagged. He felt sad that she was afraid of him. Sad that she even had to fear the violation of her body.

'Look.' He reached out to rest his hand on hers as a reassuring gesture but then reconsidered and withdrew it.

'I'm not going to do anything you don't want me to do ...'

There was a pause.

'I believe you,' she said assuredly, nodding slightly.

'That's good,' he responded, patting his thighs. 'They're soaked, so the bra and panties have to come off.' He turned towards her to read her face.

She looked at him ruefully.

'Not on the first date.'

***

The house was old but had a modern open plan layout. Instead of pillars to hold up the roof, Igor had zoned it with partial walls, showing the old stone which he liked, along with chunky robust oak shelving units.

In the snug, there was a fireplace and on the adjacent wall was the front bay window, looking out onto the front garden and mountain beyond. This had a very deep, well-loved looking, tan leather sofa beneath it.

The dining-cum-kitchen area was built with entertaining in mind, even though he wasn't going to be doing any. There was a twelve-seater beech table that he had reclaimed and restored.

Like most projects in the house, he'd thrown himself into the process of rescue and improvement but did not enjoy or bother with the ensuing results. That was, if he got round to finishing it, which he hadn't. He'd lost interest in the house after a minimal effort of fixing only one bedroom. It felt pointless. His job, work relationships, in fact, any kind of relationship, as well as himself, were neglected.

He had toys but didn't play with them. The digital radio wireless speaker in the kitchen area was covered in a film of dust, as was the high-end turntable and amp in the snug. These looked incongruous with the rest of the house, which was rustic and slightly shabby.

He'd gone to significant trouble and expense to have all the utilities, given he was so remote. He was an engineer by profession and could turn his hand to most things. He'd set things up for family living that was never going to happen. He knew this, even when he was doing it. Now he hated it all and was uncomfortable living in it. It always felt dark and the ceiling was too low for his liking. It felt oppressive.

He had resigned himself to being solitary with his dog, remaining in the familiar state of lonely unhappiness.

He wasn't short of opportunities to meet someone if he tried, but he didn't and hoped to remain invisible. He'd lost his libido which meant he had lost everything. There was nothing left. Not even that. He decided he couldn't seek out female companionship because no one was going to put up with a scarred and angry bastard that couldn't get it up.

The woman he'd just rescued though, had said he was handsome. He reflected on this for a minute. In a moment of vulnerability and considerable physical compromise, it was one of the first things she had come out with. But then her judgement would have been considerably impaired, or maybe this was all part of the plan – the play.

He walked up to the full-length mirror on the wall between the bedroom and the main bathroom.

He couldn't stand looking in the mirror usually, sick of the sight of himself. He tried to look objectively, as a third party, and assessed the reflection.

He was six foot three, just teetering, he thought, on the cuddly side of fit and athletic. It had been some weeks since he'd worked out. He was well-built and muscled. He patted his stomach. He had a latent six-pack, but he could get that back fairly quickly, he mused.

He leaned in to examine his face. His father was originally from Uzbekistan and his mother was Ukrainian. He looked like both of them but in different ways. He had a Middle Eastern type of face he thought, always stuck though, with his dark eyebrows in a permanent scowl over Slavic green-blue eyes. The navy-blue ring around the outside edge of his irises meant they were striking against his light brown complexion. All in, he thought that he wouldn't look out of place in a cage fight, outside a nightclub, or cast as a hitman in a violent action movie.

He considered his face to always appear tired. He hadn't had a decent night's sleep in over a year and looked much older than thirty-six. He tilted his chin up and rubbed the stubble. Maybe he should shave, but that would look like he'd made an effort, so he dismissed it. He always had his dark brown hair shaved off to a number one all over. He stepped back and shrugged his shoulders.

If she'd come to kill him, maybe he should just fall for it. There were worse ways to go he pondered, but didn't suppose that there were many targets that would fail miserably at being seduced, owing to a lack of erectile function. He couldn't even manage being murdered with dignity. Scornfully, he laughed at himself, moving off to investigate the food situation.

There was nothing in the fridge or cupboards. He went back to check on his patient.

Having previously helped to remove her clothes, he'd taken her temperature, blood pressure and listened to her heart and lungs. Thankfully, these were all fine. He'd worried about her going into shock and her rapid pulse, so had yoked up IV fluids by hanging the bag on a wire coat-hanger from the wall-lamp. He'd put up a litre on a slow flowrate and would see how she went with that. He didn't want to overload her, so would keep checking.

He'd left Nisba comfortable and lying down in the bed, well wrapped up with the dog lying next to her, peering intently into her eyes. Although Nisba had accepted his dressing gown, she had still insisted on keeping her wet bra and knickers on.

He knocked very gently and pushed the door a couple of inches further ajar. He expected her to be sleeping but wanted to be sure she was decent.

He was taken aback to find that she was sitting on the edge of the bed with her head between her knees, talking to herself. As Nisba came up, her face was white and clammy, keeping her hands over her nose and mouth, breathing slowly and deeply.

Crouching at her feet, Igor waited for a little while, judging when it would be a good time to speak.

'Tell me what it is I can do to help you.'

'I need to phone work,' she whispered. 'They were expecting me and there was stuff I'd said I would do, so that means I've dropped them in the shit.'

'We can do that. We've not found your phone yet, but we can sort it. Is there anyone else I can contact for you?'

Earlier, he'd called his friend and Operations Director, Raj, to coordinate some assistance, which comprised a couple of men and diggers to clear the debris. They were going to try and locate the phone for him. Igor didn't bother in the end about asking them to look for anything else.

He considered Sophonisba to be fragile, anxious, a vulnerable woman in trouble. He did not consider her assassin material He was feeling good about being able to help her.

She turned down the offer of calling any friends or family, which surprised him.

'Do you know your work number…and I'll call them for you.'

Nisba held up her hand.

'Just a second.' On closing her eyes, she paused and then recited the number.

'Please tell Tan Chico that I'm really sorry I missed the session. I'll also help him with the prep for the new project when I'm…'

Turning slowly, Nisba lowered her head to rest on the pillow and closed her eyes.

'Don't worry, I'll call your boss and I'm sure it will be fine. I expect they can manage without you for a week or so,' he offered, trying to sound reassuring.

He'd put the contact details in his phone.

'Get some rest,' Igor said as he walked out of the door. He was already dialling.

The name Nisba had given him had sounded familiar and on hearing Tan Chico's voice, he knew immediately who he was.

Igor remembered spending most of an evening speaking with Tan at a charity event he'd organised in Tashkent a couple of months back. Tan was from Mexico originally and had been brought up in the States hence his American accent. Tan had also worked for oil companies in Houston. Their paths had crossed briefly there.

Tan recognised Igor straightaway and recalled the fundraiser they'd attended.

'I'm phoning on behalf of Nisba…um...' Igor paused, realising he'd not had a chance to look at her passports yet or ask her, so didn't know her last name.

'Nisba! You know where she is? We've been calling and calling.' There was a commotion at the other end of the phone. Igor had to hold it away from his ear it was so loud. He heard several raised voices in the background firing questions at Tan.

'What's happened? We're worried sick about her. We were wondering if we should report her missing.'

Igor had not had time to think about the consequences of the incident, least of all the effect on the people around her. He wasn't very good at that these days. He was relieved though, that he had some sort of confirmation that she was benign. Not a threat.

'I'm pleased to let you know that she is safe and…um, well,' he said.

'Thank God. Thank God. We thought something terrible must have happened, for her not to call or text. We've been out of our minds, worried about what we're going to do without her.'

'What is it that Nisba does for you exactly?'

'She's our CEO.'

It took a moment for Igor to compute this information.

'...And my Business Coach,' Tan added.

Impressive, thought Igor. Then he dropped his head. His unconscious gender bias had let him down again. His sister was always going on about it and now he understood what she meant.

'I see,' said Igor.

'So, what happened?' asked Tan suddenly.

Igor hesitated to allow himself some time to create a suitable version of events.

'She got lost and ended up at mine. And then...got caught in a landslip...'

'A what?'

Igor decided he did not want to relive any of it at that particular moment, so diverted their attention back to Nisba.

'She's with me at the moment; recovering. She has some cuts and bruises. The Prixakent bridge is impassable and the river has burst its banks, so it will be some time before she can get home or ...wherever. The Shogun is out of action for now.'

'Ah. That's our pool car for rural based clients. You'll take good care of her, won't you Igor?'

'I will...I am. Don't worry.' There was a pause.

'You couldn't be holed up with a better person, Igor. She's a great friend and a pleasure to work with.'

'We absolutely love her!' another voice chimed in.

'Yes...yes, that's true,' responded Tan, 'but...I'm just going to step away for a second...go somewhere quieter.'

There was a brief silence.

Tan was back on the line.

'There's something that might be helpful for you to know. I mean I don't think I'm breaking any confidences because she's quite open about it...'

Igor held his breath. Please don't tell me she's gay.

'She has *ADHD* with autistic traits, and there's other stuff as well...'

Igor didn't really know what this meant. He was intrigued and concerned at the same time.

'What do I need to be aware of?'

Tan explained that it wasn't the same for everyone, but Nisba had a combination of traits that weren't immediately obvious. She was a pro at hiding them. One was sensory overload. Going to the supermarket, parties or a meeting even, with audio visual, people talking, having to think and write notes; this was a complete nightmare for Nisba. She often used ear plugs to filter everything out so she could concentrate but had impressive hyper-focus and analytical abilities.

Tan continued. 'I would imagine that she will be extremely stressed about being helpless and out of control. Being hemmed in, stuck in bed and dependent on someone else for her needs...loss of her routine, structure – bad news. Also, that brain of hers is turbo-charged so needs to be stimulated and stretched, otherwise...'

'Otherwise?'

Igor was becoming concerned now that his new house guest might prove to be a handful.

He was struggling to take care of himself, let alone someone else with issues.

'Well...intrusive thoughts that sort of thing. She can get a bit down if she has time on her hands. She swims like a gazillion lengths a week to help with that. And feelings...well, that's the main thing to be wary of. She gets totally overwhelmed. No middle ground, so her coping mechanism is to make out she doesn't have any, using humour – a lot.'

Tan mentioned about no three dimensional spatial awareness, particularly navigating and directions.

No shit.

He was advised not to bother with verbal instructions either – *write them down.*

'...So how the hell does she do the job then? It sounds impossible.'

'It's a struggle but no one can tell,' replied Tan. 'She helps us all play to our strengths, and she plays to hers. But all that high performance and work ethic...she just wants a family, you know...a big brood.'

Tan went on to explain the kind of work that Nisba and he did, until they'd been on the phone for about forty minutes in all.

'Well Igor, I'm sorry the call was under such circumstances. But...'

Igor waited.

'With hindsight, I am glad you two have met...'

Igor could sense that Tan was grinning on the other end of the telephone.

'You're a lucky man,' Tan chuckled. 'Don't blow it!'

Igor rested the phone, screen side down on his knee for a minute and reflected on what he had just learned.

Tan had also confirmed for him that Nisba was single. Apparently – 'she had binned off the dickhead boyfriend the year before.'

Suddenly life had got interesting.

He felt quite honoured to have such a well-loved and impressive guest under his roof but was worried about his ability to take care of her and not make her unfortunate predicament worse.

It sounded very complicated being Nisba.

He needed to go back and check on her. It had been a little while.

The door was still half open. He looked through the gap. Nisba was curled up in the foetal position. Her head was resting directly on the mattress. Igor could just about see that her hands were clenched into fists with the canula free arm underneath her chest, her fist jammed up to her chin.

Misha was lying next to Nisba, resting her head on her paws, earnestly watching for any movement. Misha appeared to have lost interest in him but at times showed there was a conflict between her loyalties. Igor felt a little bereft but found it heart-warming to see the comfort she was offering this intriguing woman.

Nisba looked small, vulnerable and in defence mode. Her hair was still plastered in mud and he observed the congealed and cracking mud on the arm he hadn't cleaned up.

It was hard to imagine, that this sorry looking woman, according to Tan, guided and directed sixty-seven colleagues located around the world, transforming organisations and how their senior leaders behaved and functioned in the workplace.

Tan had told him that she was – 'particularly skilled at breaking down people's negative perception of themselves and creating new thought processes to bring about more positive work and life outcomes…'

It all sounded very corporate, but interesting, and ironic he thought. Maybe, she had been sent by God after all, and he had changed fate.

Thinking about Nisba's achievements and battles, Igor was now feeling a bit of an underperformer. Having been so bogged down in guilt, pain and trauma, he'd overlooked his position of privilege and capabilities. He was not being true to himself.

Igor owned a winery, just under ten thousand acres in total, of vineyard and fruit farm, with the livelihoods of almost three thousand people at stake. He found this a drain and resented the winery, having inherited it from his father.

He could and should do better he thought, suddenly wishing to make room for something more positive and constructive.

He found himself looking forward to Nisba waking up.

She was awake, but he knocked gently.

'Please come in,' Nisba answered, propping herself up with some difficulty.

Igor suddenly felt she was at a disadvantage. He had learned so much about her and all so deeply personal.

'Hey…how are you feeling?'

'I'm fine thank you.' The response showed a brave smile, which he was not convinced by.

'May I take your temperature and blood pressure again?'

She presented her arm for him.

Looking at her intently whilst he worked the sphygmomanometer, he listened.

'You're still a bit fast,' he said.

Nisba explained that she was always a bit fast, living with tachycardia and arrhythmia. She'd forgotten about it.

'What with one thing and another...'

He'd given a nod in acknowledgement. He'd stop the fluids. Nisba went on to ask him about his medical training and how he came to have such an elaborate first-aid kit, but noted he wasn't up for giving much away.

'Field medicine,' he volunteered, quickly changing the subject. 'I spoke to Tan.'

'Oh. Thank you. How is everyone? I hope they're OK. I left Tan in the shit a bit.' Nisba looked down at her hands, sighing with regret.

'All good. They know that you will be out of action for a while and that you are in safe hands. As it happens, I know Tan from a thing in Tashkent last year.'

'Oh...how funny.'

'He and your team speak very highly of you. Anyway...they'll be fine. Tan says you are to take your annual leave. You've broken the carry-over rule...not practising what you preach.'

'Oh blimey, what am I supposed to do with all that? I'll have to find something to do.' She laughed, looking around the rather empty and undecorated room.

They chatted for a while about things they liked doing. He played the guitar and sang. A closet rock-star she had said. He thought that was funny. Nisba laughed at her inability to be really good at any one thing, because she spread herself too thinly: constantly distracted by new interests.

She was also quite emphatic about the fact that she was from Cheshire, not Greater Manchester.

Nisba turned down an offer of food, which was a relief, seeing as there wasn't much in the way of sustenance. She didn't have much of an appetite she'd said.

Igor spent some time venturing to ask the next question.

'How do you feel about having a bath or shower? It can't be comfortable having all that mud in your hair.'

He noted the anxiety grow in her eyes and what they appeared to be saying: How was this going to work? She could barely lift her arms or carry her own weight.

Making the best suggestion he could, she was just about OK with it.

He helped her into the ensuite which was warm and with a walk-in shower. Aiding her with the removal of the dressing gown, Igor observed she was still sporting the underwear she had arrived in. He was working very hard not to look at her body, the texture of her skin…

He threw the gown away onto the little chest of drawers by the sink. He shut Misha out and proceeded to help Nisba sit down in the shower. She sat hugging her knees, appearing to stare into the distance.

'OK…so…' He began to talk her through it, probably more for his own reassurance than hers.

He kept his T-shirt on and having taken off his jeans, this left him in his trunks. He'd thought carefully about it. He would get soaked but that didn't matter.

There was a rain shower head and a handheld which he grabbed. He switched on the shower, running it away from her until it was a nice temperature.

'I'm going to sit behind you and wash your hair. I'll try to be quick so you don't get cold.'

He felt wholly inexpert and inept. Igor was normally good at everything practical he turned his hand to, but this was well outside his usual skillset. He wondered fleetingly, if it would have been such a big deal, if he found her completely unattractive.

She didn't complain, even though he was convinced he was hurting her, pulling bits of twig and grit from her hair and working the dried mud out.

Handfuls of her hair also came out which he found alarming.

Nisba reassured him that this was completely normal and that no doubt it would block his shower. Her hair apparently, was a force to be reckoned with and had a life of its very own. Other than that, the process was in silence. He did his very best to be gentle and not get shampoo in her eyes.

A wisp of blood appeared in the water, curling its way from where she was seated and around her feet becoming darker, spreading outwards towards the edges of the shower tray.

'No… no!' She bent her head and placed her hands over her face making a mournful moaning sound. 'That's just not fair.'

'No, it's not.' Igor acknowledged, even though he didn't think she had been speaking to him specifically.

'It's only blood,' he said, gently swooshing it away with the shower head.

He felt bad for her; after all the indignities of the day, this did seem a bit below the belt.

'Trauma can bring on a period. Don't worry…it doesn't bother me. I can go and get you your um, you know…things.'

He showered over her shoulders to keep her warm and Nisba lifted her arm to brush water out of her eyes. It was then Igor noticed it. The hot water had melted away dried blood and a crust of mud, opening a gash in her armpit. It was about three inches long, quite deep and was bleeding. A rivulet of blood ran down the side of her body, dripping off into the water.

'It's not your period, Nisba, you're bleeding from a wound.'

She made a relieved groaning sound.

'How come you couldn't feel that?' Igor asked. 'That must be very painful.'

'I don't know. I hurt all over.'

'You'll need stitches.'

'Oh bugger, really?' Nisba sounded down-cast. 'I don't have to go to hospital, do I?'

'No, we won't make it to the hospital. We're a bit stuck for the moment because of the …' Igor rubbed the back of his head. 'I'll make some calls and see if we can get a doctor out, one that can come from the north. In the meantime, I'll have to clean and dress it and pull it together as best I can, otherwise it won't heal properly.'

Igor quickly returned with the part finished bag of saline from the bedroom, a towel, tape and dressings.

'I'm going to have to flush it out, dry you off and then dress it. It's in an awkward place. No – you don't have to take your bra off. You can do that in a minute. You'll have to keep your arm close to your body afterwards and not move it around, OK?'

'Yes, understood.' Nisba nodded. 'Thank you very much.'

Once he'd done his best to bring the sides of the wound together and dress it, he manoeuvred himself out of the shower.

'I'll leave you to this part now.'

Nisba's hair appeared black against her face, all wet and slicked back. Her eyes were dark and smudgy around the edges with drops of water caught on her long black eyelashes. She seemed to be getting more beautiful, he thought, distracted for a moment, just looking at her, taking her in. She had striking features. If he'd had to guess her heritage, he'd have said Greek or Moroccan maybe, but her pale unusual eye colour and auburn tones in her hair led him to think that was probably not all. He noticed her full lips and dark arched natural eyebrows.

Earlier, whilst washing her hair, he'd noticed that she had a threadlike gold chain around her neck. He could see now that it had a tiny pendant. A star, six pointed – the star of David.

She was full of surprises. His first thought was, she was brave, given she was a single Jewish woman in a predominantly Muslim country. Her status could not be without difficulty and potentially, danger. His second was a despairing, dragging sensation. This could be complicated. He hoped it wouldn't be.

Igor had an additional momentary worry that the doctor might be prejudiced and not provide the proper care she deserved. He would make sure that they would and was prepared for having to sort out his Rage if this occurred.

It was Friday night. He hoped he would have the opportunity to make the next one better for her and that she would still be around for that to happen.

He passed her the shower gel.

'Just throw your…erm…' He waved his hand at her underwear and then to the pile of his own clothes on the floor by the door.

He could see that she had clocked his tattoo, the Ukrainian trident covered most of the inside of his left forearm.

Their eyes met briefly.

'We both have our symbols,' she said with a nervous smile. Her little star was glinting in the bathroom spotlights.

Igor felt that he should say something reassuring to indicate that she wasn't stuck with some sort of closet Neo Nazi or Muslim Extremist.

'You're in safe hands, Nisba. Nothing has changed. I just want you to know…' That was the best he could come up with.

He had told the truth, but he had also lied.

***

The day had become clearer as it wore on, with the sun just beginning to show signs of setting. It was about 7pm when Igor went outside to assess the damage while he waited for the doctor to reach the meeting point. He was relieved that Dr Saparov, a Ukrainian private doctor was able to come out. Because the bridge had been destroyed, Igor would have to take a detour across some fields in his truck to pick him up.

A great deal had happened in just ten hours, he thought.

The men had done a fast and effective job of clearing most of the debris from the track, the river itself and surrounding areas. They had turned the Shogun back over and checked it thoroughly. Indestructible, it hadn't suffered any major damage, mostly cosmetic to the inside which would come right once it had completely dried out. This would take a good few days. It was surprising that only the passenger side windows had been shattered by hitting the rocks. The exterior was badly scratched and dented in several places.

It was an old Shogun, so no Sat Nav or mod cons with a basic looking radio and CD player. You can tell quite a lot about a person from the state of their car interior, Igor thought.

There was a lot of stuff still in it, much of which had escaped the mud. He flipped open the lid of the centre console to find a wad of receipts, a half-eaten packet of biscuits and a small bottle of water. In the back footwell were some sodden books. One looked like a novel in a language he didn't recognise. He carefully prised the pages apart. Maybe Finnish. The other was a book of word and letter puzzles. They looked very challenging to Igor, noting that they'd all been completed. There was a sports bag – waterproof, which was lucky, containing what looked to be work clothes. A green dress, black heels, stockings and a black jacket. He stopped himself from thinking what she would look like in them, well, in some of them anyway. He'd bring the bag in so they wouldn't get damp.

He moved round to the front passenger side and opened the glove compartment. A cascade of CDs tumbled out. He picked them up one at a time out of the footwell, examining each one with interest, before placing them on the front seat.

Reggae Hits Volume 1 and 2, a disco compilation. He smiled. Oasis, *(What's the Story) Morning Glory?* He wasn't surprised by that and nodded with firm approval. Beyonce – same again. Nina Simone – he didn't know the name. Maybe he would know it if he played it.

He turned over the last one. Classical. Opera: *Prince Igor and the Polovstian Dances on the Steppes of Central Asia* by Aleksander Borodin.

He broke into a grin and gave a nod of acknowledgement. He pulled out his phone and typed in the details. Despite no longer revering Russian composers, he would listen to it in the truck at some point. He was curious.

***

On his return, Nisba was sitting on the bed with her knees drawn up and arms wrapped around them.

Her hair was suffering from a lack of product and Igor's heavy-handed blow-drying. It stood up big and frizzy like a dandelion clock. She'd told him it looked like he'd given her electric shock treatment. Misha lay next to her on guard.

Feeling pleased he could cheer Nisba up, he walked quietly in.

'I've got something for you,' he said sitting on the bed next to her. He held out her phone.

'Oh, thank you! How did you find it?'

'It was in the centre console so survived quite well. I called in a favour with a mate after the…um…to get your truck cleaned up and he found it. His brother runs a mobile phone shop so I asked him to dry it out, just in case. You'll have to unlock it though, to see if it's fully functional.'

They had offered to unlock it for him. Tempting as it was, he turned the offer down.

'That's incredible…thank you so much and also for sorting the car out so quickly.' Nisba smiled broadly looking at the phone.

Igor decided not to bring up the repairs he'd arranged.

Her face fell, screwing up her eyes as she slowly tapped the numbers to unlock her screen.

'It seems fine,' she whispered.

'I guess you will need these.' He handed her a pair of glasses, smiling at her reaction.

'I've brought your stuff in by the way. I'm sorry about going through your private things, but I opened your suitcase to check there wasn't anything important…like a laptop or something. All the clothes were wet and muddy so I put them all in the washer-dryer. The knapsack is fine though. I didn't go through that,' he said reassuringly, recalling boxes of tampons.

She laughed and then put her hand to her chest, wincing.

'It's alright. I appreciate that. Did you by any chance find any nightwear…you know…pyjamas or something. There are some, somewhere.'

'I'll take a look, but you're in pain,'

'A little bit.'

'Right.' He knew what that meant. 'I'll get you something.'

He stood up and was in the doorway when she called to him.

'Igor...'

He paused.

'You are a very kind and decent man. Thank you.' Nisba swallowed hard and rubbed her chest. 'I consider myself very lucky that I... um... landed at your door and not someone else's.' She turned to look at Misha next to her on the bed who could now tell they were talking about her, twitching her ears and eyebrows.

'What a clever dog you have.'

Igor came back and sat on the bed.

'You could look at it, that if you'd landed at someone else's door, you wouldn't have been caught in a landslide.' He looked over at Misha. 'Misha is a failed cadaver dog.'

Nisba raised her eyebrows and laughed. 'No, she isn't.'

Igor smiled in agreement.

'By the way,' she continued, 'is it just you in the house...or erm, is there a...'

'What? Mrs Igor? No, there isn't.'

'May I ask another potentially insensitive question?'

'Go on,' he replied, looking at her from under his eyebrows.

'Do you have any alcohol in the house?'

Igor laughed. 'What do you need?'

His phone rang.

'That's the doctor. I'll go and pick him up. Don't go anywhere.' He smiled. 'Oh, and it might be best to save that drink until after he's been.'

***

Dr Saparov appeared diminutive standing next to Igor. His face was smiley with high cheek bones and permanent crow's feet. Nisba guessed that he was in his early sixties.

He walked into the bedroom carrying what appeared to be a flight case. Igor was providing Saparov with a hand-over of where he was up to with the treatment of the wound. Igor sat on the bed next to Nisba and introduced them. For some reason he felt quite proud to be doing so.

Igor had known Dr Saparov, since he was twelve from when he lived in Ukraine. Although Igor had been born in Tashkent, he had been brought up in Kyiv. Saparov was their family doctor and had treated his mother.

The Doctor offered his hand to Nisba, nodding and smiling.

'How do you do, Nisba? I've been hearing all about it.'

They exchanged a firm handshake.

Nisba was delighted to meet him and apologised that he had to come out and at such a late hour. He waved his hand to dismiss it.

'Not at all. You are a very interesting case.' He rubbed his palms together.

'I'd like to ask you some questions before we make a start on the wound. I know Igor will have done an excellent job of checking you over, but let's just see how you are, now that you've had some rest.'

Nisba found his manner calm and friendly which put her at ease very quickly. Igor stood up to leave to give them privacy.

Nisba caught his hand. 'It's fine,' she said shaking her head. 'Please stay.'

Nisba assured Dr Saparov that he would probably be disappointed. She wasn't at all interesting. Yes, she had arrhythmia and tachycardia but wasn't living with anything else that might be relevant. There was the possibility that she might have costochondritis, an inflammation of her chest bones. She'd had it before, but had full motion and senses in her body and didn't have any other serious cuts that required his attention and no, she didn't have any abdominal, diaphragm or kidney pain. She had no allergies to any medication or anything else that she was aware of. He confirmed that her lungs were clear. He advised that Nisba would have an impressive array of bruises. At present, they were red and pale blue but would develop nicely into pieces of modern art and that she wasn't to forget to take pictures to show her friends.

The approach to suturing the wound involved her having to lie down on the kitchen table. He needed a good light and for her to be at a decent height.

Igor assisted Nisba out of bed, supporting her as they made their way past the kitchen. Her suitcase and some of its contents were still spread out across the floor. As they neared the dining table, Igor felt her sag suddenly, but he caught her.

'Damn. Sorry about this.' Nisba placed her hands over her nose and mouth and began to breath slowly.

'I'll be alright now,' she confirmed a minute later. Composing herself, Nisba smiled brightly as Igor replaced his arm around her and walked her over to the table.

They'd already spread a sheet over it. Using a chair, she carefully climbed up. She was asked to lie on her stomach, turn her head to the side and place her arm above her head, resting it on the table. Once in position, Nisba reached out her free hand, feeling around for Igor. He it took it, placing his other hand over the top of it. He sat on one of the kitchen chairs, leaning forward, so he was level with her.

'You'll be fine,' he whispered.

This didn't escape the notice of Dr Saparov who smiled to himself. He'd already observed how tender and gentle Igor was with this girl. There was trust and a level of intimacy between them. He was very happy for Igor and hoped that something would come of it.

'Right my dear, as I explained before, I'll give you a local anaesthetic around the wound. I'll also be squirting some into it. You won't feel a thing. I'll do some deep sutures and then the ones that you will see. I'll do my best needlework for you…don't you worry. I'll give you a tetanus shot and a course of antibiotics for good measure.'

Nisba began to chat a lot to distract herself. Igor and Dr Saparov went along with it to maintain the distraction. By the time he had finished, Dr Saparov said he'd felt like he'd had an interview; probably the most enjoyable he'd ever had. Now that she had his full life story, he was quite keen to know how and why she ended up in Prikat – at Igor's house.

***

Nisba had been on her way to a client – a winery. She was going to meet a colleague at another company in Tashkent but had thought it a good idea to arrange this initial meeting with the winery – Chateau Prikat, as it was on the way. It was last minute and wasn't in her diary so Tan wouldn't have known to make enquiries there. She also wasn't one for spontaneity but did try at times to push herself out of her comfort zone. The directions she had been given weren't very good, but then any directions she said, wouldn't be of any help, unless they were drawn out with very clear landmarks. She'd had a call with someone called Raj Pereira, who provided them because the person she was originally due to meet had left the company and had just been replaced. She would be starting from scratch with this person and didn't even have their name.

Nisba had gone very wrong, even though she had followed Raj Pereira's instructions closely. They had taken her miles away from the site location to where there was no phone signal. She'd spotted a house on the hill through the trees, so decided to pull off up the track and ask for directions there.

Nisba grinned, waving her free hand. 'And the rest, is history.'

Igor raised his eyebrows and rubbed the back of his head.

***

Igor returned with a tumbler containing an enormous shot of whiskey.

Her eyes widened.

'That'll knock me out.'

She took it carefully. It still hurt to move and she was barely able to take the weight of it.

After taking a gulp, she offered it back.

'I won't be able to drink it all.'

Igor took the glass, hesitated and then sipped it slowly.

He'd made a policy of never drinking by himself or having much in the house, knowing it could become a dangerous dependency. It was enjoyable though, to feel it burn its way down, and to have some company. He was enjoying the instant rapport that they seemed to have established. He passed it back.

'I'm not much of a drinker,' Nisba said with conviction, her face serious. 'Only for medicinal purposes.' She grinned.

There was a silence for some minutes.

'I had assumed you were a Muslim man, Igor...you don't observe?'

'Mmm.' He drew a deep breath and looked up at the ceiling. 'It's complicated.'

'Complicated is my middle name.'

Igor smiled. He wasn't going to dispute that.

There was another silence.

Igor sat forward, resting his forearms on his knees and linking his fingers. He looked at the floor. He was venturing into territory not visited for a long time and wasn't sure of the way.

'You don't have to talk Igor...silence is just fine.'

He was surprised by her intuition and turned to look at her. She had been observing him. Their eyes met and their gaze was held for several seconds. Nisba was reading him, he thought, and it appeared to be making her sad. He noticed her eyes slide away, looking to the ceiling, blinking and then she closed them.

'I'll leave you to get some sleep,' Igor said, getting up. 'If you need anything, anything at all, I'm in the sitting room. I'm not far, just shout.'

'Thank you, but what time is it now? I've lost track.'

'Just after Midnight,' Igor replied, consulting his watch.

'It's late. You must be knackered after today's shenanigans. Are you staying up?'

'No...I'm going to bed. I'm on the sofa.' Igor turned towards the door.

'Oh, that won't do! I'm not in a spare room then?'

He sighed. This was awkward.

'No, this is my room. There is only one and the sofa is fine, in fact it's more comfortable than the bed,' he added, to make her feel better.

She made efforts to get out of bed screwing her face up in pain.

'No…no. Don't get up. Please. You're not ready.'

'But I should be the one on the sofa. This is terrible Igor. I've invaded your house…left a trail of devastation behind me…' She waved her right arm about, keeping the other firmly by her side, as instructed.

He liked how she spoke. So dramatic, he thought.

'It's alright…don't stress about it.'

Running out of energy to maintain the protest, Nisba flopped her arm to her side and hung her head.

'I feel so helpless,' she whispered. 'It must be so terrible for people who are stuck like this all the time. Sorry, Igor. I'm a crap patient…you need to be able to get on with things…and have I been stopping you from going to work?'

He stood, slowly shaking his head, giving a slight smile.

'I'm getting cold …' she said, looking about her, figuring out how to get back into bed.

'Will you let me help you?'

'Yes…thank you.' She took his hand for support.

He swung her legs back up onto the bed, covering her up to her chin. He found himself suddenly very close to her.

She shyly avoided his gaze. Without touching her, he gently brushed some hair out of the way, which had flopped into her eye.

He stood up quickly. The temptation to kiss her took him by surprise.

'You must be hungry,' he said to distract himself.

'I am a bit peckish, now that you come to mention it.'

He nodded. Right, she must be starving.

'I'll go and see what I can do'.

***

The offering was paltry in his opinion. He explained he hadn't been expecting visitors but Nisba was delighted anyway. Igor was relieved that he had some bread left. He had a scrape of butter, so decided, given she was English, two very thick slices of toast wouldn't go amiss.

He apologised for not having any marmalade, which Nisba found amusing.

Whilst she ate, they chatted and at the same time he brought her knapsack through into the bathroom so she could get ready for bed. He encouraged her to spread out and make herself at home.

He explained that he wasn't being weird or anything, but it was best if she didn't lock the bathroom door. If she came unstuck and needed help, he wouldn't have to shoulder barge it. He would use the main bathroom. He'd dug around in amongst her clothes and lingerie and found her some nightwear.

Igor was crestfallen when she laughed at what he'd brought her.

Nisba didn't have the energy to go and look herself, so got ready for bed. It took a long time to do everything with the limited movement in her left arm.

Igor was about to knock on the bathroom door to check on her because she had taken so long, when she suddenly opened it.

She was wearing the nightwear. A pale turquoise satin slip with spaghetti straps, the hem coming to just above her knees. He noticed Nisba had also done something to her hair. It was in waves, like a 1940s Hollywood movie star.

Caught out, he swallowed hard. He liked the old American and British movies, especially the black and white ones and Nisba looked like she had just stepped out of one.

'Could you have found anything more immodest?' she asked, pulling at the straps.

He was lost for a minute.

'I can't see anything wrong with it.'

She chuckled as she walked away to get into bed. She pulled on his dressing gown frontwards like a straight-jacket and sat up in bed.

Igor found that Nisba could literally talk for England. She had a great deal to say about many topics but then she would come to an abrupt stop, losing her place, often veering off onto something completely unrelated and then there would be silence. These silences weren't awkward and gave space for reflection. He liked that. It hadn't gone unnoticed that she also had a way of getting information out of him, when he could actually get a word in. He could see why Doctor Saparov had given so much away. It was after a particularly long pause, when she suddenly asked another one of her probing questions.

'You're not just a humble farmer, are you?' She was smiling in a conspiratorial way. 'That was a rhetorical question by the way – you don't have to answer it…'

He took the bait. Before answering, he lifted one leg up on the bed to get comfortable followed by the other, drawing his knee up with his arms linking them around his ankle.

He responded with a mischievous smile, awaiting her assessment.

'So…what are you thinking? Nightclub bouncer...cage fighter?' There was a longer pause. '…Assassin?'

She laughed and was embarrassed about it. He didn't mind.

'I am a farmer. I grow fruit,' he said, which was technically true.

She wasn't going to be satisfied with that and he knew it.

'C'mon Igor, what fruit? What do you grow and what do you do?'

'You know, a few grapes and some other soft fruits,' he answered modestly, shrugging his shoulders. But he knew she was on to him.

'You can't pull that English understatement bollocks on me, Igor.'

They laughed.

It was only then that he informed her that he was her client, not that he had been aware of it until she'd been speaking to Saparov. It had been arranged by management and not a decision he had been involved with.

'So, I would have ended up meeting you anyway, without having to suffer force majeure?' Nisba said.

They both pondered on this a minute. Igor wondered what action he would have taken if the landslide hadn't happened. He probably would have driven to site so that she could follow him and then ask for her number since he was her client. There would be a reasonable excuse to invite her to dinner. He would have to do something nice like that once she was recovered, he thought.

He changed the subject.

'So...CEO at thirty-six, that's impressive.' He paused. 'I looked at your passports. I had to be sure you were who you said you were.' The corners of his eyes creased and his eyes twinkled.

She grinned and shrugged to say that it was fine. She glanced at the passports still sitting on top of the bedside table.

It transpired that they were both December babies. Nisba was born on the 18th and Igor on the 28th of the same year. Nisba smiled.

'I'm older than you then.'

'Mmm, but the years have been much kinder to you.'

'I suspect life has generally been a lot kinder to me, than it has been to you,' said Nisba, not looking for a response.

'Interesting,' Igor commented, changing the subject again.

'Your passports; a UK and an Estonian citizen. I've worked on every continent in oil and gas but have never met an Estonian.'

They found they had something else in common. Whilst he had worked on big noise exploration and production projects all around the world, she had undertaken human resources work on behalf of smaller independent oil companies. This had been her first introduction to Uzbekistan. This had also taken her to Kazakhstan when she decided she'd change sector, going in for other sectors including charities and NGOs, in the Congo... She came to an abrupt stop.

'...and Angola.'

He noticed that she was jiggling her foot violently, under the covers.

Igor had also worked in Angola and was about to tell her when she cut him off suddenly.

'Tell me about what you can play on the guitar...'

Igor stretched out at her feet, placing his hands behind his head.

They talked for several hours, covering numerous topics: music, the miserable time they'd both had at school, Brexit, politics in general and art. They discovered that they both gave blood. She described where she lived on her maps app, showing him a satellite view of a large detached 1920s house surrounded by oak trees, with double-bays and terracotta tiles, like fish scales he thought, all over the front. He cut short a fantasy of a surprise visit, knocking on her front door and being welcomed inside.

They agreed not to talk about the war.

Part-way through the evening, Igor shut Misha out, sending her to her basket. Misha had been unhappy with the level of attention she was being paid. Nisba and Igor were far too interested in each other and she did not approve of the lack of distance between them on the bed.

On his return, Igor said he'd considered the possibility of Nisba being a Mossad agent, or a Russian spy. Her Estonian passport was good cover. He'd figured that if she were going to dish him a dose of Novichok, she would have done it by now.

He felt bad, sensing that she understood he wasn't joking.

Nisba explained that her dad had been a Second World War refugee, fleeing Soviet occupation of Estonia. He was a toddler when he arrived in the UK in 1948 but had died when she was little. It was sudden. Her parents had her very late in life. She had been long awaited. Her paternal grandfather had been murdered by the Russians and other relatives sent off in cattle trains to Siberia.

Her mother was born in Tunisia, a *Maghrebi* Jew, born just after the Germans retreated in 1944.

Her mother and father were a controversial match, but a successful one.

Igor could relate to this, as his parents' marriage was a rebellion on both their parts. His mother Karolina died when he was thirteen of cancer and his father Sherzod, had died three years previously, in 2020. They also were of different cultural and religious backgrounds. His father was Muslim and his mother was raised as Christian Orthodox. His grandparents were both disappointed with the choices that his parents had made. Apart from that, he couldn't relay an interesting or romantic backstory like she had.

Nisba was sorry that he lived with so much loss and then appeared to spend some time deep in thought. After which, she concluded, that if he were an assassin, he needed to beef up his legend.

They chatted until Igor didn't reply any more. He was out. She remained sitting up so as not to disturb him, switching off the bedside lamp as quietly as she could, and closed her eyes.

Nisba was contemplating the possibility that, whilst she thought she had survived being pulled from the mud of the landslide, she might in fact be in a coma.

She'd taken the wrong turn and had come upon Igor, the most attractive man she had ever seen in her whole life. He wasn't pretty. He was on that edge of handsome and not. Very sexy, she thought. He was also very likeable, understanding and easy – just perfect.

As she closed her eyes, Nisba began her process of highlighting thoughts for deletion. Deleting would minimise any effect of having an emotional or physical reaction. This needed to be achieved as soon as possible, to limit the damage.

When he'd helped her back into bed, she'd had a strong desire to kiss him. This recklessness frightened her. She'd met him only twenty-four hours ago and just wasn't that kind of a woman. Never had a one-night stand. Strictly long haul.

The tenderness with which he had washed her hair and handled her bleeding, made her heart crumble a little bit. It was a kind act but also, so intimate somehow. She felt that Igor had gone above and beyond to make her feel comfortable, safe, providing such excellent medical care. But Igor was way out of her league, so forming an attachment was foolish. He was sure to have a stunningly beautiful Uzbek, or gorgeous, blond leggy Ukrainian girlfriend somewhere. Humiliation was starting to creep up on her, concluding that she was just a baby bird that had fallen out of its nest, only to be rescued by a lion.

He seemed very decent and – gallant. Men were men and usually took an opportunity when presented. Maybe he's gay, she thought fleetingly. That was an arrogant thought – don't flatter yourself Nisba. You're not all that, she scolded.

Then she became fatigued by it all.

His sad sea green eyes, infectious laugh, deep crunchy voice (not to mention his physique), well, she was definitely not going to be moved by any of these things and was therefore not at all interested. Not one bit. Especially, not in his compassion and gentleness, dammit.

Nisba knew that he could kill her with one hand in a second, but she was unafraid of him. She was afraid though, that he would be her undoing. She couldn't afford it.

Despite his strong, intimidating appearance, he seemed vulnerable, sad and alone. Then she slept.

Day 2 Saturday

It felt like a few minutes later, but it said 5 am on her phone. Nisba wasn't sure if she was asleep or awake. Her brain couldn't quite figure out what was happening.

Igor was still at her feet. He was lying on his side, hunched up, shaking violently to the point she thought he was having a seizure. Nisba knew what to do in this situation but prayed that he wasn't. He was saying something, not words. He was definitely not awake. She was relieved that it was a nightmare, but the severity of it was so great, it shook the whole bed. Nisba found it disturbing to watch. It must be so terrible she thought, tempted to snap him out of it.

That was not a good idea, she concluded.

Nisba instinctively started to whisper and then very slowly pulled her legs out from under the covers and lay on her side behind him. She told him that it was going to come to an end very soon, until eventually, she was speaking in her normal voice, softly repeating the words. Very gently, she had begun to stroke his arm, barely touching him, gradually becoming firmer. She was prepared for him to fight her off. She wouldn't be upset if he did, but the shaking had subsided and so had the sounds.

Nisba tentatively put her arm round his waist to comfort him so her hand was on his stomach and moved a little closer. Her nose was touching his T-shirt in between his shoulder blades.

She felt Igor take her hand and hold it close to his chest.

***

Nisba awoke. On opening her eyes, she felt pleasantly warm and had slept well. Not moving, she realised her head was resting on Igor's chest. He was lying on his back and her right arm lay across him with her hand resting on his left hip. She had one leg over his and could feel his heart beating.

Nisba could tell he was awake. She didn't move.

Igor's arm was wrapped around her and was absentmindedly drawing circles with the tips of his fingers gently on her bare shoulder. He changed the pattern every now and again by stroking her with the side of his thumb.

Nisba wondered what he could be thinking. Turning her face into his chest she breathed in to give herself some time to figure out what to do next.

She needed to be breezy, like nothing had happened and wish him good morning or something.

Nisba lifted her head just as he looked down at her.

It was a gentle affectionate kiss initially. They tentatively sought out another and then hurtled toward the edge of the cliff. Deeply, with desire and relief, they both bathed in the sheer joy and pleasure of it.

Igor couldn't remember the last time he had felt such an emotional response to a physical act. Heat and desire surged from his toes to his face. He buried his hands in her hair and had turned Nisba slightly, so he was almost on top of her. It was so intense; he thought his heart might give out.

They teetered on the edge for about ten long seconds but simultaneously dragged each other back.

With their foreheads touching, Igor whispered breathlessly, fearful and full of regret.

'You're my patient – in my care and vulnerable. I've taken advantage, which I said I would never do.'

He'd crossed the line and was sure to have lost her trust. He breathed heavily, feeling drunk from it all.

'No,' Nisba replied, 'that wasn't you. It was me.' There was a pause. 'I think we just got caught in a storm for a second and it's blown over now. I'm not myself. I was out of order.' Nisba smiled brightly and briefly.

She wasn't looking for any reply and Igor didn't answer, giving her a squeeze. She gave him one back.

'Thank you for looking out for me,' Nisba said suddenly.

Detaching herself from him, she suddenly felt bereft and chilly. She lay on her back and then turned her head, looking at him intently and seriously.

'I will do the same for you.'

***

Fuck. Shit. Damn. Bollocks.

Nisba threw her head back and looked at the ceiling, shaking her head. She pinched herself – not in a coma then. But she had broken all her rules and proceeded to talk herself out of any positive conclusions.

I am the nearest woman. That's why. He's a man – so, you know, he'll take what's on offer.

Nisba puffed out her cheeks and exhaled, convinced that they had rapport, chemistry even, but then plunged into doubt.

They had become friends and she considered herself lucky. She was still here to think about it because of him and his dog.

Nisba was very aware of her weaknesses and vulnerabilities, struggling to set internal boundaries and look objectively and rationally at emotional situations, making decisions that took self-preservation into account. Often acting rashly based purely on emotion, she'd then have to pick up the pieces later. It cost her. Her friends seemed to be able to make calm judgements that avoided later fall-out. Nisba had developed tools to help her be more like them, forcing her to step back and provide a rationale, employing an objective assessment process.

He'd saved her life. Yes, he had, but that didn't mean she owed him hers. She would be a good friend, but this did not require her to enter into any self- destructive behaviour or disproportionate grand gestures. Tick. Did she actually like him other than just really fancy him? Tick. Did she believe in him? Was he fundamentally a good person? Tick. Were his politics and values sound? She'd checked those out on day one. Tick. He hadn't engaged in any kind of coercive behaviour. Tick. He hadn't demonstrated any dodgy personality traits. Her training had helped her pick up on those. Tick. Had she fallen for him because he had been kind and taken an interest in her. Pause. Oh dear. This is what had happened to her previously. She had deep rooted low self-esteem and any kind of validation and approval from a Nice

Kind Man was a danger zone. So, this was probably another of her hyper love-bombing reactions.

Did he respect her? Hmm, yes, she thought he did. Could she confidently introduce him to her mother? For the first time in her life, she would be proud to and look forward to it. Her mother was broad-minded – pragmatic. She didn't consider matching religion or ethnicity to be a guarantee of suitability. There was the same caveat, the non-negotiable for Nisba though, that her heritage and traditions would be accepted and accommodated. Could she introduce him to each of her friends without any anxiety? As above. Tick. Would she and could he be the…she stopped there for now.

Out of the questionnaire she had a couple of areas to look at and assess further to arrive at definitive answers. A score of less than 100% would not do.

Nisba looked at her phone. She wasn't going to allow herself to spend any more time on this, to avoid obsessing. She would have to think of something else, which was difficult, needing answers straight away, to put it to bed. She would have to enter into something gruelling or taxing to shut it down; like teach herself Japanese or something.

She kind of hoped he would do something that would be a cross on her questionnaire. It would make life so much easier. Then she would be able to walk away with no regrets, no pain.

Nisba didn't have these problems with work so much. Work was objective and did not involve emotion unless it went seriously pear-shaped, which wasn't very often. She had stopped the coaching and counselling as she discovered it was emotionally draining for her, leaving too little left. But this – this was something else. The consequences of the decisions she made now, could last a lifetime. She needed to stop the noise in her head, keep her ideas tidy and not forget to watch her own back.

Nisba couldn't get it out of her head. Playing it back, recalling how she had felt kissing him. It was the most sensational and wonderful moment, unable to bring to mind an instance when she had felt like that before. It was something she knew was out there now but had never been within her grasp – to feel so much for someone.

She recognised that this was lust, attraction and a dopamine hit, which she was not allowed to act on. Another rule. But Igor had a rare kindness not present in her previous partners. Her differences and challenges had been frequently combatted, highlighted or teased. How she *wasn't*, was always the thing. The magnetic quality of Igor, she found, was that her wiring, her factory settings were accepted. He had stuff too, which was perhaps why he was non-judgmental and easy going. She really liked him for it, feeling she could just be herself – apart from try not to fall flat on her face for him.

She'd always been with the wrong man, never realising that she could have had higher expectations, often tolerating poor and sometimes cruel behaviour. She never dreamt in a million years, that someone so handsome and attractive as well as lovely, could possibly be attracted to her. Maybe it was possible. Then Nisba felt sad and tearful, feeling sorry for herself, having found everything she had been looking for, having had a glimpse of what could be, but couldn't have it. She would be going home soon, having to leave it all behind. Knowing what she was missing now, was hard to come to terms with.

She went round in circles for a while.

It was still exciting though, the promise of what might be, but she would not allow herself high hopes. There was nothing he had said or done to warrant them. The majority of his family members in both Ukraine and Uzbekistan were Muslim, and although he was lapsed, the chances of Igor seeking to hook up with some random Jewish woman that had fallen at his feet, were slim to none. It would be controversial and they'd both had their own personal experience to draw upon about that. It really was all in her head and a waste of energy. His life was here. Hers was there. That kiss had to be the first and last incident of crossing the line. Having to protect herself, she could not give herself to him, only to be let go. That would take her down the road to self-destruction.

She would be well enough to leave in a few days. It was just too soon, but then not soon enough. The more time she spent with Igor, she figured, the harder it would get.

***

Igor had been worried that Nisba was afraid of him. There was a lot about him that was ugly, he thought and not all of it was visible. It bothered him that she could see it. The way she looked at him sometimes, he was afraid that she could.

Yet, Nisba wasn't running away, metaphorically or physically. She had been caring towards him – loving, even. There were times when she looked at him, seeming so genuinely pleased to see him, he could feel his inner stoniness warming up and his mood lifting. He found her an empathic, kind and giving person, so she was probably like that with everyone. But his presence in the world seemed to matter now and he cared what Nisba thought of him.

Igor admitted to himself that he was a bit in awe of her. This was a new state of being for him.

He was impressed by her resolve and level of self-awareness. How she did that job of hers, he had no idea, or why she continued to put herself through it. Her mental and emotional stamina were worthy of respect. He was envious. In this regard, she was tougher than he was, he thought.

He'd learned from Tan that Nisba had coached him to be a better leader. He was seventeen years her senior and shared that she had completely changed his working life for the better. He was one of many colleagues and clients she had helped. If he had a problem and not just work-related, Nisba was his go-to person. She was an expert problem-solver.

So, Igor would not be the one who screwed Nisba Maasik, just because he probably could, whilst she was frail, with her defences down. She was his friend and he wished to get to know her better. He was genuinely interested in who she was. He'd earned her trust and had also made a promise to Tan Chico.

He rubbed his face and shook his head slightly. He still had a non-alcoholic hang-over from that kiss, thinking – he had gone from being a dead man forty-eight hours earlier, to alive, virile, and having ungentlemanly thoughts about her on a regular basis. He no longer had to worry about performance issues.

Previously, there had been little emotional involvement in his sex life.

He had been married to Feruza because he was fulfilling a family expectation. His life had been mapped out for him by his father and unhappily, Igor had fought hard to get away overseas to work, doing what he wanted.

He hadn't wanted the family business either, but he was the only son. His older sister Mila, as the only daughter, was much less able to rebel or be seen to dishonour the family. The irony being, she would have been far better suited and capable of running it.

Coming from wealth, they'd had the best education in Ukraine, money could buy. Mila had a Master of Business Administration. She was a real talent having gone to Oxford, but their father crushed it. He enjoyed the kudos of telling people how erudite and clever she was, but he was never going to allow her to fly away and fulfil her dreams.

Feruza didn't want to marry Igor and he wasn't in love with her either, but he liked her well enough and desired her, so was accepting of it. They had been married five years by the second invasion of Ukraine. She was attractive in a cool, aloof sort of way. Tall, long straight black hair and large brown eyes. Her face never showed what she was thinking but he knew she was still in love with Oleksii, one of his childhood friends. Always had been. It was draining and emasculating to know and feel that she was always thinking of Oleksii and therefore, he could never please her.

He had hoped for children, but none came. He had the theory for a while that there never would be, that she would leave him and go to Oleksii.

In his wildest dreams, Igor imagined Nisba to be an enthusiastic and generous lover. The chemistry between them was, he thought, like magic. Or maybe he was just hopeful and foolishly optimistic. But there was this other thing they had, that he couldn't quite put his finger on. He searched around for it. It was a mutual understanding about things, a kind of solidarity. When Nisba said she had his back, she had meant it.

He was excited by her and felt – that was it – accepted. He really hoped that she would want him, desire him and be able to find a space for him in her life.

If she did, then he feared dragging her into hell. He couldn't guarantee keeping her safe or keep her safe from him. It could get dark. She didn't deserve it.

He did consider though, when Nisba had comforted him, this was the best sleep he'd had. He'd slept soundly for six straight hours, something he had never achieved since the war. He wished every night would be like that, but she was clearly a sensible and together sort of person, having made herself clear in the politest possible way, without sounding presumptuous. He recalled, with hidden disappointment and feigned indifference, her telling him, she could only start something that had a future. Not being there for much longer, she wasn't looking to make any attachments. She had been business like about it and he respected her for it.

But it was too late for Igor, living in hope that this would change.

He didn't know the exact date she was leaving the country. Nisba had said; 'In a week or so.'

He hadn't asked specifically because he really didn't want to know. It was not a reality he wanted to face up to yet.

***

Tan Chico's phone
Tan: 21:38   How's it going? How's Nisba doing?
Igor: 21:40   Very well thanks. She's doing great.
Tan: 21:41   Great news! (Thumbs up)
How are you two getting along? (Grinning emoji)
Igor: 22:00   What happened in Angola?

Tan: 22:01   Can you take a call?
Igor: 22:02   Sure

Incoming call from Tan Chico

'Hi Tan.'
'Hey. I'm glad to hear that she's recovering well. Nisba's sent me a couple of texts but always puts a brave face on things, so I wanted to get the real picture.'
'Sure,' replied Igor. 'It was a miracle that she wasn't more seriously injured. Anyway...she seems at home and more relaxed now...'
'So, how are you finding her company?'
Igor could tell that Tan was fishing for gossip. Igor paused too long for his reply and Tan laughed. He wasn't being unkind. Tan was a gay man. Igor would be spared the Alpha Male back-slapping bullshit. Igor changed the subject. He couldn't take the high hopes of Tan when there weren't any. It was getting him down and he wanted to know about Angola.
'It's a very sad story actually,' announced Tan. 'It's had more of an effect than I think she lets on of course. It was when we were in Sumbe, working on behalf of a women's charity. She was acting as an Interim CEO as a favour for a former work colleague. It didn't even happen to me, but it was the most terrifying thing I've ever experienced. Nisba was outside in the carpark, and we were all in the office when she was held at gunpoint. I saw it from the window.'
Igor was not prepared for this, having an urge to hang up and take cover.
'He was a sixteen-year-old, whose mother had died. He didn't feel that she got the help she needed so...you know, he went off the rails. He was waving the gun around and screaming. He didn't know what he was doing, so he could have easily blown her away without even meaning to!' Igor could hear the outrage and fear in Tan's voice.
'The phones don't work half the time out there and there was no signal, so we couldn't call for help or anything...

She was out there for what seemed like ages – talking him down. He handed her the gun in the end. Nisba walked him in with her arm round him.' Tan paused, requiring some time to recover from the memory. 'When the phones were back up, she wouldn't let us call the police. Anyway, Joao, that was his name – Joao Domingos, he ended up working for the charity. Smart kid, you know…sorted out all the IT. He'd got his life on track and was able to support his little sister.'

Igor braced himself.

'A few weeks later, he was killed. Knocked off his bike by a truck – hit and run.'

Igor paced, shaking himself down.

'That's the only time I've seen an emotional reaction…well, I heard it,' continued Tan. 'When Nisba found out, she sent us all home. I didn't leave though. Didn't like the look of it. She locked herself in the ladies' room and screamed the place down. It was horrific. She'd cried and screamed so hard, she had that haemorrhaging around her eyes – you know, those little red dots. She had them for days.'

Igor swallowed hard, because of the lump in his throat and gathered his thoughts.

He'd worked in Angola on a discovery there and had hired one of his former colleagues to come and work for him in Uzbekistan. Igor made a mental note: Angola – a topic to be avoided.

'You like her,' Tan said. It was a statement with no judgements.

Igor didn't reply. He closed his eyes feeling defeated.

'Well. She thinks you're *alright,* so that means she really likes you,' said Tan laughing.

'I don't want to sound like some overbearing avuncular asshole, but all I can say is – just be very straight forward. Very literal. She can't interpret subtle behaviour when it comes to the opposite sex. Also, no overblown romantic gestures – you'll freak her out.'

Igor attempted to interrupt, but Tan was carried away with resolving his dear friend's love life.

'The thing is, Nisba doesn't believe she deserves to feel special, so when she does receive any positive affirmations, she gets overwhelmed. It might feel like a rejection to you, but she'll show her affection in her own sweet way. Anyway...I wish you both the best of luck. I'm really pleased that she's finally met a gentleman who will appreciate her.'

Igor felt awkward thanking Tan for his approval and well-meaning advice, still crushed by the fact that nothing could happen. He was tied to his wretched life in Uzbekistan and Nisba had hers, in England. He'd also learned for himself, that her understatement could be inconsistent. Being *alright,* did not always directly translate to being *really great.*

Igor went back to join her. She'd fallen asleep sitting up, phone in hand and with her glasses on.

It hurt to look at her.

Day 3 Sunday

Nisba had insisted on getting up.
She made her way about like an old person, limping and shuffling, using the furniture for support.
Once the morning painkillers kicked in, she became more able-bodied. Misha followed her around fussing and whining.
Pleasant smells had emanated from the bathroom, but it looked like a bomb had gone off. After Nisba had finally emerged and before Igor could pass comment, she stressed that she hadn't finished and would tidy up.
Nisba warned him that she wasn't very tidy in general.
This was her first proper introduction to the house, other than her journey to the kitchen table for the stitches. She had not paid too much attention at the time, too busy avoiding the embarrassment of fainting.
Igor was making coffee when she entered.
She looked different with clothes on. He was glad that he hadn't passed any comment on that out loud.
Nisba's hair was a particularly big statement this morning. In fact, everything about her he observed, was more dramatic than usual, now that he was able to get the full impression of her. She wore jeans (tight, he noted, not without pleasure) and a black silky shirt that was slightly fitted. The sleeves were rolled back to her elbows. He leaned against the kitchen island looking at her, for far too long. Igor then sprang back into action as she walked about. He tended to the coffee.
'You have such a lovely house, Igor. And what a great view at the front. May I take a look out the back? I have no idea where I am, or about my surroundings.'
'Sure – help yourself.'
'Can I borrow these?' She pointed to an enormous pair of navy-blue rubber clogs left by the utility room door. She didn't know where her own footwear was.
He gestured with his hand, smiling.
'Go ahead.'

Shuffling out via the utility room, she disappeared off through the back door. Misha bounded after her.

She was gone a long time, at least that was how it felt to Igor.

Nisba returned, animated, making flourishing gestures.

'You live in the most beautiful place in the world. I have never seen anything like it!'

He was trying to remember what it was like. Yes, he supposed the terrain was very beautiful with the snow-capped mountains in the distance and rolling countryside – and there was the lake.

They chatted for a while and then she continued her tour of the house whilst she drank her coffee. She was very interested in his bookcase in the Snug.

He was surprisingly highbrow she noted, laughing to herself – for an assassin. He had quite a few American classics. She recalled him telling her he had been to university in the US.

There were numerous Ukrainian novels, including works by Ivan Franko. Most surprisingly, as she went along the shelf, it was appearing more and more like her own bookcase at home. He had Jo Nesbo, some Lee Child novels and JK Rowling mixed up with philosophy and history books. On the next shelf, she spied 'The Lorax' by Dr Seuss and 'Paddington at Work' by Michael Bond in English. Two of her most favourite storybooks.

'My niece left those behind a year or so ago. I keep forgetting to take them back,' Igor called, from the kitchen.

'Flippin 'eck,' commented Nisba. 'I've got the same combination of books in my sitting-room at home. I hope we're not related.' Which she immediately regretted. How bloody stupid!

Igor looked aghast.

The terrible, yet absurd scenario of being long lost twins, separated at birth, crossed his mind for a nano-second.

He quickly changed the subject, bringing up the possibility of going for a walk at some point and then about what she might like to eat. Nisba hadn't eaten a proper meal for several days.

Igor made a suggestion.

'How about getting out of the house? You've been stuck indoors in one room for a while. What about a shopping trip this afternoon? The shop is north, so we can get there by road, no problem.'

He studied her face carefully. The combination of surprise and a noisy supermarket was probably not her idea of fun. He'd suggested *later*, to give her some time to think about it.

'That sounds like a really good idea,' she replied, smiling. Her eyes were looking away. She was thinking about it.

***

The sunshine was breaking through when they convened outside the front door.

'Can I drive?' Nisba asked suddenly.

Igor caught his breath.

'Sure.' He could have said the insurance wouldn't cover her to drive, but it did .

They climbed into his red Toyota pick-up.

Nisba patted his big thigh.

'You'll be fine,' she grinned.

She drove like a man, he thought. He sighed, correcting himself. She was a skilful and assertive driver, only occasionally expressing low level road rage at junctions and on the freeway. He'd found that funny. He had been wholly distracted by her, never once paying any attention to his surroundings for a potential threat, like he usually did.

She parked.

'Not a white-knuckle ride then?' she quipped, unbuckling her seatbelt.

It was a large supermarket. Igor noticed the underlying thrum of air con, electricity and people's voices. It wasn't something he'd ever really noticed or paid any attention to before. He looked at Nisba's face. Her expression was as if she was undertaking complicated mental maths.

He touched her arm.

'Will you be OK?'

She looked surprised.

'I...umm. In the call with Tan, he did tell me some things...'

'Oh, he did, did he?'

Igor was in charge of the trolley. They chatted as if they did it every week, making their way up and down the aisles efficiently because she didn't want to spend any more time over it than they really had to. He was fine with that. It was a chore in his eyes. Nisba had written a list and had a pen. Igor had it all in his head.

Once they'd done with the food, they moved onto the other aisles where there were bizarre combinations of items such as Snickers multipacks, bird-food, drain cleaner and children's toys.

Igor picked up what he was after and pushed the trolley back toward Nisba who was crouching down, reaching for something on the bottom shelf.

She came back up and stood, sticking her chest out, holding two toy fried eggs in front of her breasts.

Igor regarded this with a poker face, raising one eyebrow. He slowly lifted his arm, pointing up toward the CCTV.

Her face made him laugh so hard, it hurt. Nisba walked quickly back towards him, holding her hands over her face, mortified.

On her return to his side, someone was trying to get past them.

Igor slipped his arm round Nisba's waist to guide her out of their path. He left it there much longer than he needed to. While they were recovering from the laughter, their heads still together, he had another strong desire to kiss her but then a voice behind him called out his name.

'Mr Mirzeyakamov – I thought it was you. *Salom.*'

'*Salom* – how are you?' asked Igor, turning to the woman. 'But it's Igor...please, or Mr M, if you like.'

The woman appeared to be in her early fifties. She had sparkly brown eyes.

Igor spoke in English.

'This is Nisba...um...Nisba, this is Mrs Ismailova.'

'Zeinab,' the lady interjected.

'How lovely to meet you, Zeinab.'

Zeinab Ismailova smiled delightedly at Nisba, looking intently into her face.

'Zeinab just started with us on Friday,' explained Igor.

'Ooh, and what is it you are doing?'

'I'm the new site manager,' Zeinab replied, looking a bit daunted.

'Ah, so you run the show!'

'Yes, that's right.' Zeinab laughed. 'Getting them all in order. I already can see a few things that need to change.'

She gave a nervous look toward Igor and then gave Nisba a conspiratorial wink.

Nisba and Zeinab chatted for a while. It transpired that Zeinab was there to shop for supplies. She'd volunteered to help prep for the big work event taking place in a couple of weeks' time.

This was something the winery did annually for the colleagues in production, the warehouses and their families. Apparently, Mr M (Zeinab had learned) was big on doing that sort of thing, but didn't often show up. She went on to say that she was one of the very few women in the whole company and that her hire was controversial, but she knew that Mr M had very much supported it.

They agreed that both she and Nisba had a lot to talk about.

Igor busied himself looking at something he didn't need.

When they finally wrapped up, Zeinab touched Nisba on the arm and said goodbye and walked briskly over to Igor, who was only a few meters away.

'When you come to the event, you must bring your wife with you – she's lovely!'

Igor suddenly felt a crashing, falling sensation. Zeinab had turned away and walked briskly off back down the aisle, swiftly turning the corner.

Igor looked down at his shoes, breathed in heavily and looked up. Nisba was examining the shelves again, reviewing their list, tapping the end of her pen against her bottom lip. She turned and met his gaze, breaking into one of her killer smiles.

His chest constricted.

She would be gone by then. Not there anymore. In another country. Thousands of miles away. How could he get her back to having it like this? Just doing simple hum-drum stuff. He realised that he had been enjoying himself. Experiencing happiness. He had been, for the last three days and for the first time in years. He did not want to let go of it.

The clamour of the music and throng of people clawed at him.

He understood now why she wore earplugs. The pains in his chest had turned into a creeping sense of terror and hopelessness. He was going to die; he was sure of it. He rubbed his face to get rid of the sensation and placed his hands over his ears.

There was a startling smack and crash of glass bottles in the next aisle.

Igor ducked instinctively, resting his hands on the floor to steady himself. His ears were ringing and he began to gasp, in Ukrainian.

'Got to get out. Got to get out.'

In the distance, he could hear a calm rushing sound and then an English voice telling him he was safe and that she'd get him out.

Igor remained crouching, looking at the floor. He could see her feet and then another pair, rapidly advancing, but they came to an abrupt halt about half a metre away.

'Yes…thank you for your concern.' She was speaking Russian now. It wasn't rubbish at all!

'Everything's fine…please give him some space. Thank you. Thanks very much.'

Her feet turned to the others. 'I'll be back for the trolley.'

Feeling her hand on his back, Igor staggered up. She took his hand.

'C'mon, Igor, let's get you outside for some air.'

She walked him back to the car still holding his hand. He chose the passenger seat which made her smile.

'Here.' She handed him her phone and then the headphones, disentangling them.

'Put these in and close your eyes. I'll be back in a few minutes – alright?'

He nodded.

Nisba walked off to go back for the shopping.

On her return, she found he'd put the seat back and was resting, listening with his eyes closed.

She'd put on a classical mix, which included 'Cavalleria Rusticana', some Offenbach and Elgar's *Enigma Variations*. Not what he would ever have thought of, but he found it calming and beautiful.

She climbed into the driver's seat and looked beside her at Igor, gently stroking his arm.

'Are you ready to move? Get back home?' she asked softly.

He nodded.

She set the Sat Nav as she was unable to recall the directions in reverse.

Nisba didn't pass any comment about the bright blue SUV she'd noticed arriving at the supermarket at the same time as them, which was now pulling out as they were leaving. There were two men in it. On their return to Igor's truck, the men had been waiting for them, before moving. Nisba was sure that one of them had been taking photos.

The SUV was now two vehicles behind. She drove for two miles and at the first opportunity, took a sudden wrong right turn, too late for them to react and follow.

Making a U-turn, Nisba re-joined the main highway. The SUV was now about five vehicles in front. She tailgated the small lorry in front for cover.

The SUV did not come to the house.

She pulled up outside the front and walked round to the passenger side, opening the door for Igor.

He removed the headphones and gathered up the wires.

'Thank you,' he said quietly, handing them back. He stepped out, feeling calmer, but embarrassed and exhausted. The reality of losing Nisba was still hurting.

Once indoors, Nisba said she would sort the shopping. He was to go and chill out for a bit, but he started to shift shopping bags.

'I should help you,' he whispered.

'There's no need. Go and have a lie down. It's important to take care of yourself.' She lifted a bag onto the island and began to unpack it.

Her eyes were sad and large. 'I'll join you in a bit.'

He made his way over to the sofa.

***

Nisba wondered if she'd been imagining it – about the SUV.

Her guts were telling her she wasn't.

She considered Igor's position. From what she had managed to extract from him, she ascertained that he was quite a powerful man.

Whilst he was sleeping, she did some research on her laptop.

It was rather strange reading about him, the man she was staying with.

Come on, Nisba, she thought. Be honest with yourself. The man you've fallen for – you're in love with this dude.

Chateau Prikat grew grapes for wine production. It was also a grower of fruits which were dried for export. The plantation overall, was huge. She calculated that the view from where she was sitting, would be his land, as far as the eye could see.

She swallowed hard. Nisba had always been afraid of failure but most of all, she feared success, which might become unbridled – uncontrollable. She had been accustomed to struggling growing up and somehow held herself back, avoiding opportunities that might take her places or put her up front – on stage. She preferred to remain low profile, which was not always easy as a high achiever. People often wanted a piece of her. So far, she had achieved success by remaining behind the scenes. Her colleagues who enjoyed the exposure, were the ones more visible and in the public eye. It worked well for her, the company, and for them.

Igor's position was very much in the public domain and of interest.

She discovered that he had previously been the Mayor of Prikat and was responsible for the livelihood of nearly three thousand people. He had a role to play and there would be those who would want to take him down. There always was, she thought.

Nisba looked at other similar businesses in the country. There was serious competition in her view and there was also another fruit farm located south-east across the river, not that far away.

There was also the fact that he had fought for his country. He had said, although he was an Uzbek citizen, his soul was Ukrainian so he had volunteered immediately. Igor's background and capabilities may have led him to be someone important in the war.

From personal experience, Nisba understood what happened to people who defied the Russians, no matter where they were in the world.

She had to catch her breath from a heart palpitation. Wired fast as she called it, was quite stressful and tiring.

Maybe this was the reason he was remote, in a part-finished house, trying to be inconspicuous. Some outbuildings were falling down. On first impression, from the outside, the property appeared neglected and unloved.

His high profile scared her. Although he had made attempts not to have one, Igor's chance to have a completely normal kind of life could be difficult to achieve, plus, he was clearly unwell. He needed some help.

She would pick her moment to find out what the situation was with his work and if he was aware of any malign forces that might explain the tail. She wondered if he would be able to talk to her about his PTSD.

Nisba needed to check her flight details again, unable to remember whether it was the 26th or 28th, hoping it was the latter.

The flight was in fact booked for the 6th of March – sixteen days away. Deadlines and expiry dates made her anxious, so she double-checked her visa. Twenty-seven days left.

Ages. Nothing to worry about.

Nisba wondered for how long she could legitimately stay with Igor. She would be well enough to leave, days before her flight. Not ready to leave, any time soon, there was the hope though that her vehicle repairs and the reconstruction of the bridge would take a long time.

***

Igor woke at about 11pm and looked around him.

The moonlight was breaking through the inadequate curtains, drawn across the snug window above him. He found he had a quilt laid over him and Nisba curled up asleep at his feet at the opposite end of the sofa, her head resting on her hand.

He sat up. She would be cold, he thought. Nisba stirred.

'Come under the quilt,' Igor whispered, 'it's freezing.'

He wasn't worried that it sounded like a proposition. It wasn't. And it wasn't taken that way.

He would not push her boundaries, however, if she did show any sign of interest this time, he was not going to fight her off.

After today, he realised he had a lot of work to do before he could consider being anything other than just a friend to Nisba. Again, she had shown kindness, fortitude and profound empathy without judgement. He had not known anything like this before.

He couldn't just let her leave without doing something. Even if she didn't want him, she seemed to have become one of the best friends he'd got. Life would be better with her in it, in one form or another. He prayed for the first time in a decade, that life would find a way, where she would stay, or at the very least go and then come back to him.

He wrapped the quilt around them. There was nothing more healing than being close to this wonderful woman, he thought.

'Goodnight, Nisba. Thank you for looking out for me today.'

'Goodnight, Igor…I hope you can sleep well.'

Day 4 Monday

Since Nisba was feeling a lot better, Igor thought he would go into work for a bit.

He had distanced himself from The Plant (as he called it) for a month or so and felt more energised to reconnect with it. From a couple of emails, it sounded like he needed to be there in person and find out what was going on.

Nisba, who was supposed to be on leave, was setting herself up at the big table with her computer to do some work.

He was gathering his laptop, charger and other items.

'You have the run of the house, do whatever you like in it except, don't burn it down. I'm not precious about anything in it, so don't worry about breaking anything or going through cupboards to find anything you might need. OK?'

Great. Nisba had liked the sound of that. She'd make herself useful.

She would talk to him when he returned home, picking her moment carefully. The last thing she wanted to do was to stress him out and trigger something.

'If you go outside – don't go too far or get lost,' he said, smiling.

Nisba added him as a contact in her phone and then as a Friend to her tracker app.

He didn't have the app, so he downloaded it and accepted her Add Request.

'Until you delete me, you'll know where I am at any time – anywhere in the world,' she announced and then regretted it. She did not wish to see the screen with their initials showing they were a continent apart.

His face had dropped and he began looking about him for something he couldn't find.

'Right,' he said. 'I'm off.'

They stood there looking at each other for a few seconds. He dropped the bag and stepped forward.

They hugged. It was as if they were already at the airport saying good-bye. It was long. They broke apart. Igor turned away without looking at her but she caught his hand to pull him back. Her eyes still wore a smile, but this quickly evaporated.

'Be careful out there.'

He blinked a couple of times.

'I will,' he replied slowly and left.

She heard the engine start up and the truck scrunched away.

Nisba turned to look around her. She found herself in a stranger's house. His energy and soul had left so suddenly, she felt quite alone. Usually, she enjoyed her own company, lots of space and silence, but this felt peculiar.

Nisba was thankful for Misha's company, who was now looking expectant.

After locating her coat and boots, Nisba went outside and asked Misha to show her the way.

There was a blue tennis ball in the long grass. Nisba picked it up and stuffed it in her pocket.

The back garden was a field of about an acre. The flower borders were overgrown, with the grass standing at almost two feet high. This led into some woods. Near the entrance stood a mountain of logs. There was also a large tree stump and an enormous axe which was leaning up in a log store close by. This was almost full, with a gap at the top. It would be great for a game of hide and seek, she thought.

Misha ran on ahead into the woods.

'Wait for me!' Nisba called.

They had been out for nearly an hour in the ancient woodland, which smelled mossy and earthy. Along their way, Misha joyfully jumped in and out of the river, as if seeking approval and validation from Nisba after each jump and shake. Back on the path, Nisba threw the ball. Initially, Misha hadn't quite grasped the idea that she should bring it back and drop it so it could be thrown again. By the time they were back at the house, she'd cracked it.

Nisba was hot and fatigued. She had forgotten that she wasn't on form and would therefore be slow to bounce back.

'Whew! Now then Misha, how about some water and a treat?'

Nisba entered the back door and stopped dead.

Someone was in the house.

She could smell it. The smell of another person – a stranger. She possessed a keen sense of smell and could tell immediately; it was a woman.

Misha gave a tardy bark as she ran through into the kitchen area.

Nisba was scared. Could this be the stunningly beautiful girlfriend?

Nisba thought briefly, that if she herself were Igor's girlfriend, she certainly wouldn't be too chuffed with him having a woman to stay, especially one that he shared the same bed and sofa with.

She ventured in. There was a tall woman with her back to Nisba, standing, silhouetted in front of the sitting-room window.

Nisba's heart felt like it was throwing in irregular beats, so she had to catch her breath.

'Hello,' Nisba called out tentatively, in English, following with *privyet* – hello in Russian.

The woman turned and walked towards her. As she came into view, Nisba noted a strong resemblance to Igor but she had hazel eyes and a fair complexion.

The woman didn't give a greeting and there was no introduction. She spoke fluent English with an unexpected home counties accent.

'So, how are you finding living with my brother?'

The question had a disapproving tone.

Nisba wasn't sure if she should respond or assume that this was a rhetorical question.

'Fine, thank you. I'm Nisba it's um…nice to meet you.'

'Mila Rakhmanova.'

'Hello, Mila.'

Nisba didn't feel comfortable offering tea to Igor's sister in her brother's house but wasn't quite sure how else to break the stand-off.

'How about some tea?' Nisba suggested, not making any moves.

Mila walked to the kitchen and made a start, much to Nisba's relief. Mila carried on speaking, with her back to Nisba.

'You know he's sick don't you...?'

Nisba didn't answer.

'He thinks people are following him all the time and want to kill him.'

Nisba swallowed. Her mouth had become suddenly very dry, hoping the tea would come soon.

Mila had put the kettle on and lined up the tea-making things. She turned round suddenly, leaning against the kitchen unit and looked straight at her.

'I don't know what kind of a woman you are Sophonisba, but it's very odd to be staying here – out in the middle of nowhere, a single woman with an unmarried man…well, a widower. Aside from that, are you not afraid of him?'

'No,' replied Nisba, the wave of adrenaline beginning to swell.

Bloody Hell. His wife had died!

Mila slowly shook her head.

'And the night frights. All that screaming and shouting? I find it terrifying!'

Nisba supported herself on a stool at the island and jiggled her foot, remaining silent.

'Well, you certainly seem to have made a big impression on him,' continued Mila, raising her eyebrows. 'So much so, I was curious to come and meet you.' Mila almost gave the hint of a smile.

Nisba was very pleased and surprised to hear this and felt she ought to make an equally good impression back, so did her best.

'Well, I'm glad you've come over. It's my first day by myself…um… so it's very nice to make your acquaintance, Mila, and have some company. Shall we sit on the sofa? We bought some cake and biscuits yesterday, so I'll go and get them.'

'You've been out shopping? Well, that's...well I am surprised. Igor hasn't been living in this house very much at all, until very recently. He was staying with us most of the time, but I had to ask him to leave. He was scaring the children. You know – in the night.' Mila took a seat at the far end of the sofa.

'Ulvi – my husband, wanted him to stay, so he could keep an eye on him. They're close you see, but I had to put my foot down.
I think now, he spends most of his time with that work colleague – Raj. He was struggling with leaving the house and had a phase of not going into work at all.' Mila smoothed her trousers and turned to observe Nisba's face for a reaction. Appearing mildly disappointed, she continued.

'It's sad how the war has damaged him. He had such a terrible time. We were terrified he wouldn't make it – especially as he was let down so badly.' Mila checked Nisba's face again. 'You know...by that awful wife of his – Feruza.'

Nisba's heart felt like it had stopped momentarily.

'Yes, I'll have some of that, thank you.' Mila proceeded to busy herself with taking some Halva, placing it on the plate Nisba had just provided.

Nisba felt that Mila was quite enjoying the effect of her words. It seemed to spur Mila on to volunteer a lot more information without any kind of encouragement.

'Dad was very controlling, to the point he had it all set up that Igor marry his best friend's daughter. A fellow Uzbek also living in Ukraine, a Muslim. Anyway, Feruza left Igor. She'd been having an affair with his friend Oleksii. Apparently, they had been a secret item all along. She went off to be with him and a week later, they were killed in a bombing raid. Igor had already gone to fight and Oleksii...well I'm not sure how or why he got out of it...'

Nisba couldn't eat the Halva. She felt sick.

'So...Igor's gone to work, he's been out shopping, he's even texted me to find out how I am, which is quite out of the ordinary, and you two seem to be getting along ...very well, by all accounts. Curious.' Mila smirked.

Nisba was trying not to smile at this point. They did get along so well and ...she recalled their kiss.

Nisba glanced at Mila, but Mila had already found her out.

'All women find Igor attractive you know,' Mila said, smiling now. 'He just has no idea. He could probably have any woman he wanted, but he doesn't. He's just not like that. He's loyal and...' The smile suddenly faded. 'Just be careful with him.'

'I don't blame you for your concern Mila and I will be...I am being,' Nisba responded almost whispering, finding it a struggle to speak.

There was silence for a couple of minutes. Mila broke it.

'I hope you are fully recovered from that awful accident. I suppose there is a special connection formed with the person that's saved your life...I imagine that's something that will last forever.'

'I hope so,' whispered Nisba, without thinking.

Mila regarded Nisba for a few seconds and stood up to examine the items on the mantlepiece over the fireplace. She ran her finger along it, examining the resulting dust and raised her eyebrows.

'So...a daughter of Abraham – how interesting.'

That's the term given to converts, actually, thought Nisba, but she wasn't going to quibble.

'Do you have a Jewish name?' Mila asked.

'Yes...a Hebrew name. Mine is Rivkah – Rebecca.'

Mila nodded approvingly and then looked at her intently.

'You don't need to worry about any disapproval about *that* from me. Our mother brought us up to respect difference – even the Jews.'

Nisba coughed to stifle a laugh.

'Right,' she said, walking away from Mila to the kitchen to hide her grinning face. 'More tea?'

'What will you do?' asked Mila, suddenly sounding concerned.

Nisba turned and looked across the kitchen at her. She really wasn't sure of Mila's position. Was this a show of female solidarity, empathy, or a question to potentially humiliate her. She plumped for the latter.

'Be a good friend,' answered Nisba.

Mila raised her chin and gave her a wily look, just like her brother, thought Nisba. Mila nodded her head slowly and then began to smirk.

'I'll watch this space with interest.'

***

'What do you make of that Misha?' asked Nisba, as she threw herself on the bed. Misha joined her.

Nisba propped herself up to stop her heart racing so she could reflect on what had just happened. It took her a while to climb down from these kinds of encounters. After playing it all back, several times over, she was unable to draw any conclusions. Nisba couldn't make up her mind whether she liked Mila or not and was not at all sure what Mila thought of her. It shouldn't have mattered, but it did.

Nisba forced herself up and moved off to explore the kitchen and utility room, to help change the subject in her head. Immersing herself in some cleaning and odd jobs would occupy her mind.

Nisba found a large stash of PPE in plastic bags along with an extensive array of medical supplies. This was far in excess of a normal first aid kit, as if Igor were prepared for carnage.

After a while, she located most items she was looking for but had to do a bit more delving to find the cleaning products. Nisba did not want to feel like she was rifling through Igor's things, so was careful not to move items about too much. There was a pile of towels in a cupboard next to the sink. She pulled one out. Something very heavy was caught up in it which thudded loudly onto the quarry tiled floor.

It was a gun.

Nisba looked at it for several seconds. A 9mm semi-automatic pistol, she noted.

Misha had rushed over to see if it was edible but soon retreated. Nisba breathed in heavily. She wasn't surprised somehow. War would leave one never wanting to be defenceless and vulnerable she guessed, and ordinary life – peacetime, would never really be normal or peaceful. She ran through her checklist very quickly to ensure that her response was a normal one. There were no definitive conclusions. As a Brit, finding guns in your hosts house wasn't an everyday occurrence. Even a neurotypical person might struggle with this one, so she gave herself a break.

Unshocked, Nisba picked it up and checked it. She wasn't unfamiliar with guns. Since her incident in Angola, she had taken it upon herself to face up to her fear and learn how to handle and fire them. The magazine was full. The safety was on. Nisba put it back as she found it, inside the towel.

There were two.

The other was in the bedside cabinet. Momentarily, she felt afraid. Nisba had a vision of Igor holding her at gunpoint in a rage. It seemed implausible. There was no reason to be more afraid of him now than before. Perhaps she should be. Her new friend seemed to be living in fear, being followed by mysterious people, for unknown reasons. She had to ask herself the question: how much you have to love someone, to not feel a strong desire to run away.

This would be a lot. She knew she was in deep and breaking all her rules. How brave or stupid was she?

Igor was probably looking forward to getting his life back. She believed the chances of him feeling the same way to be a ridiculously long shot.

Nisba had known Igor barely four days and for her, life had changed.

***

Igor was looking forward to returning home. It had turned into a long day. Things were not running smoothly at the plant. It was now requiring far more of his attention to resolve the issues. He was resentful, as this would mean less time spent at home with Nisba.

It felt so different driving back to the house, knowing that she was in it. He expected that she would be working on her laptop, despite being on leave, or maybe needing to go back to bed. Either way, he was still excited about it.

When he arrived outside the house, all the lights were on and as he climbed out of his vehicle, he could hear music.

He opened the front door and walked in. Something smelled very good. He hadn't ever come home to cooking smells in this house. He spotted her in the kitchen. She hadn't heard him over the music, which was playing extremely loudly. Nisba had connected her phone to the wireless speaker. He had come in part way through the full-length version of 'Papa was a Rolling Stone' by the Temptations, before the lyrics kicked in.

Nisba was as if in a trance, totally unaware of him, wrapped up in the rhythm of the music. She could move. Slow. Provocative. Igor exhaled heavily. He didn't want her to stop. But then she clocked him, killed the music and beamed at him.

'Sorry about that!'

Before he could answer, she had bounded up to him, giving him a hug and a peck on the cheek.

'Good day then?' he asked recovering from the surprise. He had liked it. He'd never had a welcome home like that before.

'Yes, very good thanks, how about you...how was your first day back at work?'

'OK, thank you,' he replied looking about him, sharing a few dull details about it.

'Looks like you've had a busy day,' he concluded.

Everything looked different somehow. It was much nicer than how he'd left it.

There was a vase on the table, all bright and shiny with some flowers in it. The lamp in the corner on the bookcase that he could never get to work was now glowing amber against the wall. The only items that had been moved, he noticed, were his flag and wooden lady on the shelf. These were now dust-free and placed centre stage. All her stuff had been rounded up, no longer strewn across the floor. He began to see that he lived in a nice house.

'I hope you don't mind,' said Nisba. 'I like to be busy, so I tidied up and did a bit of dusting. I was conscious that you've experienced a bit of a home invasion. It must be hard to have a stranger in your house…'

Yeah, really hard. He smiled to himself.

'So…umm…I thought I would do something but wasn't sure how to contribute...'

Igor interrupted her.

'You don't have to do anything, Nisba…it's great, but for the record, I don't like the idea of you stuck here, cooking and cleaning because you feel you have to pay your way…it's not a role you should feel you have to fulfil.'

Nisba's eyes widened slightly and then she tilted her head on one side and looked at him, opening her mouth to say something, but didn't.

He continued to look around.

'You found a light bulb then?' he asked, looking at the lamp.

'No, I just rewired it.'

He blinked a couple of times and smiled. 'Right. Of course you did.'

'I don't think the person who did it before knew what they were doing.'

The dig wasn't lost on him. The corners of his eyes creased. His eyes twinkled. She liked it when they did that. A lot.

'There were a couple of other things I wanted to talk to you about.' Nisha said turning to him as she took the lid off the pot on the stove, giving it a stir. Nisba spooned out some of the lamb *Plov* she'd made, holding it up to Igor with her hand underneath for him to taste.

It met with his approval.

'Let's talk over dinner,' she said.

***

Igor was embroiled in a land dispute. It was an issue he had inherited from his father, when he took over the running of Chateau Prikat three years ago. He then left in February 2022 to go back to Ukraine and spent four months fighting, returning to Uzbekistan to recover, after being wounded. He was determined to go back but had been assessed as unfit and a liability.

Running the business was not something he had wanted to do. Before taking over the winery, he had established a career working for a super-major oil company. He'd resided and worked all over the world, in Houston, Trinidad and Tobago, Sharja, and Angola, to name a few places. He enjoyed the technical challenge of projects, as they had momentum, a beginning, middle and an end. Whilst the winery business was highly successful, he found the pursuit of maintaining Business as Usual, dull and unstimulating. He'd gained 6 Sigma Black belt and having trained others to that level, felt that everything necessary to maintain quality and maximum efficiency of production had been fulfilled. He didn't relish the idea of being responsible for all those families' livelihoods. His heart wasn't in it, mostly because it wasn't his own creation. He'd had a hard job freeing himself of his father's control, considering his father was still doing it, beyond the grave.

The nearby farm owner, a man named Shulkin, claimed that Sherzod Mirzeyakamov – Igor's father, had committed a land grab and fenced off acres of land that didn't belong to him. This included a section of the river. Igor had examined the deeds which showed that the river was clearly a shared boundary. Unable to live with any kind of aggravation, Igor had agreed that the arrangement revert to those in the deeds; however, this hadn't satisfied Shulkin. He had wanted more. Igor regretted setting a precedent. He'd known, deep down, that the issue would never be resolved. Not ever.

Igor had killed Shulkin's son.

It was in the context of war. Shulkin was Russian and his younger son, Igor Shulkin (an unfortunate coincidence that they shared the same name), was fighting on the Russian side.

Shulkin also owned farms in Russia, where his two boys were brought up.

In Igor's view, the land was a distraction, a petty feud – but this was inescapable. He felt an ongoing low-level threat from Shulkin and was intimidated on an irregular basis. It was unpredictable in timing, nature and severity. It was, therefore, hard to judge what it would lead to; hence, Igor feeling the necessity to defend himself.

The other thing that he thought she ought to know – Shulkin was Jewish. Igor had therefore killed a fellow Jew.

Igor braced himself. He was going to lose her, he thought, watching Nisba picking at her food. His chest began to hurt. He tried to turn himself to stone so he wouldn't feel the pain of her reaction. Surely, she wouldn't want to be under his roof any longer and would want to get away.

'Is that who is following you?' she asked suddenly, looking up.

His eyes widened and he paused for a moment.

'I thought I was imagining it. My thinking can be ...um, distorted sometimes.'

'It's real. Igor.'

Placing his cutlery down on his plate, he rested his elbows on the table and held his head in his hands. He then rubbed his face and studied her, hoping to get a clue about how she was feeling and what she might be thinking.

'Do you want to leave and stay somewhere else until...?'

'No,' she said, interrupting him.

He was bewildered. Relieved. Amazed.

She said she was upset and angry – but not with him.

Nisba told him that she felt that Igor was unlucky, in so many ways. If he hadn't killed Shulkin's son, it would have been someone else and they may not have survived to go on to be tormented by Shulkin. It just happened to be Igor. Shulkin had come out to Uzbekistan to reside and farm the land there, which as fate would have it, was attached to Igor's father's estate. And about killing a Jew... There was a pregnant pause. Nisba had forgotten what she was going to say so Igor held his breath until she resumed.

She understood his dilemma, appreciated even, that it would be a thing for him to worry about, but she did not see this as personal. It was an unhappy coincidence; just like the son being named Igor. What did bother her was that the guilt of taking a life, all the lives that Igor had probably had to take for survival and for the liberation of his country, was in his face– every day. Inescapable. How would he ever be able to heal? He had survived and left the war, but the war hadn't left him. It was so unfair and cruel. Nisba jiggled her leg which made the table tremble.

They sat in silence for many minutes. Igor picked at a hole in one of the table mats. He was thinking that she had a sensible logic and a way of laying things out. It had been helpful to tell someone about it, out loud. He felt he'd got more of a grip on it somehow.

'Oh – and I almost forgot,' exclaimed Nisba, waving her hands about. 'I met your sister today!'

Igor's jaw dropped. This was followed by a deep groan as he laid his head in his arms which he rested on the table.

She laughed. 'Oh, don't worry Igor…me and Mila – we're like that!' Nisba held up her crossed fingers.

'Fuck, Nisba. Was she a bitch to you?...I'm sorry. She can be so judgemental and self-righteous.'

Nisba wasn't going to disagree with him on that point and highlighted that his rather scary sister was the least of their problems.

'That was an excellent dinner by the way,' said Igor getting up to clear the table.

'Thank you. It was a pleasure making it. I love to cook. I quite fancy doing some baking tomorrow.'

Igor decided there and then that he wanted to marry Nisba.

There were many reasons why, aside from the baking, of course. The thing that mainly did it for him was the fact she could re-wire a lamp. The fact that nothing about him seemed to put her off, was a close second. But there was more to come and there would surely be limits to her friendship.

The fact that she would be leaving in a few days had been placed firmly to the back of his mind.

Day 8 Friday

They had begun to establish a routine, spending most evenings in the snug with a film on the TV that they never actually got around to watching. They'd talk until 2 or 3am cramming their life-stories into the time they had together, each learning as much as they could about the other.

Igor had nearly choked on his beer when Nisba told him about her two house-rabbits: *Randall and Hopkirk*. She had to slap him on the back for several seconds until he recovered. Whilst he had been tickled by it, this came as no surprise. She'd taken it as a compliment when he'd said she was – eccentric.

Igor taught her some Ukrainian phrases, which he found hilarious when she repeated them back.

It was very tempting for Nisba to stay up and fall asleep with him. Unable to trust herself, she dragged herself away to the bedroom.

Igor would lie awake on the sofa, hoping she'd fall for him. There was still time. He'd told her that she could stay as long as she wanted, even if the road and bridge became clear. He prayed she would stay until the day of her flight but saw no reason for her to stay any longer than she needed to. He wished for the floods to remain for a lot longer and that the work on the bridge wasn't progressing quite so quickly.

He would get ready for work, whilst Nisba set herself up at the kitchen table with her laptop. He made the coffee for them and since he'd bought more bread, toast was a regular feature at breakfast.

They sat at the kitchen table chatting about the day ahead. Nisba would go for her usual walk with Misha and have their customary cuddle and snooze on the bed afterwards, as the walk and fresh air still knocked Nisba out. She told Misha all her secrets and Misha reliably kept them.

Nisba and Misha had a dynamic that Igor found entertaining. They appeared to have full length conversations with Misha hanging on to everything Nisba said, tilting her head in response to key words. Igor didn't mind that he had no mastery over Misha anymore. She had been a good friend when he was in need. Now, he was just in awe at the capacity for dogs to have such empathy and intuition.

When Misha was sent to her basket, she sauntered off, throwing herself down with her back to them, making a loud *huff*.

'Don't sulk, Misha,' called Nisba. Misha held her big black silky head slightly turned, to spy Nisba in her peripheral vision.

'Yes, you are! I can see you are.'

Misha then proceeded to rearrange herself, giving another *huff,* sneaking a look round to make sure Nisba was watching. Misha lay down with her head on her paws, still with her back to them. They laughed.

'Such a special dog. I can't imagine life without her.'

Nisba immediately regretted saying that. Of course, there would be life without her. She rubbed her forehead.

Nisba then had to refocus.

She had her sights set on the teak garden furniture outside. It had been neglected for so long; it had turned green with algae. As the days were growing longer and were clear and bright, she thought it would be nice to sit out. Cleaning it would give her something to do. It was important for her to be occupied on something physically or mentally demanding and this would satisfy on at least one count. She promised she wouldn't overdo it...

The front door suddenly banged wide open. A man of South Asian appearance stomped confidently in and strode up to Igor, slapping him on the back.

'Come on man, we're late!'

Igor turned to Nisba.

'This is Raj – Raj, this is Nisba.'

Raj turned his head briefly, held his chin up and looked down at her for a second. Then he turned his back.

'Hi.'

Nisba had been getting up to acknowledge him.

'Hi,' she replied, but he was already walking away toward the door.

Dickhead.

His manner was very different from when she had spoken to him on the phone, only a few days ago, when he had provided such poor directions.

Igor scowled, stood up, grabbing his rucksack and laptop. They left. Raj slammed the door behind them.

Nisba could hear Igor's voice outside.

'You're a fucking rude bastard...'

She heard the truck doors slam and the engine start up.

Smiling to herself, she sat back, putting her feet up on the chair opposite, and sipped her coffee.

Nisba was suddenly startled by the front door flying open again. Igor strode over to her and leaned down so his face was close to hers.

'I'll see you later,' he said softly and gave her a quick kiss on the cheek. She suddenly caught his arm, pulled him close by the sweater and gave him a firm kiss on the lips.

'Just be bloody careful out there, Prince Igor.'

They heard Raj blasting the horn.

Bloody Hell, Nisba! What the hell did you do that for?

Igor walked back to the truck, elated. He was still smiling to himself as he climbed back into the truck.

'Right. Let's go,' Igor commanded, slapping his thighs, still with the vestiges of a twinkle in his eyes.

'For fuck's sake,' muttered Raj rolling his eyes.

***

It had been a long, hard day. There were delays in production when previously there had been none; before he'd taken his eye off it all. Faults with the machinery, an unprecedented level of staff absence, not to mention a fight that had broken out between two supervisors in the warehouse. These were just a few of the items he had to deal with.

His Director of Operations; namely Raj, was spread too thinly, so Igor felt compelled to step in. It was all this kind of 'shit' as he saw it, that he couldn't stand. The new site manager, Zeinab, seemed very good and on the ball. She'd informed him that on the upside, the fire drill had gone surprisingly well but there were a number of financial queries she wished to discuss with him the next day.

He was very happy to be home, once he'd finally got away.

Initially, he was unable to find Nisba in the house, looking around for a while, until he eventually located her in the back garden.

Nisba had tied her hair up, which formed an explosion on the top of her head. She waved at him with a wire brush in her hand. Her broad smile gave him a rush of adrenaline.

They greeted with a hug. He wished it had been longer. Igor could smell the ozone on her skin. He just wanted to scoop her up and take her to bed.

Then he remembered that she was too heavy for such a romantic gesture, so it would have to be then and there in the long grass. He noticed her cheeks were pink and her skin dewy, making her pale gold-coloured eyes glow.

Not realising she had been talking to him that whole time, he was caught off guard.

'...so, is that OK then?'

'Yes, great,' he replied to cover himself. In his mind, he was still there in the long grass with her.

His sister was right. A woman couldn't walk across a room without being assessed for sex.

But she had such a nice ass in those jeans and her vest top showed off her breasts, which were quite ample, for someone with such a tiny waist. She had a voluptuousness about her, but she was fit, toned and golden brown in the evening sun. He couldn't take his eyes off her.

He did respect her for her brains too, he really did. He didn't like to think of himself as a typical man. She was, after all, the whole package.

He recalled a conversation he'd had with his oldest friend, Yuri. They had known each other since they were five. They were in the same unit in Ukraine. They were sitting in hell on a pile of rubble, sharing a cigarette. Yuri had said – 'all that men were designed for was to fuck and kill and that's why men should be banned from positions of power. They were pre-programmed to instigate wars. War was therefore inevitable and endless, so women should rule the world.' It was an unexpected statement from the hardest man he knew, who looked like an assassin. Was an assassin. Igor was inclined to agree with him.

Then he remembered that he had something for Nisba in his truck. In the meantime, she'd put some music on. Despite having worked physically hard all day, she seemed highly energised and giddy.

He wasn't gone very long, but by the time he'd come back, Nisba was getting down to 'Crazy' by Gnarls Barkley and was singing – loudly. She could sing alright. He was pleased about that. Fitting song choice he thought. She was definitely crazy – just like him.

Nisba held her hands out to him, smiling. He felt shy, but took them, wondering what was going to happen to him. It was quite seductive, he found. Placing his hands on her hips, she slipped her arms round his neck. It was just dancing, he thought.

There was a hiatus when the song came to an end. They remained close together as he looked over her shoulder whilst she examined her play list.

She quickly swiped past the song from the film *Dirty Dancing* to Abba and 'Dancing Queen.'

Good save.

'But before we get stuck into that,' said Igor. 'I've got something for you.'

He handed her two cream coloured dinner candles. Nisba gasped. And then he produced two silver candlesticks.

'I can't believe it. How thoughtful of you.' She appeared taken aback.

'Go ahead. Please. Do what you would normally do on a Friday night.'

She set them up on a mat on the kitchen table. He handed her some matches and turned the lights down.

It was an aspect to Nisba he'd never witnessed before. It was intriguing. She recited the blessing in Hebrew.

'*Baruch ata Adonai, Eloheinu Melech ha'olam…*' Concluding with: '*Shabbat Shalom.*' She then turned to him.

'*Shalom*,' Igor replied. '*Salam Alaikum.*'

'*Wa alaikum assalam,*' she responded in a whisper.

They hugged and held it for several seconds

'Thank you,' she said into his neck. Igor thought he was going to burst.

Then she broke away.

'Our tune!'

She was like someone who'd been drinking, Igor thought, but Nisba didn't seem to need that to lose herself in dancing around the kitchen, doing her moves and singing along. Misha was also getting involved, prancing about, grunting loudly and occasionally jumping up on her back legs.

Igor couldn't resist pulling his phone out and taking some video. When Nisba saw him with his camera, she hugged Misha who was on her hind legs, her big paws resting on Nisba's shoulders. He caught a sweet moment when they were both grinning at the camera.

The Abba song seemed to embody everything about Nisba, joyful yet melancholy and kind of heroic. He couldn't quite believe what was happening in his kitchen or to him. He was having fun, enjoying her crazy, nostalgic old song choices. Up next was Barry White – 'My first, My last, My Everything.'

They waltzed around the house, Nisba in her bare feet and Igor twirling her around every now and again, dancing close together holding hands and then stepping back, arms extended. Nisba became hot and out of breath, forgetting she was injured. The pain killers were wearing off, but she kept going.

Igor felt that her energy had altered the fabric of the house. He gazed around him. It was warmly lit by the lamp she had fixed and the candles were flickering, reflected in the mirror. He found there was something extraordinarily dream-like and magical going on.

His mind flicked back to the dark, dusty and cluttered room, only eight days ago and to how he had felt then. Alone, tormented with no motivation to live his life. He returned to the here and now.

'Are you not tired yet?' Igor shouted over the music.

'No. I can go all night. – C'mon Igor, what's next. You choose!'

Day 9 Saturday

'You must be deaf, blind and fucking stupid,' said Raj, as he and Igor drove toward the plant.

'It's been obvious from day one, she's got the hots for you. You should just get in there while you can and then you can get on with your life.'

'...Get on with my life?' Igor repeated, furious. 'With this fucking millstone of a winery round my neck, having to work the weekend and listening to your misogynistic bullshit...'

Raj shrugged as he negotiated a roundabout.

'So, fire me and get a different ops director...find someone else to watch your ass.'

Raj rested his elbow on the edge of the window, steering with just one finger.

'You just can't see it. She's taken over your life.'

Raj turned to Igor, taking his eyes off the road every now and then.

'She's taken over your house, got you running home for lunch...it wastes so much fucking time, when you should be at work, helping me sort all the shit out. Not to mention commandeering your dog. It doesn't even obey you anymore...and what do you really know about her?' He shook his head, looking at Igor again.

'Keep your eyes on the fucking road.' Igor waved his hand at the windscreen. 'For fuck's sake Raj. And just stop all the Nisba bashing. It pisses me off. You don't know her...she's twice the man you are.'

'Fuck, man. You are ruined.'

***

Nisba had made a great job of finishing the teak garden furniture and had also cut the grass. There seemed to be no end to her grafting, thought Igor, soon becoming anxious that now fully recovered, she would run out of projects and be on her way, imminently. She'd already stayed longer than he had hoped for.

They pulled the table out into the evening sunshine. It was clear and bright, but cold as the evening was wearing on.

Since she had gone to so much trouble, they were determined to sit out and enjoy it. He'd never used the table before. In fact, Igor reflected, he had never sat out in his garden before.

They brought their dinner outside and had poured the end of a bottle of Chateau Prikat red wine into tumblers. He didn't possess any wineglasses which they laughed about.

They chit-chatted, commenting on how very peaceful it was, with the birdsong, the sweet and hopeful smell of freshly mown grass.

They both heard it.

Igor froze.

'I'm not expecting anyone.'

Misha barked and ran round toward the front of the house.

'Get indoors,' he whispered to Nisba and then headed straight for the log store, grabbing the axe.

It was difficult to hear over the din of Misha's incessant barking. The car engine they'd heard had come to a halt. The vehicle must have come right up to the front of the house.

Nisba, somewhat bewildered by the extent of Igor's reaction, reluctantly retreated to the back door to enter the utility room. She remained in the doorway, wondering how serious this was.

They waited.

A man appeared.

Misha barked and barked and barked.

The man held his hands high up to his shoulders his face wincing and flinching against the din and menace of the dog.

Nisba could see Igor drop the axe.

'Ulvi!' he shouted, smiling. Igor called Misha off but she curled her lip back, baring her teeth, sustaining a deep guttural growl. Igor beckoned Nisba to come out. She quickly attempted to quieten Misha down. Her reaction ceased for a few seconds, but then soon ramped up again.

Igor apologised several times to the man named Ulvi, shutting Misha in the utility room, where she continued to bark for some minutes behind the door.

'Nisba, this is Ulvi, my brother-in-law – Mila's husband.'

She was relieved, having heard very good things about Ulvi.

'Delighted to meet you.'

Noting large brown eyes and a generous beard she judged him to have a pleasant face. A religious man Nisba also observed. He was wearing a long white shirt over his trousers and a *doppi*.

'Likewise,' Ulvi replied, smiling, focusing on her eyes.

'I've heard all about your adventure with the landslide and hope that you are well.'

He'd looked past them at the table set out with the food and wine.

'I'm very sorry to be interrupting your meal. I was just passing and thought I would look in on you. It's been a while, Igor, and I've been thinking about you...here all alone... but clearly, I see you have company.' He grinned, turning to Nisba.

'It's fine...please sit and have something to eat with us,' offered Igor, gesturing toward the table.

'Oh, no. Thank you.' Ulvi waved both his hands, affirming the negative response. He was softly spoken, with a gentle and calm manner.

'I'll leave you two to...I understand that you will only be here for a few more days?' Ulvi asked, again turning to Nisba, giving her a commiserating look.

Nisba and Igor exchanged glances. Igor didn't appreciate the reminder.

Nisba suppressed a sigh.

'Yes, that's right, although I'm pretty sure Igor and I will be staying in touch.'

Why did I even say that? Her brain and mouth didn't always synch. She rubbed her forehead.

Ulvi nodded with a smile.

'Well, Igor, let's not leave it too long for a catch-up. I'm keen to hear about how you've been doing. I am very sorry that you are no longer able to stay with us.' He looked down regretfully. 'Anyway, I hope to see you soon,' and then nodded to Nisba.

He made off, back round toward the front of the house.

'See you later,' she called.

Igor looked puzzled. 'You won't see him later.'

'No, I know,' Nisba replied. 'It's what you say…instead of bye. It doesn't matter if you'll see them in ten minutes or ten years. Maybe it's an English thing.' She shrugged her shoulders.

Igor added this to his growing list of English idiosyncrasies.

Nisba reached for her tumbler and emptied it with one gulp.

'He's never come here to see me on his own before.' Igor rubbed his chin. 'I think Mila has updated him on the gossip and so he wanted to meet you. He's been worried about me. I bet they think something's going on between us,' he ventured, smiling, looking carefully at Nisba.

She deliberately didn't make eye contact.

'Ah well,' she breezed, looking at the grass. 'Is there any more wine?'

Day 10 Sunday

'You're not in any rush then?' asked Raj, helping himself to the morning coffee that Igor had prepared for Nisba. Raj didn't offer her any. They were alone temporarily, together again. They'd had a few encounters. He was never friendly and openly antagonistic.

Nisba looked up from her laptop.

'What do you mean?'

'You know...to get back home.'

She didn't reply, thinking momentarily about his accent; still unable to place it, landing on English public school interspersed with Mid-Atlantic.

He filled the silence.

'I get it. You're in love with him and you're what?...waiting for the fairy tale...something to happen? – *Don't go Nisba – stay here with me.*' He feigned an extra deep voice and Ukrainian accent.

Nisba laughed. Raj's face dropped.

'Wow, Raj. That was really not bad. Not bad at all!'

She sat back in her chair. Raj leaned against the range cooker swigging his coffee, his face showing calculation of what he might say next. Nisba beat him to it.

'Igor needs people around who really care about him, and I happen to be one of them.'

Raj looked impatient and gave an irritated sigh.

'He can't do anything as long as you're around. It's interfering with his work *and* he won't be able to go on his holiday.'

Weasel. Nisba pursed her lips.

'Igor is his own man, Raj. He will do what he wants, when and however he wants.'

Igor returned via the backdoor through the utility room. He'd been dealing with a brown rat that Misha had caught. He knew that they resided in his woodpile but had never done anything about it.

'Did you find it?' asked Nisba, as he took a seat at the table. He got up again, noting Raj with her coffee and went to pour himself and Nisba a cup.

'Find what?' asked Raj.

'The rat's nest,' replied Nisba quickly, glancing at Raj. 'Apparently, one is never more than two metres away from a rat at any given moment.' The corner of her mouth turned up a little.

Raj brashly responded.

'You should put poison down,' he said and gestured by dragging his finger across his throat.

'No, you can't do that. You'll kill everything,' retorted Nisba, irritated.

***

Igor broke the silence.

'You don't like Raj very much.'

They were about to have their Sunday night dinner. Feeling he'd been robbed of his weekend; Igor had brought work home with him. He wanted to be around Nisba rather than alone, late in the office. He used to stay behind every night, avoiding the fact that he had no life, other than keeping his employees paid.

It was pleasant and helpful to talk about his day, offload, but not too much.

'He has no manners,' Nisba responded, sitting back in her chair, spreading her hands out on the table. 'They're important.'

'Mmm. He has…trust issues. I don't think he likes you much either. He's probably intimidated by you.' Igor peered over the top of his glasses which he used for screen work. '…or he fancies you.'

Nisba laughed. 'Or he fancies you!'

Igor hadn't thought of that, he had to admit. But dismissed it out of hand, amused. He knew Raj a lot better than she did.

'I think he liked having you all to himself,' continued Nisba. 'Anyway, he won't need to put up with me for too much longer, so I don't know what his problem is…it's not as if I'm your girlfriend.' She shrugged. That statement pained her. Composing herself, she carried on.

'I don't like his manner. It's like a low-level sort of bullying. He won't like you having anyone around who will call it out, especially if they've got your back. I expect he's telling you that you're pussy-whipped and that you spend too much time with me and I've made your dog's allegiance change places.' Nisba studied Igor's face carefully.

He looked straight back at her.

Fuck.

He felt very uncomfortable and that throw-away comment about not being his girlfriend, that had cut him.

Nisba gave a sad smile and nodded slowly.

'When you're vulnerable, you need to have your wits about you. There is a certain type of person who enjoys taking advantage, taking charge and telling you how your life should be. I used to be with someone like that – a long time ago,' she said, bringing the cutlery over.

'I won't bore you with all of the details but it was slow and insidious. I didn't realise it was happening until one day…a visit to A&E later, I had to do a runner, otherwise…well, I may not have made it.'

Igor's jaw dropped. The look of shock on his face made Nisba uneasy, feeling she'd over shared and regretted it, remembering his lack of resilience. For her, it was like talking about someone else now, but it had taken her twelve years to reach that point.

'Carry on,' he replied in a whisper.

Nisba appeared to brace herself.

'I left in the clothes I stood up in. I went to my friend Faye's. I'll tell you about her some other time but… he found me. Stalked me for months, so I know what it feels like to be followed, intimidated and live in fear of your life. Wondering – will it be today? And there's no escape. Not even in your own head. Afraid to go to sleep because he'd hunt me down in my nightmares. Sometimes, I couldn't tell if I was asleep or awake …you know…him coming through the window or the walls. So, what I am saying is, it can start so low level that the toxicity is undetectable.'

Igor's chest had expanded and his knuckles were white. He had a strong urge to break something or go and chop some logs.

She leaned over, placing her hand on his and then squeezed it, shaking her head slowly.

'Don't take it on, Igor,' she whispered gently, looking into his eyes. 'It's been owned and dealt with.'

How was it, he thought, that so many smart, amazing women wound up with such fucking morons.

'But you do so well. You seem so – together,' he said quietly. 'What's your secret?'

Nisba laughed.

'I don't want to shatter any illusions that you might have about me. I think you will be disappointed to learn just how screwed up I am.'

He shook his head, looking at her intently. He was amazed how much they had in common and was now beginning to understand their bond, the connection they had.

'Everyone struggles, Igor. Don't believe anyone who makes out life's a breeze and perfect. Like Mila for instance. She's done everything right. Loving husband, children, respectable…feels like she's earned the right to judge? Don't believe it. Everything comes at a price, one way or another.' Nisba made her way back to the range cooker to check the pot on the stove. She continued talking with her back still turned and then stopped, apologising for losing her train of thought.

'I was going to say something profound but forgot what it was.'

She paused for a moment and then resumed.

'Yes, sorry. I think I was trying to say, that life is about trying to be the very best version of yourself, for you and for others, despite everything, that's what Judaism and Islam teaches us, right? And Jesus.'

He swallowed. She'd got his attention.

'I haven't experienced…war, like you have but I've inherited my parents' trauma…it can't be helped. It gets into your bones. It was hard, but I am really proud of my bizarre up-bringing.' Nisba smiled, poofing her hair with her hands.

'Things haven't exactly gone according to plan for me either. I think I must have unconsciously hit a fork in the road and gone left instead of right. Who knows where I was actually meant to end up. I've spent too much time trying to figure it out...find the person I would have been, if I hadn't been traumatised.' She began to pace and flick her pencil back and forth between her thumb and forefinger. 'Taking the decision to pull off the motorway I had been on for so long and risk getting completely lost, was terrifying, but it had to be done. I just knew that the destination was worth taking the risk for.' Nisba stood still for a minute and put the pencil behind her ear. It disappeared in amongst her spiral curls.

Igor listened intently. Nisba had come to sit down and borrowed his pen. She'd lost her pencil. He noticed she wrote a couple of words down on her note pad. He had learned that she often had to do that, otherwise the idea would just drop out of her head. Her mouth couldn't keep up with her brain, she'd said.

'In the meantime, you have to take time to understand that it is a journey. A process and that along the way you must admire the scenery, take comfort in the beauty you could easily overlook, you know...things like the trees, the sunset, listening to the birds. Because appreciating them – it's sort of, healing.'

Igor nodded, looking down at the curled-up corner of her note pad and continued listening, in silence.

'If your sense of perspective has been completely messed up by something, it becomes a Thing that interferes with everything. A creature. You need an expert trainer to help you be able to deal with it.'

She began to break off the wax that had dripped down onto the silver Shabbat candlesticks.

'Go on,' Igor urged.

'I think it's a bit like those owners who have dangerous dogs they can't control. It's a nightmare for them and everyone around them. They're terrified of it. It dominates and ruins their lives, until they can get a dog whisperer or whomever to fix it. And then, life is transformed. You can look forward to going for a walk, free from fear and whatnot…'

Igor now rested his head in his hands.

If she left now, she had left him with a gift. They were only a few simple words but they had resonated. She'd left him with sufficient empowerment to be able to change his life. It was all logical, practical, and made sense now. No matter how many times Dr Saparov and others had said that he should get *help*, it just hadn't landed for him. But now, he would definitely see about getting a psychotherapist or someone, to figure out what would best meet his needs. It had suddenly become urgent. He was so overwhelmed by this moment of enlightenment, he asked suddenly:

'You can see my Creature, my Dog?'

Nisba pressed her lips together and nodded slowly.

'Yes, I saw it the moment we first met.'

She fiddled with her hair and discovered the pencil. 'You only get one time on planet Earth, Igor and if some fucker…or something trashes it…you have to give your mind, body and soul the best chance, so you aren't robbed of it. Otherwise, they win and you're not living at all.'

Igor sat there not saying anything for some minutes, still gazing downward. He then looked up. 'You're still here.' he said. She could really do without his problems he concluded.

She sat in her chair swinging back on two legs and then suddenly rocked forward.

'Yes, I'm afraid so. I said I would look out for you, and I will, but I can't save you, not from your creature…beast, anyway. Only you can do that, but not by yourself. You mustn't try doing it alone. Anyway, you won't be alone with it. It will be hard, stirring it all up, but you'll always have me to talk to…' She looked up shyly, meeting his gaze and then quickly disconnecting, continuing to jiggle her leg.

Igor was still nodding slowly, coming to terms with what he had heard. He could literally feel his brain changing. His thought processes were taking different and unfamiliar routes.

He realised that in certain ways, he was also vulnerable. He needed to be more aware of what was going on around him and less self-absorbed and preoccupied, otherwise, he could easily be swept along by a negative slipstream such as Raj, or someone else. He knew Raj was wrong about Nisba and she wasn't completely right about Raj. Igor judged her to be good though, and with his interests at heart.

'So…what happened to you recently?' he asked.

'Ah – that.' She shrugged her shoulders. 'Well, I was strung along for a long time. He knew what I wanted, but he kept saying – 'next year, next year,' and then eight years down the track, on the last day, he said: 'Oh yes, I always wanted to have children – I just didn't want them with you.' She gave a dramatic *Ta-dah!* flourish with her arms.

'Fuck!'

She stood up and placed her hands on his shoulders, slipping her arms round him, burying her face into his neck.

He placed his hand on her forearm to hold her there for a minute and closed his eyes. Then she let go.

'I'll put the kettle on.' She walked quickly away toward the kitchen.

Shit. He hung his head because he realised that he loved her and there were so many reasons for her not to love him.

***

It transpired that they were to see Ulvi later. A day after his visit.

They were invited to the house. It was a beautiful sunny day, unusually warm for February, so they would be in the garden for lunch. They were to park at the back and come in through the garden.

It was like a holiday brochure, Nisba thought, with mature fig and maple trees around a large sweeping and well-manicured lawn with a kidney shaped swimming pool.

The beauty of it made Igor and Nisba smile.

'I heard that you love to swim, Nisba,' shouted Ulvi, waving.

'What do you think?' he asked, gesticulating toward the turquoise pool. 'You can come and swim whenever you want!'

Mila didn't look so sure about that and Nisba noticed.

They took seats in the shade under the cream canvas of an enormous parasol.

It wasn't long before Mila had appeared with a tray laden with plates of *samsas*.

On catching sight of Igor, his young niece and nephew suddenly scrambled out of the house, shrieking with delight, running across the lawn towards him.

'*Dyadya* Igor! *Dyadya* Igor!' They hurled themselves at him, proceeding to treat him like a climbing frame.

Igor pretended to fight them off, stumbling around with Aziz who was six and a half, on his back and Alina a year younger, clinging onto his leg as he walked around; her two little feet on top of his huge shoe.

It was so much fun; they wanted him to go around the whole garden again – faster.

Nisba wasn't convinced about them being scared by Igor's night frights.

They ended up in a heap on the other side of the garden. They all laughed at the spectacle.

Nisba sighed. He was just wonderful. It hurt.

Mila introduced their children properly to Nisba. Alina immediately asked Nisba if she could play with her hair.

'Of course.'

Igor grinned. Mila looked slightly anxious. 'Don't let her do anything you don't want her to,' she warned.

Nisba laughed. 'I'll be fine!' she replied, taking Alina's hand. They disappeared off to Alina's bedroom for a salon appointment.

'Well Igor...' smiled Ulvi, sitting forward, rubbing his hands together. 'I think you and I have some catching up to do!'

Mila suddenly felt left out. After a few minutes, she went to check on Nisba, to make sure Alina hadn't gone too far.

***

It was good to be back with the Rakhmanov household, Igor thought, with the hustle and bustle of family life. He had missed it. He'd also missed Ulvi. Ulvi had been the only person he felt he could open up to.

He found Mila hard to connect with. He often felt that she didn't want him around or that she was jealous of his friendship with Ulvi. Igor frequently felt judged by her, for falling short and for being unwise.

He wasn't sure if the arrival of Nisba would compound this or have the opposite effect. Nisba was so goddam likeable, funny and good for him, he thought, so failed to see how his sister could possibly disapprove of their…friendship.

Ulvi was a good listener. No judgements, just absorbing what he was told and then making the odd observation. It was comfortable and helpful, he found.

'What is it about her that makes you think – this is it. She's the one?' asked Ulvi leaning forward, elbows resting on his knees, fingertips touching.

There were so many things, Igor pondered. He had to think about them all.

They had a bond, a deep connection which had been forged more or less straight away. It was mysterious – like magic. He trusted her. In addition to that, she made him laugh – a lot. She was an oddball, and he really liked that, how she tiptoed around in socks full of holes, yet on the flipside, she was probably worth more than he was.

Ulvi was amazed to hear this.

And then there were her brain powers, Igor explained. She was competent. At everything, despite fundamental challenges.

Ulvi sat up and leaned forward finding this interesting.

'What do you mean, brain powers?'

'Nisba has super-sensitivity to certain things. She's clever, insightful and empathic. Knows how I'm feeling and what I'm thinking because Nisba has been through stuff too. She can see stuff others can't – like patterns and things…sees things through a different lens.'

Ulvi raised his eyebrows.

'That sounds extraordinary – almost scary.' He looked taken aback.

'I like it. She's helped me. Keeps me sane. I was losing it – and now I'm not.'

Ulvi nodded thoughtfully.

'So, you are feeling better then? Having fewer episodes?'

Igor nodded.

'I can tell now, when I would usually have one. I'm also sleeping a lot better. I am beginning to look forward rather than backwards. I realise I had been getting through each day still living in the past…you know...back there…' He waved his hand about.

Ulvi sat back and looked at the sky, digesting what Igor had told him. Once he'd collected his thoughts he asked: 'So, what's your next move?'

Igor turned to look at Ulvi, squinting into the sun.

'With Nisba,' Ulvi expanded. 'Do you think this is a good time for you right now to get…involved? I'm just concerned for you, that's all. Also, it's not just about what you have in common, it's what could potentially divide you…your differences; they're significant, to say the least.'

Igor nodded thoughtfully and then sat up, rearranging the cushion behind his back.

'We're two people bringing very different stuff to the table. It's people on the outside that generally have the issue. I don't see it as a negative thing or potentially divisive.'

'Perhaps you should,' said Ulvi in a grave tone. 'What about if you have children? How would they be brought up?'

Igor laughed.

'I haven't got that far yet.'

Ulvi joined in with some mischief in his voice.

'But you'd like to, right?'

Igor grinned starting to feel a little uncomfortable but then reflected.

'We've both been brought up in that context. It won't be a compromise for me. I have no relationship with the Almighty. I'm not religious. Ironically, she has suggested it might be good for me to try and find a way back…make peace…' Igor rubbed his chin. 'I've also made the decision to see someone. To get professional help.'

'Really?' Ulvi raised his eyebrows suddenly, looking more serious now.

'That's a brave step. Re-living it all.' Ulvi gave a little shrug. 'She's certainly making a big impression on you, Igor. Just be careful. Just because you really like her, doesn't make her right about everything.'

Igor gave a slight smile and nodded.

'Thank you for trying to keep me grounded and maintain my sense of perspective.'

There was a brief silence.

'So, what's your plan?' Ulvi asked suddenly, leaning forward to pick up his glass of apple juice.

Igor smiled, his crow's feet beginning to form.

'I don't really have one. I just don't want to let her go, that's all.'

Ulvi nodded. The seriousness fell from his face. He broke into a grin and gave Igor a couple of encouraging slaps on his leg.

'Sounds like a need for action!'

***

'Oh, Alina. What are you doing now?' exclaimed Mila, in the doorway of Alina's large pastel pink and yellow bedroom.

Nisba was sitting cross-legged on the pink fluffy rug. Her hair had been combed out and had a middle parting with a hair slide pinned on each side. She was holding her hands out for a manicure. Blobs of nail varnish were being applied. Alina was undertaking her task with such a high level of concentration she was sticking her tongue out and her forehead was furrowed.

Alina had short straight black hair in a bob with a severe fringe, otherwise, she resembled her mother. Both children did. They had her hazel eyes with the splash of green.

'So, madam, what colour would you like your toenails?' Alina asked with wide expectant eyes.

'Ooh…I can't decide – what do you think, the blue or the pink?'

'Oh Nisba,' whispered Mila, getting down onto her hands and knees to inspect the damage.

Alina proceeded to alternate the blue and pink. It was not a neat job.

Mila got up again and left the room.

Once finished, Alina sat back on her heels and asked. 'Are you and Uncle Igor going to get married?'

Nisba laughed. *I wish.*

'I only met him a week ago.'

'Mummy says…' Alina began.

Nisba braced herself for a monumental breach of confidentiality.

'You can be married to someone for years and not know them…so that doesn't matter,' replied Alina, assessing her handiwork.

The logic was blinding. Nisba blinked several times to digest it.

'So, will you say yes?' questioned Alina, her eyes wide again looking intently into Nisba's. She was so close; Nisba could feel her warm breath on her face.

Nisba proceeded with caution. 'Umm. What do you think I should say?'

'Yes. Because then you'll be my Auntie.'

'Oh, I see,' replied Nisba with a serious nod.

Mila reappeared at the door. Nisba wasn't sure if she had overheard.

'So, Madam,' announced Alina, 'what do you think you would like next time? What date should I book you in for?' Alina opened a little pink notebook and waved a pencil with a flower-shaped eraser on the end.

Meeting Mila's gaze, Nisba's joy fell into her stomach. She felt the prickle of tears. She was enjoying herself far too much.

'Right. Come on Alina,' said Mila briskly. 'I think that's enough for now – don't you? I think it's time we went back outside.'

Nisba swallowed hard, got up and straightened out her trousers.

Mila cast her eyes over Nisba's hair momentarily and then walked away toward the staircase.

Day 11 Monday

Nisba didn't know what to do.

How long should she leave it? Misha had run on ahead into the woods and had not come back. They'd walked together for about half an hour for their usual morning outing. Nisba had thrown the ball for her, but Misha had picked it up and run off with it into the distance. She would usually come running back at full tilt after a few minutes. It wasn't unusual for her to be distracted by a ground squirrel or a hare, but she never left Nisba alone for very long.

Nisba sat on a log to rest. She'd been running to try and catch up with Misha, calling as well as whistling for nearly twenty minutes. She was afraid to go too far in case she got lost.

Misha had probably made her way to the lake, she thought. Igor had told her that she'd caught a fish once, but this was still roughly over a kilometre away.

Nisba had avoided texting and alarming Igor unnecessarily. She would only do that once it had become seriously concerning.

That moment had come.

***

Igor pulled down the back of the truck. It looked like he was going to lift Misha out but changed his mind part-way. He wasn't ready. Taking off his coat, he laid it over Misha's body, turned away and walked off, disappearing round the back of the house.

Nisba didn't want to leave Misha alone but understood Igor needed to be. She stroked Misha's soft silky fur, speaking to her for a little while until she could feel the pending tsunami of emotion. She cut it down by walking away suddenly, back into the house, not really knowing what to do.

Igor chopped wood for two hours.

She could hear the thud, thump and thwack over and over and over.

And then it stopped. Nisba stood up to go and see.

It started up again.

After another twenty minutes, the light was just starting to fall. Taking the largest drinking glass she could find; she filled it with water and ventured out of the back door. Nisba observed Igor about fifteen meters away. The mountain of logs beside him had become even higher. He'd taken his shirt off despite the cold. She'd never seen him do that before. His light brown skin was shiny with sweat. A cyclone of rage and power, his huge arms swung the lethal axe with precision. His muscle development was impressive, with the V muscle just visible above the waistband of his jeans. They had dropped down low, because of the physical exertion. Not that she was looking. She gulped hard to compose herself.

Nisba was afraid to startle him, so made as much noise as possible as she made her way over.

Then she saw it.

His back. The scars.

She discerned three bullet wounds. Not neat. Smash and grab. There were also what she thought to be multiple stab wounds and several slashes.

He suddenly caught sight of her in his peripheral vision. He quickly turned to face her, taking a couple of paces backward so she could only be in front of him. Igor was breathing hard and swung the axe so the head thudded onto the ground. He leaned on it.

'You shouldn't have crept up on me like that – I could have hurt you.'

There wasn't anything to say to that. Nisba held out the water, trying to judge his mood.

'Thank you,' he said without looking at her. He gulped the water down so fast that it spilled down his chin and onto his chest. He wiped his mouth with the back of his forearm. Igor then looked squarely at Nisba for a moment, as if looking for a sign of what she might be thinking.

He stretched sideways still facing her, to grab his long-sleeved T-shirt from the woodpile and pulled it on. It became patchy from the sweat. Igor rubbed his face and head with his hand which he then dropped down by his side. He was ready.

'Let's bring her in.'

***

Igor retrieved a half empty bottle of Cognac from the sideboard, placing it down heavily on the table, followed by some tumblers. He poured two very large shots, pushing one towards Nisba.

She held up her glass as did Igor.

There was a long pause, observing each other.

'To Misha.'

'To Misha.'

Her bottom lip started to wobble. Taking a gulp, she blinked hard looking at the ceiling to stave it off, but it took hold. The sob erupted.

He stepped towards her and took the glass, putting it down on the island. He wrapped his arms around her. Nisba had to stand on tiptoe to reach his neck, where she buried her face, muffling the sobbing noises. She could feel his scars through the warm damp material and couldn't resist rubbing his back affectionately. To her, he was still the most beautiful man she had ever seen.

It took many minutes for the sobbing to subside.

His skin and T-shirt had become wet and she needed to blow her nose.

'You're all snotty – sorry,' Nisba gasped in between hiccupping breaths. He didn't reply and didn't let go.

***

The man with the digger, who had cleared the debris from the landslide, was asked to come back to the house. He was visibly upset to be asked to dig a grave; a grave fit for a grown man, as Misha had been pretty much that, at full length.

He cut it in the back garden just in front of the entrance to the woods. Climbing down from his cab, he spoke briefly to Igor to say he'd come back to fill it in once they had said their goodbyes.

Misha was wrapped up in a sheet and lay on another, so they could lower her in slowly.

Nisba had written her a letter. It was with great difficulty that she had done it. Goodbyes were the worst and hardest things for her to cope with. Any kind of parting had to be swift and understated, otherwise her emotions and sobbing would be uncontrollable. She'd laid the folded note close to Misha's heart, squeezing her big floppy lifeless paw, blinking very hard to stay in control.

'I found her ball,' said Igor, producing it from his hoodie front pocket. 'Should we keep it or bury it with her?'

It was still wet and a bit slimy, so he held it between thumb and forefinger. Nisba thought for a minute before taking it from him.

She could smell it. Something sickly and sweet. She held the ball up to her nose briefly.

'It's not going in with her,' Nisba replied. Igor didn't like the look on her face.

He took it back and smelled it.

'She was poisoned.'

***

Sent from Nisba's phone:
Monday 27th 16:00
Hi Mum, Sorry I haven't written for ages. All is well.
Having a good time here in Uz. I'll be home soon and will
let you know when, so we can do something nice :o) XXX

Sent from Faye Ubosi's phone
Monday 27th 16:12
Hey Niz. Not heard from you for ages. Wots happening?
Is it next week you're back? We need to catch up.
Either way let's set up another virtual date with a glass

of wine ASAP. Sorry. Can you get wine where you are???!!
:o):o):o)

Monday 27ᵗʰ 16:13
Nisba:
I know a man who can…

Monday 27ᵗʰ 16:14
Faye:
Bloody hell Niz!!!. I hope you're not doing anything crazy!!?
Can you take a call?

Monday 27ᵗʰ 19:28
Faye:
Niz – where did you go? Sounds like we need to chat!

Monday 27ᵗʰ 19:30
Faye:
Missed call to Niz

Sent from Tan Chico's phone:
Monday 27ᵗʰ 23:14
Hi Nisba, I hope you're making a speedy recovery! Not heard from you for a while so wanted to check you were OK. Igor tells me you are doing well but working too hard on stuff around the house and making him fat with all your cooking and cake baking. Sounds like he enjoys having you around! :o) ;o) Let me know how it's all going!!xx

Tuesday 28ᵗʰ 09:00
Jaguar Land Rover - Cheshire
Dear Sophonisba,
To date, we haven't received a reply to our recent Correspondence regarding an appointment to review your vehicle options. This is a reminder that your Personal Contract Plan for your Range Rover Vogue will finish on

Wednesday 1st March.
Your options are to return the vehicle, pay the outstanding balance of £49,000.42 or take up a new agreement.
Please get in touch with me as soon as possible to discuss how you wish to proceed.
Rob

Tuesday 28th 09:27
NHS Long-hill Hospital
Cardiology - Appointments
Dear Sophonisba Maasik, this is a reminder about your appointment on 4th March at 9.15 am for your annual routine follow up with your Cardiologist.
Please confirm your attendance by clicking the link below.
Appointment Confirmation

Sent from Amara's phone:
Tuesday 28th 11:23
Hey hon. Just to let you know that my elective caesarean is a week on Thursday!!! Can't wait to see you and for when you are 'Auntie'!! Text me when you land and we can talk
properly then. lots of love x x x

Sent from Mum: Rose Maasik's phone
Tuesday 28th 12:02
Hello dear. Glad to hear that all is well and looking forward to you getting back. I've had to get the boiler man back out. He treats me like a batty old dear and told me off for going up a stepladder to clean my windows! Honestly, anyone would think 80 was old. The structural engineer is inspecting the house regarding the cracks in the front bay on Thursday so could do with some help from you with the insurance claim and the letter to the builder. The movement is much worse than when you were here last. I'm afraid the front of the house is going to collapse! I forgot to let you know that my dear friend your Auntie Loretta died on

Friday. Anyway – so sorry to bother you with all of this whilst you are so far away. Off shortly to drive some real old dears to their hospital appointments Xx

Day 12 Tuesday

It was very quiet in the house without Misha. Nisba found the absence of another soul depressing. She reflected. It wasn't just that, she and Misha had a special connection. Misha was a one-off. Yet someone had snuffed out this amazing, beautiful creature and destroyed their strange, unique symbiosis.

Usually, Nisba relished the quiet when she couldn't get it, but now, with no choice in the matter, she didn't like it. It was becoming harder to occupy and entertain herself. The spark that had reignited following her accident had petered out.

The idea of Shulkin attacking an innocent creature was a new low, she thought. Disturbing.

Nisba spent hours, sitting, staring into space and when she snapped back into reality, she couldn't remember where she'd been.

Nisba had just counted the strands of the fringe on the Persian rug, when she spotted a bright blue SUV through the sitting room window – the SUV from the supermarket, slowly making its way up the track.

She got up and ran.

Crisis status meant her brain was operating in optimal mode. Her first reaction was to hide the kettle she had just boiled, in the cupboard under the sink. She grabbed her bag and slung it across her shoulder. It must not look like she was in. She then crept out of the back door which was open. Closing it carefully, she very quietly took the key, locking it from the outside. Fortunately, the front door was always kept locked.

Nisba then darted to the log store.

Hurting herself as she squeezed through the gap between the logs and the roof, she fell down the back. The logs had been arranged so they didn't touch the walls. This was lucky, otherwise valuable time would have been spent piling up logs to hide herself from view. Then she remembered about the rats.

It was impossible to move, squashed in the gap, lying on her side. Nisba had to check her phone which was jammed in her jeans back pocket. She was determined not to be one of those morons in the films, who left the sound on, only to be given away by some stupid ring tone.

Unable to get it back in her pocket she awkwardly stuffed it down her bra. It was pitch dark in the log store, damp and full of cobwebs. Owing to the lull in the drama, her body had begun to realise what was happening. Her elbows and knuckles stung. She had to force her head down low, so the blood wouldn't drain. She did not want to faint in there.

Her view to the outside was completely obscured, so she could not get sight of them.

Nisba waited and strained to hear.

There were two sets of footsteps on the gravel.

They spoke Russian.

'The dog's out of the picture. We just need the other bitch now,' one man said.

'I think she's gone out. The house is locked,' said the other.

'Get in and check the house. She's not been going anywhere.' The footsteps were becoming fainter.

'We're not leaving until…'

She could no longer hear them. Nisba pulled out her phone with difficulty and typed the message to Igor:

They're here

Nisba closed her eyes so she could hear better. She wasn't sure whether what she heard was the car engine starting or not. Unlike those morons in the movies, she was not going to come out of her hiding place too soon either. She would stay put, for as long as it took, holding the phone in her hand for some light and to see if Igor would respond. She didn't expect him to. He was smart and not unfamiliar with situations like this. He wouldn't risk giving her away. She would just have to wait. Closing her eyes again, she waited. And waited.

She opened her eyes. She could hear shouting.

A voice getting nearer.

It was Igor.

The app wasn't overly precise, but he could see she was nearby.

'In here!' Nisba shouted.

***

Igor sat at the kitchen table, his face contorted and his knuckles white. He could handle the menaces and intimidation; but would not tolerate this extending to Nisba.

Nisba was an innocent, who had inadvertently walked into a warzone. He felt he had lured her in, tempting her to stay.

He'd been playing a sick and selfish game he thought, pretending he could have the life he yearned for. He'd got away with it for a little while, having the time of his life, stealing precious moments.

Igor looked up as she walked back in from the bathroom. He observed she was filthy, covered in grazes and was coming down into a post-adrenaline slump. He couldn't do it to her any longer.

He rubbed his face and then ran his hand over his mouth and chin. His stone-cold shields of old had gone back up.

Nisba seated herself on the opposite side of the table.

'Tell me,' she said sadly, looking at her hands, knowing she was speaking to someone different now.

Igor bent his head. There was no nice way of doing this. He placed his hand over the car key and pushed it across the table toward her.

'The bridge opened this morning. The Shogun is ready – you're free to go.'

There was silence for a few seconds.

'Am I,' she responded, toneless. Not a question, but a statement.

'You're not safe here,' he continued firmly, struggling to maintain the shields. He used to be expert. He couldn't look at her.

'Please leave.'

'I see,' she said, expressionless, standing up. The chair scraped back against the stone floor. There was a pause.

'I'll be back in a minute,' she said suddenly and quite breezily.

Igor was taken aback. He felt crushed by her response. It was cool, off-hand and unfeeling, he thought. He'd hoped for some show of sorrow. Regret. Something. But she must have gone off to pack up her things.

So, he couldn't even look up to watch her go, holding his gaze on a mark on the stone floor, teetering on the edge of wishing he'd never met her. Never laid eyes on her.

She'd returned to the bathroom. He heard her lock it. She'd never done that before.

He sat there waiting, for what, he wasn't quite sure, stuck in the nightmare, feeling sick and rejected.

His phone rang.

'Raj – not right now...yes I'll come back later. Look, I don't need your shit right now. And yes – this *is* more important...' Igor hung up.

It seemed like Nisba had been in there for ages. He got up to take a look. The bathroom door was now ajar. He knocked and on getting no answer, he gently pushed it further open with his forefinger.

Empty. She must have come out while he had taken the phone call.

He then went to the bedroom, finding Nisba lying flat on her back on the bed, with her arms out to her sides. Her eyes were closed and she had her head-phones in. The phone was lying on the bed next to her. He very carefully turned it round with one finger to see what she was listening to.

'Wonderwall' – Oasis.

He was confused. If he were going to play any tune for *her* on his guitar, it would be that one.

He noticed her face was wet. Her top lip and the end of her nose were red and swollen. She had been crying. Hard.

He felt wild for a minute with sorrow and bewilderment.

He couldn't think of a single time in his life when any girl or woman would have ever cried over him. He knew goodbyes were overwhelming for Nisba so was prepared that this was the only reason. They were friends. Close friends, he'd thought. Been through stuff together, so this would be hard.

He sat down next to her on the bed. Hopeful, sad and feeling desperate, realising that each of their means of coping had hurt the other. He promised himself; he wouldn't let that happen again.

She opened her eyes.

'I can't walk away, Igor.' She struggled to make eye contact. Her eyes slid back to look at the ceiling.

This is what he had always wanted and hoped to hear from her. He found it agonising. He needed her to stay so badly and wanted her to know. But having dragged her back from the brink, he now had to push her away.

He swallowed. 'You have to,' he said, massaging the scowl lines between his eyebrows. 'But one day, it will be sorted out…'

'What if it isn't ever sorted, Igor? How can I live in some Cheshire village surrounded by footballers' wives, knowing you're here. In mortal danger. I can't keep you safe from over there. You're my friend.'

He gave her a sad, weak smile and leaned in to comfort her.

'Please don't – it's just too hard,' she said, managing to avoid a croak. 'But please may I stay until the morning. Can I leave at the same time you go to work? Then I'll make my way to the airport.'

He was relieved. He'd imagined Nisba packing up the Shogun and driving off, not knowing where to go or what to do. She wouldn't be able to face Tan, or anyone she knew; she was too proud. He wasn't sure what she would even say to Tan. What would he, himself, say to Tan?

Igor was still fearful, wondering what else could happen, between now and then.

He nodded.

'But you'll have to come back to work with me, you can't stay here by yourself.'

***

They drove to site mostly in silence.

Zeinab met them in reception.

'*Salom,* Mr M. Oh, and Mrs M too. How lovely.'

Igor caught Nisba's eye. Before today, she probably would have found that amusing, making some dry and witty comment, but he noticed her bottom lip wobble and her eyes fill up. She'd turned away blinking hard.

He'd never bothered with correcting Zeinab and now he felt he'd let it go on for too long to do anything about it. That wasn't strictly true, of course. He had to admit to himself, he'd allowed it to happen because he liked the idea of it.

Nisba noticed a pretty blond woman on reception; Russian to hazard a guess, who looked pleased to see Igor, as she appeared pink and flustered. He'd politely acknowledged her, returning his gaze immediately to Nisba. This woman was not pleased to see Nisba.

By nature, Nisba was not competitive. Despairing of her looks and hair most of the time, this, today – she found quite gratifying.

She was given a tour. It was a huge site with spacious, well-appointed offices; open plan with several vast production areas which she could only get a glimpse of through the small windows in the double doors. They were unable to enter these controlled areas.

Nisba had given a little wave to a petite local woman who popped her head out from behind a filing cabinet in Finance. Very neat and chic, unlike herself, thought Nisba. This was the only other woman she had seen, apart from Zeinab and the receptionist.

Maybe it was how she was feeling that day, but whilst the physical environment was pleasant, the atmosphere was not what she had expected. It was uncomfortable. Igor seemed ill at ease. The members of staff seemed wary about the boss and an unknown woman being shown around. Nisba had visited a great many workplaces across many different sectors throughout her career, and this, she thought, was not somewhere she would enjoy working. Recalling that it was the previous site manager, who had been 'let go', that had booked the meeting to look at changing things, she could see why. And then she had a thought. A big thought. It was important.

'Is that alright with you Nisba?' asked Zeinab.

Igor was standing behind Zeinab, signalling a nod for Nisba. He could tell her focus had been elsewhere and she not heard a word.

'Yes. Of course, great,' Nisba replied quickly, getting the message, with no idea what it was about.

The thought. It had evaporated. It had dropped out of her head.

They were now heading for lunch in the canteen.

Nisba was cogitating over the fact that she still had the rest of the day to get through. Her head was full of noise and felt like gridlock traffic. There was still the evening and then the night. How was she going to do it? The tour was a convenient, temporary distraction but what about when they had to return to the house?

***

Igor picked up his guitar.

He needed some sort of outlet. Since Nisba's arrival, he had looked forward to playing it again.

He was a clever and talented self-taught musician. He could hear something and then pick it out on his acoustic guitar. Nisba had told him she admired these abilities.

When he'd asked her what he should play, she'd said: 'Dancing in the Dark,' by Bruce Springsteen. It was what he used to play, before he met her, when he was angry and full of self-pity.

It would be odd to play that now. He wasn't in that place anymore. He'd think of something else.

Feeling sad and conflicted, he reflected.

Nisba struggled to communicate her feelings about anything but had shared with him that she was a big fan of poetry, which had surprised him. Her explanation was that – 'all the songs we know are poems; written by poets and poets who are musicians.' He saw her point.

She was definitely wrong about her not having a romantic bone in her body. She had been bold, contradicting her own words.

He considered the songs she had played for him in the kitchen, whilst she waited for the food to cook. She couldn't prep and listen at the same time.

He'd been paying too much attention to her to pick up on the significance of the lyrics. But now he did. There was one; very beautiful and very original, he thought – 'Symphony,' by Clean Bandit. He searched for the words on his tablet.

The second verse was definitely his, he thought, and picked it up from there. It had to be much lower for him. He played a few bars to warm up, to bring him to the right part of the song. The second line was almost impossible for him to finish. He could just about say the word – *healing.*

As he continued, he realised, she'd been trying to tell him something all along. The lump in his throat hurt so much, he had to get up and stretch his face and neck to get rid of it.

The other song, he remembered, was quite different. A dance number by Pink. Not really his thing, but she'd also played this numerous times. She tended to do that. Apparently, that was one of her traits. He wondered if he could play it back for her, to somehow tell her in return – because, he realised, he hadn't. Not out loud. He hadn't been as brave as she was.

Igor sat back down and fiddled about.

He became lost in it. Uninhibited. Passionate, finding it profound. So apt, Igor thought. He was also pleased with his rendition, discovering something new about his abilities, thinking he would add this song – 'Trustfall,' to his repertoire.

Nisba had suddenly appeared at his side.

He could barely look at her, the pain it caused him. Nisba's eyes were streaming with big plopping tears, blinking and swallowing so hard, she was gulping.

He put the guitar down and went to hold her.

'Please don't comfort me…I just can't deal with it.'

He then held her face in his big hands and looked into her eyes.

'Yes, you can. It's me,' he urged, wiping the tears from her red puffy lips with his thumb. 'You don't have to mask for me, Nisba. Just let it go and stop fighting with yourself. There is nothing wrong with showing emotion, showing me emotion – not today…'

Gasping, her shoulders shuddered. 'That was so good…what you were doing… on the guitar.' She could barely get the words out.

'I need to know…' Nisba then looked down and fidgeted with her fingers. It took her a moment. 'I just need to know if there is a way back for me?...back to this.' She waved her arms around at the room. 'Back to you. When I said, I can't walk away, I mean…I can't walk away, from you, because…shit…because...' Nisba looked down at the floor and rubbed her forehead.

She'd told him everything he needed to know. He wrapped her up in his arms in a big full body bear hug. Her feet left the ground.

'I am deaf, blind and fucking stupid, aren't I?' he said, resting his chin on the top of her head, then pressing his cheek against hers.

'Yes.'

They laughed.

'But you did say…' said Igor.

'I know.'

He held her tight to him again.

'I can't breathe, Igor,' she mumbled, muffled and smothered by his chest.

He released his grip.

'Ah that's better,' she said more clearly, drawing a deep breath. 'I feel much better about everything now, but the other thing is…I absolutely need to know, that nothing will happen to you.'

'I survived battle – just about…I'm sure I can manage Shulkin in Prikat and his heavies.'

'It was clear who your enemy was then, Igor, but I'm really not so sure who it is now.'

He released her suddenly, placing his hands on her shoulders, looking closely into her eyes.

'What do you mean?'

'It's just a feeling. I feel a pattern and can't put my finger on it. I just don't think things are quite as they appear to be.'

Nisba had scary insight, he thought, so was taking her very seriously. He was suddenly filled with dread and anxiety. He had to stay safe. Alive. There was a pressing need to devise a plan to sort it out, so he could live the life he wanted – with Nisba.

***

Igor didn't want to be around whilst she packed up her things, so he went outside to fill her Shogun with diesel and carry out some unnecessary maintenance.

He liked having all her stuff around. He especially liked having scanty lacey panties in amongst his laundry, as well as removing copious amounts of her hair from the shower trap.

He felt physically drained but emotionally charged. His heart was beating unusually fast.

Igor had reached the point of being unable to find anything else to tinker with and it was getting late. He turned to go back into the house, feeling sad, yet hopeful.

He reached as far as the rug in between the sitting room and the dining room. Nisba was filling a glass of water from the kitchen tap. He noted she was wearing the turquoise satin slip. She'd not worn it since the night she arrived.

Nisba put the glass down and turned round, leaning back against the sink. It was not just the way she looked, but the way she looked at him. Igor could feel his hands trembling, his heart pounding.

He instinctively knew that she had made a decision. She would throw caution to the wind and would have no regrets.

They walked purposefully towards each other.

Sliding her hand over his shoulder, she stroked the back of his neck and kissed him. Igor could feel his pulse in every part of his body. Their lips parted for a deep, long, hungry kiss.

He then buried his face in her neck and kissed her shoulder. The strap of her slip fell off, down to her elbow.

'May I touch...?'

'Yes,' she whispered, interrupting him with a kiss.

He took her a few steps back until she was against the table. Nisba lifted herself up onto it, wrapping her legs around him. Pressed hard up against her, he kissed her shoulders and then moved his way downwards, gently caressing her breasts. She was unashamedly uninhibited about how much she was enjoying him. He found it thrilling.

She drew breath, as he knelt down and stroked his big hands up her thighs, pushing the slip up to her hips. He brushed his lips against her skin, gently progressing along the inside of her thigh. Feeling his hot breath, she was intoxicated by it and groaned with pleasure and anticipation.

***

Nisba knelt astride him on the bed, stroking his chest and stomach. She leaned over him, whispering between kisses.

'Are you ready?'

'I've always been ready.'

They laughed breathlessly, their noses touching.

Igor pushed back her hair. They'd had a very brief conversation about contraception earlier. Neither of them had any.

They both gasped as he entered her. His hands gripped her buttocks as he pulled her closer to him, so he was deeper inside her. Nisba then sat up, flinging off the slip and shook back her hair.

He could see her – glorious and beautiful – Igor was enthralled by her body and what was happening to his.

In his fantasies with Nisba, he had been in control – masterful, manly and heroic, in his view. He should have known better.

This was an event with equal participation, initiative, and generosity. It was in turn joyful, passionate and intense. He loved that she was noisy and that he made her scream. He'd never ever been that way, but now, with Nisba, he let everything go.

There wasn't an inch of their bodies that they each hadn't kissed, stroked or tasted, by the time they had fallen exhausted into a heap. Then they slept, skin to skin, in each other's arms.

They awoke at 5 am. This time Igor was masterful, he felt, cradling her in his arms beneath him, they made love, slowly – eye to eye. It was a fitting finale, triggering each other to arrive at the same time.

Day 13 Wednesday

They packed their cars, slammed the doors of their respective vehicles and stood looking at each other.

They smiled nervously. Igor pulled up his jeans which didn't need pulling up and fiddled with the waist band. Nisba inspected the hem of her shirt and then looked up.

Steeling herself, she walked over to him. They stood very close together but not touching. They had agreed that they would not hug or kiss. Nisba looked at her feet for a little while, trying to steady her breathing.

Igor broke their rule by taking her hand, reaching with the other to her face, stroking her cheek.

She looked up into his eyes. She could do it. She would do it.

'I love you, Prince Igor.'

'I love you, Mrs M.'

The corner of her mouth crept up. She then turned to go, looking back briefly, giving him a mischievous twinkle of her eyes.

Igor smiled, placed his hand on his heart. He was feeling unwell from the emotion of it all.

'See you later,' he said.

'See you later,' she replied. Nisba climbed up into her Shogun and pulled the door shut.

Igor got into his truck.

She observed him gesture through the windscreen for her to go first.

He connected his phone and would be ready to press play. He had forgotten all about it. This was the right moment to listen to it.

Nisba had only one song she could bear to listen to. Happy. Sad: 'Together in Electric Dreams', by Phil Oakey and Georgio Moroder.

The rest of the journey would have to be made in silence, to debrief, to de-compress.

They wound down their windows, to wave at that moment when Igor had to turn off to take his route to the plant.

They had both checked they weren't being tailed and would continue to do so, checking in with each other on arrival at their respective destinations.

The music would now be a distraction from the lump in their throats and the tears creeping up, blurring their vision.

They pressed Play.

***

Nisba hated airports. Limbo. A sort of no-man's land.

She inserted her earplugs. For her, it felt like walking into a rock concert, although Tashkent Airport wasn't particularly big or flashy. She floated around as if under water. Waiting.

Nisba was not good at waiting. Now that she had left, she just needed to be gone, teleported home and moving forward.

She purchased a book of crosswords. This was part of her airport ritual. Unable to apply herself to any kind of creative thinking or ongoing concentration in such an environment, this was a perfect way to pass the time. It would keep her sufficiently entertained and challenged and therefore away from negative thoughts or a panic attack.

Nisba had already received Igor's confirmatory text. She logged hers, stating her safe arrival and that no one was following her, checking discreetly around her on arrival, in the queue for check-in, security and through into the lounge waiting room. Seating herself in a position with a view of the whole area, she could not be forced into a corner, without alerting others.

Nisba set alarms on her phone to check the gate. As an experienced traveller, she knew how likely it was to be distracted and easily miss her call.

She hated having to run to a gate, so put her phone on vibrate and turned up the volume. She did not want to miss contact from Igor either.

Nisba then spent some time people-watching, wondering if there was anyone else feeling the way she did, exhausted in the most wonderful way, her body fizzing and her skin – hot. Her head was slightly hung over with fatigue.

Nisba had to crush hard the fact that she had no idea of when she would see Igor again. It was this kind of emotional situation that caused her mind to pop up negative and irrational scenarios that caused unnecessary anguish: She'd get home, never to hear from him again, never taking her calls, or responding to her texts. No explanation. No closure. Left bewildered, alone and dashed. It took some minutes to shake this off and refocus. Back to reality.

Igor was consulting his immigration lawyer and had given Nisba his details as she would provide information regarding sponsorship. This lawyer had advised Igor previously, sorting out all his former visas for working and living overseas. It was hard to say how long the process would take.

She flicked through the pages of her passport, admiring all of the stamps for a moment and checked again the days left on her extended visa for Uzbekistan, as an employed foreign national. Eighteen. Nisba knew this but had to see it for herself, again.

Igor seemed so far away now but she took comfort in that she could still feel him and that he was still inside her.

Nisba closed her eyes. They were stinging and tired. She understood now what all the fuss was about. About Love. She always felt on the outside, not a member of the club everyone else was a part of. But now she was.

Right now, she just wanted to be back, skin to skin with him again, feeling his big warm hands stroking her.

Swallowing the painful lump growing in her throat, she opened her book of crosswords. The shapes danced off the page and big splashes of tears plopped onto the black and white squares.

***

Two and a half hours had elapsed and she'd done sixteen general knowledge crosswords. They just weren't hard enough.

Then the gate was open, so she made her way. It was the usual long, slow, tiresome shuffle, like cattle, from A to B.

There were three people in front of her in the queue to board when her back pocket buzzed.

The queue was now moving quickly. Making a judgement call, she stepped back to allow a few more people in front.

It was an unknown number, not Igor.

She pressed the green handset icon, then quickly regretted it, wondering if it was some threatening phone-call, then thinking it could be Igor, using another phone.

'Nisba. This is Doctor Saparov…where are you?'

His tone was urgent. She didn't like it.

'It's Igor – he's sick. Very sick.'

The floor started to sway away from her. Nisba bumped into two people who weren't very happy with her. She grabbed at the rail nearby. People continued to file past, ignoring her. She found herself on the floor.

'I'm just at the gate,' Nisba managed to say. 'I'm coming,' she said. 'I'm coming!'

The remaining passengers continued, stepping over her.

'I thought you should know.' Saparov sounded more serious and foreboding. 'Be as quick as you can.'

Nisba sat there for a few seconds. Her brain wasn't computing, she felt nothing. This was normal. It was simply too big to comprehend; experiencing a kind of 'malfunction,' as she called it, but would 'reboot' at any minute. Nisba examined the floor tiles whilst she was down there. They were big, greyish beige and highly polished with the fluorescent square lights reflecting off them.

One of the two ladies at the gate desk was speaking into a radio. One crouched down on her very high heels to address Nisba, to ask her if she was alright and if any medical assistance was required. The woman's face was unnecessarily heavily made up, she noted, and her perfume was so strong Nisba could taste it.

'No, I'm fine, thank you, but I won't be boarding the plane.'

The lady turned away and proceeded to speak further into her radio.

A young man in a fluorescent yellow jacket appeared.

The lady informed Nisba that it was too late to disembark her luggage. It would go on to Manchester via Istanbul.

That was the least of her worries, Nisba thought. She had to get out and into a taxi, to get back to Prikat, as fast as possible.

The young man didn't speak, just using hand signals, as he escorted her all the way back through the process, through the barriers, through security, passport control and then out of the airport. She could only go as fast as the man. He was taking his time.

'I'm really sorry. I'm in a hurry…it's a, it's a – umm family emergency.'

He didn't seem to hear her and continued like they were taught at school, not to run down the corridors.

Finally, she was outside, blinking in the bright sunlight.

She ran to the taxi rank but there was a long queue. Throwing up her arms, Nisba appealed to Jesus.

He was forthcoming.

Breathless, she jumped in and began to provide a lengthy explanation of where they were headed. She wasn't 100% convinced he'd got it and wasn't overly sure she had either.

Nisba had pulled out her screwed-up map to show him. On mentioning an amount in US dollars her destination suddenly became a lot clearer.

She then called Dr Saparov back.

There was yelling and groaning in the background. Nisba could barely hear him. The din was Igor, almost screaming at one point. It made her skin prickle with goosebumps.

'I'm on my way in the taxi.' She had to almost shout.

'I'm so glad you are coming back. We're at the house. He won't go to hospital. Perhaps you can talk him round.'

'I'll do anything.'

'I know,' he replied kindly.

There was nothing else she could do but will the traffic and the taxi driver to get her there. It would take an hour at least. It was busy. All the lights were against them.

Nisba leaned forward from the back. Grasping the side of the front passenger seat to support herself, she spoke to the driver, taking him by surprise.

'Sorry. Sorry. My…my…umm….umm…husband is ill. He needs me. Can you get me there as fast as you can?' she asked, pulling out a couple more dollar bills.

He didn't say anything in response, but she could feel the acceleration as he jumped the approaching light.

He chuckled.

'Thank you!' She sat back, leaning her head against the headrest, and closed her eyes.

'Please God. Please God.'

***

Igor knew something was wrong when he'd arrived for work. He had stomach cramps and felt sick.

The pain had developed into sharp stabs. He'd experienced knife wounds in the past, and this felt exactly like that. It was starting to make him double-up in agony, so he called Saparov. In the past, he would have tolerated it, allowing it to take its course, even if it meant killing him, but he had made a promise to Nisba and to himself, that he would take care and be responsible about his health.

By the time Saparov met him at the plant, Igor was squirming on the bathroom floor, sweating, gritting his teeth and trying not to make any noise. He did not want to raise any alarm other than to Saparov.

Igor believed Raj to be somewhere in Production.

He was wrong. Raj was shouting and banging on the door which Saparov had locked to keep any possible employees out. Raj had thought Igor had been ignoring his calls and texts.

'Open the fucking door, Igor,' shouted Raj, sounding scared.

He put his ear to it. He jumped back as Saparov suddenly opened it wide.

Raj's face froze with shock on seeing his boss and friend, writhing on the floor tiles.

'What the fuck is happening?'

Saparov didn't reply to the question.

'We need to get him comfortable and somewhere I can treat him… he won't go to hospital. It's no use us driving him there – he won't comply.'

Raj nodded with understanding.

He drove them to the Prikat house with Saparov and Igor in the back. Igor lay prostrate across Saparov, sounding like he had taken a bullet to his lower abdomen.

They dragged him through the front door, almost tripping over the rug and across the open plan area, onward into Igor's bedroom.

Saparov and Raj exchanged glances.

Igor hadn't wanted Nisba to tidy up. He wanted to come home to it and do it himself.

His clothing, pillows, underwear, as well as her slip, formed little heaps, scattered about on the floor. The sheet had been stripped off the bed and was screwed into a ball by the door. The covers were in a tangle across the bottom of the bed.

Raj rolled his eyes and Saparov laughed inwardly. He was pleased to see that their relationship had progressed. The amusement was short-lived, as he tended to his patient.

Igor threw himself onto the bed lashing about, not knowing what position he could take up, as there was no relief. There had been some seconds in between the sensation of a blunt knife slowly drawn across the inside of his bowels. The pain took his breath away and now, it didn't relent. Feeling faint, sick and feverish, Igor was convinced he was going to die.

He shouted for Nisba, feeling wretched and powerless, knowing she'd be thousands of feet up in the air, on a plane.

Saparov laid his hands firmly on Igor's arms.

'Hush, hush…ssh Igor – you'll hurt yourself. Take it easy.'

Igor continued to pull at the mattress cover, throwing himself left and right, clutching his abdomen and then his head.

'Look at me Igor…look at me.' Saparov wished to calm him. He had spotted the note on Igor's bedside cabinet.

'Can you hear what I am saying?' shouted Saparov, as gently as he could. Igor, straining, grunting, suppressing his pain, clenched his teeth.

'Yes.'

'She's left you a note.' Dr Saparov smiled and patted Igor's shoulder affectionately, as he handed him the folded piece of paper.

Saparov turned to Raj. 'Come on, let's give him a minute.'

Raj rolled his eyes and mooched outside, following Saparov.

They waited outside the door.

Igor unfolded the note, a page Nisba had torn from her planner. He could see that she had written the whole song out; all three verses, but he barely got past the title: [1]'The First Time Ever I Saw Your Face.'

Dr Saparov heard Igor break into a sob.

'Go and make some tea Raj, I'm gasping,' whispered Saparov, patting Raj on the shoulder.

It went quiet for a few seconds and then the sobbing erupted. Unstoppable. Uninhibited.

It brought a tear to Saparov's eyes, but the flush of emotion receded quickly, as his focus was channelled onto keeping this man alive.

***

The driver dropped Nisba off in the layby, adjacent to Igor's property and she paid him generously.

She ran all the way up the track, past the spot where Misha had found her in the mud, stumbling and panting, her heart feeling like it was trying to pump itself out of her body.

Overheating, Nisba tore off her jacket as she ran. Flinging the door open, she threw the jacket along with her bag across the floor. The house smelled different, of illness, vomit, and something else.

It was quiet. Still. No shouting. Raj was in the kitchen, holding himself up against the island. He did not look up.

She hesitated, her hand hovering over the bedroom door handle and then she grabbed it to walk in.

Igor lay motionless on the bed. His skin was a greyish purple colour.

Dr Saparov was sitting on one of the kitchen chairs by the side of the bed, his head down, his hands resting on his knees. His eyes were closed.

She was too late.

Suffocating, gasping for air, the room began to sway and white bubbles formed in front of her eyes. The sound was muffled, like she'd dived under water. She flapped about, to keep herself afloat.

Then she detected a faint voice beside her. It suddenly became louder.

'Nisba…Nisba,' Dr Saparov called out, as he held her up, preventing her from collapsing.

'He's sleeping. He's sleeping!'

She was confused. Her eyes had told her brain that he was dead. Slowly learning that she could undo this thought, her brain quickly rebooted.

'What are the symptoms?'

'I think it's a form of food poisoning but I'm not sure which type…he is sweating, has bloody stools, lower abdominal pain and vomiting. It could be Shigella, Campylobacter…'

'What kind of pain?'

'He says it's like knives – long drawn-out cuts, not short stabs.'

'I think I might know what it is.'

Dr Saparov was ready to listen to any suggestions

'E-coli.'

'That was on my list,' he replied, peeling off his gloves. 'What makes you think that specifically?'

'I've had it.'

Nisba sank down onto the bed and took Igor's limp hand.

Dr Saparov squeezed her shoulder.

'If it's haemorrhagic, he must go to hospital as he might need a blood transfusion,' he explained.

Nisba nodded in acknowledgement. 'I'm worried about his kidneys,' she responded.

'*HUS* is a risk, but he has been taking on fluids and electrolytes and there's been no vomiting for a while so…he seems OK, for the moment. There's no peripheral oedema, but it may happen.'

Igor had a canula in the back of his hand. It was the easiest place to insert it, despite the thrashing about. Nisba could see that he had soiled himself. It was bloody and his shirt was stained with vomit. He'd pitied her for the loss of dignity, the violation of privacy and of her personal space to save her, but this was just cruel, she thought. She decided to help clean him up, once he was awake.

'What have you given him?' Nisba asked.

'I've started with the IV paracetamol and antibiotics. He can have codeine, if the pain gets worse, but I would rather he didn't. That will slow his bowel movements. We need, whatever it is, to pass through him as quickly as possible. He must keep taking in the fluids, no matter what. I'm hoping it won't get to the point that he needs morphine.'

Nisba noticed that Igor's other hand was holding her note.

'I told him I'd contact you,' continued Saparov. 'He can't find his phone. It's vanished.' He shrugged his shoulders.

She narrowed her eyes.

'Right.'

'He won't know you're here,' commented Saparov, his lips forming a smile. Nisba smiled back.

She leaned over Igor.

'No!' called out Saparov. 'I'm sorry Nisba. Until we really know what the situation is, there can be no kissing…or intimacy, of any kind. You'll need to take measures to sanitise your hands and ensure that that there can be no transfer of anything.'

She understood, nodding sadly.

Nisba then turned to face Saparov.

'Thank you for everything...everything you're doing. Please can I ask that you don't give him anything you haven't prepared yourself or let him out of your sight. And don't let that – weasel, Raj, anywhere near him. Also...if you should feel unsafe in any way...' She was going to tell him about the weapon in the bedside table but decided against it. It was unfair to burden him and it would sound a bit extreme.

'...Will you call me?' she asked, making for the door and then looked back at him. 'I'm going to see a man about a dog...Saparov looked puzzled.

A little voice came from the bed.

Nisba ran back over to Igor. He reached his arms out to her. They hugged, becoming entangled in the IV tube momentarily. She muffled some sobs into his shoulder, apologising for not being able to kiss him.

'Dr Saparov won't let me.'

Igor made a half laugh, half coughing sound.

He then mumbled into her neck. 'You must not approach Shulkin. Not without me. That's important. Tell me you won't go. We plan things together – alright? He mustn't know I'm unfit. We stick together on this.'

Nisba nodded. She knew he was right. Everything they did had to be planned and sanity checked. She would not leave his side.

Saparov looked at a loss and rubbed his forehead.

'Is it best if I don't know, or are you two going to explain what's going on? And would you please be careful about contact.' His amicable and charming demeanour was starting to wear thin.

'I'm sorry, Yevgeny,' sighed Igor, with both his hands covering his eyes. 'I've brought you into a shitstorm...' He then winced, turning onto his side, curling his knees underneath him. Nisba took his hand. The pain was returning. She finished what he had been trying to say.

'Shulkin poisoned Misha and I wonder if he's done the same to Igor.'

She also brought Yevgeny Saparov up to speed, about them being tailed by the SUV, the intimidation Igor had been subjected to, and about her most recent visitors.

'I believe he was poisoned in the canteen. I was there. Igor had something different to me and Zeinab... and there was a new member of catering staff she didn't recognise. I remember her telling me.'

Nisba could tell, that the possibility of she and Igor being mentally unstable, paranoid and delusional, had crossed Saparov's mind. Igor had form.

It scared her a little. They had no evidence. It was all purely circumstantial, having nothing but their own testimony, suspicions – and fears.

Saparov thrust his hands into his white coat pockets and assessed Nisba's face. He knew that she was thinking what he was thinking.

Screwing up his face for a couple of seconds, he then relaxed and began to nod.

'But you have to understand, as a doctor, I have an obligation to keep my patients safe. If I have any reason to believe that you are in danger, I must inform the police. Also, if the culture comes back as E-coli 0157, this is notifiable. The chances are that the plant will have to be shut down.' He turned to Igor. 'To what extent do you think that would be convenient to Shulkin?'

'Very. It could ruin us,' hissed Igor through gritted teeth. 'I think he would like that.'

Igor groaned at the thought of the 2,800 employees that depended on him. He had insurance, but that was just money: this was reputational damage. It would be a disaster. The competitors would just swoop in and take his customers.

'This Zeinab...she needs to be contacted immediately,' stated Saparov. 'Find out how she is.'

'I'll do it,' volunteered Nisba, turning to Igor. Then put her hand to her mouth. 'Mila! We forgot Mila. We must contact her, to let her know you are poorly.'

Igor wasn't so sure. He'd agreed about Nisba speaking to Zeinab, but he really wasn't in the mood for Mila.

He'd felt bad he'd not caught up with Ulvi. An update was overdue, but if he told Ulvi he was ill, Ulvi would certainly tell Mila.

'Unless you think I'm going to die…let's not contact her yet.'

***

Nisba was thirsty and had a banging headache, so needed to visit the kitchen. She would have to face Raj.

He had remained there, knowing that for now his presence was not helpful or wanted. But he wasn't going to leave.

Nisba emerged from the bedroom and closed the door quietly behind her.

They were silent initially, as she reached for the painkillers from the top shelf of the kitchen cupboard.

After filling a pint glass with water, Nisba gulped the whole lot. She then slowly placed the glass down, as if trying to do it without making a sound.

'Tell me Raj, what is your job exactly,' she suddenly commanded, looking him straight in the eyes.

He was startled.

Raj had a young face for a man of thirty-four, so Nisba considered that perhaps he had grown a beard to make himself look more mature.

He wasn't an unpleasant-looking chap either. A bit on the short side for her taste at 5 ft 10, but on reflection, he was actually quite good-looking and clearly worked hard in the gym. It was a shame he was such an arse.

Raj found Nisba irritating because he thought, against his better judgement, she was pretty hot, and smart. Igor was a lucky bastard on that front. He himself, generally wasn't.

He had to give her the credit, that nothing seemed to pass her by, and that he could not manipulate her.

He folded his arms.

'I'm Director of Operations…'

'Yeah and what else?'

Resistance was futile, he thought. She would needle him.

'His bodyguard.'

Nisba nodded.

'You're not a very good one though, are you?'

Raj couldn't fight it.

'Touché,' he replied, stuffing his hands into his jeans' back pockets, twisting his mouth into a wry smile.

Nisba smiled in return. She was too fatigued to laugh but was relieved in some way that the impasse had been broken.

'So, you'll have checked me out?' she asked, tracing the pattern of the marble of the island with her index finger.

He nodded.

'I'm not that interesting.'

He broke into a grin.

'I had some concerns about you – your background. I needed to understand why you were here. I admit, my attempt to keep you away didn't work…well it made it worse in fact.'

Nisba raised her eyebrows, realising that by leading her astray with his bad directions, he had unintentionally brought her straight to Igor's door.

'I needed to shield him from any shit you might bring his way,' Raj continued. 'Your work with organisations investigating war crimes in Ukraine really doesn't help. You're an issue magnet. He's probably got a bullseye on his back, courtesy of the Russians. Other than that, there's a lot less to you than meets the eye.' He grinned. 'But I completely understand your motivation to do stuff like that, given your family history, but as far as my job's concerned – you're a liability. I've been trying to keep him vigilant, but now he's gone all soft and distracted.' Raj rolled his eyes. 'I know I've been a shit to you and you probably think I'm a nasty bastard…it's not felt great, but I'll be ruthless when necessary. It's just how it is.'

She bent over the island, resting her elbows on it, feeling the cold marble through her shirt sleeves.

'Look,' he said, walking over towards her. 'Let's bury the hatchet. I know you'll walk over hot coals for the guy and that's fine with me.' He held out his hand.

Nisba stood up straight and tilted her head on one side and narrowed her eyes, observing Raj closely.

'Other than money, what's your motivation?...there's something you're not telling me.'

Raj withdrew his hand, feeling confronted, but thought about it for a few seconds. He would give her something.

'I owe him my life – and pretty much everything in it.'

They shook hands, firmly, for several seconds.

***

Until the results of the bloods and sample came back, Nisba had taken instructions from Dr Saparov on how to take care of Igor. She'd made notes. Saparov had other patients and some family commitments to see to. Meanwhile, he would have to leave her alone with only Raj on hand to help.

Nisba felt bereft when he departed, now responsible for Igor's life and wellbeing; she feared him declining, crashing – unable to take remedial action.

Dr Saparov couldn't think of anyone else more trustworthy, or capable to leave him with, other than at a hospital. He found her to be decisive and authoritative. So different from their first encounter, he thought. He would also heed her earlier request.

He was fascinated to hear from Igor that Nisba was the founder and director of a successful global consultancy. On looking her up on the internet, he found that she had received industry awards and impressive testimonials. He was witnessing her power and strength now and the love she had for Igor.

Nisba felt a pang of guilt about calling Raj a weasel. Whilst she worried less about Raj's behaviour towards her now, she was not convinced by his competence to keep Igor safe.

Raj remained in the kitchen, perched on a barstool at the island. He would leave Nisba to deal with the vomit, piss and shit, he had said. That was not his bag.

He had installed, very discreetly, several cameras around the property, so he could observe any activity on his laptop. He felt it should have been done sooner, so he would have got a look at the two men who'd come to the house. Raj conceded that he had not been an effective security detail, although Igor had sent him away, several weeks prior to Nisba's arrival. Igor had told him he was going to take his chances.

In Raj's view, Shulkin's menaces to date had been none life-threatening in the main, with nothing to indicate who was directly responsible. He and Igor would be followed, but only occasionally. Initially, Raj had wondered about Igor's state of mind and if he was imagining it. He wasn't, regrettably. Weeks would elapse, and then it would happen again, so it was hard to judge the level or frequency of the protection required. Tyres would be let down in the night, dead birds posted through the letter box. The police had pulled Igor over, having been reported as a suspected drink-driver. They'd also had the Drug Squad with dogs raiding the packaging plant, owing to a tip-off about suspected drug smuggling. He was unsure of the local police. Igor was a well-respected pillar of the community – he was straight, but this was not the case with all police officers in the area.

The worst and most sinister incident was when Igor had been about to get into his truck to go to work. He'd glanced downwards, to find a red laser sight trained on his heart. It was following this that he had to persuade Raj to stand down.

The operation at work had become resource heavy, as it had to be carefully monitored to prevent the opportunity for a hoax, or someone planting something.

Raj had to fire the last site manager for using company funds to purchase items for personal use, such as laptops, audio equipment and cameras. Not of huge value, but he had to go. Raj and Igor had their suspicions that if he were removed from the equation, other things they couldn't prove might resolve themselves, which they did.

***

Nisba would give Zeinab a call, but first she wanted to make Igor comfortable, wondering how she could approach this without him feeling undignified or embarrassed. The first step was revisiting the PPE she had found in the utility room. It appeared to be overstock from work.

Nisba grabbed some gloves, hand sanitiser and antibacterial soap.

She and Saparov had devised a plan, in case Igor needed a blood transfusion or any other intervention beyond their skills and facilities.

A hospital visit would set Igor back psychologically. They agreed this would have to be carefully managed.

Saparov explained to Nisba about Igor's war wounds. His carotid artery had been nicked and suffered a pneumothorax, caused by one of the bullets to his shoulder. He had been close to dying, bleeding out, trapped on his stomach, buried under rubble. Initially, he was caught out in the open, trying to reach one of his men. When he was found, Igor was lying on top of the man, in an effort to shield him. In hospital, Igor spent many weeks of his recuperation on his stomach, unable to move, which had been very difficult for him. The young man, Volodymyr, who was only nineteen at the time, survived.

Igor was propped up with pillows, sitting very still, aiming to conserve energy. He held a plastic cup full of electrolyte fluids. As Igor was unable to reach the bathroom, Nisba had brought him a glass wine carafe to urinate into. There wasn't much else to hand.

'I'm going to take your clothes off,' she said with a grin.

He could barely talk but managed a weak laugh.

'And then I'm going to give you a bed bath.'

'Sounds good…you can do whatever you like to me.'

Nisba had several cloths for different jobs, three bowls of hot water, kitchen roll and two bin bags. Some blankets were warming on the radiator in the en-suite bathroom. She'd not done anything like this before.

When Nisba was eleven, she contracted E-coli along with four other pupils at school. The biohazard team from the council had to come to the house to collect stool samples. They had to shut the canteen down and the school, for an industrial clean. She ended up in hospital for four days. They had been out for the day with her Auntie Loretta and Amara at the seaside, when she rapidly deteriorated. They all thought she was being over-dramatic – as usual. When they'd reached the beach, she'd lain groaning on the sand, wishing she was dead. It was at this point they realised they couldn't ignore her.

The nice doctor in A&E had said that if they'd waited any longer, Nisba would not have made it. After a blood transfusion and two days in ICU, she was moved to a general ward. It took over a month for her to get back to normal.

Nisba was fearful for Igor but hoped that he might be more physically resilient than she had been. Fortunately, the intervention of Dr Saparov had been early and swift.

Nisba unbuttoned Igor's jeans. He helped by moving himself about, so they could be pulled down. He was less bothered than she expected and wondered how this would have played out if it had occurred before they had become intimate – before having the best sex they'd ever had in their entire lives, she thought, smiling to herself.

Then the apologies started to follow. Things were getting a bit messier as she got to his trunks. For him to know that this was all in a days' work, she chatted about what entertainment she could lay on for him.

'Not that sort of entertainment.' She laughed, shaking her head at him.

Nisba suggested moving the TV in, but he'd said that the aerial wouldn't work. She could get some music. He shook his head. Or read to him. Something jolly and benign. He nodded.

She knew what it was like to be stuck in that small room, with only just space for the bed, the bedside cabinet and a chest of drawers. The view from the bed was of cream walls with no pictures, just the windows with twelve panes in each (she'd counted them) on the right, and a plain blackout blind. It was a very nice big mahogany bed, like a French antique. It would need a new mattress, but for now, he lay on several towels.

She was quick with the hot and wet kitchen roll to clean him up.

Igor started to laugh which she was glad about. Nisba was not sure she would have been quite so good humoured, if she were in his position. In fact, she concluded, she'd have rather died than have Igor wipe her bottom, on the first day they met.

Afterwards, she'd disposed of the kitchen roll, peeled off her latex gloves, when he suddenly took her hand. His eyes were teary. He opened his mouth to say something, but no words came out. Nisba leaned over and they hugged, holding each other for several minutes.

She then bathed him from top downwards. The sensation of the hot flannel on his face was invigorating. He held it over his eyes for a while, before letting go for her to continue. They had another laugh about him becoming aroused. It didn't take much these days.

Igor was such a beautiful man, Nisba thought, and he had the most incredible body. Yet he had been worried about her finding him unattractive because of his scars, as well as being a 'nut-job' and being on someone's hit list. This, in his opinion, didn't make him a particularly eligible bachelor. But for all his brutal strength, inner killer and troubled soul, Nisba had discovered that Igor was quite soppy and romantic. At least one of them was.

As Igor had done for her, she went to pull the blankets from the radiator and laid them over his shoulders, tucking them in around him.

'Just let me know when you need me to clean you up again,' she said, as if she'd asked him if he'd like another cup of tea. She kissed him on the cheek, and they held their faces together.

At that moment she felt violently protective. If someone was to come and try and hurt him, she would want to fucking kill them, she thought. It shocked her.

Then she noticed his cup was getting empty, so refilled it and opened another sachet of electrolytes.

'I'll phone Zeinab now. Then I've got some life admin to do.' She rolled her eyes. 'After that, I'll see about rustling up some chicken soup and find something to read to you.'

***

Zeinab's mobile went straight to voice mail.

Nisba went on to catch up on her emails, conducted some online banking and called Faye, to help her out with returning her car to the dealership and sorting out a few other bits and pieces. This was all on the pretext that she was stuck in Uzbekistan because of work – for now. Everything was fine and that she would catch up properly, soon. Faye was not convinced because of the tantalising text she'd received. Faye knew Nisba and that she was playing for time, so wasn't going to push her. She would come clean soon enough. Nisba could not keep a secret. Faye could see Nisba's location on the Friends app. Nisba had been away from her Tashkent apartment in a remote rural location for just over two weeks now. Near vineyards.

Nisba wasn't emotionally ready to convey her reality. She would soon – just not today. The call to her mother would also have to wait.

Nisba couldn't make any promises of when she would be back either because she couldn't. She was someone who kept their word and was not very talented at lying.

Raj remained outside, fiddling with the cameras, as he had detected a blind spot.

Nisba returned to the bedroom. Igor was sleeping.

Her text to update Dr Saparov was a positive one and he was very much encouraged by what he read, but it was only day one of the symptoms manifesting themselves. They still had to be vigilant about HUS or nephritis – an inflammation of the kidneys, which could cause lasting damage.

It was only 3pm, but Nisba decided to prepare dinner whilst Igor didn't need her.

There was a whole fresh chicken in the fridge, which she swiftly cut and deboned.

Chucking the carcass into a big pot on the stove, she left it skin-side down to fry off a bit. She set the timer on her phone for ten minutes, so she wouldn't forget about it.

Whilst that was on the go, Nisba peeped round the door at Igor. He was so still; she had to concentrate very hard to see if he was still breathing. In a moment of panic, she rushed over holding her face close to his, to discern his shallow, hot breath on her lips.

She closed her eyes and breathed out.

Dear God, don't do that to me.

She stifled the hot prickling of tears.

One day short of a fortnight ago, she had vowed that she would remain a batty old spinster with her house rabbits, and over her dead body would she ever lose her head because of a bloke again.

Nisba today had absolutely no reservations about her feelings or her actions. She believed them to be wholly rational and well judged.

An alarm went off on her phone. The sound of a claxon. It had made her jump, wondering what it was for, having become so distracted by the laundry and other tasks. Nisba then threw the other ingredients into the cooking pot. Once she'd added seasoning and water, the lid went on and it was left to simmer. The kitchen smelt like roast chicken dinner.

Next, she would get creative and make some *matzo* balls. Nisba hoped this would be a gentle and nourishing meal, if indeed Igor had any kind of appetite at all.

Raj returned via the back door.

'That smells bloody good.'

'And how are you getting on?' she asked, leaning on the island and rubbing her face, suddenly feeling very tired.

'All fine, but you've been on the go for hours. You never stop. So intense!' said Raj filling the kettle. 'I'll make you a drink.'

Nisba was surprised.

'...And you've not eaten all day,' he commented, peering into the breadbin. 'I don't want two patients.' He turned and rolled his eyes and then gave one of his crooked smiles. 'Do you trust me to keep an eye on him for a bit, while you have a break?'

No, she didn't.

She hadn't said anything out loud, but he read it. He looked down at his shoes.

'For what it's worth Nisba, I hope I'm lucky enough to find someone who has my ass, like you've got Igor's.'

Nisba was taken aback and felt bad. It was just that she needed to be able to say to herself that she'd taken every step to protect Igor, eliminating the remote possibility of anyone getting to him. There was also the unfortunate possibility that Igor may get worse anyway, and then she couldn't know for sure if he had been got at or not.

She swallowed hard. 'I am sorry, Raj.'

He nodded sadly and then appeared to shake it off.

'I think we have good coverage. If you have a minute, I'll go out and try approaching the house and walk around it without being seen. Let me know if at any point you can't see me.' He turned the laptop round towards her. There were eight windows on the screen, showing a variety of angles of the house.

Nisba watched him leave the property and walk away down the track.

He veered off suddenly, scaling the fence and ran across the pastureland, through the fruit trees that formed an orchard on the right-hand side of the house. The sensor picked him up and a light came on. The relay successfully triggered all the other lights placed around the property. He then ran up to the cottage, working his way round the back, hugging the walls. Very slowly and quietly, he opened the back door, only to be met by Nisba, who was waiting for him with her kitchen knife.

'That's pretty good, Raj.'

'You can put that down now,' he said, sidling away from her.

She returned to the stove, checked her pot, put the timer on again and grabbed the crust of bread that Raj had found. Having poured herself another glass of water, she selected two books, tucking them under her arm.

'I'm off to read him a story,' said Nisba, with a hint of a smile, ready for Raj to poke fun.

But he didn't.

'Wait for me,' he called.

***

It was getting on for 5.30pm and there was still no word from Zeinab.

Worrying that her UK number may not be recognised, Nisba decided to send her a text. As site manager, Zeinab would probably work well beyond contracted hours, so hoped that Zeinab might return the call that evening, once she'd finished. There had been a lot going on. Nisba recalled that Zeinab mentioned having an in-depth session with the finance director to review all financial activity and to get to grips with the state of the profit and loss account.

Raj informed Nisba that he would have to leave soon, to go and check in on the night shifts, having lost confidence in the supervisors since the fight in the warehouse. He needed to be sure that the handover went smoothly

'I won't be gone for the whole shift. It's less than ideal,' Raj said, dragging his fingers through his hair. 'We could do with some extra help. Speak to Igor, he's sure to have a suggestion. Anyway, I aim to be back for that dinner you're making.'

***

Nisba found herself feeling sorry that Raj was leaving. He wasn't such an arse after all and she knew that she had hurt him, by not trusting him.

Igor was thrashing about again. The pain came in waves. Nisba was unable to keep both an eye on the laptop and attend to his needs. It made her nervous. She went as far as jamming the kitchen chair under the handle of the bedroom door. Igor mustered a laugh at her protectiveness.

If someone came, hopefully the lights would be a deterrent. They could really do with Misha, she thought, sadly.

Igor was becoming fed up with drinking so much fluid. Despite curling up to ease the pain, he was hungry. Nisba had brought him a hot water bottle, which he held close to him.

He said he would try the soup and *matzo* balls, unsure what he was letting himself in for.

Helping him on with a sweater as it was becoming chilly, Nisba tucked a tea towel into the neck. Igor was unsteady with the spoon, having little strength to even hold the bowl, so she held it for him and spooned the soup, allowing it to cool, first blowing on it and testing it against her lips.

His face creased into a smile. He loved her wide concerned eyes and the way her black eyelashes swooped out to the corners, her cupid bow top lip and big curly hair. She would take a dim view, he was sure, but he thought she looked like a Disney Princess. He'd watched enough of the films at Mila's with his niece and nephew, to know.

'What's the verdict?' she asked, grinning.

He nodded slowly. 'Very good.'

She loved his crow's feet and the way he looked at her from under his moody eyebrows. He was ridiculously handsome, and the way he spoke; so sexy, she thought. Deep, crunchy but soft, and the accent…

He wanted the whole bowl and all the 'dumplings,' as he called them.

She hovered with the last spoonful when her phone rang.

It was Zeinab. Nisba placed the bowl down and gestured to Igor that she would take the call, mouthing who it was.

'Hi, Zeinab. Thanks for calling back. How are you?'

'It's not Zeinab, this is Elias Ismailov – Zeinab's husband.'

It took a second for Nisba's brain to compute the words and the deep voice. His accent was French.

'Oh, hello – is everything alright?...I called earlier to check in on her because...'

'I'm at the hospital,' he said flatly.

Nisba blinked several times, to help her think.

'I'm very sorry to hear that and…and how is she?'

'She's in the High Dependency Unit,' he responded, struggling. She could hear it.

'Oh no. Do they have the results yet? – do they know what it is?'

There was a long silence.

'Of course they know what it is.' He sounded angry and incredulous.

Nisba could hear her heart beating. She hated being the cause of upset and distress.

She continued. 'Igor...umm...Mr Mirzeyakamov is not too good either. He's...'

'What! When did this happen?'

'It started this morning...'

'What started?' He sounded irritated and impatient now.

Nisba was bewildered. Then a creeping sensation started up her neck and across her forearms.

'I'm sorry Mr Ismailov – what has happened to Zeinab?'

'She was in a head-on collision on the Kangli Road, driving home from work last night.'

Nisba's heart felt like it had stopped and then thundered into action, the beats tumbling out of synch. She caught her breath, coming to terms with the news.

Igor reached over placing his hand on her arm. Nisba turned to him. Her face told him it was bad news.

Pressing the phone face downward against her chest, she explained.

Igor gestured to take the phone.

'I must speak to him.'

She nodded, handing him her mobile.

Igor flexed his shoulder muscles, breathed in looking at the ceiling and then suddenly, the polished, professional, owner of Chateau Prikat was speaking.

He introduced himself as Zeinab's employer, expressing his shock and concern.

Elias informed Igor that she was stable but had sustained a head injury as well as breaking one of her legs. She had been very lucky in a way. Her 4x4 vehicle had done its job to protect her and Zeinab was expected to make a full recovery, but it might be slow.

Elias was anxious about the fact that Zeinab had only been in the job a couple of weeks and feared that she might lose it. She could be off for months. They had both just relocated back home from France. Elias was waiting for his new job to commence in a month's time.

Nisba knew that healthcare was free in Uzbekistan and that employees received sick pay, but Igor had added that Zeinab was highly valued. Elias was not to worry at all about the provision of care for Zeinab. Igor would personally see to it that his employee welfare programme would apply, despite her short tenure, and he would also sort out compensation as fast as possible.

With Elias's permission, he would enquire about her tomorrow evening and see about an opportunity for a visit. If Zeinab were in a position to receive a message – to please send his and Nisba's regards and wishes for a speedy recovery.

He concluded the phone call and then flopped sideways with exhaustion and groaned.

'Was that alright?'

'Spot on. You covered everything that's within your power Igor.'

She then shook her head.

'Poor Zeinab. How traumatic and awful.'

Igor nodded in acknowledgement.

'I'll have to contact Raj to get it all organised, straight away,' he said.

'About Raj…'

'I don't think he's corruptible or untrustworthy, Nisba. He's protective. He's afraid of failing me and feels like he just has. Raj has a strong need to reciprocate, so it's a difficult dynamic for him.'

Nisba nodded with understanding. She was denying Raj that chance.

She wasn't going to probe about the reason, but Igor was more forthcoming than she expected.

'I met Raj on an exploration and production project. We were on an offshore support vessel, off the coast of Nigeria…we were attacked by pirates.'

He waved his hands about. Nisba didn't ask for more details. *Bloody hell!*

Nisba shook her head. What a life. Igor just didn't seem to be able to get a break. She imagined a dinner party with her friends Faye and Amara, with their respective husbands in the safety of her kitchen diner, back home in Cheshire, and the kind of anecdotes Igor would have, compared to them…

'On the occasion I was attacked by pirates…whilst I was busy defending my homeland…when I was poisoned by an avenging Russian...'

She rested her head in her hands. Things would have to be put right with Raj.

Igor kept forgetting that he didn't have his own phone. He had tried to remember when he had it last. It lived permanently in his back pocket, to the point it had left an impression faded in the denim of his jeans.

He was upset about losing the video of Misha and Nisba dancing together in the kitchen and the only photo he had of Misha, or Nisba for that matter. There was no other record of Misha, apart from his memories and her grave.

They sat there a while in silence, sharing the moment of sadness.

Nisba's eyes were drawn to movement on the laptop.

'Someone's coming.'

She removed the chair from the door and turned to Igor.

'I'll get the one in the utility room.' Nisba gesticulated at the drawer of the bedside cabinet.

Igor rubbed his head.

'Shit, Nisba.'

It was a bizarre feeling. She knew what to do. Something just carried her along with total clarity and courage.

Grabbing Igor's enormous hoodie, she pulled it on quickly, remembering that she had no clothes other than those she was wearing, and that her only possessions were the items squeezed into her hand luggage. Her brain began to do a stock take of the items in her toiletry bag.

Nisba unfolded the towel in the utility room cupboard and took out the pistol, laughing wryly to herself. What would Faye say now? It was all a bit incongruous, for a Cheshire girl to be toting a gun in Uzbekistan. However, her experience in

Angola had changed her perspective. Nothing was the same since. It was hard for Faye to understand. She tucked the gun down the front of her jeans. It was cold, heavy, and made them feel very tight.

Did it make her feel more powerful? Less vulnerable? No, it didn't. She felt dirty. She didn't want to hurt anyone and could not legitimately brandish a gun, without having one pulled on her. In fact, there was nothing legitimate about it. Unsure of what she was dealing with, Nisba was determined to be prepared, but felt slightly sick.

She made her way toward the front of the house with the laptop cradled on her left forearm, her hand supporting the open screen. Although the light was falling, she could clearly see a dark coloured vehicle making its way up the track. A hatchback, struggling with the potholes stopped and a man got out, jogging the rest of the way. Not wearing a jacket; it was clear to see that there were no concealed weapons.

Placing the laptop gently down on the kitchen table, she thrust her hands into the hoodie's front pocket to disguise the bulge and waited for him to knock on the door.

'Hi there – who is it?' she called out breezily.

'Good evening. It's Miguel Dos Santos... I'm Mr M's warehouse manager.'

Nisba could see him through the glass as she walked toward the door. A black gentleman smiled and waved at her. She knew that accent very well.

Nisba opened the door wide and stepped back.

'Hello,' she replied smiling back, rapidly scanning his body with her eyes. In one hand he held a phone, the other was empty by his side.

'You must be Nisba,' he responded, grinning.

'I am indeed. Good to meet you, Miguel.' She pulled out her hand. He shook it.

He wasn't looking to come in. Apologetic for the intrusion and coming unannounced, he explained he was passing Igor's track on his way home.

'I found this in one of the break-out areas.' He waved the phone. 'I recognised the dog, and I guessed the lady must be you, from what Raj and Zeinab have told me.' He held the screen up to her.

She saw herself and Misha grinning at the camera. Igor had set the photo as his home-screen.

She swallowed the rush of emotion and then wondered what Raj would have said about her.

'Thank you very much for returning it. Igor will be so pleased and relieved to get it back.'

Nisba deliberately didn't offer any explanations for him not coming to the door or being unavailable. Her instincts told her that it was best that no one knew he was out of action.

He seemed keen to leave, so she thanked him again for coming by and bid him good evening.

Nisba watched him run back to his car, reverse for a distance and then do several attempts at a three-point turn, before driving carefully away.

She ran straight back to the utility room to get rid of the gun and then re-joined Igor, who was lying on his side with his eyes closed.

'I'm awake,' he mumbled.

'One of your colleagues…Miguel Dos Santos found your phone!' She waved it at him.

Igor manoeuvred himself slowly to sit up. Nisba helped him with his pillows and sat next to him on the bed.

'He's Angolan, isn't he?'

Igor looked up. He'd put his glasses on and was looking over the top of them at her. He did look very cute in his specs, she thought.

'Yes, he is.'

'Mmm.' She nodded. 'I loved working with the Angolans, even though I had a bad experience there. Well, a couple, actually.'

Igor nodded. 'Tan told me, about the young man…only because I asked him. I got the impression something bad had happened.'

'It's OK.'

'But you say that wasn't the only thing?' he asked. How much worse could it get? He then regretted pursuing it. It could have waited.

There was a pause. It looked like she really didn't want to go into any further detail. There were other things on her mind, and this would require a 'Transition' as she called it. Jumping from one emotional state to another, or to another less interesting topic could be very uncomfortable and fatiguing as it often involved too many 'Steps.'

'Well, I dunno...I had a hunch the two things were connected. I was convinced Joao was put up to it...manipulated by bad people. We helped women in extreme poverty, providing access to health care, family planning, that sort of thing. I somehow ended up getting involved in a case, uncovering a fake birth control pills scam.' Nisba waved her hands about and then buried her fingers in her hair. 'Abortion is only legal to save women if they are at risk of dying, or if they are raped...or where there are birth defects, so they can be forced down a dangerous and horrible path, if they have an unwanted pregnancy. So that's what was happening. Someone was creating misery and then making money out of it.' She shook her head. 'I didn't feel safe after that, and then...anyway. We're a right pair aren't we? Trouble seems to follow us about.'

Igor was shocked. She put herself out there. Stood up for what she believed in. She was a brave woman, he thought.

'C'mon Igor...stop thinking about that. Remember your phone,' said Nisba, nudging him.

He unlocked his phone using face ID. There were a screenful of notifications, numerous missed calls, thirteen Call App messages – and one SMS.

Igor sat up with a start.

Nisba could feel it. The chill. Fear.

It was one word:

Max

'Who's Max?' whispered Nisba, her eyes wide.

'I am.' Igor replied downcast. 'He can't bear to call me Igor. You know...like his son. Maxim is my middle name, so I was called Max in the army. Too many Igors. It's what *he* calls me.'

'Shulkin?'

Igor nodded.

They sat in silence.

'Will you reply?'

'No.'

Nisba sat looking down at her hands and ventured to put her hand on his. He grasped it and pulled her in. They held each other for several minutes.

His phone buzzed.

They didn't move for a few seconds.

'It might be someone else,' Nisba offered, hopefully.

'It's him.'

Friday 6pm. Bring her with you.

He sat bolt upright.

'What is it Igor – what does he say?'

He shook his head. 'Shit,' he muttered under his breath, showing her his phone. Her eyes widened even further as she looked back up at him, her mouth dropping open. No longer just a bystander and a support to Igor; she was now suddenly involved – a protagonist.

'Fuck,' said Igor, rubbing the back of his neck.

He texted back:

No

The reply was almost by return:

No Nisba. No deal

'What!' Igor shook his head.

There was a ping.

It was a message via the internet call app. Someone else.

'It's from Ben Shulkin, his older son.' Igor heaved a sigh. 'It's strange to say…but he's a sort of – friend,' he said, looking bewildered as he turned to Nisba.

Nisba still with wide eyes, wondered what this could mean.

She's the key. No danger.

They exchanged glances.
Ping.

You have my word

They held each other's gaze.
'This is an invitation to Shabbat dinner,' Nisba mused out loud, looking at the ceiling.
'I think you're right.'
'Is their mother still alive?'
'No.' said Igor very sure. He was picking at the blanket.
'Any other women in the family?...is Ben married?'
'No, why?' Igor furrowed his eyebrows. He'd picked a ball of fluff the size of a marble.
'It's tradition for the woman of the house to light the candles. If there isn't one, the man does it, but I get the feeling…'
'We're not going, Nisba and you're not having to do anything. If you're lighting any candles on a Friday night, it's in your own home…here – with me.'
Nisba stroked his face. He placed his hand on top of hers, holding it there.
She had a strong urge to call him Sweetie Pie, Baby or Honeybun, or some such term of endearment. She didn't, but something was definitely going on with her, she thought.
'I wonder if it's a parley, you know, like in [2]*Swallows and Amazons*…[3]*Pirates of the Caribbean?*'
He wasn't getting it.
'This could be the pathway to a truce…an accord, Igor.'
He looked doubtful.

'If there's a chance, I think you…we… should take it,' Nisba said holding both his hands. 'Why don't you speak to Ben Shulkin and see if you can find out what it's all about. He can choose not to reply, or he could take your call.' She shrugged. 'But at least you've tried. It just might be a way forward to…I don't know some sort of closure…a settlement or something.' Nisba let go and ran her hands through her big hair. It sprung back and then flopped forward, so she tossed it out of the way.

'I think it's significant, Igor, my being Jewish. I vote that we go. Can it get any worse?'

Igor raised his eyebrows and then rubbed his lower abdomen. She had a point.

He was still recovering from his mortification of the whole situation. Dragging her into his miserable, sordid affairs. He couldn't believe it. She'd come back. This beautiful, incredible, bat-shit crazy woman had come back to him, prepared to walk into the lion's den with him. He was scared for her.

Igor exhaled puffing his cheeks out. There were two people in his life now, that he most wanted to avoid: Nisba's mother and her friend, Faye.

He threw up his hands, conceding defeat.

***

Igor had a bad night.

The pain was excruciating so Nisba had to set up the IV paracetamol again. Dr Saparov had texted earlier in the evening to say he would be over in the morning.

They needed to explain to him that she and Igor had a dinner date on Friday – the day after tomorrow. She was unsure how Igor would be able to manage. He was determined to show that the poisoning had not affected him. This was going to be a stretch.

Igor was determined to get to the bathroom on time. It wasn't so much about shitting himself, he said, it was about Nisba not having to wipe his ass again. There weren't many women, he supposed, that would find this an acceptable activity in the first three weeks of a relationship; perhaps after fifty years of marriage.

Everything was a mess. Their first 'date' was being fattened up for the kill by his nemesis. Then again, it might be their second. He'd tried to take all her clothes off on what Nisba had termed their first.

He prided himself on being a gentleman. Upstanding and proper and yet he was sitting on the toilet with his head in his hands, whilst Nisba wrapped a hot towel around his shoulders.

He would make it right, make it up to her as soon as he could.

Nisba didn't have any clothes, so she wore one of Igor's T-shirts, threw on his dressing gown and went to prep some food to leave out for Raj. Igor had phoned Raj to let him know the phone had been found and was now back in his possession, as well as to update him on the situation with Zeinab. This meant a new role for Raj and a vacancy back at the house, for a bodyguard.

Igor knew just the person to call.

'Max!' shouted Yuri down the phone. 'You bastard, it's the middle of the fucking night!'

Day 14 Thursday

Dr Saparov was relieved to inform them that it wasn't E-coli 0157 but E-coli all the same, and therefore still a threat to health, but self-limiting.

They should continue to be scrupulous with the hygiene as it would still run its course over the next five or six days.

He was pleased with Igor's progress, but less than impressed about him wanting to go out for dinner the following night.

'You should be resting in bed and drinking the electrolytes – not fine dining.'

Nisba pointed out that it wasn't a frivolous excursion, but more of a face-off. It was their first proper date and neither of them wanted to go on it.

Dr Saparov with one eyebrow raised turned to Igor, who was trying not to laugh.

'She's right, Yevgeny. I just have to get through it, so I'll need your help. Again.'

Day 15 Friday

Nisba's hand luggage comprised what she called her survival kit. From experience, as a regular traveller, she carried the basics for every-day living, albeit in miniature, in case her main luggage went astray, as it had done on several occasions over the years.

With only the jeans, black top, jacket and black trainers worn for the flight, she had nothing else, so nothing suitable to wear for the dinner at Shulkin's.

'Do you think it would be weird to ask Mila if I could borrow something,' Nisba asked Igor.

They were sitting up in bed, sipping cups of tea.

'Yes and her stuff wouldn't fit you. I think it would be too big. She's much taller than you.'

He hadn't caught up with Mila yet. He would though – to inform her that he and Nisba were an item. A couple. Serious.

He anticipated disapproval. Not just because she was Mila, but because it was a stretch for people to understand. A woman, turning up out of the blue, Jewish, and they had only known each other two weeks. Ulvi could accommodate it, he was sure, but Mila would require time.

'If you go into the utility room, there's something in there that might be of interest. I forgot all about it...at the very back.'

It made him smile when he heard her whoop with delight from the back of the house and then run back.

'You are just the best...! What do I call you by the way?'

'Igor,' he replied, raising an eyebrow, looking puzzled.

'Oh, you know! What do I say to people...what's your title?'

'Mister.'

She rolled her eyes. 'Do I say...my partner?'

He wasn't a fan of that.

'Boyfriend?'

Igor shook his head. It sounded like they were at school.

'...Lover?' she asked, lasciviously. He nearly spat his tea out.

That was just the sort of thing Nisba would say to people, he thought. She was naughty. A provocateur. He understood why she'd got into trouble at school.

Nisba emptied the hold-all, shaking out the green dress. It was a bit crumpled, so she hung it up in the bathroom along with the jacket. It would do nicely. It was a wrap over; just one button, Igor noticed, securing it in place. It had lantern sleeves with covered buttons on long cuffs. She pulled out the shoes and an unopened packet of lace-top hold-up stockings.

Nisba caught Igor's eye. He'd pretended not to notice. She grinned.

'That was a question I forgot to ask you,' he said. 'How come you were dressed for a hike when you were on your way to a business meeting?'

'I'm a secret agent, Igor, don't forget...' She laughed. 'No, I have to be careful. I usually change in the car. Anyway, how ridiculous. Can you imagine me tottering up your track in heels and a flappy dress in that wind?'

Yes, he could.

'And the underwear?' He rubbed his face recalling the moment he pulled her clothes off.

'What about the underwear?'

'Well, it was unexpectedly...umm, sexy – for a woman out hiking...' His eyes began to crease at the corners.

'I wasn't out hiking,' she replied quickly, her forehead beginning to furrow.

Igor smiled. He remembered that certain humour was lost on Nisba. He couldn't tease her.

'I like nice underwear,' she continued. 'And my mum taught me, one should always have nice clean underwear on, in case you get mown down by a bus or...well, in the event of being rescued by a handsome prince.'

'I see...so you were prepared.' Igor smiled, his eyes twinkling.

Nisba nodded seriously.

'And they have to match. I can't leave the house unless the bra and knickers match, or at the very least – coordinate. It's just how it is.'

Igor decided that this wasn't an issue he would have much difficulty with.

He dragged his mind back to the task at hand.

'Right,' she said. 'The major Jewish festivals...tell me what they are again...'

***

The house was very different to Igor's, more of a villa or plantation house. It was large, rendered white with many tall windows. It had an Art Deco feel to it, Nisba thought. The front porch was made entirely of glass.

Igor and Nisba climbed out of Raj's Discovery and found each other's hand, grasping it tightly.

'Good luck,' called Raj, from the driver's seat. 'I'll be right here. Just call or text if you need me.'

Nisba turned to him and swallowed. 'Thank you, Raj.' Her mouth was dry. He gave a brief wave of his hand in acknowledgement.

They were met at the door by Ben Shulkin. His demeanour was friendly and apologetic. He was a little taller than Raj and of slight build. He had large smiley round blue eyes and an unkempt beard. A mass of dark brown curly hair almost hid a blue and white *kippah*.

It took some time for him to walk down the hallway. Igor had explained to Nisba earlier, that Ben suffered from Relapsing Remitting Multiple Sclerosis. One of the two reasons he didn't go to war. The other – he didn't want to. He didn't agree with it.

They were ushered into a large, long hallway with a chandelier. He shook hands with Igor vigorously and took Nisba's gently, giving a small bow.

Nisba noticed that the chandelier had twelve candle-shaped bulbs, in amongst the crystals. The floor was tiled with black and white marble and bucolic oil paintings hung on the wall in ornate antique gilt frames. There were nine of those in all with one hanging about seven degrees down to the left, off the horizontal. She was tempted to straighten it, but then the scenario of the picture crashing to the floor, breaking, the ensuing apologies, embarrassment and major awkwardness, played out in her head. She would keep her hands to herself.

Ben pushed open one of the six heavy panelled doors, leading off the hallway, holding his arm out for them to go in. Nisba's high heels clopped on the marble as she made her way through, still hanging on to Igor's hand for support.

It was a vast and grand dining room, with a thick sage green velvety carpet, which her heels sunk into, a table laid out with sparkling wine glasses, vintage china and silverware. It was all unexpectedly beautiful, Nisba thought, with early spring flowers in a glass jug placed in the centre. It was set for five. She couldn't account for the fifth person.

At the very end of the table, in front of the bay window, which had the curtains drawn, was seated a very small and very thin old man. He was jaundiced.

This wasn't what Nisba had in mind at all, expecting to be intimidated by a large brute of a man, or a sinister looking one, stroking a white Persian cat. Igor gave her hand an even tighter squeeze.

Unsure if she should smile at Shulkin, say 'hello', or just do nothing, she looked to Ben and then to Igor discreetly, for clues. A small voice broke the silence. He spoke in English with a strong Russian accent.

'Please forgive me for not getting up to greet you,' said Shulkin. He was hiding breathlessness. 'Do sit.'

He patted the place on his left and smiled at Nisba. She just knew it – the place setting with the candles in front of it.

Igor moved to sit next to her.

'Max,' stated Shulkin, patting the table on the opposite side. Igor hesitated. 'Nothing bad is going to happen to her,' assured Shulkin, with a hint of a smile.

Shulkin then turned to Nisba and offered his hand. She swallowed and looked to Igor; she didn't want to do anything he would disapprove of.

He took her hand and placed his other cold and bony hand on top of it.

'How wonderful to meet you,' he said sweetly, with a smile that brought a glint to his watery olive-coloured eyes. Just a little bit creepy, she thought.

Ben took the seat next to her. He started to fill in the awkward silence with chatter about the traffic in the city, the new bridge and flood water and hoped that she was fully recovered from her accident.

'Yes…fighting fit thank you,' Nisba replied confidently, with a breezy smile. Igor was proud of her, but felt weary, having a strong desire to move his plate aside and rest his head on the white damask tablecloth and close his eyes. He was too tired to be angry, but his patience was starting to wear thin.

The dining room door opened. Another guest strode in, a man of a build, height and menacing appearance almost equal to that of Igor . He seated himself next to Igor. This man didn't make eye contact with anyone, and there was no introduction. Ben looked embarrassed.

Igor was angry now. This was a provocation, he felt. This man was Shulkin's heavy. His protection. A man called Rustam Rashidov. He had seen him before. Nisba could see Igor's lips purse and knuckles whiten.

He wanted to thrash it out now. Get it over with. Nisba's face had said: 'Let it go', but this was Igor's show. He was entitled to get satisfaction.

'You look like you wish to say something, Max,' said Shulkin, holding his wineglass up to the light. Ben shuffled up, nearly knocking his chair backwards and made his way over to the sideboard for a replacement.

'You killed my dog,' hissed Igor bitterly, between clenched teeth. Nisba braced herself. Her head was pounding with anxiety. There was no undoing this.

Shulkin's eyebrows shot up with surprise. He looked over to his man. The man shook his head.

'That was nothing to do with me,' responded Shulkin curtly.

Nisba could feel the blood draining from her head. The thought she'd had at Igor's workplace had just come back.

Igor continued, suppressing his rage.

'You poisoned me and…you sent people to hurt Nisba.'

'Absolutely not,' replied Shulkin assertively and without hesitation.

Nisba prayed she wouldn't faint at the dinner table. The room was starting to sway and her skin prickled.

'I think she's figured it out – she's a lot smarter than you isn't she, Max?' Shulkin replied, appearing amused, as he studied Igor.

Igor was furious and confused. He sat there, everything clenched, blinking.

Shulkin then turned to Nisba and looked her square on.

'So, Rivkah…are you ready?'

Igor and Nisba were both shocked in equal measure. How did he know her Hebrew name? Nisba's brain made a rapid calculation of the nodes in the network: Mila to Ulvi to family member to workplace to colleague – to Ben?

She turned to Ben.

He looked bewildered.

Another contact then – and back to Shulkin.

Her brain was noisy now, having a puzzle to solve which she had the urge to deal with right away, not wanting to drop any threads. It was important.

But she was on stage. All eyes on her. The puzzle was hogging all her attention. The spark plugs in her brain had been ignited by the new drama. It was loud and overwhelming. The excitement of it made her tremble. She was no longer in control.

Shulkin repeated the gesture toward the candles.

Nisba took up the box of matches. Her hands were shaking. She broke one.

Feeling exposed, tested, she lifted her trembling hands around the flames, closing her eyes.

'*Baruch ata Adonai eloheinu melech ha-olam…*' It was said, relying entirely on muscle memory.

It failed. Nothing. A blank.

Her eyes then met Igor's. She read his face and hands. It's alright. You're doing just fine. Start again.

Shulkin observed these micro signals, enjoying the chemistry between them.

Nisba started from the beginning, trying not to think too hard, allowing the words to flow by themselves. She recited the whole blessing, with relief.

'*Shabbat Shalom*,' was muttered around the room.

'Very sweet,' commented Shulkin, shaking out his large crisp linen napkin.

Ben stood up to conclude the ritual, reciting the blessing over the wine and the *Challah*. His father had looked on critically. Ben then returned to his seat, relieved, but then turned apprehensively to glance at Igor and briefly to his left, at Nisba.

Shulkin looked down at his lap and rearranged his napkin, smoothing it out over his knees.

'Now Max. Do you know why you're here?'

There was no reply. Igor was irritated. Feeling manipulated and patronised.

Shulkin proceeded anyway.

'I won't live to *Yom Kippur*, so the time has to be now. Today.' Shulkin sat forward, steadying himself, with his hand made into a fist on the table. The frailty and lack of oxygen to his lungs, were suddenly apparent.

Nisba felt like the air had been sucked out of the room and filled with an odourless suffocating substance. She could barely take a lungful. Igor held his breath.

'Do you know what *Yom Kippur* means to a Jew, Max?'

There was a protracted silence.

'It's the day of atonement and repentance,' Igor responded gravely, and paused, 'for your sins.'

He was glad of Nisba's crash course. She was right that he would be tested, potentially belittled, or humiliated for a lack of knowledge. He didn't like where this was going.

'Very good,' Shulkin acknowledged; surprised, nodding at Nisba approvingly. 'And now that you have Rivkah by your side, I have been reflecting...'

There was another long silence.

'I forgive you – for my son...for *my* Igor.'

There was a loud crash inside Igor's head. His breath caught in his throat. He swallowed hard. Then the storm settled. He found that he didn't feel any better. There would be strings attached.

Ben looked hopefully at Nisba, her eyes widening.

'I should love my living son more and stop looking backwards. There is such a short road ahead.'

Nisba heard genuine regret and sadness in Shulkin's voice and demeanour. It took him a few moments to compose himself. He showed some vulnerability, but it appeared there was a limit to this. He did not show any more.

'You will bring life into the world, Igor. Yes. I call you by your given name. I don't want you to die. You must not die.'

The silence that ensued made Nisba's eyes hurt. They were unusually dry and stung. She regarded Igor's face but was unable to tell if he had understood the inference.

The rest of the meal was conducted mostly in silence, broken occasionally by Ben's nervous small talk. Nisba and Igor helped him out with some benign chit chat. Shulkin didn't touch his food. He sat and listened. She noticed that his eyes were closed, most of the time.

***

They stood in the grand hallway where Ben brought out their coats. He attempted to help Nisba with her jacket but only made it more difficult. There was nervous laughter. She wanted to get out and would happily have run out into the cold night without it.

Shulkin slowly followed, shuffling with a stick. His face looked sickly and more jaundiced in the cold light of the hall chandelier.

He shuffled up to Nisba, facing her, a little too close for politeness and reached up a hand, bruised and taped with a canula, to touch her hair. She supressed a flinch and looked him in the eyes. He was dying. Death was imminent. She could feel it and smell it, sensing that he had wasted time. Far too much time. Nisba suddenly felt very sad; maybe it was the post adrenaline crash, she thought.

She cleared her throat. '*G'mar chatimah tovah,*' she said, gravely.

'*G'mar Tov,*' Shulkin replied, nodding magnanimously.

Then his face suddenly brightened, as he brushed a curl out of her eyes and turned to Igor with satisfaction.

'Such beautiful daughters!'

***

Raj drove them home. The journey was in silence.

Igor and Nisba sat in the back together holding hands, leaning on each other for support.

It would take Igor a while to come to terms with the idea that the threat posed by Shulkin had been lifted. It had become part of him, a way of life. It would leave a scar. He'd need to talk about it with Nisba and his psychotherapist.

He realised that before he'd met Nisba, he wouldn't have had the self-awareness to think clearly about it. He would have been caught up in the emotion, the victimhood, as well as the guilt of being let off the hook.

It was a 'Thing' to be dealt with, rather than be consumed by. It was a major step closer to the life he wanted. He turned his head to kiss her on the bridge of her nose. She looked up at him with a tired smile, kissing him gently back on the lips.

'Thank you,' he whispered.

She tilted her head.

'For saving my ass.' She stroked his head. His hair had grown. He looked less severe. Less brutal. He'd also developed a beard, which he had to tidy up, before they'd come out.

They arrived back at the house. It was quiet. All the lights came on, as they parked up outside. Raj had been monitoring the property via the laptop on the front seat.

Nisba was surprised when Raj came round to open the vehicle door to help her out. Igor shuffled over to exit the same way and leant on Raj. Igor was ready to drop with exhaustion and pain. The codeine Saparov had given him was wearing off, as was its slowing effects on his bowels.

He had to wait for Raj, who insisted on going in first to take a look around. Once all clear, Igor made his way swiftly to the bathroom.

Raj chucked the car keys on the kitchen table. Nisba kicked off her shoes and groaned with relief, as she wriggled her toes.

'So?' asked Raj, his eyebrows raised and hands out, expectant.

Nisba smiled and breathed in. She was still needing to debrief in her own head, have a longer period of silence to decompress.

'Let's wait for Igor.' Nisba tiptoed over to the kitchen. 'Are you hungry?' she asked, opening the fridge.

'You bet. I could eat a scabby horse.'

They heard Igor start up the shower in the en-suite. Nisba excused herself for a minute. Igor had just finished his shower as she leaned her hand on the glass.

'Are you alright, Sweetie Pie?'

He stood, Adonis body dripping, and wiped the water out of his eyes and from his face.

She yelped as he grabbed her round the waist pulling her into the shower and kissing her. She was soaked.

They laughed.

'I'll just starve out here... don't mind me,' shouted Raj, from the kitchen.

'I'm not sure how it happened...it just came out!' Nisba whispered to Igor, her face, incredulous. Then she was conflicted. Her training would say she was infantilising him, but it was a genuine term of endearment.

'I quite like it,' Igor replied, his face serious, pushing the hair out of her face with his wet hands.

'Don't worry...I'll make sure it never happens in front of Raj.'

'I'd appreciate that,' said Igor, grabbing the towel.

***

They perched around the island on the barstools, whilst Nisba put together some sandwiches, or 'butties,' as she called them.

Igor relayed a verbatim account for Raj of the evening's events, with expletives and some ranting.

Raj was suitably outraged and joined in, commiserating with Igor.

'What a fucking manipulative, creepy bastard!'

Nisba sat quietly listening, dabbing the wet patches on her dress with a hand towel.

After about twenty minutes of this verbal exertion, Igor had had enough. 'What are you thinking, Nisba?'

She was miles away.

And then she was back.

'Your problem lies at work…at the winery,' she said. 'I'm not sure who or how exactly for the moment, but it's far more dangerous than Shulkin.' She twizzled around on her barstool a couple of times.

'But you have an idea what it is?' asked Raj, wiping his mouth with kitchen roll.

'Yes, I think so… and it's all about to get a whole lot worse.'

***

'A coup?' Raj looked at Nisba both shocked and puzzled.

Igor sat with his head in his hands at the island.

He'd taken his eye off the ball, through being dragged down by guilt, pain and hopelessness. It was only a theory, and Nisba did have a tendency to catastrophise. She admitted it. However, it was not unfathomable, Igor thought.

He was vulnerable, as she had said, and could easily be taken advantage of. A target. Wealthy and powerful. He certainly didn't feel it now.

'I hope I'm wrong,' said Nisba, 'but I think if we look at things through this lens, then we might see things we didn't see before.'

Sliding off her bar stool, she went to stand beside Igor. She stroked his head and down the back of his neck. He turned and put his arms around her waist, pulling her towards him.

'Don't you worry Swee..Igor…we'll sort it out,' she mumbled into his neck.

Raj looked away, back at his laptop.

'When do the reinforcements arrive?'

'Tomorrow,' replied Igor. He held Nisba's face in his hands and began to kiss her. One button. Just one button, he thought. He could barely contain himself. She closed her eyes, trying to control her breathing, wanting to comfort him, pleasure him and escape into the joy of being close to him. Feeling the warmth and the smell of him.

'Right…fuck off you two. I can't be doing with all this pent-up sexual tension,' snapped Raj, rolling his eyes. He made his way over to the sofa with his rucksack and laptop. Flinging himself out full length, he leaned over to get his headphones, placed them over his ears and closed his eyes.
He then opened them again.

'Go on!...I won't be able to hear you.' He pulled the throw over himself and stuffed some cushions behind his head and closed his eyes again.

They stood up. Igor held his hand out to Nisba.

'Good night, Raj,' they said. He didn't answer.

Day 16 Saturday

'We need to go and visit Zeinab,' Nisba announced over breakfast. She had her mental arithmetic face on, observed Igor.

'What for?' asked Raj. 'It's a nice thing to do but where does that get us? I am sure there are other things we should be prioritising.'

He got up to check the toast and plunge the cafetière, which he then brought over to the table.

Nisba placed her palms down on it and stared into the middle distance.

'Right now, I can't see anything more important.'

Raj raised his eyebrows.

'Zeinab was looking at the profit and loss account and then had a car accident, putting her out of the picture for God knows how long,' continued Nisba.

Igor and Raj exchanged glances.

'Yes, but she said she was having sessions with the FD, to get to grips with it…because she was new,' replied Igor.

'After, she had some financial queries that she wanted to talk to you about,' challenged Nisba.

Igor had only mentioned these things in passing, when Nisba had asked him about his day. These facts though, had been logged, cross referenced and computed. He'd not attached any significance to them.

Raj widened his eyes. Then bit into his hunk of toast.

Nisba's mind suddenly leapt to the idea of toast and Marmite. She really fancied some. They didn't have any. She'd have to get a jar.

'We need to follow the money,' resumed Nisba, picking up her train of thought. 'Zeinab will set us on the right path. I'm sure she found a leak…some fraud.'

Raj looked doubtful. 'We're not missing any money, are we?'

Igor shook his head slowly. He didn't think so.

'Not that you can see,' said Nisba. 'You got rid of someone doing it openly. A perfect distraction from a more sophisticated means of fraud. You may have been lulled into a false sense of security.'

'You're really running with this – aren't you?' said Raj.

Igor sat in silence, rubbing his head.

'Buck up, man… we've got the A-Team on this.' Raj slapped Igor's back so hard, he jolted forward.

Igor was unsure, but then the corners of his eyes started to slowly crease and his eyes twinkled.

His oldest friend Yuri had been a sniper during the war, before medical discharge owing to epilepsy brought on by his head trauma. He was a curious combination of as hard as nails and soft as butter. He was a builder in Ukraine now and a private investigator on the side. Vlod, another former soldier, dogged, brutal; albeit non-verbal now, had been integrated into their unit. Inscrutable and a bit mysterious. He worked with Yuri who had taken him under his wing. And there was himself, a former soldier but a tactician and strategist. Raj: a 'jack of all trades,' tech savvy and able to blag his way in and out of anything, and then there was the brains of the outfit – Mrs M with her unique skills and strengths.

Igor nodded.

'I think for once, Raj, you are right.'

Day 18 Monday

Igor was wondering if he could ask Nisba to go in by herself. They sat in his truck, waiting for the other to make the first move.

They'd parked up at the hospital, after the usual driving round and round to find a space.

'Would you prefer to wait in the car?' she asked.

He really appreciated her innate ability to read his mind, his feelings. This was going to be tough.

'Don't torture yourself, Igor. If it's going to set you back and do you no good, it's not the right thing to do. You don't have to be a hero,' she said patting him on the thigh, 'you're already one in my eyes.' She grinned.

She was just the best woman, partner, wife…whatever she should be called – in the world, he thought.

'I can do this.' Because she was with him. He could and would move forward and overcome.

They walked some distance following the signs, finally arriving at the reception area.

For Nisba, it was the smell. She also found the joviality of the nurses and doctors misplaced, versus the misery and tragedy playing out behind each door. Being surrounded by other people's pain and anguish was deeply upsetting and stressful for her.

Nisba got as far as a vending machine in the corridor near to Zeinab's ward, when she began to feel the blood draining from her head. The sensation of feeling overwhelmed, like she had been, at eleven years old, in hospital, was creeping up on her.

Bending over with her hands on her knees, breathing slowly, eyes closed, she encouraged the blood to return to her head and calmed her heart rate.

Igor was feeling tired. He had been liberated from one conflict, only to be launched into another. He hoped he would have enough energy to battle on. Deep down, he knew that he would.

He hadn't felt that before. The absence of despair. He recalled the morning before meeting Nisba and the gut wrenching, maddening sensation of utter hopelessness. The abyss. Instead, there was hope, as he had a clear view of a future now. He had his hand on Nisba's back. He was not going to allow his rock to sink.

He took her hand and walked her over to some orange and black plastic chairs to regroup.

***

Zeinab was sitting up looking surprisingly well, smiling and happy to see them. Although the rosiness of her complexion and sparkle in her eyes had waned, it was a relief. They had been prepared for tubes, drains and a drowsy, deathly looking patient and the awkward task of thinking of something to say to her husband.

Elias had gone home for a while but would be back later. He'd refused to bring her work laptop and had brought his idea of what might be helpful. Zeinab rolled her eyes, inviting them to eat the grapes and take the flowers.

Igor had recalled himself failing miserably at locating pyjamas for Nisba. It was a man thing, he thought. A chronic failure to understand a woman's needs. Pathetic. Nisba understood his needs, and he would definitely make the effort to understand and meet hers. He'd also seen it in Mila. Just after giving birth to her second baby, worrying about what to prepare for her husband, for dinner. He turned to look at Nisba. He was determined for her not to suffer like that.

It was ironic then, that Zeinab was now asking him how he was. She'd heard he had been poorly.

'Just a spot of food poisoning,' Igor replied, waving his hand dismissively. He was starting to sound like Nisba, he thought.

'Did you see my emails about the insurance claims and the other items?' Zeinab asked, looking worried now. She folded the edge of her blanket over a couple of times and then unfolded it again.

He hadn't, he'd been out of action.

Nisba had been rehearsing in her head about how she could ask Zeinab what she was concerned about at work and what had caused the accident. How to get to it, without coming across as nosey and tactless. It was like a maddening itch that had to be scratched.

Her tactic was to sit on her hands. She often found that her hands and mouth were somehow connected. The more she waved them about, the more verbose she would become. Sitting on them would shut her up and make her stop and think.

Igor saved her the job.

'Tell me what was on your mind?' he asked, pouring her a glass of orange juice.

Zeinab shrugged her shoulders a little.

'I'm new and don't wish to start making waves, but there is an unusual amount of activity…financial transactions for a relatively simple operation, once you get to know the set up. My gut tells me, someone has their hand in the till. I think you should take a look at it, just to be sure.'

Zeinab fiddled with her wrist band.

'There's something else?' Nisba asked, placing her hand on top of Zeinab's.

Zeinab swallowed, opening her mouth to say something and then rested her head back on the pillow and closed her eyes.

'I must be going out of my mind.'

Both Nisba and Igor shook their heads. Their faces told her that they wanted to hear what she had to say.

'I have this horrible feeling that I've stumbled on something. Perhaps I'm paranoid but I can't shake it off. I was on the Kangli Road. It's single carriageway and I overtook a vehicle which kept slowing down in front of me…touching the brakes. When I pulled out to overtake on a straight, it suddenly accelerated and started to race me. Then another vehicle came up behind them, which left me no room to slow down and pull back in, by which time, there was a vehicle coming in the opposite direction. They did their best to avoid me, going into the ditch – but I clipped their wing and went into a spin. I don't remember anything after that. Apparently, the two vehicles drove off. I was told that the husband and wife in the oncoming vehicle were OK and were the ones who called the police and ambulance. They didn't get the number plates unfortunately and neither did I.'

Zeinab put her hand to her forehead.

They were shocked into silence.

Nisba ran her hands through her hair and exhaled and squeezed Zeinab's hand.

'Do you remember anything at all about the vehicles?'

'It was a blue 4x4, bright blue…the one that forced me into the oncoming traffic. That was in my statement to the police.'

The hairs on Nisba's forearms and above her knees prickled. Her heartbeat became loud and fast. She could see Igor rubbing his face.

The scope of this problem was suddenly becoming bigger, Igor thought. He needed more men; he calculated in his head. As in people, manpower in general. He wasn't excluding women, he confirmed to himself.

He could see Nisba making similar calculations. She had gone far away, staring down somewhere at the floor.

They would have to report Nisba's incident with the two men, they decided. It was a pressing matter now. They had vital information about the blue vehicle.

Nisba had the number plate.

***

Igor and Nisba had returned to sit on the orange and black chairs, sipping from plastic cups of water. Igor's was tiny in his huge hand, almost crushing it.

For the first time, Igor had to contemplate leveraging his position, calling in some favours and pulling some strings as Zeinab would need protection.

Igor was disappointed in himself, considering that he had been too passive about everything. He needed to step up and protect himself, his family and his business. Accustomed to carrying a burden and being weighed down, he needed to cast this off. It had become a habit. It was crucial; to safeguard the future and the life he knew that was possible. It was now within his grasp.

'I need your help – again.' Igor looked down at his hands. '…Your…abilities.'

Nisba reached out and placed her hands on his.

'You want me to find out if you are being robbed.'

'Yes,' he whispered. 'Yes, please.'

'It sounds like you need a forensic accountant or an excuse for an audit…but this has to be strictly off book, doesn't it?'

He nodded.

She'd do it.

Nisba explained what she needed. It would need to be procured without raising the alarm.

Igor was concerned, that this work would take up her time and energy, away from her own business.

She would sort it she said, but Tan was owed an update.

'I think it would be nice if we did that together – don't you?' Igor said, smiling.

She laughed. 'Oh yes…that would be fun, but we'll leave the peril, threat to life and ex-military back-up out of it.'

Igor nodded in agreement.

He then consulted his watch. They would go into Parkent as it was the nearest big town to Prikat and then head back home. He knew people in the police, at Parkent.

They'd be back in time for Yuri and Vlod's arrival.

***

There wasn't a great deal more they could do, other than report the harassment.

Whilst Igor was treated like a minor celebrity at the police station, in short, there was nothing to prove that the same vehicle was involved in Igor's site manager's accident and the threat made towards his 'lady friend.' Nisba had not been able to identify the men, as she hadn't seen them and had only just about heard what they were saying. It wasn't against the law for the vehicle to come to the house, even uninvited and technically, not against the law to follow someone to a supermarket. There was nothing to prove that the same vehicle was involved in both incidents. They were sorry about the dog; however, the crime of exterminating a canine wasn't high on their list of priorities.

Igor and Nisba had known what to expect before they went in, which was why they didn't report it in the first place. But now, following Zeinab's 'accident,' they felt compelled to. They knew that whatever happened next, would tie into these events and then this report would become significant.

They agreed that they wouldn't be angry, disappointed, or frustrated. It was a tick box exercise, a moral duty, given that in their opinion, the men in the blue SUV had attempted to murder or deliberately put Zeinab out of action. They would have to take their own steps to prevent further incident and pre-empt any malign acts against Igor's business.

***

When they got back home, Yuri and Vlod had already arrived.

Igor laughed as he pulled up to the front of the house, next to a large shabby American-style camper van.

Nisba wasn't sure what to expect, but she was quite excited to finally meet two men that Igor had talked so much about.

They had been *there,* together, sharing that experience of hanging on to the hairlike thread between life and death. They'd taken turns to ensure that the thread was never broken.

Igor couldn't wait for Yuri and Vlod to meet Nisba.

Raj had furnished each man with a beer and was doing his best to converse with Yuri, whose English was limited.

They formed a group in the kitchen.

As soon as Igor entered through the front door, Nisba felt a special charge in the air. Yuri turned to see his friend walk in. He put down his beer and walked over in silence towards Igor, who held his arms wide.

There was a very long silent bear hug, with much back slapping.

Yuri stepped back. 'Fuck, man! You got fat.' He slapped Igor's flat muscly stomach hard with the back of his hand and looked round at the others grinning.

'It's great to see you too, Yuri.'

Igor then turned to Vlod, who was looking quietly at the floor.

He was a slight, pale young man of twenty, with short spiky brown hair and serious grey eyes. Igor grabbed him like he was his long-lost son, holding him close for about ten seconds. He croaked something Nisba didn't understand and when he'd released him, Igor had tears in his eyes.

It was such a joyful moment, but Nisba had the urge to blub. There was something very beautiful about this coming together of men who had this shared history. She was thrilled to see Igor so happy with his comrades.

Yuri was short. Really short, observed Nisba. He had biceps bulging out of his black T-shirt, like white cobblestones, with brown dead-straight hair, pale sky-blue eyes and a hare lip scar. There was another scar which split his left eyebrow in two. He looked pretty mean, she thought and noted he had the same tattoo as Igor.

Yuri turned to Nisba. She grinned at him, wondering what kind of introduction she would get.

He then held his hands high above his head and bowed down, as if to worship her. On his way back up, he placed both of his hands on his heart, smiling.

Nisba stepped towards him and gave him a hug. She'd put the Ukrainian Igor had taught her to good use.

'It's fucking great to meet you!'

Yuri and Igor laughed, hard.

Yuri stepped back holding her hands, grinning at her and then turned to Igor, nodding with approval.

There was a lot of testosterone in the house, thought Nisba, but she didn't feel uncomfortable or left out. It was great to be surrounded by so much laughter and bonhomie.

Nisba took a moment to study Vlod, who stood quietly, shoulders hunched, close to Yuri, for what appeared to be shelter, holding tightly on to his bottle of beer.

She had learned that Vlod hadn't spoken since he and Igor were pulled out of the rubble. Igor had attempted to save Vlod's life, shielding him from gunfire and flying debris.

Apparently, Vlod, also a volunteer, with 'specialist knowledge' (Igor would not elaborate on what this was) had not been particularly chatty before that either, struggling to make eye contact and to interact.

It was obvious to Nisba. She could see him counting the books on the shelf and the tiles on the walls below the kitchen cupboards.

She caught Vlod's eye, but he quickly glanced away.

Nisba walked round into the sitting room area and headed to the low sideboard that the TV sat on and pulled out a pack of cards.

She leaned round the oak units forming part of the partition between sitting room and kitchen. Vlod was looking to see what she was doing. She waved the pack of cards and beckoned him with her head.

He walked over.

Nisba sat on the rug in front of the fireplace and split the pack and laid two piles of cards out, one in front of her and one for Vlod.

He sat down opposite her, cross legged.

This game didn't require any words.

She began a card layout, five cards wide, like Patience. First, face up, the rest, face down. Another one up on the first card and down on the others and so on, until the sequence was complete. She then laid the remaining cards in a pile in front of her.

Vlod copied her, laying his pile out in front of him and waited.

Nisba began to take the card from her pile and gestured him to do the same with his. She laid the card face up, next to it.

She then examined her own row of cards. The two cards now facing up in front of them, was a four of clubs and the other, a three of hearts. The suit didn't matter, but the number value did. She took a two of diamonds from her five-card array and placed it on his Ace followed by a five of spades onto the other card – a four of hearts. She demonstrated an up or down, numerical sequence, playing either pile or both at the same time. He caught on quickly, rapidly following her eight with a nine, ten and a Jack. Only one card at a time could be placed, no cheating with multiples. She nodded, grinning.

'Very good.'

As the cards from their five card layouts were taken, they were able to turn the downturned cards over to reveal more playable cards. Pausing play briefly, she slapped the piles, to see which of them was the smallest.

'You want zero cards at the end…so you hit this one – OK?' She pretended to slap the smallest pile.

He nodded.

'Good…now faster.' Nisba gestured to rev up and go as fast as they could.

She used to play this during breaktimes at *Cheder* and was a 'Grand Master' at it. They'd called the game Spit. She had no idea why.

The game had the desired effect; a full-on violent attack on the cards ensued, although Vlod was a fast learner, Nisba was too quick for him, hitting the smallest pile a fraction of a second before him. They had begun to attract an audience.

Yuri, Raj and Igor came over and perched on the edge of the leather sofa to watch the drama unfold on the rug at their feet.

Nisba and Vlod hadn't noticed, as they were totally hyper-focused, their hands a blur, both oblivious to the shouting, groaning and beer-fuelled cheering from the spectators.

This was interspersed with moments of complete silence because of the building suspense, when the cards were turned and neither of them had anything to play. They kept turning until the moment came when the crashing about and tumult of cards recommenced, accompanied by a good deal of swearing and laughter.

Raj wanted to beat Nisba, so he was up next. They'd all had an excellent demo so were each clamouring for their turn at playing the Grand Master, or whoever was able to beat her.

Vlod had almost smiled, looking up at Yuri, who was seated on the sofa, resting his hands on his knees, nursing his beer. Yuri leaned forward and patted Vlod's shoulder like a father, and nodded, grinning with approval.

Igor was emotionally overwhelmed for a moment.

Nisba caught his eye. She mouthed a lustful kiss at him and grinned.

Igor smiled behind his hand that held his bottle of beer, trying not to laugh. Yuri nudged him hard with his elbow and laughed heartily. He'd caught her in the act.

At 4 am, Raj had to accept that he would never beat Nisba. He was thrashed in turn by Yuri and then by Igor.

Vlod and Yuri finally left for the camper van and Raj took up his place on the sofa.

It wasn't possible to sleep all night with the headphones on and he didn't possess any ear plugs. He wasn't a great sleeper at the best of times, but the hardest part about sleeping on the sofa these days was, no matter how quiet Igor and Nisba tried to be, he could still hear them.

Every goddam night, every fucking morning and sometimes in the middle of the night, he complained to himself. It was amusing initially, hearing them tumble about, suppressing the giggles, but after a while, it started to make him feel lonely, unloved, and horny.

Day 22 Friday

Nisba was thrilled to have so many people to cook for.

This particular morning, she'd been baking bread and making piles of pancakes at the same time, delivering them hot, to the table.

The big table was strewn with discarded half-lemons and sticky jugs of hot golden corn syrup. Granulated sugar had been spilt in amongst the coffee cups and pots of black tea.

Yuri, Vlod and Igor had decided they were going out for a ten kilometre run.

Igor used to do this regularly. He admitted it was ambitious, given he was out of condition, following his bout of E-coli.

He had to maintain his figure, he'd said. Yuri had passed quite a few comments about it in Ukrainian, which weren't complimentary. Nisba could tell. She'd also put on a bit of weight herself. The top button of her jeans was too tight to do up.

They'd all spent the last few days together, enjoying each other's company, cooking, eating and drinking with Igor and Nisba acting as a tag team providing the hospitality. They aimed to be normal for a while, before battle commenced.

In the meantime, Raj had been bringing home spare screens, cables, a keyboard and some sticky note pads from the store cupboard at work, bit by bit, so as not to draw attention. He'd done it late, when no one was about. He'd fiddled with the CCTV camera at the back of the buildings, to ensure that no one would see him. He'd even purloined an ergonomic leather office chair.

Yuri and Vlod equipped with military style binoculars, had disappeared off into the landscape each day, to check out for any evidence of short or long-range surveillance on the property.

Raj was feeling unusually useful, enjoying the sense of value he was adding. He was Operations Director after all and applied these skills to the present situation. Inwardly, a part of him regretted preventing Nisba from having her meeting with the new site manager – Zeinab. Maybe this would have caused things to have panned out differently, but then the situation with Shulkin could never have been resolved without her.

With a heightened sense of responsibility, he went as far as checking the whole house for bugs, taking Igor's phone apart and examining its set up before they commenced discussing their plan. He found nothing, concluding that the phone was taken away to avoid Igor being able to seek help, but they, whoever they were, had been too late. Raj couldn't figure out, how the phone had been taken in the first place. He continued thinking aloud for a while.

Igor began to clear the table. The table had been restored for this very purpose. He smiled as he began to clear up the breakfast detritus. He would do the housework, whilst Nisba went to set up her new office.

Yuri wouldn't allow Nisba to carry any equipment from the vehicle into the bedroom. He spoke in Ukrainian to her and she responded in English. They conversed like this for about an hour, even having a laugh, until the room was rearranged with the bed shoved into the corner against the wall, and a desk created from an old door and cupboards. She arranged a two-screen set up with all the cables ready for a third: Igor's laptop.

Yuri moved off outside to have a cigarette with Vlod.

Raj had hired some additional 4x4s. He'd complained, as he parked them in the only outbuilding without any crap in it. 'How did one man accumulate so much shit?'

They'd have to take more circuitous off-road routes away from the property. The main track had been closed – impassable, owing to resurfacing work, which it clearly needed. They put up some 'No Entry' signs to that effect.

They would rota the use of the vehicles and ensure that they would do everything in pairs, varying their routes to work. Essential journeys only.

Thinking of what had happened to Zeinab, Raj had purchased dash-cams, to be on the safe side.

One of them would always have to be at the house to protect Nisba.

Raj had informed them that he had already started his campaign of 'being a complete arsehole at work.'

'Thanks, Nisba, it requires more effort than you'd think.'

***

Nisba didn't believe that they could have done much running.

They were gone hours and returned without so much as a bead of perspiration.

Yuri placed his hands on his hips, consulted his watch and then showed her his steps. His English seemed to be selectively bad.

'Blimey. 23,000 steps. Did you carry Igor most of the way?'

Igor laughed.

'We did some walking around the grounds too.' His face then became serious and placed what they'd found on the table.

A box with some pink blocks of rat poison and a half empty packet of Camel Blue cigarettes.

They'd been found relatively close by, and not far off the road. A vehicle could quite easily have parked in the layby for someone to be able to climb the embankment, up and over Igor's fence and watch them from there.

It would have taken perhaps a second person to get ahead of Nisba in the woods and plant the poison, along with something tempting and apply this to the ball, for good measure. They figured that it would have to be a significant amount, to take down a dog the size of Misha.

Igor and Nisba hugged each other. It would have been a horrible death. Rat poison was essentially a blood thinner. The other men looked dejected. It was a shitty move to kill the dog, they said, agreeing they were dealing with some serious scumbags.

Nisba felt uneasy. The world wasn't quite how she perceived it to be. Going about her business, she had been watched, with a plot hatched against her. Feeling violated and shocked, she absent-mindedly shook her head slightly, her eyes fearful.

It was sensed by the others. Yuri patted her on the arm to acknowledge it.

Nisba needed something to take her mind off it.

She raided the fridge, fancying some cheese, chutney and crackers. She hadn't fancied any of the pancakes and was now suddenly very hungry.

Grabbing Raj's headphones off the island, she waved them at him.

'May I borrow these please?'

He gave her a thumbs up whilst deep in conversation with Yuri, which appeared to involve a significant amount of sign language. They were seated at the kitchen table with pen and paper, discussing the findings so far. Vlod looked on.

Raj found Vlod completely impenetrable, but didn't underestimate the processing that was underway. He had learned, since meeting Nisba, to appreciate the value of difference and not judge it. Igor had warned him that Vlod could be unpredictable, likening him to a terrier. Quick. Destructive. It was best to leave him to it, rather than be proactively friendly.

Raj had also found that he was feeling more comfortable in his own skin these days. He'd always found himself lacking because he had unconsciously compared himself to Igor and therefore, was always in his shadow. The contribution he was making to this situation mattered.

***

Nisba seated herself at her new workstation, fiddling with the levers on the black leather office chair, shunting up and down. In her opinion, the hydraulics and adjustment features for reclining and twizzling round were excellent.

Igor held his laptop under his arm and looked at the ceiling.

'No rush,' he said, the corners of his eyes creasing.

She suddenly sat up in position, rubbing her hands together and then apologised for appearing excited about the prospect of identifying embezzlement. But she was. It was the puzzle.

'I get it,' Igor said. He opened the laptop and logged in to the finance, purchasing and banking systems and showed her around them briefly.

He had offered to provide her with a detailed company overview and how it all worked, but she had turned that down. The only thing she did want, was a 'Who's Who', with role titles, core responsibilities and what their assigned authority levels were, with respect to payroll and payables.

She needed to be an uninitiated outsider, able to look at the numbers objectively, after that, she would come back to him with any further questions. She knew in principle and from direct experience, how businesses worked.

Igor had drawn up the structure of his organisation, with details of the finance team, as Nisba had expressed most interest in them. There were a couple of basic questions in the first instance, which Igor answered for her.

They had a third-party payroll, a company called Seyf-Pay, where monies were transferred monthly for office staff and fortnightly for warehouse and production. HR was also outsourced. The wine tasting tours, although part of the same company, was a business unit he didn't get involved with running very much. It was highly lucrative, seasonal, but straightforward, unlike production.

The company was a Limited Liability Company (LLC) with Igor, Mila Rakhmanova, Zeinab Ismailova, Raj and the FD, a man named Dav Uzmanov, as Directors.

'If you were to be bumped off – who benefits?' asked Nisba chewing the end of an orange highlighter pen.

'Mila.'

'What if you were married?' She wasn't being provocative. It was an academic question.

He broke into a smile.

'You would.'

Nisba had been concentrating, rocking slightly backwards and forwards. She blinked several times and then bit her bottom lip to stifle a smile.

'I'm working on a suitably witty retort… but I can't think of one.'

Igor looked relieved.

'I thought you were going to say that you would turn me down, you wouldn't *'want a bloody winery.'* ' He mimicked her with quite a convincing Manchester accent.

She nodded.

'You read my mind. Anyway...' She twizzled back around on her chair.

He knew that Nisba hadn't dismissed the profundity of what he had said. She would process it, and her sincere and emotional response would come out later, when he least expected it. For now, she was overwhelmed and somewhat distracted.

She had a couple of other things to ask. Aside from the highest overhead costs, she wanted to know where the business was spending its money. What were the priorities for investment.

Igor didn't mind that Nisba would know the intimate details of the financial health or otherwise, of his business.

She said she would be very happy to tell him about his *EBITDA* and if his gross profit ratio was good or not. He knew that she would.

Igor also didn't mind about her knowing what his salary was.

Nisba was now starting to tap away on her keyboard, looking intently at her screens.

'I'm not in the slightest bit interested in your net worth, Igor. I only want you for your body – you know that.'

He did. He could tell.

Igor went to leave, stifling a grin. She would need to be left to it, with no distractions.

'Igor,' Nisba called, turning her chair around and removing her headphones. Her hair flopped about. She looked at him over the top of her glasses.

'Yes?' His hand hovered over the bedroom door handle.

'Are you prepared for the outcome?' She pulled off the glasses.

He rubbed his forehead. No, he wasn't.

'Prepare for the worst – hope for the best?' She smiled optimistically.

'Right.' Igor massaged the scowl lines again between his eyebrows.

'I don't mean to be flippant,' Nisba said, tucking her feet under the chair. 'It's shit it's come to this. I am very sorry about it. Things will get worse, to get better. Each step we take though, is one step closer to cutting the head off the snake.'

He walked back over to her, bent down and held her face in his big hands, giving her a big, long kiss on the lips. She grabbed his buttocks and gave them a squeeze. He moved to her neck.

'Right. Stop it now.' She laughed. 'Otherwise, we're going to have to barricade the door and we'll never hear the last of it.'

He made for the door again, smiling to himself.

'And before you go…I forgot to ask,' Nisba said, spinning round on the chair. 'How long have I got?' She knew it was going to be tight, considering they had to behead the snake within eight days. That was when her visa ran out. She really would have to leave then.

Igor scratched his head and regarded her from under his eyebrows.

'Dav Uzmanov, the finance director is on holiday in Vietnam. He's due back on Wednesday morning, so you have…four days.'

'Shit!'

***

Day 25 Monday

Raj had begun to notice cliques forming within the operational staff on the shop floor of the warehouses as well as during breaks and in the canteen.

Given Nisba's theory, he was looking at things differently now, trying to recall when this first began. He began to notice other things.

There were two team leaders in particular, that seemed overly interested in the shift rotations – which supervisor was on, off, and what Raj's role entailed, whilst 'that woman' was in hospital.

There were also questions about annual leave and specifically, the cover for Saturday, the day of the event.

Zeinab as site manager wasn't popular, even though they had no reason to dislike her. Having gained most of her experience in France, she was not considered local. She was a woman, on the wrong side of fifty, in what they perceived to be a man's position, but proving to be irritatingly effective.

Igor was viewed as remote, privileged, and uninterested. They were partially right. The longer serving permanent staff members were aware of the reason for Igor's long absence and subsequent return many months later. Igor was generally liked by them; he had the sympathy vote.

Raj had always been 'one of the boys,' despite being an outsider. He was respected because he was fair, consistent, and most importantly, he made the men laugh. The dim view of senior management was his way in.

He'd thrown in a couple of free external breakfast and lunch runs and splashed around some derogatory comments about Zeinab and company ownership in general, ensuring that both nightshift and day supervisors and their respective teams were privy to this.

He needed to be considered potentially on-side of any mutiny.

Despite it breaching a range of human rights and company policies, Raj had set up hidden cameras in the non-working environments. This included coverage of not only the breakout areas and canteen, but also the locker room and the toilet cubicles.

He was not overly amused that he would be able to watch people take a piss, shit, take their clothes off and do… whatever.

Leaving the house surveillance with Igor, Raj used a new and bigger, more powerful laptop for work, to accommodate the site surveillance.

They needed to find out fast, who was corrupt and who was straight.

Raj sat in his office, with his feet up on the desk, popping peanuts into his mouth, finding it quite addictive, people-watching.

Entrapment was also thrilling, tapping into the dark side and the baseness of humanity.

He watched.

And waited.

Day 26 Tuesday

Nisba had spent several hours the night before, studying the profit and loss, purchase, sales ledgers and recent banking activities. After cogitating well into the small hours, she had a number of questions for Raj.

She aimed to work as efficiently as possible, accruing lead time where she could. It was important for her to remain sharp.

To spot trends, she found it necessary to go back at least two years, so there was a high volume of material to work through.

Nisba texted Raj. They weren't communicating on email, as a precaution.

Hi Raj. A few questions for you. What is the usual headcount ratio versus volume production for this time of year? Can you put a face to the name of every single employee? Do you have photo ID for them all? That's most urgent. Who is responsible for setting up suppliers, new starter payroll etc What happens to the waste? Just curious! Please may I have a flipchart or paper and marker pens? Ta :o)

The reply was swift.

Can I call you? Will be easier

Nisba tutted. Easier for Raj. She was in flow and didn't want the disruption and drama of a phone call. It could knock her off course, but she needed the information quickly and accepted that she always had to adapt to other people's ways of working; it didn't usually occur the other way round.

On opening the Notepad function, she conducted a brain dump of every thought in her head, with Actions and Questions, creating a To Do, Work in Progress and Done chart. Her brain was a tornado. Whilst the ideas were flying around, she could keep going, but if the weather changed, they could easily all fall to the ground and then evaporate. She had to capture them all quickly, for safe keeping.

A separate tab was created for each topic, which included Payroll and Suppliers, amongst others.

Nisba had typed up her questions ready, so she could record the responses straight into Notepad.

Raj had stepped outside of the office building to speak to her.

It was the first phone call since burying the hatchet. She'd wondered how it would go. It was blowing a gale at his end; she could hear it tearing up their conversation.

'Hey Nisba – how's it going?'

He was surprisingly chatty and friendly, she thought, remembering to be the same in return. Nisba was champing at the bit for answers, so could easily forget to make customary polite small talk. As the questions were written down in front of her, she was able to relax and roll with it. If she hadn't prepared like this, she'd be in trouble; becoming immersed in the conversation and forgetting altogether what the purpose of the phone call was.

It was challenging to listen and type, so she repeated out loud everything she heard and typed it, to make sure it made sense. It was not possible for her to listen to Raj and summarise at the same time. As a result, a full verbatim account was noted down.

30% waste (on starting grapes – pomace, seed, lees and water) Volume goes up and down climate-depending however our yield is consistently high on average per acre for both wine and table grapes. Circa 5 and 9 tons per acre respectively. That's around 3,500 bottles of wine per acre (times that by 10k acres). Staff heads should be stable or reducing not increasing at the moment.

Off- peak is circa 100 office staff, plus 1,800 operational (indoors/outdoors). Peak season, Ops alone, can go up to 3,000.

Profit margin is typically 40% – please tell me this isn't going down.

We sell pomace (to flour/dairy industry) the rest is green waste and goes to landfill. Not much recycling going on in Uz.

Accounts Payable person, Shazmina I think she's called and Dav the Finance Director is the 2nd level of approval for payroll payments/all other payments she makes. We have flat management structures – way too lean, too many direct reports and little admin support. Both junior and senior colleagues have massive workloads/scope of responsibility. Org needs to be redesigned. Growth has occurred too quickly.

'That's great, thanks. Can the approval be overridden?' Nisba enquired.

There was a pause

'Yes, it can. Dav the FD can award this wholesale, to Shazmina.'

'Like, when he's on holiday,' said Nisba.

'Shit.'

'Mmm. And the employees? Can you vouch for every single one? What I mean is, can you determine who really exists and who doesn't?' There was a silence. A very long silence. 'Are you still there?'

'Yes…and no, I can't. I'll need help with that. I take it you need this – ASAP?'

She did. The payroll date was imminent.

'Yes, that would be rather helpful. Thank you.'

Raj walked back into the building; preoccupied, ignoring Irina on reception, who had asked him if all was well.

***

Five minutes later, there was an urgent knock on Raj's door.

'Come in,' he called, looking intently at his emails, then glancing up. He aimed to appear unrattled by the previous conversation.

Miguel Dos Santos had taken a couple of steps into the room. He was tall. Slender.

His body language was combative, breathing hard through his nose. His hands were clenched into fists.

Raj had barely said 'hello', when Miguel threw an A4 sized, fat brown envelope across Raj's desk. It nearly flew off the other end, but Raj caught it.

'What's going on?' Miguel demanded. MDS, as he was known amongst close colleagues, was usually impeccably polite, diplomatic, and never swore. Raj had never seen him angry. Until now.

Raj was pleased to see that his efforts had yielded such a good result, so soon.

'Shut the door, Miguel and sit down.'

There was some hustle and bustle outside.

Miguel didn't want to sit down.

'Tell me what's on your mind, Miguel,' asked Raj, leaning on the desk with his elbows, twiddling with his pen.

'I'm not going to stand by and let you run this operation into the ground,' Miguel spluttered.

Raj raised his eyebrows.

'What makes you think that I'm doing that?' Raj sat back in his chair, stroking his bearded chin.

This nonchalant reaction irritated Miguel. Raj had widened his large brown eyes. Innocent, puppy dog. A face worthy of punching, he thought as Raj appeared to be enjoying himself.

Miguel smouldered with annoyance, his eyebrows furrowed and he pursed his lips.

'It's been tough for the last few months, keeping the operation on track…and you constantly undermine my efforts.' Miguel threw his hands in the air.

'I've been putting measures in place to combat the sloppy attendance, the lack of observation of safety procedures and then you reward the bad behaviour with deliveries of *non kabob* and southern fried chicken. And now you're fuelling the rumour mill, the staff malcontent…and today – you're literally throwing money around. Something's up and it's pissing me off. I'm not letting you destroy this business…Igor's business.'

Miguel, having finished his rant, dropped his hands down by his sides. He had broken out into a sweat and quickly wiped his top lip with his thumb and forefinger.

Slowly nodding, Raj puckered his lips and then smiled.

'Thanks, Miguel, but please do take a seat for a minute.'

Raj began to text, which exasperated Miguel.

To Igor M's phone
From Raj Pereira: *I've caught a fish*
Igor: *How big?*
Raj*: The biggest*
Igor: *MDS?*
Raj: *Yep*
Igor: *Great result*

There was some hullabaloo outside. Several warehouse colleagues were standing very close to the door. Raj could see the shape of them through the frosted glass wall of his office.

The conversation would have to be curtailed.

Raj texted to MDS:

Am with you on this. Can't talk here. You need to leave this room soon. Can you meet at Igor's tonight?

Ping.

'I think you should answer that,' said Raj, gesturing with his eyes.

MDS looked puzzled. He slowly pulled his phone out of his back pocket to check his messages.

He looked up, bewildered.

Raj put his finger to his lips.

'Shhh…'

MDS paused for a minute. He looked down at his phone, considering his response. He texted back.

7pm

Raj nodded and continued to text.

I'll send some instructions on something we need help with. It needs to be done fast.

MDS stood up, nodded and then made for the door.
Before MDS grabbed the handle, Raj quickly caught up with him.
'Slam the door on your way out, and make sure you look pissed off.'
MDS slammed the door and looked pissed off.

***

Nisba emerged from her office, into the brightness of the rest of the house.
Igor looked up from the sofa. He'd just received good news from Raj but kept it to himself for a minute.
She'd would need some quiet time before engaging in conversation.
He'd learned that she would walk away from her task, once she had hit full capacity, so there would be no room for anything else for a little while, so he'd save all the questions he was dying to ask. It seemed fair enough to him, and not a big adjustment to make. He hoisted himself up from the sofa, always an effort, as it was so soft. He began to roll up the rug. He hadn't finished sweeping.
Yuri and Vlod were out and about in the wilderness.
'It's just us then?' Nisba asked provocatively.
Igor grinned. She always had capacity for sex, it seemed. He was glad about that and always happy to oblige. She'd told him that she hadn't ever been like that, before. Now, she couldn't get enough of him. Just his presence turned her on.

He realised he'd had more sex with Nisba in two weeks, than he had in the last three years, with Feruza. That was how sad, loveless and barren his marriage had been. He understood why that was now. She didn't want him and was getting it from someone else.

On reflection, he realised that he had been in an abusive relationship. He was shocked and felt some shame, as Nisba had done. He recalled the times when Feruza had swung at him, hitting him in a rage, seeming to enjoy dysfunction, the drama, and hurting him, with her words and fists.

He now considered Nisba to be right. Lots of kissing, cuddles and great loving sex, was good for one's mental health.

He was feeling pretty good lately, all things considered. Exhausted, but in a pleasant way. Everything seemed a lot easier to deal with since the conversation they'd had about his Beast.

'First, I need something to eat. Can I get you anything?' Nisba asked, opening the fridge, suddenly ravenous, grabbing some smoked fish and pickled gherkins.

He didn't and was fine, continuing to sweep, waiting for her to share her thoughts.

Nisba perched on a bar stool at the island and munched for a while, still deep in thought. She glugged on a pint glass of water. Forgetting to drink and eat, whilst hyper-focused, was not unusual for her.

'OK so…here are my theories… and they are still only theories. I thought I'd let you know what I was considering, so if I am right, you are prepared. Is that OK?'

The whole thing wasn't OK, but her proposal was perfectly reasonable.

'I'm waiting for some info from Raj. I'm not sure how long it will take…' Nisba tailed off, picking up a gherkin with her thumb and forefinger, proceeding to crunch her way through it.

She licked the tips of her fingers.

'You have fake employees, fake suppliers and fake insurance claims. We'll know just how many employees, from

Raj, soon. I Just need to do a bit more digging with the suppliers and the bank. In fact, I'm in the middle of doing a load of bank reconciliations now. I don't think your internal controls are robust enough, so they have been taken advantage of.'

Igor's heart rate had increased. He leaned on the handle of his sweeping brush. He nodded slowly and sighed.

'If you find evidence of fraud – you can stop it?'

'I wish it were that simple, Igor. I think it's more about – who, when, and what else. You've got other vulnerabilities. And of course, there's why…other than pure greed. There's usually a cause…something that spurs someone to act.'

Igor rubbed his neck.

'It's not looking good for anyone in Finance then?' he asked.

'No, it's not, particularly for Shazmina. It looks like she sets everything up. All actions in the systems are date and time stamped in her name. I think you'll need to consider planning a timely audit. It will be interesting to see if you find a flurry of terminations and account closures.'

Nisba dropped her shoulders. She felt suddenly fatigued.

'We need to dig into her background, find out what's going on in her life etcetera…and who has remote access to the systems? I forgot to ask that before,' she added.

'No-one but me. Email is only accessible on work mobile devices, for senior management, so that's Raj, MDS, Dav the FD and Zeinab.'

'And Mila, does she have any access to anything?' Nisba pulled at her top lip.

Igor shook his head and seated himself on the stool next to her.

'She's doesn't work for the company at all – she's a director in name only. I doubt if any of the others have even met her.'

Nisba needed to go and rest her head for a while. Igor followed her. They cuddled on the bed. Igor held her in his big arms, lying on his back, thinking about his business, which felt like it was slipping through his fingers and that he'd placed an unfair reliance on Nisba to prevent it.

Whilst it was not comparable to a US or UK business in currency value terms, it was worth everything to the 2,800 families that depended on it for their livelihood. It was also a thriving business, offering wine tours to tourists, in addition to its wine production, export of juice, sultanas, and other dried fruit.

There was very little else in the area, with scarce resources, unreliable utilities, and no other employment to speak of. If the business suffered irreparable reputational damage, or bankruptcy, the whole community of Prikat and in the surrounding areas, would face an uncertain and impoverished future. It couldn't be allowed to happen.

He then realised Nisba had fallen asleep.

Smiling to himself, Igor buried his nose in her hair, which always smelled so lovely.

Day 27 Wednesday

Nisba had needed the sleep, but this meant a much later resumption of her analysis than she'd planned.

It was important that actions were recorded in the systems within reasonable working hours, to avoid suspicion. She therefore needed to be wrapped up, with all her findings and evidence, before Dav Uzmanov, the FD logged on at his usual start time of 8am.

It was now 6.49 am but the time on the bottom right of her laptop seemed to be running down far faster than usual. She found her estimate of how long a minute was wildly inaccurate.

She had checked and rechecked the data, to ensure she was closing down and terminating the correct records.

Nisba blinked and it was suddenly 7.58 am.

In all, there had been six hundred and twenty-eight fake employees, including two hundred and twenty-three still on the payroll for the next run. These comprised several administrators, a variety of production and warehouse staff, transport, pickers and packers. There were batches of staff, who had worked over peak seasons, for both table and wine grapes, from June through to October as temporary workers for harvest. She discovered, they all had the same bank details. It was a clever tactic she thought, having new starters and leavers over a long period. This covered a period of two years. It may have gone back further, but she'd had to draw the line somewhere, given the lack of time available.

Fifteen fraudulent insurance claims were made, in total. Forty-seven different fake suppliers, providing various products and services, such as machine maintenance, packaging, and organic fertilizer were involved. These claims, often for significant sums and for legitimate purposes, were processed during the busiest time of year so as not to draw attention.

While the bank details in the finance system appeared legitimate, the payments weren't processed through this system. Instead, they were issued directly via the company's banking system. The bank details used were consistent, matching those of a specific employee but belonging to a single account. A review of the finance system didn't reveal any irregularities or throw up any red flags to anyone undertaking normal everyday duties.

The pay-outs from the insurance claims, the payments made to the imaginary suppliers plus the fake employees, totalled roughly an equivalent of three million US dollars: just over thirty eight billion Uzbek Som.

Igor pointed out to Nisba that it was important to remember, the average annual household income in the country, was around $800 US dollars. This was a serious haul.

Someone was playing the long game and had planned it carefully. They would probably have had prior opportunity to practice, for this to go on so long, undetected.

Nisba thought that once such a large amount was amassed it was highly unlikely that Shazmina would stick around in her job as Accounts Payable Clerk, commuting daily in her 2014 Nexia.

It was just a thought. But for now, they all agreed, that Shazmina was their prime suspect or key accomplice and would need to be investigated by Yuri and Vlod. Neither Igor nor Raj knew anything about her, apart from the car she drove. In fact, they concluded, they hadn't really noticed her very much at all.

They didn't feel very good about this, after seeing the look on Nisba's face.

***

Finance director, Dav Uzmanov, failed to show up for work.

Igor later received a text from him, to say that his flight had been cancelled and that he would try and get back at the earliest opportunity.

'I'll be in touch,' it said.

'Mmm,' said Igor.

'Unbe-fucking-lievable,' said Raj.

Nisba sat back in her chair, rolled her eyes and buried her hands in her hair, poofing it up.

Day 28 Thursday

Shazmina was dreading it. She'd received an email from the big man himself, Mr M, for a meeting with him and the ops director.

She'd only met Igor a few times in passing. To her, he looked intimidating. Enormous, like a prize fighter. He had, by all accounts, been messed up by his war experience in Ukraine. Who wouldn't be?

The finance director, Dav Uzmanov, had told her that this made Mr M distant and angry, and it was also affecting his judgement on running the company. She hadn't seen that; it was just that he never seemed to be around.

Mr M's 'Western Values' weren't appreciated either by the site manager or FD, particularly in relation to equal opportunities. Chateau Prikat was considered a Ukrainian-run company, not an Uzbek one and this was not a popular concept, in everyone's eyes.

Lately, it was Raj Pereira who had been running the show, since the former site manager, Umar Bekov, resigned. That was all rather sudden, she had thought.

Shazmina wasn't sure why he'd left so quickly, but she was glad anyway because he was openly mean to her, being one of only three women, including Zeinab, in the whole company. He was in his forties, and she was twenty-four. He treated her like an idiot, in her opinion.

She wasn't. Shazmina had a degree in accounting. This was her second job since graduating.

The big challenge for Shazmina in relation to the meeting, was that she was in love with Raj.

Her stomach was fluttering and she was overheating. It was a dead end, she knew. He was a Man of the World. Much older. From Goa. She'd read up that this would mean he was probably a Catholic. Shazmina was local and a good Muslim. She tried her hardest to be. He would not look at her twice, she'd decided.

Unbeknownst to Raj, he made her laugh, every day, unseen from behind the filing cabinet. Overhearing his anecdotes, quips and sarcasm with Dav and other colleagues, she often found herself stifling laughter a long time afterwards, thinking about them.

Shazmina was excited though; being in the same room, and in a meeting, where he would be there and that it was about her! She concluded that it must be about a pay rise. There was no other reason she could think of. She worked hard, was never late, or sick, and put in extra hours, so was sure this wouldn't have gone unnoticed.

She paid a visit to the ladies' bathroom just beforehand and fixed her hair. It was black, very shiny and shoulder length. She'd pinned it up today but pulled some down, to form tendrils around her face.

Shazmina had a symmetrical face, with high cheekbones, almond-shaped brown eyes, and full lips. In the mirror, she saw someone very young, unsophisticated and considered her eyes too South-eastern looking. Whilst pinching her cheeks, Shazmina pursed her lips a couple of times.

She sighed, believing her reflection wasn't going to improve on further examination.

***

Raj was sitting on his desk and Mr M leaned against the cupboards behind him, with his arms folded.

Shazmina's heart gave a little flip. She couldn't read their faces. She'd walked in smiling. They weren't.

Raj invited her to take a seat.

Shazmina sat with her ankles and hands crossed so she wouldn't fidget, and swallowed hard, keeping her eyes focused initially on Igor. Her heart was pounding so hard and she was so tense, her jaw and neck were locked to prevent her from shaking.

Raj got up and shut the door firmly behind her.

She noticed that he'd had his hair cut. His beard was very neat and he wore a crisp white tailored Oxford shirt, which glowed slightly, in contrast against his brown skin. His sleeves were worn rolled up so she could see he was strong and took care of himself. But not too much. He had soft-looking lips and large expressive brown eyes. Looking especially handsome today, she thought, and hoped he would smile soon.

Shazmina didn't like being seated. Raj had gone back to perch on his desk, so they were now both looking down at her.

There was no polite icebreaking.

'Any idea what this meeting might be about?' asked Raj, turning to pick up his pen.

'Umm... no,' she replied, looking at Igor then to Raj. She was not going to humiliate herself or try and be confident by saying – *I hope it's about a pay rise. I've worked my socks off!*

Raj had raised his eyebrows. Then he gave an emphatic nod, as if he were needing time to think and then turned to Igor.

Igor stood up straight, smiled faintly and unfolded his arms.

'We've invited you in, as we would very much like to speak with you about some accounting activities. We're hoping that you will be able to shed some light on one or two areas...of concern.' He then gently pulled up another office chair, bringing it round to sit beside Raj. Igor sat forward, trying not to appear too scary or intimidating.

'In particular, six hundred and twenty-three employees and forty-seven suppliers, that don't exist,' added Raj.

It took a few seconds for Shazmina to compute his words.

Her mouth dropped open, and her eyes widened.

'Someone has committed fraud,' she exclaimed, gaping. 'How is that possible?'

Igor and Raj exchanged glances.

'Well,' said Igor smiling. He couldn't help it. 'That's a very good question, but we do have an answer.'

Shazmina leaned forward, she was all ears. Trembling with shock, her attraction to Raj's good looks suddenly evaporated. How could this happen? They had processes. Her mind was alight with the possibilities. It had to be the finance director, had to be.

'Since you've worked here,' Raj continued, 'you've set up fake suppliers, fake employees and creamed off the princely sum of almost thirty eight billion Som.'

She blinked twice and gripped the arms of the chair.

'No,' she wailed and then almost laughed. This had to be a very bad dream, or some sort of sick joke. Shazmina had an urge to cry, but she wasn't going to. Over her dead body would she be reduced to tears at work – by men.

She held up her chin.

'No,' she said, through gritted teeth. 'I did not!'

'How then, do you explain that every entry for these fake employees and fake companies, is in your name?'

Shazmina gasped for air, her eyes darting from Igor to Raj and back again.

Igor held his head in his hands and rubbed the back of his neck. He was not enjoying this. He knew now they were on the wrong track.

'I don't know!' she cried out, furious, no longer caring about insubordination or that her already ultra strong Uzbek accent and English language skills would deteriorate further. This was outrageous, she seethed. It was typical – the only woman in Finance.

'I only ever do fifty percent of new starters and companies,' she argued. 'Workload is divided deliberately. Segregation of duties and levels of approval...they're important – to avoid fraud!'

Raj prepared for another salvo, but Igor held out his hand.

'Thank you, Shazmina. This is difficult, I know,' responded Igor, kindly. 'I think we should take a break for a minute.'

She nodded. He was being nice now, so this made her want to cry, even more. Shazmina found herself left alone, with Raj.

She didn't care if he liked her or not. Any hope of retrieving anything out of this situation was beyond redemption. Hot, and feeling that she must look flushed, Shazmina swept the now damp wisps of hair out of her eyes and stood up. Standing at only five feet, she looked straight up at him, defiantly. Her nostrils flared just a little and her lips were puckered in an angry pout.

Raj was doing his best to maintain his Bad Cop face, but that look got the better of him.

He was making fun of her, she thought, accustomed to being derided by the FD for her ambition and the way she spoke. Raj's eyes were smiling now and the corner of his mouth crept up.

He rubbed his hand over his mouth and adjusted his face on Igor's arrival, who was carrying a tray with the wherewithal to make bowls of tea.

He placed it down on Raj's desk. Raj let Igor do the talking but kept his eyes fixed on the angry young woman opposite, studying her face and body language.

'Pull up your chair, Shazmina,' asked Igor, gesturing her to come closer. Raj went round to the other side of his desk, taking a seat opposite.

It was so hot. She wished they'd open a window or put on the air con.

Raj suddenly stood up and opened the window vent.

Her eyes slid to meet his. She quickly looked away at the tea things. Igor was a bit too close for her to feel comfortable to make eye contact with him, unused to sitting at such close quarters to a man…the boss.

Shazmina was still cross but had been thinking.

'I want to see entries, you talk about. I don't suppose you checked to see if any were recorded while I was in hospital, having appendix out!'

She sat back with some satisfaction and folded her arms.

Raj was resting his elbow on his desk and had placed his hand over his mouth.

Shazmina glared at him. His eyes were glinting, and she detected the corners creasing.

She surprised herself by having a sudden urge to thump him.

Both men were quiet for a moment and then Igor began to pour the tea.

Igor passed her a bowl.

'What would you do, if you were us, in this situation?' he asked.

Shazmina hadn't expected this question and neither had Raj.

She cupped her elbow in one hand and pulled at her top lip with the other, thinking for a moment.

'I would suspend me and rest of finance team, pending investigation and have external audit …then I would probably have to involve police.'

Shazmina swallowed hard and closed her eyes, lamenting the end of her career.

'…But you have the authority to run the payroll payments to Seyf-Pay…is that correct?' asked Igor gently.

'Yes.'

'Then you can help us.'

***

Yuri and Vlod had commenced their investigation of Shazmina Karimova, whilst she was at work. He and Vlod took a drive out to the Mirzo-Ulugbek district of Tashkent, not far from the Khamid Alimdjan metro station, where she lived. This meant at least a one and a half hour round trip for Shazmina for work, each day.

From her employee record they learned she was unmarried, and much to Igor's consternation, earned a salary so low it would barely keep the roof over her head, which in turn offered her a motive. Other than that, everything about this set-up was unremarkable.

There appeared to be nothing ostentatious about her way of life, in fact, quite the opposite. Yuri had chatted with a lad sitting in the stairwell of her concrete, 1960s functionalist-style apartment block. He was about eighteen or so, with facial piercings and highlighted hair. Yuri engaged in conversation with him, on the pretext of trying to deliver a parcel. Was Yuri in the right building and did the lad know the inhabitants of flat twelve?

Yuri had knocked on the door of Shazmina's flat first, to ascertain if there was anyone else in the property, before considering picking the lock. His knock had been answered by a nurse.

The lad was more forthcoming than expected.

'She works to support her mother – pays for live-in care, so…not exactly a great catch. The mother's sick – asbestosis so, not long now. Too much living in shitholes, like this.' He grinned, rolling his eyes, waving his hands up to the ceiling. 'Shaz is pretty hot, though…but I'm not interested.' He preened his hair and straightened his jacket. 'Too up herself...'

It was the look on Yuri's face that led him to retreat quickly upstairs, back to his own home on the next floor.

Nisba was most pleased to find that there were entries during the time-period Shazmina was laid up in hospital. She knew there would be, as soon as Raj had texted her about it.

But Nisba was also angry. This was a country where women didn't have the freedom she took for granted. Whilst education was encouraged, everything Shazmina had achieved in the workplace would have been battled for, swimming hard against the current and here she was, drowning. The perfect stooge.

***

That evening, the bottle of Cognac came back out of the sideboard, but there wasn't going to be enough to go round. Igor commented, with a twinkle in his eye, that Nisba had drunk all of his whiskey, following her accident.

Yuri disappeared out of the front door and came back indoors from the chilly evening, armed with a large bottle of Vodka, and a guitar.

The waft of cold air was welcome. They were all feeling jaded and downhearted. Yuri slammed the bottle down on the table, gesturing to Igor to get his guitar. Raj grabbed some glasses.

Nisba waved her hand to pass up on the drink. Igor had one shot out of politeness. Yuri and Vlod were professional drinkers and Raj was not far behind.

After some tuning and casual strumming to warm up, Igor and Yuri opened with 'Stefania' by the Kalush Orchestra. Everyone knew the rather catchy and repetitive tune from Eurovision 2022, but only Igor and Yuri knew the words.

This was going to get messy; Igor could tell. He and Nisba grinned at each other.

'We're peaking too soon,' Nisba whispered. 'I think they've forgotten that Miguel will be here any minute.'

She laughed at Raj's reaction, on receiving the text from MDS which confirmed his arrival.

Igor had to stop Yuri mid flow of *Chervona Ruta*, a popular Ukrainian song.

Vlod accompanied Raj outside, to run down to the meeting point, to escort Miguel back to the house.

***

Miguel wasn't sure what to expect on entering Igor's house, but a party definitely wasn't a scenario he'd been prepared for.

There was music and singing. Igor and an intimidating Eastern European looking man were strumming and harmonising what sounded like melancholy traditional Ukrainian songs. There was a two litre bottle of Ukrainian Vodka on the table, shot glasses, oranges cut into slices scattered about on chopping boards, bowls of deep-fried dumplings and good cooking smells coming from the kitchen area.

Igor smacked his strings to a stop and stood up. Balancing his guitar on his chair, he went over to shake Miguel's hand.

Miguel hadn't seen much of Igor lately. He seemed different and couldn't put his finger on what it was.

And then he did. He hadn't seen Igor smile since New Year of 2022. Back then, he had been the example of a great business leader; inspiring, engaging, generous and kind. He was a handsome *gajo,* although Igor didn't seem to be aware of it, which was no bad thing. Igor was the best project manager he'd ever worked with, in the oil industry, on exploration and production projects.

On Igor's return from fighting in Ukraine, Miguel had been shocked when he first saw him. Scowling, muscled up, like a heavy-weight boxer and irritable. He recalled how jumpy Igor had been in the production and warehouse areas, leaving quickly, never to visit them again.

It had been heart-breaking to see his role-model and friend reduced to a husk of a fighting machine.

But this evening, the old Igor he knew and admired was back.

Igor encouraged the group to make introductions.

'My name is Yuri. Igor is my friend, from five years old.' He gestured with his hand to show the height of them. 'From home, in Ukraine. I come to save his ass.'

There was laughter.

'Hi Miguel, my name is Nisba. I'm from a village near Manchester in England. I am Igor's…' They turned to each other and grinned. '…Lover,' she said, turning back to Miguel. The group whooped and laughed. Yuri drum rolled the table. '…And I'm also here, to save Igor's…rather nice ass.'

'Again,' chipped in Igor. A ripple of laughter went around the room.

Igor didn't want to show up Vlod, so quickly moved on to introduce him on his behalf.

'This is Volodymyr – Vlod for short. He is our friend,' he said waving to Yuri and himself. 'We were also in Ukraine – together.'

Miguel understood the inference. There was no further explanation required. He was humbled, feeling bad, for thinking Vlod extremely rude when they met at the layby. He needed to be more open-minded; he thought.

'And my name is Raj…' Raj joked, grinning at Miguel.

'And you're here to be a pain in everyone's ass,' quipped Igor, giving him a slap on the back. 'But carry on, Raj – not everyone knows who you are.'

'OK...I was born in Canada, my parents are from Goa, but I'm not from anywhere in particular, hence the messed-up accent. I've moved around the world since I was a kid.' He turned to Nisba, 'I spent too much time in a well-known English boarding school.'

Nisba grinned.

Raj laughed and waved his hand dismissively. She didn't need to say it out loud.

'I worked with Igor in oil and gas, before following him into this shitstorm.'

The group turned to Miguel.

'My name is Miguel...or MDS,' he grinned. 'I'm from Angola and worked with Igor for four years in the oil and gas industry, around the world. I managed to avoid Raj. I came here, three years ago to work with Igor as Warehouse Manager. I am here to find out how I can help save Igor's ass.'

There was a round of applause and shouts of approval.

Miguel was offered a shot of Vodka by Yuri. Vlod was seated next to him, watching him closely. Miguel didn't dare refuse.

Nisba stood up and slapped her palms together.

'Don't get too pissed, people – we've got stuff to do!'

Miguel watched the men quickly muster to leave the table.

This was interesting, he thought.

He watched Igor slip his arm around Nisba's waist and beam down at her, sneaking a quick kiss on the lips. They looked excited about something. A private joke, it seemed.

Nisba was definitely the brains of this outfit, he thought – the Project Manager. He was intrigued, as they filed toward what appeared to be a bedroom. Their bedroom!

As he walked in, the bed was in front of him, pushed up against the opposite wall.

Behind the door was a desk with two monitors, a laptop and keyboard. The adjacent wall had a pocket sliding door to an en-suite bathroom. He then noticed the wall to his left, festooned with sheets of flip chart paper, taped together; five by five.

Igor explained that he had given Nisba permission to draw directly onto the wall and gave a little shrug.

'It needs to be able to be pulled down and hidden at a moment's notice…just in case,' she said.

They all glanced at one another.

'Risk-averse is my middle name,' Nisba responded, with a grin.

Igor placed his hands on his hips.

'You told me it was – Complicated.'

The group laughed.

The wall chart showed a huge family-tree-style layout of more or less the whole company, with Igor at the very top with a large section dedicated to Finance and boxes drawn to denote the people in the other internal and external functions. This included Seyf-Pay. The company's contact there had been vetted by Yuri and observed for several days and considered to be straight. Miguel saw his own name, further down the hierarchy, under Raj, to whom he reported directly.

Nisba handed each man a pen and a pad of sticky notes, the large sort; half of A5.

She had switched to her corporate collaboration mode. She would pay the price later.

Prolonged engagement with people and intense social interaction she found exhausting. In some instances its impact was of exhilaration, great excitement, but this could also be emotionally draining.

On the walk over to the house, Miguel had been provided with the full outline of Nisba's theory and what they had found out so far. It had brought him to a standstill. He could offer no argument to the contrary. This validation was worrying for everyone.

'Whatever you know, whether it's about specific people or just observations, please write it on your pad, stick it on the wall somewhere, or by their name, and share it with the group. We're interested in motives, inter-relationships, opportunities…all that kind of thing,' Nisba explained.

Igor went first and added a sticky note next to his own name.

Nisba/Mrs M

Raj rolled his eyes.

'He's got a point, Raj,' challenged Nisba, her face serious. 'I'm a target, so let's think about why that is. Write it down, Swee…Igor. We need everyone to be able to see the whole picture, very clearly, and how events and people inter-relate.'

He was the only one tall enough to continue writing on his note, once it was stuck down. Igor was left-handed, Nisba noted; like she was.

1)Misha eliminated - protects Nisba at home
2)Nisba threatened - protects Igor. 2 men sent - WHO??
3)Nisba – in the way/ future beneficiary

His pen moved across to Mila.

'Are you sure you don't think it's Mila?' asked Igor, sounding weary.

'No, I'm not sure – but I don't want it to be. It doesn't make any sense,' Nisba replied, looking round at the rest of the group and then turning back to Igor.

'Are you OK for us to discuss your family? This is all getting rather personal.'

He waved his hand.

'Go ahead, Nisba. Let's just get it all out there.'

She nodded in acknowledgement and waited for Igor to provide the translation for Yuri and Vlod.

'OK, as it stands, Mila is doing alright …' said Nisba, twiddling her highlighter pen.

Igor interrupted.

'That means – really well. Just for the benefit of the group, when Nisba says; 'a bit,' she means, 'a lot'. When something is 'alright,' it's 'really good' and…'

There were murmurings within the group. Yuri shook his head and threw his hands up, laughing.

'We were saying that there is no motive for Mila, as the present arrangement benefits her. Removing Igor or me from

the equation, doesn't really make any difference in terms of her financial gain. She also had a significant inheritance.'
Nisba chewed the end of her pen.

Igor backed this up to add that Mila owned prime real estate in Grand Mir in Tashkent. A six-bedroomed villa with a swimming pool. Ulvi made a mint, holding down an extremely lucrative sales job in pharmaceuticals. They didn't want for anything. Private healthcare, schools and nice cars. The cost of this though, was that he spent more than six months of the year, in total, away overseas.

Raj raised his eyebrows. Nisba winced.

'He feels compelled to be providing equally to his wife – it's important to him,' explained Igor.

'Mmm. So, if it is Mila, it's about something else.' Nisba shrugged and continued. 'Control? Getting what's rightfully hers as the heir?' She wrote it down.

Nisba's pen then moved to Dav Uzmanov, the finance director, since no one had anything else to add.

'I think this is your man,' stated Nisba, confidently. She turned to Yuri and Vlod. 'We need to know everything there is to know about this dude.' She tapped the wall with the end of her pen.

Yuri nodded with understanding. Igor began to translate again, for Vlod's benefit.

Nisba turned to Igor.

'You know that there's absolutely nothing wrong with Vlod's English.' She looked to Vlod. 'You understand every word I say – don't you?'

Vlod pursed his lips and looked away.

'There you go.'

Yuri's eyebrows shot up. He and Igor were wrestling with the shock and amusement.

Raj then stepped forward with his sticky note.

'Dav is married and goes on holiday to Vietnam – a lot. On his own. He's there now and not rushing to get back home, it seems. He's the only colleague I know that leaves the country for holidays.'

'Thanks Raj, that's really interesting.'

Raj stuck it up.

'Is it?'

'Yes,' she replied. 'Whilst Uzbek Som is one of the lowest value currencies in the world, in Vietnam, you double your money. At the moment, 1 Som is worth 2.4 Dong.'

That was just the sort of thing Nisba would know. Raj found her an infernal smarty-pants sometimes.

'It's not the value of the currency against GBP or the US Dollar…it's what it can buy you here, or in Vietnam. And if you've already amassed some Sterling or USD, you could have the lifestyle of an oligarch,' she continued.

'Very true,' interjected Raj. 'Soms are worth absolute jack. So that means, your handsome prince here, if you take him home with you, isn't a millionaire after all – he's only worth 400 quid.'

Igor laughed. Nisba didn't. Raj invoked that look again, thought Miguel. Twice in one day.

Miguel wondered if she was going to slap him but considered her too dignified and intelligent for that. Raj could be a real *pau grande* sometimes.

'And by the way…who hired him?' asked Nisba, gathering her thoughts again.

There was an awkward silence. Raj looked to Igor. Igor looked to Raj who then ran his hands through his hair.

'We had a recommendation, from Mila.'

Nisba's pen was suspended in mid-air for a moment. She blinked about four times and was about to say something but then changed her mind.

Her imagination wasn't liking it, so veered off towards something else. What date was it, and how long had she been at Igor's? Just under a month now. She felt a sudden and pressing need to call her mum and Faye. Also, Amara would have had her baby by now, and she had not been sufficiently attentive, as a good friend should be. So full of the drama of being around Igor, and immersed in the work, it was like nothing else existed. Shocked by the recollection of her life in the UK, the desire to text at the very least, became urgent. Her mind played out the whole scenario of hurt, disappointment, apologies, and regret.

She would have to retreat straight away to the bathroom with her phone to send something, otherwise, the distraction would result in a half-hearted effort and output.

Igor sat down on the end of the bed, leaned his elbows on his knees and then held his head, rubbing the back of it.

Miguel began to feel uneasy.

On return from the bathroom, feeling a good deal better, Nisba returned to the task at hand, with alacrity.

'This guy has resources, expertise, opportunity – motive is greed for now, but there's more to this than meets the eye. I smell a rat,' Nisba mused, chuntering to herself, noting some of the key words on the paper. 'One thing I've learned in life is: if you smell a rat – it's usually because there is one.'

Vlod then stepped forward. There was a hush as they watched him stick his note up, in between the stick man and woman drawings Nisba had made, of Zeinab and Dav Uzmanov, the FD.

Igor read it out:

'Umar Bekov, the previous site manager – who is he to the others?'

'Bloody hell, Vlod, that's a good shout,' said Nisba. There was acknowledgement all round. Yuri gave him a firm slap on the back.

They continued in this vein for a couple of hours.

Miguel had stuck up three notes in all. These were placed next to two warehouse supervisors. Whilst the contribution was small in size, it was pivotal. He was able to enlighten the group that they were both related to Dav Uzmanov the FD and that Vlod was right. It wasn't a widely known fact that Uzmanov and Bekov were half-brothers.

Nisba's concluding statement was that this was perhaps a family affair, therefore influence, potentially coercion, and also loyalty would be key factors to the success of an attack on Igor's business. The group needed to find out about other family members and close ties, pretty quickly.

It was highly likely that there would be further attempts to get at Igor and herself.

Miguel would need to walk a tightrope of keeping the operation functioning well, but not too well. No disciplinaries or formal warnings, to appear that he posed no threat and also as a means of getting close to those involved.

The company overall had to continue to be the Golden Goose but appear vulnerable to a hostile takeover. This, they agreed, was the only way to encourage those responsible to expose themselves.

Zeinab would continue to have the discreet protection Igor had arranged for her, maintaining the appearance of being out of commission, but kept out of harm's way.

It was vital that Shazmina continue to play the part of stooge, unfortunately.

Women, and especially women who showed themselves to be smart, would not be appreciated by their combatants. The A-Team would have to see how that played out. There was still the possibility that Shazmina, with her access could be targeted and pressured into helping their assailants.

Nisba scribbled on the wall next to the FD's name, talking through it out loud.

Was Dav the head of the racket or Umar, or someone else? Perhaps Dav was being manipulated. What role had Umar Bekov played or continued to play in this plot? Either way, they needed to disable the operation as soon as possible, before anything else bad happened, and in only three days – before her visa ran out. She then had to correct herself. Two days. At least twenty-four hours would have to remain on the visa, allowing for the journey to fly out of Uzbekistan.

The conclusion was: if anything was going to happen, it would be to the payroll, and then with the further advantage probably taken at the event, the day after tomorrow – the Saturday the ops and supervisors were so interested in.

The staff levels would be low, with plenty of distraction and noise, so when Igor, Raj and herself, would be most vulnerable to attack.

Miguel, Raj and Igor exchanged glances. They perceived the event to be low risk, based on exactly the same factors Nisba had presented. Low volume manpower and very public.

'Mmm,' said Nisba pulling at her top lip and wagging her head from side to side. 'These different viewpoints are really important.'

The group went quiet for a moment.

'There's something else though, that we are not seeing,' she resumed, suddenly reanimated. 'It's hiding in plain sight.' She turned to face their wall chart and stepped back, to survey it.

'Occam's Razor,' she said. 'Or like when you hear the sound of hooves – you usually think horses, not zebra. We need to keep an open mind and not rule out rhinoceros, deer, giraffes...' she trailed off.

Yuri had put his hand up.

'Yes, Yuri?'

'Or Ass.'

There was laughter and backslapping.

Nisba summarised her thoughts again. The payroll should be split into two. It wouldn't be a problem to pay some people early as long as no one was paid late. It was too high risk to have twelve billion Som sitting in an account to be paid in one transaction, despite having checked that the pay-run was in trustworthy hands and would reach its intended destination of Seyf-Pay.

Raj pointed out that it was a shame that Shazmina had been unable to join them. He was sure she would have had loads of information to contribute.

Nisba stopped in the doorway and turned to look at him, narrowing her eyes, scrutinizing his face.

'Just saying,' Raj said, as he made his way past her, out of the bedroom.

Both Umar Bekov, former site manager and FD, Dav Uzmanov would be investigated the next day by Yuri and Vlod. Nisba would consolidate the contributions, summarise and identify where their gaps were and prioritise the actions.

She then decided it was time for dinner.

'There's dinner?' asked Miguel. He looked at his watch. It was 10.43 pm. He'd been there three hours already.

'Supper, actually,' said Raj, grinning. 'And you can't ever leave the house, without getting fattened up by Nisba.'

***

Nisba and Igor brought over dishes of lamb *plov*, roast spatchcocked chicken, achi chook, an Uzbek salad, more fried dumplings, and yoghurt dip. Jugs of fruit juices and a carafe of red wine were added to the spread. She'd bought *patir* and had baked traditional flower-shaped breads to share.

Nisba had stuck a few of the dinner candles Igor had bought into the necks of some empty wine bottles and lit them, placing them along the middle of the table.

There was a loud friendly hum of chatter, laughter and clinking of crockery and cutlery.

Whilst he was eating, Miguel took some time to study the members of the group.

He revisited Igor. His hair had grown a little, so he was looking less like an assassin. Miguel was envious of Igor's build and muscles. No matter how much work he himself put in, he would never achieve that.

The same applied to Raj, who was Igor's gym buddy, lean and ripped, but apparently even he was unable to keep up with Igor, who would go on for hours, punishing himself. That's what it was about, not well-being or machismo; he was hooked on pain.

Raj was protective of his friend. He'd had Igor stay with him in his flat, after being kicked out of his sister's house. Raj had told him he was fearful that Igor would go out into those woods of his and blow his brains out.

Miguel studied Igor and Nisba's interactions for a little while. These made him smile. The way Igor's eyes followed her to the kitchen. How she made him break into laughter.

Miguel didn't catch it all, but there was something about having 'washed the carafe out first.'

There were gentle shows of affection, a stroke of the arm, a rub of the shoulder and the way she looked at him.

Miguel was happy to see his friend happy, loved, and in love.

The group as a whole seemed tight, like they all went back a long way. He was pleasantly surprised by the respect they had for Nisba. She wasn't Igor's woman, and Igor wasn't just her man. They were a unit and the kingpin of the group.

This was one of those teams at work, like when he and Igor worked on the discoveries offshore of Angola and Brazil – like magic. The perfect combination of people, creating synergy. These moments were brief, and one change could cause the magic to evaporate.

He felt privileged to be part of it, but also slightly downhearted

'What's on your mind Miguel?' asked Igor, looking concerned.

'I guess I'm disappointed you didn't trust me and confide in me sooner.'

Igor looked down and nodded.

'I am sorry that it looks and feels that way. I've always known you were a good man, Miguel. I hope you'll forgive me for trialling Raj's tactics on you and for testing your resolve…this could be dangerous.'

Miguel nodded slightly, in acceptance, looking around the faces of the group. They looked anxious, understanding that he had reason not to accept it.

***

Miguel had observed that Yuri and Igor were starting up again on their guitars. Tuning up and strumming.

There was the odd Ukrainian word between them, but other than that, it was that special telepathy musicians have, instinctively knowing what the other is doing and complementing it.

Throughout the evening, Nisba made an effort to mingle, drawing up a chair and chatting in turn with everyone.

Miguel had noticed she'd spent quite a bit of time with Vlod, whose eyes were always averted but looking around, listening intently, he imagined. Nisba didn't seem to notice that Vlod wasn't talking back. It was odd that, every now and again, she'd nod as if he had.

It made Miguel smile, broadly. Nisba caught his eye, smiled back, and came over to him, pulling up Igor's empty chair as he was now sitting with Yuri on the sofa in the sitting room.

Miguel had heard from Zeinab that she'd first met Nisba in the supermarket. Unbeknownst to Nisba, Zeinab was witness to her escapade with the fried eggs and had also caught her freewheeling down the aisles with the trolley.

Vlod and Raj had made their way into the sitting room, dragging out a small but heavy red leather armchair and some beanbags. The music was heating up.

Miguel was surprised to hear that Nisba had spent time in Angola. There was quite a lot about Nisba that surprised him. They began chatting about back home. She pulled out her phone and showed him photos of the rabbits, *Randall and Hopkirk,* and her mother.

He took the phone from her and held it at arm's length and then zoomed in, looked at Nisba and then back at the photo.

'She's Jewish…from Tunisia,' explained Nisba, to satisfy his curiosity.

'So, she's from Africa,' he replied with a grin. 'And why you're named after an African Queen!'

'That's right,' nodded Nisba.

'Sophonisba was a brave woman – standing up for a principle and…' said Miguel, but didn't finish his sentence. Sophonisba died for this principle, but no doubt Nisba would know the story, he thought.

Nisba was distracted by the guitar music.

'We have to go and sing along, I'm afraid!'

Yuri and Igor had just started the opening to 'Hotel California,' by the Eagles.

It was like a light had been switched on in Vlod.

He was singing, albeit off key, loudly and happily, much to the amazement of Nisba, Raj and Miguel. Vlod knew the words to all six verses.

Nisba grabbed her phone again out of her back pocket and set it to video. Slowly she panned around the rowdy, rather drunken room, receiving a wave as she went from Raj to Miguel to Vlod, a grin from Yuri and Igor, interrupting their singing, momentarily.

The tone then became melancholy with some Elton John but they were enjoying the very loud and painfully out of tune rendition of 'Goodbye Yellow Brick Road.'

Miguel noticed that Nisba was now fighting tears, struggling to explain her feelings. She wasn't observing two grown-up, damaged men having fun, but two little boys pre-war, when they were unhurt, full of hope, picking their way through western hits. She was thinking about how much time they must have spent practising, to work them out and play them so well together like that. It was poignant and it was making her cry.

She insisted she was fine. 'Don't take any notice!'

When the song ended, Nisba stood up and headed to the kitchen to replenish the supply of refreshments.

On her return, Yuri and Igor had their heads together. They appeared to be having an in-depth discussion, whispering in Ukrainian,. It sounded like they'd finally arrived at a decision of what to play next.

Yuri stopped his strings with his hand as Igor looked up at the ceiling, blinking and swallowing hard.

Yuri reached over and squeezed his shoulder, surprising everyone by introducing the next song.

'This is for… Mrs M.'

Nisba knew instantly from the first two bars.

She drew a breath and put her hand to her heart.

Igor began 'Wonderwall,' closely followed by the whole group, singing very loudly, in unison. They knew every single word.

And then they heard Igor's voice pause and break. He held back tears as they filled in the missing words for him.

Nisba's tears were big and plopping now.

Raj left the room and reappeared with a box of tissues, passing them to her.

Raj took one. Nisba laughed through her tears.

'I've got something in my eye, OK?' he said, wiping his face.

As the song progressed, the tone became more sombre, sobered by the meaning of the words. How significant, they each thought, contemplating the dangerous road ahead and not knowing exactly the nature of the danger they faced.

And there was no question. She had already saved him.

Day 29 Friday

Raj was running a bit late, feeling the effects of the night before.

Nisba was lying in, which she never did, always seeing him to his car, arming him with an unnecessarily elaborate packed lunch. He'd thought it rather sweet of her, but she'd explained it was so he wouldn't have to chance a poisoning in the canteen. She was not going to bed bath him or wipe his arse.

Raj knocked back the last of his coffee. As soon as he grabbed his phone, it started to ring.

He answered and then very quickly held the phone away from his ear.

Shazmina was shouting, distraught.

Both Igor and Nisba, who had just appeared next to him, could hear her.

'It's gone,' she wailed. 'The payroll fund…it's gone, and it says I've taken it!'

Raj held the phone to his chest for a moment to collect his thoughts. He could barely look Igor in the eye.

'Shit, shit, shit,' spluttered Nisba, thrusting her hands into her hair. She'd disabled Shazmina's accounts and created new log ins, so they – whoever they were, would not be able to continue using her details.

She had also checked the bank details were correct for Seyf-Pay and arranged for the contact at their end to confirm receipt of the first payment, the second of which would arrive early the following morning. Nothing was left to chance.

Yuri and Vlod were outside the entrance and exits to Seyf-Pay, a significant operation, located in an office off Bukhara Street in central Tashkent. They were going to continue their surveillance of the unassuming looking young man in charge of the payroll.

Shazmina was sitting in her car in the winery car park, using her personal mobile, trembling, with the heart rate of a hummingbird.

She'd had to contain herself with all of her strength when she logged into the payroll account to make the payment, which showed a hole the size of twelve billion Som.

The Credit Controller had just brought her a cup of coffee and was placing it on her coaster, when she received the call from Seyf-Pay, to say they were still waiting for the funds to arrive. Was everything in order and were they to expect it soon?

'I'll be back in touch,' she had said, on autopilot.

The advice she had received from Raj the previous day was to appear completely normal if anything went down, maintaining the pretence that nothing out of the ordinary was going on.

Raj was now complimenting her on her composure. He would come and pick her up and bring her back to Igor's, so they could debrief and re-group. She wasn't to go back indoors straight away or drive anywhere. She sounded very upset.

Raj caught Nisba's eye.

'What?' he mouthed at her, still on the phone. She rolled her eyes and despite the gravity of the situation, couldn't help but laugh.

'I am fine,' replied Shazmina, impatiently. 'There is no time. I have to go back inside, otherwise I get accused of skiving or something. I will say it's about my Mum if they think anything is wrong. We debrief when you get here.'

'Smart girl.' He was impressed.

Nisba told him he wasn't allowed to call her a girl.

***

'You must have insurance for this kind of thing,' Nisba said to Igor, who was seated at the island, his head in his hands with his eyes closed.

'If we have been remiss, then they aren't going to pay out – besides, claims take time and that's one thing we don't have.' He rubbed his face then propped his head up, resting his forehead on the tips of his fingers.

'My people are depending on their pay tomorrow. They have to get paid, no matter what.' Igor sat back, resting his hands on his head. He looked up at the ceiling.

'What about your overdraft facility? There must be a contingency plan.'

'It's not that big...we've never needed it,' he answered, rubbing the back of his head. 'I admit we're in a vulnerable position when something goes wrong. I know we need to look at our cashflow. The income from our major clients doesn't come through soon enough for us to catch up.'

'Yes, but who has a spare million dollars lying about, to pay them?'

Igor fidgeted in his chair.

'Oh! *You* do!'

Nisba rolled her eyes.

'I've got you to thank, that it's not twice that. It's not straight forward. I can't guarantee meeting the deadline. It might be a case of paying something to keep people afloat and the rest later, but that would raise the alarm. It would get out...'

'Should the responsibility sit directly with you, to put your hand in your own pocket? What about asking Mila? It's her company too.' Nisba began to bite her thumbnail. 'Will you not speak to her about it?'

'She invested most of her capital into that house and the rest would be set aside for Alina and Aziz. I don't want to ask her, because it would disrupt all their lives so much to secure the funds...besides, she'd go mad for a start...I can't face her.'

Nisba nodded with understanding, as she picked at the hem of her T-shirt. She wondered where it would leave Igor, but didn't want to ask, in case it sounded like she was concerned about his liquidity. That wasn't it. It just seemed so unfair. All that hard work he'd undertaken, before acquiring the company and the investments she knew he had made, offering him security for the future. For life, which he hadn't had the chance to live yet.

Igor pulled out his phone.

Yuri and Vlod were asked to return. Once they were back at the house, he would go to Seyf-Pay himself and make whatever payments he could and witness their arrival personally.

He made the call, to update the Seyf-Pay account manager. Nisba laid her hand on his shoulder.

'Do you need some time to yourself?...this must be so hard.'

He turned and put his arms round her waist and looked up at her.

He shook his head slightly.

'I just had other plans for it – that's all.' He smiled, resting his forehead against her stomach. 'And I guess, I'm not a prince anymore,' he said, sadly.

Nisba rolled her eyes again and gave him a kiss. 'You'll get it back. You will,' she whispered, hugging him tightly.

Igor smiled again, appreciating her optimism, but this evaporated.

'They'll want their other half Nisba…they only got part of the prize. I fear this is going to get nasty.'

***

On reflection, Shazmina had thought she had sounded insubordinate on the phone; telling Raj what to do.

All in, her week wasn't going terribly well and her general state of anger, coupled with mortification, had resulted in her becoming less inhibited. Things couldn't really get any worse, she thought.

Shazmina was no longer nervous or excited about meeting Mr Pereira again. That had worn off. She wasn't bothered. Totally over it.

Until she saw him. Unprepared, the adrenaline bounded up into her chest and eyes and she had to catch her breath.

'Come in,' he called, waving his hand toward the chair opposite his desk.

He hadn't stuck to the plan they had agreed earlier, she noted. It seemed like he'd completely forgotten about it.

She was befuddled for a second but resumed her part. Speaking loudly and clearly for the benefit of the staff milling about in the corridor.

'The printer downstairs has broken and Jasur's has run out of ink, so may I use yours, please?'

'Of course,' he replied, in a similar tone. He shut the door behind her.

'Fucking hell, Shazmina,' he whispered, cupping her elbow with his hand. 'You really are having a shit week.'

She wished he wouldn't swear quite so much and thought him unusually giddy and upbeat, given the circumstances.

They sat on either side of his desk and regarded one another for a few seconds. Shazmina thought she felt the presence of a third party. It wouldn't go away. It was hogging the air space.

She put it down to stress. Her brain wasn't computing effectively and was struggling to read the room.

'You have a theory,' stated Raj, sitting forward, looking earnestly at her.

'Yes,' she replied, relaxing a little.

'So, let's hear it.' Raj sat back.

He appeared to study her intently, as if he couldn't quite believe what he was seeing. Shazmina wondered if she looked worse than usual, having food stuck in her teeth or something. And then he looked away. Relieved, thinking he'd not seen anything of interest, she was able to present her ideas, surprising herself at her confidence and belief in them.

The fraudster was the finance director. He had the motive, opportunity and the means.

He was arrogant and with questionable values. She'd overheard telephone conversations that made more sense now than they had at the time.

There was definitely someone else pulling the strings. Someone powerful and intimidating. The FD seemed scared of them, and there was some sort of network at large within the business. Possibly a family network, that Dav was able to leverage, maybe.

There must be hidden cameras above her desk and the offices bugged. This was the only way they could know her new details. And whoever they were, they clearly had a VPN with remote access to everything.

She feared things would escalate, given that they only got half of their money. The gang would probably resort to violence or some sort of blackmail to get the rest, or whatever the endgame was.

The team needed to track down the gang leader's IP address and location. In her view, a safe assumption would be it was a computer in Vietnam. If they couldn't figure it out by standard means, then they needed an IT geek or hacker to help them find out.

If it came to that, she knew of one.

He lived on the floor above her.

***

'Hi, Tan.' Nisba waved at the camera on her laptop.

Tan adjusted his view, so his head wasn't chopped off.

'You've got news for me…I can tell.' Tan wagged his finger at her, grinning.

Igor leaned in so that their heads were together, cheeks touching.

'Hi Tan,' Igor said, smiling.

'I couldn't think of another reason why Nisba would be sticking around any longer than she needed to, in Uzbekistan!' Tan laughed.

'Yes, it's official. But I followed your advice…particularly about no overblown romantic gestures.'

'I can assure you, there haven't been any of those,' laughed Nisba. 'But hold on…that means you two have been plotting…'

Igor and Tan had no idea what she was talking about.

'Anyway, I'll leave you to talk shop.' Igor waved and moved away.

'I'll get it out of you two eventually…so all OK, workwise? No mutiny?'

'What?...no, all well in fact, we are doing just fine without you!' Tan was still on a high from the news earlier, pleased with the contribution he may have made to help bring it about.

'That's great to hear.' She was relieved. They were going to have to get used to it.

***

Nisba had warned Igor that the call with Faye may not go quite so well.

Faye had known Nisba since she was eleven, so was witness and privy to all Nisba's domestic disasters and other misfortunes, so would not be quite so optimistic or understanding. That was all.

This hadn't made Igor feel any better, explaining to Nisba that he had tried to put himself in Faye's shoes.

She would soon learn that her best and dearest friend had wandered out into the wilds of Uzbekistan, only to be pulled out of the mud by some fucked-up nutter with PTSD, keeping her in his house, to clean, cook and scrub his outdoor furniture and then mop up his vomit and wipe his ass.

Following a threat to her own life, she would then be put back to work, to counter an attack on his livelihood. She had the clothes she stood up in and no means of escape. To cap it all, they had decided after thirteen days of knowing each other, they were going to get married and last but not least, he had gone and got her pregnant.

It was a hard sell.

***

He and Nisba had agreed that it was probably best to omit the last two items of their update.

The call with Faye concluded with Igor chatting to her husband Tom, for some minutes. Igor was pleased that, in the end, it had been enjoyable. He'd done well, according to Tom. He now just needed to get past Rose, Nisba's mum. *Good luck with that.*

The call came in before Igor even had a chance to digest these comments.

He was taken aback by the resemblance. Her skin was darker than Nisba's, with tight reddish brown curly hair, going grey around her hairline. Looking extremely good for eighty, he thought.

He detected mischief in her brown eyes straight away.

'Oh Nisba – he's so handsome. Well done you! She's wasted so much time kissing frogs…and now…'

They laughed.

'Thanks Mum, so yes, here he is – Prince Igor.'

'Hello, Mrs Maasik. I've been looking forward to meeting you,' Igor said smiling, not entirely truthfully.

She waved her hand.

'Rose. Call me Rose. I hear you've been taking good care of Nisba. I understand she had a bit of a mishap…had a fall.'

Igor blinked. 'Umm, that's right.' He thought it best to change the subject.

Nisba slipped away to the kitchen, to give them some space.

There was a silence for a couple of seconds, where Igor and Rose observed one another.

'She's in some sort of bother, isn't she?' Rose asked directly, putting on a pair of glasses.

Startled, Igor found himself wanting to avoid eye contact.

'What's she got herself into this time?...or have you put her in it?' she continued, eyeing him over the top of her glasses.

He swallowed.

'It's entirely my fault.'

'It won't be,' answered Rose quickly. 'She'll have made a decision to be involved or not. I know Nisba.'

Igor didn't reply. The insight was unnerving.

There was a pause. Rose resumed.

'You could really do without this. I can see you need a break – don't you , dear?'

Igor was caught out. A lump formed in his throat and it was hurting.

He blinked several times, as he felt the flood gates straining. He realised how much he missed his own mother.

There was a silence, filled with unspoken words.

'You'll be home soon, sweetheart,' reassured Rose, nodding with a kind and optimistic smile.

Igor coughed to clear his throat and wiped his eye.

'Tell me about the cracks in your house and why you're worried it's going to fall down…I might be able to help.'

***

Igor had left it rather a long time to catch up with Mila.

He also felt that he'd timed the moment badly, making it more difficult to politely decline an invitation to a pre-Ramadan get-together.

She could be very persuasive but had always previously been unsuccessful. He gave all social gatherings a miss, unless it was just with her, Ulvi and the children, and especially avoided any gatherings where the expectation of him was as a Muslim.

He didn't observe because he considered he no longer had a relationship with God, so it was incorrect to even refer to himself as a Muslim. His war experience meant he was at the point of no return. He couldn't forgive it. He couldn't forgive himself. So, he wouldn't be a hypocrite and rub shoulders with good and nice people whose lives were entirely shaped by this relationship.

He had spoken to Nisba about it. She had a very open and questioning attitude to faith and at times admitted to being conflicted.

'I bet there will be Muslims who are privately much worse than you, so I don't think you should consider yourself an imposter or unqualified to be amongst them,' Nisba said sipping her tea. 'If anyone is going to feel that way…it's me.'

She had offered to accompany him if it would mean he would go, thinking it might do him some good. Hang out with family, speak to somebody perhaps, and find some reconciliation.

He agreed, reluctantly. He wasn't in the mood though, feeling wiped out and pillaged. It had been an expensive day, and it was starting to catch up with him.

Igor had to pay an international transfer fee of 20%, so had lost all the accessible cash he possessed.

It was the first time he'd felt financially insecure and it rattled him. There was no contingency. Everything else was tied up and would take a while to get to.

He had to admit, that there was an element of male ego involved. He liked that he could be a provider. It was important to him that he maintained equity with Nisba at the very least. He wished to avoid at all cost the possibility of her being in a position of bearing any financial burdens alone. That bothered him.

***

Ulvi had called Igor back, to make sure Nisba was coming. He had assumed she would be, but didn't want her to think that she wasn't included in the invitation.

Mila had texted afterwards to apologise. She considered it an inappropriate expectation, especially as it was Friday night. It was entirely Nisba's choice, but of course she would be welcome.

Nisba was rather touched by both considerations. She would go.

It would be a distraction they didn't really need though.

They really wanted to focus on their predicament. Also, Nisba had been excited about spending the evening with Shazmina; their new A-team member. It would be refreshing to have another woman in the mix, so she wanted to light the candles and stay in. The prospect of uprooting herself was unpleasant, especially socialising where she didn't really belong, and there would be complete strangers.

Raj had been right about Shazmina having information to add. Shazmina was also very kindly bringing some clothes for her to borrow.

Igor was concerned about the falling out he'd with Raj, the previous day.

He hoped things wouldn't be awkward.

***

The previous day

Igor looked at Raj through narrowed eyes, assessing what he had just said. Raj was seated at the kitchen table for breakfast. Igor stood, looming over him.

'You're not the right man for her, Raj…unless you're really serious about proving me wrong.'

Nisba walked into the kitchen wearing Igor's dressing gown. Feeling the tension, she offered to leave.

'He's lecturing me about Shazmina,' Raj responded, with some bitterness. 'Feel free to join in…'

Igor continued. 'I have a duty of care. She's my employee and I got her into this mess. You're a director…her senior. It could be seen as an abuse of power. She's also very young, culturally worlds apart and probably…you know, innocent….so that makes her vulnerable.'

'That's not what I see,' snapped Raj, interrupting him.

Igor raised his eyebrows and thrust his hands into his pockets.

'Ok…so, you're right about all of those things,' sulked Raj, 'but she's not defined by them. She's got grit. At only twenty four, look what she's achieved in this…society. Educated, ambitious, independent. She'll end up as Finance Manager if she's not careful, after this shitstorm has passed – aside from the fact that she's…she's…'

'Stunning?' offered Nisba with a smile.

Raj gave a crooked grin and waved in acknowledgement at her.

He sat back in his chair, folding his arms, and proceeded to brood.

Nisba and Igor exchanged glances.

'Who are you? And what have you done with Raj?' asked Nisba grinning.

'Whatever you might think of me, Nisba, I'm not a total bastard.'

'But you have been,' interjected Igor, '...with women.'

Raj shifted uneasily and then looked embarrassed, avoiding Nisba's gaze.

'I didn't have particularly good role-modelling and I've had some crap experiences. I didn't know what good looked like...until now.' Raj waved his hand in their direction.

'Hmm,' replied Igor. 'I'm still not going to stand by and let you seduce this young girl...woman, sorry.'

Raj frowned. 'You must have a very low opinion of me, Igor.' He leaned forward on his elbows, cradling his head with his fingers. 'I'm not looking for a conquest...I'm looking for a soul mate – a piece of what you two have got...'

'...And lots of Hot Sex,' added Nisba.

Raj gave another crooked grin and jiggled his leg.

'Who's to say, she doesn't want that?...Oh, come on, Igor. Lighten up. For fuck's sake.' Raj threw his hands down onto the table. 'I don't want to fuck it up, OK. I don't want to mess her up, either. So...I'm not going to do anything.' Raj ran the fingers of both hands through his hair. 'Jesus. I don't know if she even likes me.'

'Judging by your meeting with Igor...accusing her of stealing millions of dollars, if she did like you – she probably doesn't anymore,' smirked Nisba.

Raj rubbed his chin. He wasn't proud of their Good Cop, Bad Cop routine, but felt he had just been judged by two people he respected.

He stood up and stomped over to the front door, slamming it behind him.

'He's upset,' said Igor, placing his hands on his hips.

'Is that possible...about a woman? About anything?'

Igor nodded and broke into a big smile, turning to look at her.

'Oh dear,' responded Nisba, affectionately. 'He's got it really bad.'

***

Shazmina spent some time studying Nisba's wall chart. She nodded, her finger following the notes as she read.

Nisba reminded herself that everything that Shazmina did at work and with the A-Team, was in her third language. Her English was very good, but she had quite a strong Uzbek accent, that required Nisba to concentrate in order to tune in.

'What about Irina Volkova?' asked Shazmina, looking again at the chart. 'She does not seem to be on here.'

'Ah…she's in the 'Carpark,' said Nisba smiling, pointing to the cluster of orange sticky notes to the top left of the main chart.

'Is she a friend of yours?' asked Nisba tentatively.

'No.'

'Oh.' Nisba waited for Shazmina to elaborate.

'She is from Russia. We are same age and started at Prikat Winery at same time, but we have nothing in common. We are very different people. But she is good worker and could do far more.' She paused for a few seconds and then resumed. 'I think, she is um…how to say this…'

Shazmina pulled at her bottom lip.

'Go on,' said Nisba, touching her arm, encouraging her to continue.

'She is having affair with Dav Uzmanov.'

Nisba's eyebrows shot up.

'It's not common knowledge. I umm, saw them, you see.' She laughed, a little embarrassed. 'I overhear things, because people forget I'm there, behind filing cabinet.'

Shazmina picked up a marker pen and pulled the lid off.

'Irina wanted to take three week holiday. Zeinab turned it down, because it was very short notice and for too long. Zeinab approved one week, but Irina appealed. Mr M compromised in agreement with Zeinab that Irina could take two, if she set up rota to cover her reception duties, but I know she was determined to get it because Dav had asked her to go to Vietnam with him.'

'Ah...I see, leaving his wife at home presumably?' asked Nisba perched on the edge of the bed, stretching her legs out.

Shazmina nodded, replacing the lid on the pen.

'There's more.'

Nisba sat up straight.

'He went without her.'

'Oh...Let me guess,' said Nisba, jumping up.

'He took someone else!' they said, both at the same time.

'But...Irina does not know,' added Shazmina.

'Ouch,' Nisba replied, not unsympathetically.

'Irina is lovely person, but she thinks that man is answer. You know, to take care of her. Pay for everything. She likes to be charmed... but we get along well. We are organising, you know, The Event together. She did not take holiday and instead has taken over many things from Zeinab. Very organised. She had many ideas for The Event and worked hard. I've been glad of her help because I am busy with month end.'

Shazmina went on to say that she was feeling uncomfortable about the cameras and other devices that might be in place. They agreed that they would have to devise ways of preventing unauthorised access to all accounts and any means of purchasing anything.

Everything would have to stay in place as it was; to avoid raising the alarm, but they agreed a plan to mitigate the risk of further financial losses.

'There is other thing...' Shazmina said cautiously, as they walked out of the bedroom and back into the kitchen area.

'Umar Bekov, the old site manager, has herd of goats. Very pretty. Pre-school children go to feed them. I umm...I think that might be source of E-coli.'

She pulled an anxious face, looking at Igor.

'You mean to say that I ate goat shit?' he asked, placing his hands on his hips.

Nisba and Shazmina exchanged glances.

Igor rubbed the back of his head. 'I'd appreciate it if you didn't share that with Raj – I'll never hear the last of it.'

**

Igor gave Shazmina a brief tour of the house and outside, if she wished to sit there – in case she wanted to get away from Raj.

'The constraints of work don't apply here…just be yourself. I'm Igor – he's Raj, so no Mister this or that. And just to be clear – Raj has no authority over you. You still report into the FD, so whilst he's away, anything urgent…you come to me.'

Shazmina smiled.

'Thank you. Does this mean I can be rude to Raj, without being disciplined for insubordination?'

Igor was pleasantly taken aback. He wondered if perhaps Raj had met his match.

'Yes, it does,' he smiled. 'But he could always put in a complaint about you.' Igor turned away, so she couldn't see his face.

Nisba and Shazmina then went back into the bedroom to do Girly Stuff. Apparently, it was allowed for them to call it that, but not OK for Raj or Igor.

There was an awkward silence between the two men for a few seconds.

'Look…I'm sorry I was hard on you, Raj,' said Igor rubbing his hand over his mouth.

Raj gave a slight shrug and opened the fridge, pulling out two bottles of beer with one hand. With the other, he gave Igor a heavy slap on the back.

'C'mon Sweetie Pie – let's drink these outside!'

***

'You're so brave,' said Shazmina. 'I don't think I could do anything like that.' She sat on the end of the bed, watching Nisba try on her clothes.

Trips out were restricted to critical only. A shopping trip down to the *Ippodrom* was therefore out of the question.

'How do you know? I never expected to have a company, employees and stuff and work in Central Asia and Africa. I've surprised myself. Pushed myself. Sometimes it was very scary – still is. But that's good…no guts, no glory and all that.'

Nisba pulled down a T-shirt. It was a bit tight.

'My boobs are enormous these days.' She groped them playfully. 'I think everything you've brought is great. I love this.' She held up a long blouse with a traditional pattern in shades of red and gold. 'I think I'll wear this, over those white jeans for this evening.'

Shazmina was thrilled to receive such approval.

'Anyway, Shazmina…think big, like you have been doing. You're a lot further on than I was at your age.' She paused halfway through folding.

'Sorry…that sounded really patronising. I didn't mean to sound parental but I was living on my friend's sofa, homeless, in a mess…broken hearted and with no money. You're on track, clever, self-sufficient so you have choices, which is what it's all about.'

Shazmina nodded. Everyone had their story, their struggles. She was amazed, as Nisba seemed so confident – self-possessed. It was impressive that she had achieved so much and in such a short time.

'I just don't know what else I could do…or where else I could go,' Shazmina responded, shrugging her shoulders, looking down at her hands.

'The world is a big place. Uzbekistan is not the only country,' continued Nisba pulling the white jeans up, unable to fasten the button. 'And Raj is not the only man.' She smiled, tentatively.

Shazmina looked up horrified and then groaned, placing her head in her hands. 'Is it so obvious?'

'Don't worry, the men are clueless. It will stay that way; don't you worry about that.'

Nisba sat down on the bed next to her.

'You have more power and autonomy than you realise,' Nisba said.

Shazmina looked up at her with surprise.

'It depends on what you want. You really do have the power to alter your universe if you want to. I learned a bit late. It's a state of mind. Take control…don't let life or people happen to you, is all I can say. Self-esteem and a sense of my own worth is something I wished I had discovered much sooner. However, it doesn't sound like you need any pep talks or words of wisdom from the likes of me.' Nisba slapped her hands onto her thighs.

'I do. I did. Thank you,' Shazmina replied. 'I don't know anyone like you. You know, successful and…so empowered. It's been so inspiring and – helpful.'

Nisba stood up in her outfit and slipped her feet into some shoes.

'You look amazing. You would look amazing in potato sack!' laughed Shazmina.

'Aw…thank you. Well, I might need one in a couple of months or so.' Standing in front of the mirror, Nisba proceeded to stick out her belly.

Shazmina gasped. Nisba put her finger on her lips.

'Raj doesn't know yet. Igor is going to break it to him at the right moment.'

'Congratulations! How long have you and Igor been married?'

Nisba laughed.

'Oh, we're not married. We only met four weeks ago.'

Shazmina's jaw dropped, and her eyes widened. 'Woops!'

'No…no, not at all. It just happened a helluva lot sooner than we expected. It's what we have both wanted for a long time…so why try and avoid it?' Nisba shrugged her shoulders. 'We knew that we wanted to be together – this was it.'

Shazmina gaped and then laughed hard with her hand over her mouth 'How wonderful!'

There was a knock at the door.

'It's time to go, Nisba,' called Igor from the other side.

'Right. Thank you so much for the clothes and the chat – it's been lovely,' Nisba said, adding the finishing touches to her mascara.

Shazmina was still recovering from Nisba's bombshell. Nisba laughed and gave her a hug.

'Like I said, you really can alter your universe. It can happen in a day – or years.'

Shazmina nodded. Still smiling with disbelief.

Nisba turned back to look at her.

'Oh, and er...I do hope you have a pleasant evening. I am sorry that we have to leave you all alone with Raj. But I do know he isn't...sorry – that is.' She beamed, as she left the room.

Shazmina's mouth dropped open again.

***

The front entrance to Ulvi and Mila's house was gated. They waited several minutes for the gates to part before moving forward. They were interminably slow.

Yuri had insisted on driving them and muttered under his breath. He didn't like the idea that they could be hemmed in with no quick escape.

'I think you're being over cautious. We're safe here, Yuri,' reassured Igor.

This was one place Igor felt he could relax. Nisba could sense this and felt a degree of normality, peacefulness and freedom from the confinement of the farmhouse.

Yuri turned into a shaded spot, under an acacia tree to the left of the house, which was villa-style with an arched portico.

It had been another unusually warm day. The sky was still deep blue and cloudless. Nisba loved the weather in Uzbekistan. There were over two hundred sunny days a year.

The front door was ajar. Before they knocked or called out, Ulvi appeared, welcoming them in.

'Did you not drive, Igor?' asked Ulvi, curious, looking out and around at the forecourt.

'No. I have a man.'

Ulvi laughed with surprise, as he spied Yuri, looking menacing in the front of one of the A-Team's 4x4s. He hadn't spotted Vlod, who was sitting low in his seat.

'He should come in and join us!' smiled Ulvi, waving into the hallway.

'No, no. He'll be quite happy there, thank you.'

'I really think he should. There'll be plenty of food for one extra.'

Igor didn't reply.

Mila appeared and seemed in a hurry, making her way past them and out towards her car which was parked on the opposite side to Yuri.

'Are you leaving, Mila?' called Igor, surprised.

'Ulvi says we need more drinks.' She appeared conflicted, not wanting to leave.

'Don't go Mila…I am sure it will work out.'

Igor turned to Ulvi.

Ulvi hesitated, seemingly unsure to begin with, but then conceded, sighing with some impatience.

'Well, I expect we'll be fine.'

There were fewer people there than Nisba had expected. She still felt the early onset of mild panic. It was also quite noisy, with loud chatter, traditional music and the two children shrieking.

She didn't mind the chaos that children bring at all. It was having to behave properly and make small talk with adult strangers that was the difficulty.

The hall floor, she noticed, was an intricate Islamic tile pattern. It had a motif that was repeated many times. What a complete nightmare it must have been to work it all out, she pondered, for whomever had to lay it – and damn it, had she switched the oven off? She was pretty sure. Yes. On revisiting the tile pattern, Nisba also noticed two large suitcases and a laptop bag. Ulvi apparently was going away again for work, that evening.

She felt Igor's hand on her back.

'We don't have to do this you know,' he whispered, in her ear.

'I think we should,' she whispered back.

'So, how's the winery?' asked Ulvi, leading the way along the hall. 'I expect these days; it practically runs itself!'

Igor was still not in the mood and especially not for discussing the winery.

'You've done well, Nisba. A man who's independently wealthy – unlike us, who really have to work for a living…' Ulvi grinned and patted Igor's arm.

He then melted away, leaving them in the main reception room with the food and groups of people.

'It's been a breeze,' muttered Igor.

Nisba rubbed his back, wondering if perhaps it wasn't such a good idea after all, sensing the brewing Rage and bewilderment. Such a thoughtless and stupid thing to say to a man, damaged by his war experience, she thought. In her view, Ulvi was a tactful and kind sort of person, so this was puzzling.

'Let's go outside and get away from this crowd,' she suggested, taking his hand, leading him across the Persian carpet through the sitting room, towards the terrace.

They stepped out into the fading evening. The sunlight was orange and low, glowing through the leaves of the surrounding trees, making them appear a luminous fluorescent green.

They walked around the side of the house. Igor leaned against the warm stone and pulled Nisba in and held her tightly to him. Tilting her chin up with his forefinger, he looked into her eyes, sweeping away some stray curls.

'That's better,' he smiled. They began to kiss.

They hadn't noticed Alina, who'd come out and followed them.

She ran away, back through the doors into the room and began to shout in Russian.

'Mummy! Mummy! Uncle Igor and Nizzbaar are in the garden – kissing!'

Mila's face showed displeasure and looked anxiously at Ulvi, who laughed, as did everyone else around him.

'Oh, come now, Mila. He deserves a bit of happiness. He should enjoy it whilst he can – it won't last.'

***

Nisba took a seat on the unoccupied cream leather sofa in the middle of the room. It faced the buffet, which was laid out on an enormous oval mahogany table.

She needed some respite from the throng, having done her bit, working her way around the room, making polite conversation in Russian, which was always an effort.

Nisba sneaked in her pink travel earplugs. They weren't hugely effective, but they took the edge off. Filtering out most of the din enabled her to order her thoughts and as a result, figure out her emotions.

She felt like she was alone in a little boat, floating about on a choppy sea, which slowly seemed to calm.

Nisba surveyed the room.

Opulent, yet tasteful. Spacious. All items were high end or antique. There was a lot of cream marble, amphoras, ornate mirrors with cream and gold frames. At her feet was a large square Persian rug. It had a slight sheen to it in the sunlight. Silk, she supposed.

Everything was immaculate, unlike her own house. Hers was what she would describe as – lived in.

People formed clusters around the room. All men, she suddenly observed, and wondered where Mila's friends were. She'd not been introduced to any yet.

There were voices behind her. Male voices. Two.

Nisba instantly pulled out the earplugs, the roar of the room rushing to her ear drums. She closed her eyes, to hear better and then opened them wide.

Her skin pricked and crawled from her right wrist up to her jawline. She recalled the smell of the log store and the fear she had felt.

The two men who had been sent to get her, were directly behind her, less than two feet away.

Nisba's eyes swept the room in front of her to find Igor. He was deep in conversation with a man with a long beard, wearing a *doppi*. As if he sensed her, Igor lifted his eyes and they connected.

He'd received her transmission seeing her terror and the two men standing behind her.

Igor immediately turned his back on her, excusing himself to the bearded man. Igor pulled out his phone from his inside jacket pocket and held it up, as if he were dealing with a text but in need of his glasses.

Nisba knew he was taking a selfie photo or video to record their faces. She felt blessed to have such a smart, intuitive, and competent partner…lover...and then had the sudden urge to laugh. Stop it, Nisba.

She sunk low into the softness of the sofa. Her heart beat so fast and hard, it was making her hands tremble. Sitting on them, she conducted another survey of the room, suddenly feeling surrounded by a malign force.

The faces appeared contorted, grotesque, intimidating – all looking at her.

Mila suddenly reappeared from the kitchen with more platters of food. The sea of people parted for her, making appreciative noises.

It was a difficult thought – Mila. What was her game? This was something Nisba struggled with. People's intentions. They were hard to read. She could sense emotion in people but not their agenda necessarily. This is why she had to lay thoughts out on paper, having to detach herself in order to identify a pattern, or strategy.

Nisba got up with some effort. The sofa seemed to be pulling her back down into it. Not daring to look about her, she moved directly over to Mila on the pretext of asking her if she would like any help. Nisba followed her into the enormous sparkly kitchen.

'I was expecting families…' said Nisba. 'Who are they all?'

'They're people Ulvi knows,' Mila replied, sounding flat. 'He has an extraordinary amount of relatives. The other people due to turn up are unable to come until later.'

Mila began to place items into the bottom tray of the dishwasher.

'He has five brothers and too many nephews to count.' She looked up at the ceiling. 'Two are supervisors at the winery.'

Mila then turned to gather up cutlery from the top of a tall pile of dirty plates.

'I don't agree with family members working for the business,' she continued. 'Apparently one of them had a run-in. Embarrassing.' Wiping her hands on a dishcloth, she shook her head, displeased. 'I don't know what became of the maid,' Mila muttered. 'She was due to help with all of this. Anyway…as I was saying, he was accused of something by another colleague. I'm not sure what, but it got out of hand and he retaliated in a fork-lift truck. Naturally, he was fired. Now he's at a loose end.' She rolled her eyes. 'He's a little shi….there he is, with his cousin.' Mila took Nisba's arm and showed her to the kitchen doorway, through which was a view into the reception room.

Mila nodded her head toward the back. Nisba didn't want to look. She knew exactly who they were.

A sense of foreboding had started to creep and crawl its way across her skin around her jawline, spreading its heavy tentacles into her chest, to trigger the sensation of suffocating. Nisba began her well-practised counterattack, pinching herself and looking for something distracting, happy thoughts, a mantra; 'humpty dumpty sat on a wall, humpty dumpty…'

Mila then went back to the pile of plates. 'By the way, Ulvi's not leaving until tomorrow now. I think it's because he wants to spend more time with Igor and…'

Nisba's attention was suddenly caught by the front door closing. It was done slowly to be very quiet, to avoid drawing attention.

The panic attack immediately withdrew.

Nisba quickly darted back to scan the main room to see who it was that had left and then ran to the front door, opening it ajar to peek out. She flung it open and ran out into the yellow floodlight, flailing her arms about at Yuri, pointing to the side pedestrian gate.

'Follow him!' she mouthed, 'now!'

Vold climbed out of the vehicle and ran.

Stepping back into the hallway, panting, Nisba bent over to recover her wits.

'What's happening?'

She glanced up.

Igor was looking worried.
Nisba had noticed that the laptop bag had gone.

***

Mila was suddenly by Igor's side.
'Is everything alright? Are you unwell, Nisba?' she asked.
Nisba looked pale and shaken.
Igor explained that she needed some air and then she would be alright. Perhaps a glass of water.
'Ah, 'I see,' said Mila giving Igor a significant look and raising her eyebrows before retreating to the kitchen.
Nisba and Igor exchanged glances. That could be their excuse, but they didn't want to use it. Not yet.
Igor's phone buzzed.
'He's on his way back,' Igor read, looking perplexed 'Ulvi, that is. That was a text from Vlod.'
Nisba was trying to formulate the words, but Igor's phone buzzed again.
The men were now starting to move into the hallway as if preparing to leave. She and Igor were suddenly surrounded.
He shuffled to get closer to her. Huddled with their heads together, Igor showed her his phone.

Vlod - Today 21:07
Go to toilet. Open there

Igor shrugged, slightly confused. Nisba's eyes were wide and fearful.
Igor headed for the downstairs bathroom. Nisba held him back for a second.
'I'm sorry,' she whispered.
Igor locked himself in the bathroom and sat on the toilet seat and opened the text from Vlod. Igor noted that Vlod had sent it to him personally, not via the A-Team Group Chat.
Attached was a series of photographs and a short video, a bit grainy, as it had been recorded at maximum zoom.

***

Raj and Shazmina's evening was going well.

Keen to impress, he had prepared a meal for them and laid it out on the island.

Nisba had strategically placed two wine-bottle candlesticks on the island and had winked at him on her way out.

'Piss off,' he'd mouthed at her, disguising a grin with a scowl.

But he lit them.

He'd set the food out at the corner of the island so that they were perched on the barstools at right angles to each other.

Since speaking to Nisba, Shazmina felt different, no longer at a disadvantage. She wondered why this was, trying to put her finger on it.

Looking in the mirror in the bathroom a few minutes earlier, Shazmina had viewed her reflection. This also appeared different to her and somehow, the way her body filled the room. The relationship she had with her physical being had altered.

Entering that bathroom as one person – unsure, fearful, falling short, she had come out as another, with a sense of worth, self-advocacy, a degree of peace and excitement for the future.

Raj looked up as Shazmina came into the kitchen. He could see it.

He had to ask himself how it was that he had never really seen her before.

She was a force and so pretty. He was unexpectedly nervous.

***

Their conviviality was shattered by the lights illuminating outside. They'd heard no vehicle, and Igor had not yet been in touch.

Shazmina froze.

'Get down,' Raj whispered, taking her hand to help her off the high stool.

'Go round there.' He pointed toward the back of the island, the space between it and the kitchen cabinets. She crawled away.

'What will you do?' she whispered, turning back.

'I'll be right with you.' He had followed but continued on round into the utility room.

She heard him open and close a cupboard. He reappeared on hands and knees and then sat up next to her, leaning his back against the kitchen cabinet.

'Alright?' he asked, as she watched him aghast, checking a gun.

'I think so,' she replied.

He grinned.

'I'm sorry about the rude interruption of our…'

'Date?' she offered, with a little smile.

Unexpectedly bold, he thought. He was pleased she'd said that.

He would be able to give Igor a run for his money on First Date anecdotes.

There was an urgent tap at the front door.

They looked at each other.

It tapped again.

Raj knelt to get up. She put her hand on his arm.

'Be careful.' she pleaded in a loud whisper, her other hand to her forehead. 'I'll be annoyed if you die.'

He really wanted to kiss her.

'I'll do my best not to annoy you. Just promise me – no matter what happens, you stay right here, OK?'

He didn't wait for a reply and worked his way round the room, avoiding being a target from the window or the front door. The layout of the house was unhelpful in this regard, providing little cover.

'Who is it?' Raj shouted, from under the kitchen table in his best Russian.

'Rashidov. Rustam Rashidov.'

Raj thought he was prepared for the unexpected, but found he wasn't.

'What do you want?'

There was a pause.

'I want to speak to Max...Igor Mirzeyakamov?'

'You deal with me,' replied Raj. 'What do you want?'

At that moment Raj's phone buzzed. He was conflicted for a second. Should it wait... but pulled out his phone.

From Igor. Two words:

It's Ulvi

Raj's mouth dropped open.

Rashidov continued.

'I have information you need...Lev Shulkin sent me.'

Raj raised his eyebrows.

'...about Ulvi Rakhmanov.'

Raj was usually a sixty beats per minute kind of guy but his heartrate shot up to over ninety and he felt the effects in his throat.

'What about him?' shouted Raj. He would not be tempted to open the door.

'...Who he really is.'

Raj was tempted to open the door.

He had to think for a minute, taking a look around to make sure Shazmina was not in view. She wasn't. Whilst she appeared to be a compliant sort of person, he had begun to realise she was far from it. He found that very exciting, and distracting.

'You're not coming in!' Raj shouted. If Shazmina had not been there, he would have taken steps to ensure the man wasn't armed and probably let him in. He was not going to take any chances with her life.

He was beginning to think he might need an interpreter. His Russian, whilst sufficient for most work-based interactions, had its limitations.

His phone buzzed again.

He answered.

'It's me,' Shazmina whispered.
'Yes, I know,' he smiled.
'Would you like some help with your Russian?'
'Is it really that shit?'
She didn't answer. He gave a nod and smiled.
'Right…stay on the line. Can you hear him, OK?'
Yes, she could.
 'You need to know tonight,' Rashidov shouted.
Raj whispered it back to Shazmina in English, to check his understanding. He was correct.
Raj's phone buzzed again. It was the text update from Igor he had been waiting for, to know that the car headlights signalled the arrival of friends.

2 minutes away

Raj immediately replied:

Rashidov outside. Armed? Here with info on Ulvi

***

'We've got a visitor,' announced Igor.
Yuri negotiated the grassy bank, exiting the single carriageway and took the off-road route up to the house.
Yuri and Vlod were in the front, with Nisba and Igor in the back.
The beam of the headlights illuminated a man who held his hands up, flinching and wincing against the brightness of the light.
'Shulkin's man,' cried Nisba.
'I'll go talk to him.' Igor turned to let himself out.
'Shit, Igor!'
'I cover him,' replied Yuri smiling, pulling out a Makarov pistol.
'Blinking 'eck. I hate guns,' muttered Nisba, sinking low into her seat.
Igor slammed the truck door shut.

She could hear muted voices outside the vehicle.

Igor approached Rashidov, patted him down and turned him around to face the house.

Whilst Rashidov was a big man, Igor was still an inch or so taller and broader.

Rashidov placed his hands on his head, interlacing his fingers and began to walk towards the front door. Igor held him at arm's length, to the side of him, so Yuri could have him clearly in his sights.

Igor held his phone to his left ear, to instruct Raj.

'We're coming in – Rashidov first.'

***

Rashidov opened the door by kicking it, so that it swung fully open.

Raj watched him slowly enter and take in his new surroundings.

The A-Team had a rule of not revealing the use of weaponry of any kind, even as intimidation. They would not visibly stoop to anything that could be construed as criminal behaviour, unless there was an immediate and direct threat to life.

Igor pulled out a kitchen chair with one hand into the middle of the room, well away from the table. It grated across the stone floor.

'Take a seat,' instructed Igor.

Shazmina had taken the decision to come out from her shelter, taking up a position between Raj and Nisba.

Rashidov looked at each of the group members that began forming a semi-circle around him. He appeared vulnerable and uneasy.

Sitting forward, he rested his elbows on his knees, hands clasped and looked at the floor.

He began to speak in Russian.

'I came, because your lives are in danger – all of them.' He waved his hand at the group in front of him.

The group members exchanged glances.

'Lev will be gone by,' he shrugged, '…probably in the next few days.'

'So, you no longer have a Master – is that it?' asked Igor. Rustam winced.

'Did you get all of that?' whispered Shazmina, glancing at Nisba and Raj.

Nisba nodded still looking ahead, concentrating. Raj shook his head, leaning in closer to Shazmina. His Russian, he decided, was not very good at all today, so would have to rely heavily on his beautiful interpreter.

Shazmina whispered to him, their heads close together. So close, that Nisba had to suppress a smile. They both held their gaze firmly downwards but were within kissing distance. If they looked up, Nisba was sure they would not be able to restrain themselves.

Rashidov chose to ignore Igor's question and resumed.

'Nothing is to happen to you – or Nisba. None of the intimidation you described was me or on the instructions of Lev.' He shook his head and shrugged. 'I never followed you or abused you in any way. Ever.'

Nisba and Raj looked to Igor, who appeared rigid, his face pale with shock.

Igor felt the urge to throw up, having to talk himself out of it. It wasn't a reaction he was accustomed to.

Rashidov began to speak again.

'Lev asked me to follow up on some leads…he knows a lot of people, who know people – not all good. So, Ben and I have been investigating.' He looked anxiously back at Igor and continued.

'Ulvi Rakhmanov is a Portuguese fraudster and…'

Igor held his hand up to interrupt.

'Just one second.' Igor sounded unusually stern; the stress and shock were beginning to take over. 'You are telling me; he is not Uzbek?'

'That's correct. He has no brothers or nephews – he's not even a Muslim.'

Igor drew in a sharp breath.

Nisba felt the urge to sit down. Sea sickness was swaying in on her, so she decided to take a seat.

Shazmina slipped her hands onto Nisba's shoulders.

'Are you alright? You look faint.'

Nisba laid her hand on Shazmina's. 'It'll pass, thank you.'

Nisba's move to sit down, prompted the others to follow suit.

Igor beckoned Rashidov to pull up to the table.

Igor put his arms around Nisba's shoulders to give comfort and to take it. They moved to be closer, propping each other up.

Nisba recovered and looked at the ceiling to think.

'Let me guess,' she said, 'he doesn't work in pharma sales?...he doesn't work at all, does he? Never has?'

Igor's body jolted.

'No,' Rashidov answered. 'He doesn't, and no he hasn't.'

'Holy Shit,' said Nisba, in English.

Igor had removed his arm to nurse his head. The facts were slowly landing for him.

His friend, his sister's husband, father to his niece and nephew, the man with whom he had shared his most intimate thoughts and reached out to for support, was the very force that had been pushing him to the edge, reducing him to mental destruction. It had been him – all along. Yet, his guilt and distorted thinking had led him to lay it all at Shulkin's door.

Before he'd met Nisba, it had got so bad, he'd considered ending it, shooting himself in the head or slitting his wrists in the bath.

Apart from the purchase of that house, which was made with Mila's inheritance, Ulvi had been funding his dual lifestyles for years by stealing the profits of their winery.

Igor found the treachery dumbfounding. He began to tremble, finding the room suddenly very noisy. A hissing sound began to develop in his ears.

Yuri pushed forward a large touchscreen tablet, propped up on its case, toward Rashidov.

Yuri opened the photos for him with one finger, swiping them, from over the top edge of the tablet.

The first photo showed Ulvi with his bag, welcomed with a kiss at the door of a very nice apartment by a woman similar in age to Mila, but with blond highlighted hair, bright nails and a low-cut top. The exact opposite to Mila.

Nisba gave a slight groan and then leaned forward suddenly. Something had caught her attention. She enlarged the image on the screen with her thumb and forefinger.

'Yes, that's her,' confirmed Rashidov. 'That's his wife.'

'Wife?' they all shouted.

Rashidov look startled by the outburst of outrage.

'She's a piece of work too,' he continued. He unconsciously licked his lips. He was suddenly feeling dehydrated and stressed.

Raj read the body language and got up, returning a couple of minutes later with a jug of water and some tumblers.

Raj poured him a glass and pushed it across to him and then served the others.

'Thank you,' Rashidov whispered in English, glancing briefly at Raj after taking a sip. He cleared his throat, before continuing in Russian.

'She is also Portuguese and has a company registered in…'

'Angola,' interrupted Nisba. 'I know her face.'

Nisba suddenly nursed her head in her hands.

'Oh God,' she whispered. 'It's a pharmaceutical company, isn't it?'

Rashidov was perplexed and blinked in surprise. Igor looked at her amazed.

Raj had to genuinely depend on Shazmina to get this last bit.

'And they're not just fraudsters, are they?' Nisba asked.

Rashidov shook his head. She rested her head on her arms on the table. Her sun-lightened caramel and copper curls flopped over, revealing the dark chestnut tighter curls underneath.

'They never caught them – those scammers in Angola that I told you about,' continued Nisba, lifting her head and turning to Igor. 'The fake birth control-pill manufacturer and the abortionist...that's them.' She drew in a shaky breath. 'Which leads me to believe that Joao Domingos, you know, the young lad that was killed, was probably…murdered.'

'Fuck!' Igor threw his hands up. 'What about Mila and the children?'

'They're safe, as long as they know nothing,' Rashidov answered, trying to sound reassuring. 'I'm sorry, but I don't think he will give them any consideration.'

Igor clutched his head. It was starting to hurt. His sister wasn't married at all, she was effectively, Ulvi's mistress and he, Igor, had unwittingly subsidised this bigamous set-up.

All those times, Ulvi was away on business, he was really only a mile away with the other woman or travelling to far-flung places, taking luxury holidays, whilst Mila – never going anywhere, was left behind, carrying all the responsibility of family life.

Nisba started to feel very sick. 'Excuse me,' she said, running for the bathroom.

Raj caught Shazmina's eye. She looked away quickly.

'I'm not completely stupid, you know!' he whispered.

She didn't reply.

***

Nisba reappeared, looking washed out and tired. Igor pulled her in for a cuddle and buried his face in her hair.

She was too tired to speak any more Russian.

And then she suddenly sat up.

'It was meant to happen, today!'

There was a hush around the room.

'But the plan had to change. That's why he's taking the flight tomorrow instead of today.'

She looked around at the others.

'We were literally in the lion's den today. Ulvi made sure we were both there, together. It wasn't some nice, kind, inclusive gesture…it was to guarantee I would be there.'

She turned to Igor and squeezed his hand, which now formed a fist on the table.

'Thanks to Yuri and Vlod, they couldn't pull it off. He had to abort the plan.'

Raj shook his head. 'You've lost me.'

'He wanted the rest of his money…he'd want the full amount, but we'd short-changed him. He'd need it to pay off his accomplices or… leg it, with the whole lot.'

'But Mila and the children… and all those people' Igor wasn't sure if he were making a statement or asking a question.

'He'd sent her off to the supermarket, remember? No doubt he'd have texted to add more items to her list, to keep her out of the way. I bet he's controlling…coercive. She'd do what he says. We'd have been separated off into one of those many rooms he's got in that mansion, with the help of his two 'Nephews' and no doubt there were a whole load of others on hand.' Nisba began to hurriedly comb out her hair with her fingers. 'They were all Ulvi's friends and none of Mila's, which was odd. It was not the family Do he told us it would be. And our means of getaway…well, we would have been locked in, like Yuri was worried about, behind that bloody electric gate. It was perfect.' She was now furiously pulling her fingers through the hair at the base of her head. 'He'll have called it off, as soon as he clocked Yuri. You noticed he tried to get him to come in?'

Shazmina's eyes were staring with horror, as she wrung her hands.

'He would threaten to kill you, to make Mister…Igor transfer money.' She could hardly believe what she was saying.

'That's right,' replied Nisba, patting her hair, realising how frizzy and enlarged it had become. 'It's a good job the plan was buggered, thanks to Yuri and Vlod, because…well, there isn't any money. Not yet anyway, until the next lot of invoices are paid. It's already gone to the people who've earned it.'

'Shit. That was close. Too fucking close,' said Raj, rubbing his face. 'Those two men were inches away.'

'But he will try again,' continued Shazmina. 'Tomorrow, at The Event, for sure.'

Nisba turned to Shazmina nodding.

'And then,' said Nisba, 'he'll leg it with his Portuguese tart to Vietnam. Mila will be left thinking he's gone away on business, as normal.'

Igor groaned. He felt weak with pity, anger, and disbelief for his sister. Not only this, but for the treachery, committed by his brother-in-law. Who wasn't – in fact.

'I told him everything,' gasped Igor, hanging his head in shame. 'Everything.'

He realised that he had unwittingly given Ulvi all the motives to attack Nisba and the reasons why she was important to eliminate. He'd described in detail what kind of a threat she posed. Not only that, he'd also stupidly given away that she was a worthy target. Someone else Ulvi could extort money from. This was big stuff to process.

'I must be fucking mad. I told you I was a nutjob,' he shouted; but the sound was muffled by resting his head in his arms, on the table.

'You are a good sane human being, Igor. It is perfectly normal to confide in your friends. You've done nothing wrong. It's Ulvi that's the nutjob here,' reassured Nisba, rubbing his back.

He would have to go and chop some logs soon, he thought. This was going to trigger a bad time, he could tell.

Rashidov did not understand the English words, but the emotions were clear.

'I should go. I am sorry,' he said and waved a hand toward the group. Igor and Raj, flanking him, walked him to the door and out into the night.

It was fresh and starry. The moon was just slightly more than half and very bright. The lights came on as they stepped over the threshold.

Rashidov turned to Igor.

'About your dog…sick bastards,' he said, shaking his head slightly. 'If you'd like another, I have a litter of four Doberman pups. You can take your pick.'

'Thank you for the offer,' smiled Igor. 'Fucked-up rescues are more my style,' he said. 'But maybe Yuri – he has a soft spot for Dobermans. I'll send him down to you, sometime soon.'

Rashidov smiled and nodded and then held out his hand.

Igor hesitated, but shook it, as did Raj.

They watched Rustam Rashidov walk away and then jog into the darkness, down the track.

They stood together, silent in the moonlight, still looking out into the dark, coming to terms with what they had heard.

Raj then turned to Igor, laying his hand gently on Igor's back. 'C'mon man...let's get you a drink.'

***

The mood had become sombre and quiet, following the debrief; a frenzy of outrage on the part of each A-Team member, except for Nisba and Vlod.

Nisba had pulled a pencil and notepad from her bag and was drawing William Morris style patterns at top speed, to decompress. Vlod had the pack of cards and was playing Patience, next to her. He wore Raj's headphones.

No-one felt like talking now. They sat for a long time in silence doing nothing, staring into space. Thinking.

That was when the plan began to unfold.

'We need to flush them out and ambush them,' announced Nisba, still intently focused on her drawing. She sat back to critically assess it and then put her nose back down, to refine some of the elements.

Igor nodded. 'I know the perfect place for an ambush'. He then translated for Yuri, whose face suddenly brightened. Yuri knew exactly what to do. He rubbed his hands.

Raj sat back, with his hands clasped on the top of his head, elbows out.

'...And get it all on camera,' he said, his eyes reflecting the assessments underway in his head.

He was sitting in Nisba's office chair, which he'd brought out, finding it very comfortable. He twizzled around on it and then slowly wheeled his way over to Shazmina, who was seated at the table. She held her head in her hands. Her eyes were closed.

'Alright?' he asked, placing his hand gently on her shoulder.

Shazmina looked up, pleased to see him, giving him a little smile. She had an idea.

'The Portuguese...' Shazmina came to a halt and turned to Nisba. 'What did you call her?'

'Tart,' replied Nisba, not looking up, still drawing.

'That's it. Portuguese Tart, could be leverage.'

They all nodded.

Nisba wondered if shaming another woman was bad of her. She concluded that it was not. Not this woman.

Yuri began to gather up items left on the table, beckoning everyone to gather round. Igor began a running commentary in English, translating from the Ukrainian.

Nisba had been surprised at how different Ukrainian was from Russian, the pronunciation and vocabulary. She could understand parts, but otherwise, it was difficult to follow.

She'd decided to learn Ukrainian as soon as possible. It would be important to speak it as a family.

The items on the dining table were being pushed around with a dinner fork by Yuri and occasionally by Vlod, who pointed with Nisba's pencil, making suggestions, indicating who should be where and at what moment. Timing, communication, and positioning would be of the essence.

The apple cake that Nisba had baked, now partially eaten, was the winery. This was situated at the very end of the table.

At the opposite end, tablemats formed the lake. The playing cards, now spread out in a large heap, represented the woods.

Nisba found herself to be the pepper pot and Igor, the salt. Yuri, Vlod and Raj were cigarette lighter, Igor's Ukrainian flag and the painted wooden lady, taken from his bookcase. All these would be out of sight, in amongst the playing cards – the woods.

Shazmina as the espresso cup and saucer, would be located over the other side, out of harm's way.

Raj picked up the cup.

'Do you really have to be there?' he asked, turning to Shazmina, his shoulders sagging, because he knew it would be taken as a rhetorical question.

They would be enlisting the help of Miguel – the shot glass. He would also enter through the woods.

Yuri then gestured a rewind, taking them all back to the beginning. Back to the cake – the winery. He'd taken the pencil from Vlod and like a conductor, relayed the end-to-end orchestration of the plan, with Igor continuing his translation, narrating the unfolding drama, in English.

At the finale, the room fell silent. It was touch and go. Nothing could be left to chance.

'Flippin' eck,' whispered Nisba, under her breath. She and Shazmina exchanged glances and squeezed each other's hands.

Igor invited Nisba to sit on his knee, cradling her in his big arms and rocking slightly.

Shazmina felt suddenly very lonely and afraid, with a strong need for comfort, for physical contact. If there weren't so many people around, she thought she might have ventured to reach out for it but tried desperately to keep her gaze downwards and not in Raj's direction.

Yuri caught her eye. He gave her a sympathetic smile, his eyes sliding to Raj and back again.

He then suddenly thumped the table to address the group.

'It will be fine...because…I am – alright shot!'

***

Nisba went outside for some fresh air, seating herself at the teak table she'd worked hard to clean up. She wore Igor's massive rubber clogs and put her feet up on the table.

Leaning back, she looked up at the sky. Despite the flood lighting, the black sky was so glittered with stars it was swirled with grey. Since coming to Uzbekistan, she understood why it was called the Milky Way, because it was – milky.

'You're worried about Igor,' said Raj, walking round to sit in the chair at her feet.

'Mmm.'

'What are you thinking?'

She looked out at the woods. Across the tall grass, she could see the mound that marked Misha's grave. The woods were dark. Uninviting. The entrance was like a black hole.

'I can feel he's becoming hyped. We mustn't forget, how traumatic and triggering this is for him. He's doing really well, but I worry he's going to fall apart tomorrow. It might be too much. He feels it's all his fault. If he gets overwhelmed, I don't know what will happen. He may just shut down or...I don't know. The other thing is...there is only tomorrow, The Event. This has to work. Straight after, I'll have to take the next available flight out of the country.'

Raj rubbed his beard.

They sat in silence for a while.

Then he observed her fists clench and her lips pucker.

'We'll get the fucking evil bastard, don't you worry. We're all here to help Igor. Always have been. He's come a long way. Before he met you, he was....' He trailed off. 'This is a set-back and a big deal for all of us. We'll get him back to the place he was,' Raj concluded, with large serious eyes, not entirely convinced by his own words.

He reached out, laying a hand on each of her fists. He squeezed them.

Nisba smiled. Most un-Raj-like, she thought. She looked up at him, seeing him properly, for the first time.

He had a beautiful face; and eyelashes most women would die for. She could appreciate why Shazmina was potty about him. His soul was good, she'd decided, and he was funny. She wasn't doing too badly for friends.

'Then he can just focus on what he's always wanted. You...and the baby.'

She lifted her eyes.

'C'mon Nisba. I wasn't born yesterday. Aside from the fact the two of you have been at it like rabbits...'

She couldn't help but break into a grin.

'Shall we go back in? I wouldn't want Shazmina to get jealous,' he said, with his crooked smile.

Day 30 Saturday

Igor hadn't slept. He had chopped logs for therapy and to wear himself out, but it hadn't worked, so he felt fatigued to the point that his hands were trembling. After lying awake for many hours, he got up at 5am. The Event didn't start until 10.30am, but he had many things on his mind.

He crept out past Raj and Shazmina, who lay in a cuddle, noses almost touching, fast asleep on the sofa. He could feel his strained face crease with a smile.

Such a bizarre combination. But then he was in no position to judge, he thought.

He knocked on the camper-van door. He could hear Vlod and Yuri talking inside.

According to Yuri, this was normal. Vlod could speak, but only in certain circumstances, usually one on one, when there were no trauma triggers.

Igor knew that despite his bond with Vlod, his presence would still probably switch off Vlod's ability to speak. Igor found it heart-breaking.

Yuri and Vlod were both dressed in military fatigues, ready to move. Their part in the plan was not required until the very end, but they were on hand, to undertake any role required.

There were a number of things that needed to be put in place first, by Miguel, who was already on site at the winery. He insisted on pulling the nightshift, to monitor any undesirable activity and to install more cameras.

Yuri had set up the tablet for a video call with him. They had two additional participants: Ben Shulkin and Rustam Rashidov.

There wasn't a great deal of room and the van had begun to steam up. It smelled of men. It was a faint tobacco aroma, mixed with a strong masculine deodorant, but it produced limbic emotions of fear and flight. This was not good for Igor.

He stood up suddenly, almost hitting his head on the ceiling. He then shook himself down to get rid of the creeping sense of doom and began to breathe, looking around him.

'I've got this,' said Vlod. 'Go.'

Igor was stunned. He didn't want to make a big deal out of hearing the voice he hadn't heard since being in Ukraine. At war. He wished to avoid knocking Vlod off course. This was huge progress, so he said nothing, turned to open the little door and left, jumping down from the step onto the gravel.

He stood there blinking in the sunrise. It was going to be a beautiful day, he thought, but the range of senses and emotions were the same algorithm as preparing for an assault. Battle.

Igor did not want to see anyone he cared about. He did not want to think about afterwards, because there may not be one.

He barely noticed Raj, who hurried past him, to join the video call. He certainly didn't hear what Raj was saying.

***

The event was held on the grounds of the winery.

It was a dry, fresh, and sunny day. There was no wind, so the large white billowy clouds maintained their shape in the deep blue sky.

The winery building was a purpose-built property, that had undergone several extensions to keep up with the ever-expanding nature of the business.

Igor thought it looked like a three-star Soviet-era hotel. It had a canopy at the front over the door, with the name of the company, in 1970s-style blue and white lettering. The doors and front windows were brown glass.

There were well-tended lawns down the left-hand side, leading to a wide-open field at the back, with trees and wire fencing forming the perimeter. Set back on the right, was Goods In. Today, this area had been cordoned off, with a member of staff standing nearby.

The main building was fronted by a large gravel car park, accommodating space for around four hundred vehicles, bicycles, and several shuttle buses.

The road outside was single carriageway, with parking allowed down one side, with passing spaces created by bollards.

The men on duty today were production, warehouse and vineyard staff and wore orange high visibility tabards. They were directing the traffic, aided by short-wave radios, to assist with the location of available parking spaces.

Families were beginning to stream in, having walked down from their vehicles, parked some distance away.

Irina the receptionist was considered to have gone above and beyond, organising an elaborate range of activities, food and drink stands. A roast lamb was turning on a spit at one of these, next to a face-painting tent. Fairground games, bouncy castle, bubbles and archery were also on the agenda. There would also be a magician, gazebos, music, as well as seating for the employees and their families. Irina had thought of everything.

She had mentioned to Shazmina, that she was expecting a recognition award for her troubles.

Igor found this to be the best part of running the winery; seeing the benefit it brought to so many people and the families it supported. He would usually turn up briefly, to do some polite mingling, make a speech and then leave at the earliest opportunity.

The sight of happy families, enjoying themselves, had always made him feel marginalised, lonely, and depressed.

This time, he felt afraid. Afraid for his friends, Mila, the children, and his own little family, that he and Nisba were creating. The rush of joy and excitement was soon overwhelmed by terror. There was so much to lose now.

He failed to understand why he and Mila could be betrayed in such a way. Periodically, he found himself shaking his head in disbelief.

Igor considered, if Ulvi had needed money, they could have talked about it, but this wasn't avarice, it was something even darker, committed against everyone around him. It left him feeling nauseated.

***

They each drove to the event separately. They had agreed, that if they were ambushed and picked off, it would only be one of them, so, of less value, and therefore less leverage. Igor, Raj and Nisba made use of the hired vehicles. These would be unfamiliar to those looking to follow, at least for the journey there.

Shazmina proceeded as normal in her Nexia. For continuity. Normality. She was a local, subordinate, a pawn and had to maintain that front. She understood that. It didn't mean she was comfortable with it.

Nisba parked on the road, having deliberately waited until there were plenty of people about. She had pulled her hood firmly over her head and attached herself to the back of a family group, walking along the verge, convinced that there was an aura around her, making her visible, detectable, as some sort of imposter. She pondered this, until she reached the safety of numbers, next to a magician dressed as a clown, where she texted her thumbs up signal to the A-Team Group Chat.

Raj and Igor, with spaces reserved, were able to park in the car park, at the front of the building. Shazmina created a parking space inside the gate of Goods In, since this was not in use. She was given the OK by the man in an orange tabard, owing to her Organiser status.

She remained in her car, messing about with her phone, until Raj and Igor were parked up and had merged into the crowd. It was best to avoid an encounter with them she thought, rather than pretend not to know them very well.

She had to blink away the image of Raj looking into her eyes, telling her how 'fu-fabulous, brave and – hot she was,' casting out the memory of those kisses.

They had been rather mind-blowing.

Shazmina was pleased with her forthrightness, if not a little shocked.

They had fallen asleep sitting up on the sofa, watching a film, waking up together in a heap. Raj had apologised for invading her personal space without permission and made a move to sleep on the floor.

She hadn't wanted him to and invited him back up. She understood his position. He would be very careful, ensuring she was always in control.

Shazmina chuckled, recalling Raj's crooked smile, expressing concern for the safety of his virtue, and whether or not she would keep her hands to herself.

She'd lain behind him cuddling in, her arm round his waist. He'd placed his hand on top of hers to keep it there. And that's when she asked him. If he'd like one. A kiss.

'Hmm, let me think about that for a moment.'

He'd immediately turned to face her, the sofa leather creaking and unyielding.

'I've thought about it,' he'd confirmed, reaching to stroke her face.

Shazmina got out of her car smiling to herself. It didn't last long, as she walked across the carpark taking up her position at the back corner of the main office building. From there, she had a 180-degree view of the event. She texted her thumbs up.

***

Nisba and Igor were to remain as far apart as possible but very much in view of witnesses, in amongst a crowd, close to the third-party vendors and services.

Both Raj and Miguel were required to be visible and socially attentive, making their way around their colleagues. At the same time, they needed to be vigilant, on the lookout for the 'Nephews,' trying to identify which of the numerous men on radios in high-vis tabards were in on it. It was impossible to judge.

Every facial expression, gesture and interaction was scrutinised.

There were no nods, meaningful looks or suspicious behaviour.

Everyone was chatty, happy, appearing to have genuine fun with their friends and families. No-one seemed at all interested in them, Igor, or Nisba. They couldn't detect anything untoward. It was disconcerting. Perhaps nothing was going to happen? Maybe they'd got it all wrong?

Ben Shulkin was parked, holed up in the back of a small commercial van on the road outside, close to the winery entrance.

Although it was the Sabbath and he was a Conservative Jew, Ben had made himself available. His observance could be suspended legitimately, as this was about life. Saving it.

He was feeling the pressure of being the A-Team's eyes. His thick curly hair was sticking to his forehead, his hands trembling, his eyes darting around the twenty-four windows of camera angle, on the three laptop screens in front of him, propped up on crates.

There just wasn't enough of him to go round. The adrenaline was pumping so hard it made his chest wall hurt and he could feel it pulsating in his eye sockets.

They were completely at the mercy of the local area's hit-and-miss internet connection. He was too far away to benefit from the boosters within the winery building.

They had no short-wave radio capability, so Ben's only means of communication to the group, was via a text or a call to the A-Team Group.

The camera coverage inside the winery building was now excellent, but once inside, separated and out of view from the team outside, the risk of ambush, abduction or worse, was too high. The aim was to draw the Nephews, perpetrators or whomever they were and the action, away from the site. Being lured indoors was to be avoided, at all costs.

***

At around midday, the public address system made an unpleasant whistle of feedback.

Igor tapped the microphone.

He encouraged everyone to gather round, as he wished to say a few words and then he promised to let people get back to having fun.

It was difficult, but despite his inner turmoil and suffering, Igor picked his words carefully.

He was flanked by his Senior Management Team; Zeinab in her wheelchair with her husband and personal security detail, on the other side were Raj and Miguel. There was still no sign of Dav Uzmanov the Finance Director.

'Thank you all for coming out today. It is great to see everyone with their families here at Chateau Prikat and so many children. Perhaps we are seeing the next generation of Prikat winery colleagues.' There was a murmur of laughter.

He looked about him, but not for too long, as he feared coming out of himself. It had happened before when he was in a large noisy crowd. An out-of-body experience.

'Our management team and I...' He looked to each side of him. 'We wish to thank all of those who have shown ongoing dedication, commitment and continued hard work, which guarantees the success of our company...' He paused. It was a long pause.

Raj stepped forward with a smile; to signal he could help him out.

There were many things Igor really wanted to say at this point. He had to crush the urge.

'...And to those who appreciate that we are on a journey, to improve both the employee and customer experience. Thank you for your patience and faith in us, to safeguard your livelihoods. We will continue to strive to do so...no matter what hap...'

Raj took the microphone, grinning at the crowd and patted Igor on the back.

'That's right. Zeinab, Miguel, Igor and...' Raj found it impossible to include Dav Uzmanov. '...and I, will make sure that there will be plenty more opportunities to throw wet sponges at the team leaders and for Dad to show off his archery skills.' The crowd laughed and clapped.

'...Once again, on behalf of Igor, Zeinab, Miguel and the wider management team...thank you and also thank you for the show of appreciation. It means a lot.' Raj forced a grin. He'd had enough now.

***

Raj suddenly felt thirsty. He looked about him for a drink and on the way to a stall, scanned his phone for messages, despite having earbuds which would tell him if he had any or not. He knew there wouldn't be any. Yet.

Igor checked his phone. No notifications.

Nisba peeked at her phone. No updates.

Shazmina held her phone in her hand at the ready; still nothing and nothing to report.

Miguel would have to get going soon but hadn't heard from Ben. He couldn't afford to wait.

MDS: *@Ben - Status?*
BEN: *@MDS - Proceed. On plan*

This first notification put everyone on high alert.

***

Nisba purchased a bottle of water and sipped it slowly, just to keep her mouth from being so dry, from the adrenaline. She was careful not to swig it, despite being very thirsty, to avoid needing the bathroom, having to go indoors, which was strictly off limits. She was needing it more often these days.

The weather was warming up and it was very bright. She wished she had her sunglasses, recalling they would be in an unclaimed baggage area, somewhere at Manchester Airport.

Nisba had a wireless earbud in her left ear, so could be discreetly hands free for calls. This was the first time she'd used them. She didn't like them. It was annoying, speaking to someone to find that they were plugged in and listening to something else. The right-hand earbud, she'd lent to Shazmina. Ben had borrowed her headphones, the ones with the knotted wires. More recently, they had developed a loose connection to the left ear.

Igor, Raj and Miguel liked gadgets so they had all the stuff. Nisba didn't really see the point in it; watches that told you your heart rate and when to stand up, but the wireless technology today was having its uses, and its capabilities were being put to the test.

Nisba kept an eye on the faces around her, the phone, and the magician. The sleight of hand was breathtakingly good, she thought.

The magician had a fifteen minute routine, which was repeated several times. Nisba studied them carefully. She couldn't be sure if it were a man or a woman. They were dressed in a black baggy suit with broad padded shoulders and a black bowler hat, over a red curly wig. The face was completely white, with black and red clown features. They didn't speak throughout the routine which made them all the more enigmatic.

The trick underway, was where they pulled out an enormous pair of scissors, like sewing shears, from their oversized left jacket pocket. Using their right hand, they cut up a very brightly coloured traditional patterned scarf into tiny pieces into their hat, which was empty. They had shown it to the crowd beforehand to prove it.

They then pulled out of the other pocket, a wooden spoon and proceeded to stir up the pieces in the hat, like a cake mix. As they did it, the intact scarf began to reappear, billowing out of the hat, wound around the spoon.

The small crowd of children and parents eventually dispersed, after much clapping and adulation. The magician turned their back on any potential audience to take a drink from a can of cola and then made their way off towards the crowd.

Nisba tracked them with her eyes. There was something. Something about them was holding her attention.

She moved to get a better view and proceeded to watch them lift a man's wallet out of his back pocket. Swift and delicately done. The mark never felt a thing.

Outraged, Nisba strode up purposefully, heart pounding and tapped the magician on the shoulder.

They froze.

'Give it back,' Nisba seethed, in Russian.

They suddenly swung around. They were eye to eye. Nisba blinked. Her brain needed some time to take in the visual onslaught. The make-up. The perspiration and the eyes.

They didn't back off. Instead, they thrust out their chest and threw back their chin.

'Or what?' they snarled. It was shocking. The confrontation. And it was in English.

They began to force Nisba backward in the direction of the building. Nisba looked about, spotting the side entrance in her peripheral vision.

Her phone rang in her ear. She touched it, discreetly to take the call.

'Those two Nephews who came for you are at three o'clock and possibly with two more coming your way…fast!' instructed Shazmina, urgently.

Nisba turned to walk briskly away from her painted pursuer, as she responded.

'Shit...Magician is after me so...' They were breaking up.

'What?...don't g…you're surrounded,' pleaded Shazmina. 'Ben. Tell me what can you see please? And where are…others?...Nis…needs back-up!'

There was some frantic crackling and heavy breathing.

'Sorry, I'm here,' responded Ben, breathless. 'I've texted the others to let them know, but they haven't picked up. Raj missed his check-in and Igor is with Zeinab, stuck with some people. And I've only got one ear that works. The right hand side of the headphones has stopped working!'

'I'm going to have to help her.'

'No,' shouted Ben. 'I can see her…she's OK for the moment. But I now have a visual on Raj. Miguel messaged me earlier…he spoke to someone who had a lead.'

Ben could hear the panic in Shazmina's silence. She understood a direct message meant this was something that would upset her, and the others.

'He's inside? So… he can help her?'

'Er no. He's a bit tied up at the moment.'

***

Earlier

Raj approached the drinks stand not too far from Nisba, but she hadn't seen him.

The wife of one of the warehouse operatives was serving. The warehouseman was close by and gave Raj a nod.

Raj then heard someone shout his name. He turned to look but couldn't see anyone that appeared to want to speak to him. He heard it a second time and looked again. Still nothing.

He then cast his eyes back to the lady behind the stall and was just about to pay her when a clown barged into him, seemingly in a hurry, on the way back to their set. He followed them with his eyes. Surreal. He could see that Nisba appeared to be very interested in the clown.

Raj thanked the lady and began swigging his carboard cup of fruit cocktail drink.

The day was heating up. He felt dehydrated, owing to the lack of food in his stomach, having lost his appetite. He knocked it back and instantly regretted it.

Feeling woozy, he patted his inside jacket pocket for his phone, which was no longer there.

***

Miguel felt he had done sufficient mingling and was making his way to his car now that he had confirmation everything was going according to plan.

He caught sight of a little boy running in the direction of the car park. About five or six years old.

'Excuse me, young man,' he shouted in Russian. He couldn't see any parents about.

Miguel caught up with him. 'Hey! Little man… where are you going? It's not safe. Where's your mum or dad?'

The little boy pointed in the direction of the event.

'Mummy's over there.'

'Let's go back and find her, shall we?' suggested Miguel, taking a quick look at his watch.

'I want to go home!' the little boy said suddenly, in English, pushing his bottom lip out.

'So do I,' smiled Miguel.

The little boy grinned. 'What's your name?'

'I'm Miguel,' he said, presenting a high five. 'Up high!' The little boy reached up. 'Down low!...oh…too slow!'

The boy gave a belly laugh.

Miguel then spotted a striking looking woman, breaking through the crowd, with a little girl close behind, sporting a severe haircut.

'Aziz. Aziz. Ah, there you are.' She smiled at Miguel. 'Thank you. I'm sorry about that.'

She had beautiful hazel eyes, he thought. She was very elegant. Classy.

'Mummy, this is Miguel,' announced Aziz, looking pleased with himself, having acquired a grown-up friend.

'How do you do, Miguel,' she responded with a smile. Miguel liked her. There was no caution or wariness. He usually encountered that.

'And thank you once again, for looking out for him. He's had enough and wants to go home.' The woman laughed.

Miguel stood there looking at her. There was something deep and soulful about her. Something strong and yet familiar somehow. But she clearly belonged to somebody. That was always the way. Any woman of his own age was spoken for. His wife had died when she was only twenty-eight. They were the same age and had only been married four years when it happened. He was now thirty-seven.

There was an awkward pause for a moment.

The little girl held on to her mother's legs. Her face was serious. She had been trying to get her mother's attention for some minutes.

'Mummy,' she said quietly. 'Mummy,' she said again, a bit louder. 'Mummy!' she clamoured.

'What is it, Alina?'

Miguel wasn't sure whether to leave at this point. He glanced discreetly at his watch again and at his car parked a few yards away. He really needed to go.

'There are bad people here.'

Miguel's mouth fell open.

He watched her mother laugh with confusion.

'There aren't any bad people here!'

Miguel suddenly crouched down to the little girl, to Alina's level.

'Where are the bad people...can you see them?' he asked, looking into her eyes. They were just like her mother's.

'They hurt the brown man.' Alina turned around, pointing back toward the event.

'...And then they dragged him away.'

Not wishing to scare her, Miguel maintained his composure and slowly pulled out his phone.

'I have to go...excuse me.' He looked at the woman and then turned back again to Alina, giving her a thumbs up.

'Don't worry. I'll take care of it and make sure he's OK,' he said smiling and waving.

The smile fell off his face as soon as he turned to hurry to his car. He texted Ben, sending it to his personal number. He couldn't risk Shazmina getting upset, or Igor. Igor would see red, he thought, and Nisba, for that matter. Although Raj and she made out they didn't care for each other, he knew they did.

Mila's eyes followed Miguel back to his car.

She could tell this man had enjoyed their interaction. She was flattered. It made her feel good, so it made her feel sad.

***

The only option for Nisba now, was to make a run for it, toward the gap in between the Nephews. There were four of them now. She made a rapid calculation. There was no way she could get past them. They were too close together and there was no way round them. Her only exit and chance of eluding them, was to go into the building.

'Shit, shit, shit,' she muttered.

'What is happening, Nisba?' asked Shazmina.

'I have to go in.'

There was a faint wail sound. Then it went quiet for a second.

'…. and Nisba.'

'Yes?' Nisba pulled hard at the side entrance door. It was heavy and once through it she didn't know her way around.

'They've got Raj.'

Breathless from the sudden surge of adrenaline, Nisba ran across the reception area to find a corridor, somewhere, anywhere to get to where there would be cover.

'Did you hear me, Nisba?'

'I heard you. I just need to shake off this magician. I'll be in touch as soon as I can to help…but I really have to go now and be silent.' Nisba hung up and ran.

The Nephews would also have the advantage, she thought. They would know the place inside out.

She took the first door off reception that led to a corridor, hurting her shoulder getting through it. The door was much heavier than expected. Most of the doors along it were locked. Nisba was hoping for a warehouse, an area that was large, with multiple choices of places to hide, to buy some time, before trying to locate an exit, ideally toward the back of the building. She couldn't afford to get stuck in an office, or bathroom.

Nisba was aware of her poor sense of direction and lack of spatial awareness. She had no ability to assess where she was indoors, in relation to what she had seen outside.

These aspects of her brain function were not helpful right now. Her failure could cause someone to get hurt or…she immediately shut down that train of thought.

Nisba spotted some blue, heavy looking double doors in front of her. A warehouse. She ran as fast as she could towards them, the soles of her trainers making high pitched squeaks, every now and again, on the polished plastic tiled floor.

As soon as she ran in, Nisba was blindsided by a force that threw her sideways. It was so unexpected, shocking and violent, she thought she'd black out.

Watching the concrete floor coming up toward her, she instinctively thought she must not fall flat, like when she learned to ice skate; turning sideways so her hip and elbow hit the floor first. Nisba felt a weight on her back. Heavy. Unyielding. The person's knees were now on either side of her ribcage. Their hands gripped the back of her neck.

They released one hand, tightening their grip with their knees.

A hand grasped a handful of her hair, pulling her head back.

Nisba could feel and hear – scissors. Not snipping, but cutting; hacking cuts, along thick swathes of hair. She watched, as handfuls of curls fell in front of her eyes onto the blue painted concrete floor.

This was no Nephew, thought Nisba. This had to be a woman.

Having limited movement in her arms, Nisba had to launch herself off her elbow, to turn and shift the weight, timing it to when the magician had no real purchase on her – at that particular moment when they were about to make their next cut.

Nisba heaved as hard as she could, knocking them off balance.

The magician was now half underneath her. Reaching down, Nisba pinched the skin of their inner thigh as hard as she could.

They squealed with pain, loosening their grip for a second, but they were strong, fit and determined.

She was now face to face with her assailant, who sat astride her.

The wig and hat had fallen off.

Nisba could see clearly, the grey eyes and blond hair line, sweating underneath the thick greasepaint.

'Irina! Why? Why are you doing this?'

Irina ignored her and placed her left hand around Nisba's throat. Irina no longer had the scissors in her right hand, instead, she held her phone.

Irina pressed down harder, causing Nisba to choke. Nisba wasn't sure how it had happened but found her nose was bleeding. She could taste it.

Irina held up the phone to Nisba's face, taking several photos.

Shit. She knew exactly what Irina would be doing with those. She would have to try something. Anything.

'What did Dav promise you...?

Irina blinked. With the lull in the drama and at such close quarters with her prey, Irina seemed to panic.

'You know he took someone else…to Vietnam.'

Irina's mouth dropped open.

'He used you. And Ulvi plans to be long gone with the money.'

Irina seemed to crumple and fall sideways. A pair of handcuffs clattered out of her jacket pocket onto the floor.

Nisba scrambled away on all fours and then hoisted herself up. Reeling and feeling lightheaded, she held her hands against her belly for reassurance.

Then she had to stop herself from throwing up; suppressing the retching, she breathed in and out through clenched teeth for a few seconds.

Nisba looked back at Irina whose face, although difficult to read, was distraught – tearful. The clown features were now blurring down her face.

'Oh my God,' Irina gasped in Russian, 'you're pregnant!' She clapped her hand over her mouth. Her eyes were wide with horror at what she may have done.

Nisba said nothing in response, as she held out a hand toward Irina, waiting, flicking her fingers impatiently.

'Give them to me.'

Nisba visualised the deft handiwork with which Igor's phone had been taken from him.

Irina pulled out the wallet and Raj's phone. Nisba took them, turned and walked away.

She could hear Irina begin to sob, still in a heap on the floor behind her.

Nisba now understood the real reason why Irina was pink and flustered, that day she had come on site for the tour, after the two Nephews had visited the house. Nisba was not meant to have shown up. Her appearance was a shock, the indication of a plan gone badly wrong.

***

Ben was clutching his head, his kippah in danger of becoming unpinned.

They had all been instructed not to enter the building, under any circumstances.

They had all entered the building.

Ben had tracked Igor from the event ground. He watched Igor check his phone in response to a text he had received. It was not from the A-Team. Ben saw him run full tilt toward the building, leaving Zeinab and the others exchanging glances.

'No...Igor, no,' shouted Ben, in vain. Igor did not take his call.

Igor ran straight into a trap, set upon by four Nephews as soon as he entered the reception area. There was no one now, who could help him.

Ben felt sick. He pinned his kippah back on and wiped the sweat from his top lip. He had just seen Nisba wrestling with a clown, who turned out to be a young woman.

She'd cut Nisba's hair. Her beautiful hair! Ben shook his head. What a complete head screw this was all proving to be.

And Raj...

Ben dropped his head into his hands. The plan was all going to shit, he thought, but he couldn't leave his post, his legs wouldn't carry him. His MS was particularly bad today and he, more than ever, needed to be their eyes.

***

'What can you see now Ben?' whispered Shazmina. They spoke in Russian.

'There's still no sign of Ulvi, which is the only thing going to plan, so far,' he said, rubbing his top lip again. 'Nisba was in a spot of bother but it looks like she's taken care of it...but they've got Igor – in his office. There are two of them with him.' Ben tried to swallow so he could continue speaking. His mouth was too dry, so he took a quick gulp from his water bottle.

'Raj has been captured and is in some sort of warehouse office. He's unable to move… cable ties by the look of it and…' Ben looked closely at the screen, zooming in on the image. Bastards. He decided not to tell her. 'He's umm, alone.'

He heard deep gasping breaths from Shazmina's side.

'What can you see around him exactly? Are there any doors, windows…signs? Anything!'

'They went through the warehouse into a very small office, which has a window. It's reinforced with metal bars on the outside. Wait…wait…there's a fire door or something. I can just see part of the frame...it's…'

'I know where he is.'

'Great,' replied Ben, but she'd already hung up.

***

Shazmina walked calmly but purposefully through the dwindling crowd, smiling and nodding at people as she walked past them.

Once around the corner of the building, she ran. The door she was seeking was behind the next return.

Shazmina jettisoned her Organiser vest and assessed the scene in front of her.

Putting her phone to the ear without the bud, she began to chat inanely in Russian to an imaginary, gossipy female friend.

Her hair was slipping out of its neat, smooth chignon. She checked herself out. She wore red wide leg trousers and a long-sleeved, white square neck T-shirt. Shazmina was unsure whether this was going to cut it, but then remembered one of the things Nisba had said. It's not all about what you look like – it's about your attitude. Mind-set. It affects your appearance and how people perceive you.

Spying the back of the man with the hi-vis jacket guarding the door, Shazmina made sure she was loud enough to catch his attention. She held her breath.

Allah, forgive me.

He turned round on hearing her approach.

Shazmina didn't know the face and she could tell he didn't recognise her.

Giving him the most captivating smile she could, she gave him a child-like wave, brandishing her phone.

'Can't get a signal anywhere...'

He grinned at her, unconsciously looking her up and down.

'Can I get to the toilets through here?' she asked, walking up to him.

He shook his head but was still smiling, looking down at her. He was at least a foot taller than she was. Most people were.

Her chest tightened, wondering what she would have to do to get inside.

Shazmina ventured up a little closer.

'Aw, please.' She tilted her head to one side, smiling. 'I'm desperate!'

He laughed and shook his head once more.

Tutting, she looked towards the trees and groaned.

'If you don't let me through, I'll have to go in the bushes!'

Shazmina knew what was behind them, but he wouldn't. He wasn't a regular employee; she was sure of it.

If he didn't follow, then she really was in the brown stuff and would have to take an even bigger risk, she calculated.

Walking briskly away, her shoes scrunching on the gravel, she tucked herself behind a large mature tree trunk. There were piles of broken pallets, offering a good choice of weapon. After selecting a suitable plank, she held it up at the ready, like a baseball bat.

She waited.

He suddenly appeared, stepping into the leaf mouldy gloom and looked around, furtively. Shazmina swung the plank at the back of his head.

Pitching forward, he face planted into the pine needles and pile of rotting grass clippings.

He began to push himself back up on his elbows, shaking his head, groaning.

Swiping him again, he crumpled into the earth.

Shazmina had a moment of panic, thinking she'd killed him. Bending down, she pulled the pass from his neck; the lanyard unsnapped and she then laid two fingers on the pulse in his neck.

He was fine, she assessed, but hard to say how much time she had.

Shazmina grabbed his baseball cap and slapped it on her head, then dragged off his hi-vis jacket and threw it on. It was huge and was weighed down on one side by something very heavy in one of the side pockets.

She reached in and could feel the handle – it was a gun. Wincing, she withdrew her hand. Not having ever seen one in real life before, it was shocking to her – repulsive. In the other pocket was a box cutter.

Stepping back, she regarded the man lying prostrate on the ground.

'I told you I was desperate.'

Shazmina then had a fleeting thought. Looking back at the door, at the gravel, she cast her eyes back to the man. She'd risk it.

Bending down tentatively, Shazmina pulled off his trainers and threw them randomly somewhere over the fence, followed by the socks. Sweaty socks: they therefore took much longer to remove than anticipated.

Her phone buzzed in her ear bud as she ran toward the door.

'Hey Nisba,' she gasped, swiping the pass and shoulder-barging the door open; gripping the gun in case she would need to brandish it on the other side.

'Are you hurt?'

'Not seriously,' Nisba replied. 'I'm in the corridor approaching Igor's office I think…'

Shazmina could hear the quake in Nisba's voice.

'Wait for back-up please, Nisba. Igor is in there with two Nephews, with guns. Please wait. I get Raj and then we get Igor, together…OK?'

'Do you even know where Raj is?' Nisba tried hard to hide her panic and impatience.

'In warehouse…I go there now.'

'I was just in there! I should come and help you.'

'It's too far to run…please hide, Nisba, and wait for us.'

There was a crackle on the line.

The line went dead.

It reconnected.

'…be bloody careful, Shazmina.'

Shazmina heard the *boom* of the metal external door slamming shut. Barefoot Man was closing in but hopefully, slower than normal.

Now at the warehouse double doors, she spied the office, through the small window.

Before going in, she looked about her, judging she had about eight seconds to act.

To her right were two trollies full of brown plastic trays of half-used water jugs and cups. All glass.

She grabbed two jugs and hurled them down the corridor behind her – exploding, smashing, crashing, and sloshing down the grey tiles. In case he was a talented long jumper, she swept off the trays of glasses, for good measure.

It was thrilling, satisfying, so deliciously rebellious.

She thought her brain must be playing tricks on her. There were handfuls of curly hair on the ground, as she pushed her way through the doors.

There was no one around, which was a relief but suspicious, in her opinion. Hyper vigilant, she looked about her, as she reached the office, running at the door, hoping it wasn't locked.

It was locked.

'Shit!' She was shocked at herself for swearing, and out loud.

'Raj...can you hear me?' she shouted, banging on the door.

'Shazmina...yes,' he shouted back. 'Fucking hell!'

She looked around in need of a fire axe.

'There's an axe on the wall by the…'

'Got it,' she shouted, smashing the glass to get it, with the butt of the revolver.

And then the penny dropped, regarding the hair. Goose bumps prickled up her arms.

Casting the thought aside, she wielded the axe. It was not designed with a five-foot dainty female in mind.

'Typical,' she muttered under her breath, missing the lock altogether.

'Which is quicker to break on this kind of door…lock or hinges, Raj?'

He paused. She was just awesome.

'Go for the lock.'

Shazmina could hear shouts coming from behind her back, in the corridor. Maybe Barefoot Man had reinforcements.

Terrified of running out of time, she furiously attacked the door lock.

Her mind was alight with potential scenarios. The Nephews may get hold of Nisba or tire of waiting for their money and hurt Igor, or worse – kill him. It was just all too terrible to contemplate.

Her hands were trembling, so had no precision with the axe. Being so heavy, it was hard to control.

There were several accurate thwacks but these were followed by the difficulty with pulling it back out once it had hit home. Desperation welled up in her throat. She fought the urge to drop to her knees and cry – I can't do it! I'm just not strong enough!

But this was life and death. She could do it – she had to do it.

'God is great. God is great,' she whispered to herself, over and over.

With renewed energy and verve, Shazmina made four more frenzied chops and then as soon as there was a gap, wrenched it like a crowbar, splintering the wood, and then ran at it with her whole body, falling into the room, flat on her face.

Shazmina looked up to find Raj looking down at her.

She gasped.

They'd cut him. Blood trickled down his right cheek.

'Hello,' he said, 'Fancy seeing you here.'

She scrambled up to assess his situation. A cord was tied round his neck with a slip knot. This had been tied off to the light fitting above him. Any attempt at moving in any direction, he would be garrotted.

His hands were tied behind his back attached to the back of the chair and each ankle was cable tied to a chair leg.

She cut the cord and then knelt down to free his hands.

'Thanks…so, Shazmina,' he said, stretching his neck, '…what are you doing tonight?'

She began to laugh breathlessly. Her hands were still shaking, making it difficult to attempt the necessary cuts.

'Stop it Raj… stop making me laugh. I'm...I'm hurting you. I...I can't get the blade through.'

'Just do it. If you cut me…' He trailed off. 'We just have to get out of here and get to Igor.'

He was free.

'Nisba's not with you?' Raj looked about him, rubbing his wrists.

'No…she umm. She is not far from Igor. I told her to hide until we get there to make plan.'

Shazmina handed him the revolver.

His mouth dropped open and then his eyes took in the baseball cap and jacket.

'No time to explain.' Shazmina grabbed a handful of cable ties from a bag on the desk.

'Fuck me. You are …'

'Come, Raj. Hurry…we need to move.'

They both headed back towards the pile of hair and the double doors.

They exchanged glances. Raj then pushed open the door and ran out into the corridor.

'What the fuck..,' he whispered, scrunching over the glass, picking his way, trying not to slip on the spilt water, reaching out for Shazmina.

'Ah yes, that was me,' she said, with pride, taking his hand.

A few meters along, they observed drops of blood and a partial smeary footprint leaving the scene.

Raj looked at her, incredulous.

'What?' she shrugged. 'You never seen *[4]Die Hard*?

***

They had no plan until they found Nisba.

She had hidden behind the end of a sofa in one of the breakout areas. As Nisba emerged from her hiding place on hands and knees, Shazmina clasped her hand to her mouth supressing shock.

Raj said nothing. He found that no words came out. His hunter, male, primeval instinct, stoked in his guts.

He understood it now. He could be a killer, should the moment require it. He was shocked.

'Ben tells me there are two of them,' whispered Nisba. 'One behind him and one in front. He can see them. They both have semi-automatic pistols…9 mm he thinks. So, they can hold up between thirteen and seventeen rounds…' she trailed off rubbing her chest trying to cast aside the fact that they could be using extended magazines. That could mean over twenty rounds.

Shazmina shook her head, bewildered. How did Nisba know all this stuff? And why didn't it seem to surprise Raj, that she did. Nisba's quiet, cool, serious demeanour scared her. It was like she'd been taken over by someone else.

'It's hard to guess how handy they are with the guns,' Nisba continued, 'but we can't underestimate them.' She scrambled slowly up off the floor, unsteady for a moment, and then walked away.

Before Shazmina had the chance to ask her where she was going, Nisba had pulled a fire extinguisher from the wall.

Nisba put her hand to her ear. Fortunately, she had been able to retrieve her ear bud when it fell out during her tussle with the magician. She still had Ben on the line and was able to relay what he could see.

'The office door isn't locked,' said Nisba using the back of her hand to assess her nosebleed. It had abated now, but she could feel it crusting up on her top lip and around her right nostril.

She waved, gesturing down the corridor. 'There are two more down there.'

Raj returned seconds later carrying a fire extinguisher in each hand. They were heavy but not for him. He passed the 2kg CO_2 to Shazmina, retaining the 9kg of Powder.

'You have a plan?' asked Raj, turning to Nisba.

'It's an option…I was kind of hoping there was a better one.'

Nisba had been unable to look either of them in the eye since they'd found her, trying hard to crush the fear for Igor's life and not lose her grip altogether. Nisba was also frightened that before the end of the day, she might have killed someone, or that she and her friends be riddled with bullets. The annoying thing was, she was suddenly plagued by memories of being in a school pantomime which was very loosely based on the film [5]*The Wizard of Oz*. She had played Dorothy and her lines were in rhyming couplets. With hindsight, Nisba felt she'd delivered these lines too quickly, slowing it down would have been better. She'd also had to put on a very bad US southern accent for the part. These thoughts felt wholly inappropriate, but this was not unusual. It didn't mean she couldn't focus on the task at hand, it just meant she would be shielded emotionally from it, temporarily.

'The office door opens inwards,' Nisba continued. 'So, one of us could knock to get their attention, hide from view and then hopefully lure one Nephew out.'

'They might be careful and just stick head out,' offered Shazmina.

'So…' Nisba shrugged her shoulders. 'We bonk him on the head.'

'Right,' nodded Raj looking at Shazmina, the corners of his mouth turning up into a smile. He had no better ideas.

Nisba shrugged her shoulders again. Her head drooped.

'OK,' said Raj, holding his hands up. 'Let's assume that we somehow pick one of them off, that still leaves us with one shooter, who can fire at us point blank, or at Igor, in the panic.'

He began to sweat, causing the cut on his cheek to sting. Raj sighed. 'Fuck. I have no experience of firing guns.' He turned to Nisba.

She looked at her trembling hands.

'I think you have to be the one to lead on this, Raj.'
Shazmina's eyes bulged.

Raj nodded. He knew what Nisba meant. This was his chance, to reciprocate. Step up.

'Just aim high Raj,' Nisba offered. 'But hopefully, you won't need to fire any shots at all …'

'Just so we're clear, the plan is that we pile in there and you and Shazmina, what – extinguish the guy?'

'Yes,' answered Nisba, 'with water …and umm…CO_2.' She began to sound less and less convinced by their plan.

Raj shook his head slowly. 'I think we go in; all extinguishers blazing and forget the gun – it's too dangerous. We have to overwhelm him with everything else we've got.'

They agreed, feeling slightly less afraid.

Nisba touched her ear. 'Ben…can you reconnect the call please so Raj and Shazmina can pick up?' She turned to Raj, handing him his phone. There was no time for him to react or for her to explain.

'Yes,' replied Ben, 'but they probably have Igor's phone, so you'll have to remove him from the group first.'

Nisba had set up the group so was able to remove him. There was a risk that the Nephews might see this notification and other communications, if they were able to unlock the phone. All they had to do was hold it up to Igor's face.

'OK everyone,' shouted Ben. 'Nephew One is on the phone and making for the door to leave. Get ready! He's out and coming your way *now* down the corridor. He'll be with you in…five seconds. Let him pass and jump him. Three, two, one – go!'

Raj swung the 9kg fire extinguisher, hitting the back of Nephew One's shoulders. The man lunged forward. Nisba stuck her foot out, sweeping his feet out from underneath him. There was a loud crash as he hit the floor, his phone clattering against the wall. Raj turned him over, placing his foot on the man's throat, gesturing for him to be quiet.

Raj then crouched down and punched him on the jaw,

knocking him out. Shazmina secured his wrists and ankles with the cable-ties. Then, she and Nisba grabbed his feet and dragged him behind the sofa, out of view.

The assault had been noisy. They braced themselves for more Nephews to appear.

None came.

The three of them crept toward the doorway of the office harbouring Igor and the remaining Nephew. The adrenaline was pumping so hard, it was affecting Nisba's vision. Things seemed slightly blurred. Suddenly, she recalled episodes of a cartoon from her early childhood, where all the characters peered tentatively around a door, one at a time; one head above the other. That's how she saw, herself, Raj and Shazmina now. She had to shake it off, otherwise it was going to make her laugh.

Raj was on one side of the door, Nisba and Shazmina on the other, each armed with their fire extinguishers.

They heard Nephew Two shouting into his phone in Russian from inside the office.

'Where the fuck are you?' he screamed.

'Can you all hear me?...This is Ben. Nephew Two is now coming out...counting you down!...three, two, one…'

The door was flung open.

A frenzy of foam, water spray and powder filled the doorway, billowing up into the man's face, to the extent that they were no longer able to see their target.

Nephew Two was blinded temporarily; shrieking, flailing his arms about and choking on the substances in his lungs. He lost his footing, thanks to Nisba and Shazmina's low tackle to each knee.

He fell backwards, bumping his head on Igor's desk on the way down. There was a cry of pain as he landed heavily, his arms thrown back.

Raj trod on the man's hand as he retrieved the pistol which had slid under the desk.

Shazmina pulled out another handful of cable ties from her hi-vis jacket pocket.

The man attempted to sit up to stop her, but Raj pushed him back down, resting his foot on his chest.

Despite the coating of powder and foam, Raj was pretty sure it was one of the Nephews he'd see on the video Igor had taken at the party; one of the pair who had been tasked to get Nisba when she hid in the woodpile.

She wasn't interested. Nisba had stepped over the Nephew to reach Igor, who was tied to his office chair.

Igor hadn't moved or reacted to any of the preceding action, despite having been sprayed with water and dusted with powder.

Raj moved forward to help Nisba to untie him, but she held out her hand to keep him away.

'He's shell-shocked Raj. Be careful,' she whispered. 'Best keep back and give him some time. We don't know what they've said to him…or done to him.' She recalled the photos that Irina had taken, to bait him.

Raj swallowed. He didn't know what to do. He was scared of his friend's incapacity. He found it shocking, and sad.

'We need to get out of here, Nisba, and try to recover the plan. We can't hang about,' he said.

Raj had forgotten all about Ben who was still on the line.

'How is he?' Ben asked.

'I think he'll be OK. How's it looking out there?'

'Quiet. But we've rattled Ulvi's cage. He's on his way with two men heading towards Igor's house. You absolutely have to get there before Ulvi does.'

'Right, this is it.' Raj clapped his hands, turning to Shazmina. She looked remarkably composed but Nisba now looked pale, weary, and desperate. Rag dragged his fingers through his hair.

'Nisba…you're gonna have to do something. Quick.'

'I know. Can you both leave the room for a sec?...Sorry…but I think it's the only way…'

Raj and Shazmina immediately turned to leave without question, dragging Nephew Two out into the corridor.

Nisba moved round to Igor on her hands and knees and then knelt up, turning the swivel chair round, so he was facing her.

'Hey, Sweetie Pie…it's me. Nisba. Can you hear me?'

Igor still looked vacant. But then his eyes slid to meet hers. He raised his hand as if it were very heavy and held it to her face. It crossed her mind for a nano-second that he might unintentionally hurt her.

'Nisba.' His lips moved, but no sound came out.

'Yes, Honeybun, it's me.'

He began to whisper something under his breath, but she couldn't quite hear it properly. Putting her ear to his lips, she listened carefully. It was in Ukrainian. It was close enough to the Russian, for her to guess.

'I want to go home. I just want to go home.'

Nisba nodded and rubbed his knees. Her eyes prickled with tears. He leaned forward and rested his head on hers.

'We have to get you out…right now, OK? Can you understand me?'

'Yes,' he replied quietly, in English.

'Do you remember the plan?'

'Yes…I'm alright. I'll be alright.'

'Now. We have to go. Right now, Igor.'

He stood up suddenly but then had to steady himself, resting the tips of his fingers on the desk.

'You're doing great Igor…really great.'

Nisba took his hand.

He pulled her back and buried his hands in her hair and attempted to rub the dried blood from her top lip, with his thumb.

'Who did this to you?'

'Not now, Igor.. later… and it'll grow back. Please. Do come. Now!'

Igor took her hand, as they began to run down the corridor.

***

They stumbled outside onto the gravel to find an angry man sitting on the grass by the trees, nursing his right foot. Right bare foot, Nisba noted.

Igor and Nisba exchanged glances.

The man looked up and started to shout, swearing and wagging his finger at Shazmina.

'That's your handywork I take it,' called out Raj.

They ran past her Nexia.

The event was coming to a close with only a few people remaining on the other side of the field, clearing up their stands.

They skidded to a halt.

Both Raj and Igor's vehicles were blocked in by a large truck, deliberately parked an inch away from their front bumpers.

'Mine's a mile down the road,' said Nisba breathlessly, dismayed. She was pretty sure she'd told them not to park in their own spaces.

Raj threw up his hands.

'This way,' shouted Shazmina, running back in the direction they'd just come.

She pulled out a key fob. There was a thud sound as the central locking of her little grey hatchback was released.

It was just typical. The one time she had to give someone a lift, it had to be the man of her dreams as well as her boss, and when her car was a complete tip.

'I'm very sorry,' she groaned, frantically pulling the front seat forward, throwing all her stuff over the top of the back seats into the boot. 'It's such a mess.'

'It's fine…really Shazmina. Don't worry about it,' assured Nisba, thinking of her own infinitely worse car state back home.

It was a three-door. Nisba slid into the back seat pulling something out of the footwell to give her feet room. She placed it on her knee. Raj climbed in beside her. The front seat fell back with a bang.

This left Igor outside, negotiating how to fit himself in.

'I slide it back,' said Shazmina leaning over from the driver's seat, to aid Igor's ability to get his feet into the front footwell after his backside sank into the seat. Even with the seat right back, squashing Raj, Igor's knees were jammed up against the glove compartment.

Igor had to bend his head forward to avoid hitting the headlining. Hunching his shoulders, he gripped the strap above him.

'OK. Are we all in?' Shazmina called out.

It was an affirmative all round.

Shazmina scrunched the gears and made two attempts at a three-point turn. Unaccustomed to passengers, she was suffering from stage fright.

'Would you like me to drive?' asked Raj.

Shazmina glared at him via her rear-view mirror.

'Sorry...that was out of order.' He held up his hands.

Igor had turned to look to his right out of the window. Nisba could see his eyes creasing with a smile. He looked behind him out of the corner of his eye, aware of Nisba grinning.

It was a relief for Nisba to see that Igor was back to his usual self.

'Get down everyone,' Shazmina shouted as she approached the exit, where a parking attendant was still on duty.

Igor had nowhere to go except sideways.

Shazmina wound the window down.

'Thank you!' she shouted to the man, with a big smile, to distract him from her cargo.

The man nodded and waved her on.

For a few seconds, Shazmina was unable to change gear until Igor sat back up. She revved hard and then once they were available, went up through her gears like a racing driver.

'You should have put me in the trunk,' said Igor.

'You wouldn't fit in trunk,' Shazmina replied.

Too much shit in trunk, Raj was going to say but refrained.

The car had an issue with the transmission from second to third gear. Excessive acceleration was required, in order to jump from second to fourth or second to fifth. She'd mastered the art.

The road was clear, so Shazmina put her foot down.

For about fifteen minutes, Raj began to take them through the plan again, of what to do, when they arrived at the house, each checking in that they were still clear on their roles.

'Umm...that was the turn to the house,' said Igor gently.

'Oh No! I was going too fast'

'I didn't give you enough warning.'

'Over there, Shazmina,' said Raj, pointing ahead. 'Do a three-point turn in that gateway.'

'It will take too long,' she said, under her breath and suddenly swerved to the extreme right, stamped on the clutch, yanked up the handbrake as hard as she could and cranked the steering wheel hard left. There was a gasp from her passengers, as they clung on to the straps.

The car spun around 180 degrees.

She let off the handbrake, engaged first gear and proceeded to drive on, toward the turning she'd missed.

'Fuck me, Shazmina. That was impressive,' said Raj. 'When did you learn how to do that?'

'I never tried before,' she answered, sweeping the hair out of her eyes with her left hand.

The suspension was taking a pounding. Every now and again they could hear the rub of the wheel arch against the right front tyre.

She scrunched down through the gears to take the turn.

'OK, Igor. How do we get to your house in tin can?'

Once they were a bit nearer, Igor pointed up a grassy bank. 'Do you think it can get up there?'

She stuck her head out of the window to assess the terrain.

'No, we get out and run.'

***

They didn't enter the house, but ran straight round the back, to the entrance of the woods, past Misha, where they came to a halt.

They heard the flutter of birds and the clattering call of a stork.

Yuri's signal.

'This is where you leave me,' said Igor, his head down and hands on his hips, catching his breath. He would remain behind, to lure their pursuers to the planned location.

There was a momentary flash of panic on his friends' faces. A prolonged hesitation.

Nisba put her hand to her chest.

Igor grabbed her, giving her a tight, full body bear hug and whispered in her ear. Nisba stifled a sob. Igor then let her go.

He turned to Raj. They hugged, backslapping a couple of times. When released, Raj had to cough, jamming his fist to his lips, as he turned away.

Igor looked to Shazmina who already had her arms open, her eyes wide with fear. He was very gentle. He thought he might break her in some way, if she received the same treatment as the others.

There was another clatter of bird call.

Hurry up!

Raj touched Nisba's arm and nodded with a hopeful smile, taking her hand. Shazmina took the other. They turned and ran through the woods. All they could hear was the rushing of wind and Nisba's sobbing coughs, until they emerged and scrunched onto the shingled shoreline of the lake.

The wide, bright openness was a shock to the eye. The air was suddenly fresh and full of ozone, compared to the musty smell of soil and the mossy darkness of the woods. The craggy drama of the snow topped mountains in the near distance took a moment to compute.

Raj and Shazmina were now to take up their positions of safety. No-one was to be exposed, unless deemed absolutely necessary.

Observing Nisba adrift, distraught, without discussion, Shazmina and Raj deemed it absolutely necessary. They would stay with her.

Their attention was piqued by thudding and snapping sounds. Running. Igor appeared out of the darkness of the woods, much sooner than expected.

Nisba gave a little cry of joy and relief.

Igor held up his hand, showing two fingers and thumb to Yuri and Vlod, the invisible team dug in on either side of the lake.

Three antagonists. This was fewer than they expected. One would be Ulvi.

Nisba, Igor, Raj and Shazmina hugged the tree line.

Three men suddenly ran out, past them. Their speed and momentum took them right up to the water's edge, skidding to a halt.

By the look of it, the lake had come as a complete surprise to them.

The two men, who stood on either side of Ulvi, were carrying revolvers.

Nisba and Igor, apart from holding each other's hand very tightly, were empty handed.

Igor turned to Nisba to stroke her face with his free hand and kissed her, whispering to her. Nisba looked up at him, their noses touching.

Ulvi cleared his throat provocatively, throwing up his hands in frustration.

'What the fuck is this? Do I not have your attention? If not... how about I get it.'

The man to his right, young, about nineteen or twenty, stepped forward, rather enjoying his role as the hard man.

This was clearly his first day on the job, Nisba thought, making him all the more dangerous. He removed the safety catch from his revolver, gratified with the effect.

'Right. To business,' Ulvi shouted, strident, almost screaming the words.

He looked different. Like someone else. No beard. Clean shaven, with a close, faded haircut, in jeans and a designer label white polo shirt.

Ulvi was displaying an effort of calm, to suppress his anger, spluttering his words, in a measured and brutal way.

'Give. Me. My. Fucking. Money!'

His face was distorted by the blood that had rushed to his head, making his skin appear bluish red and swollen. The whites of his eyes were pink with rage and his lips were spattered with foaming spit.

He paced back and forth about three feet from Igor, his lips pursed, looking in turn at Nisba then to Igor. Nisba shrugged and exhaled impatiently.

Infuriated by this dismissal, his apoplexy stoked, seeking an outlet.

'You…fucking Muslim cunt…Jew bitch whore!'

Nisba acknowledged this with an assessing nod.

'I was expecting something a bit more…you know – imaginative, from you, Ulvi.' She began to walk towards him, leaving Igor behind, who failed to catch hold of her.

'Fucking freak. Keep your spastic brain away from me,' Ulvi yelled.

'Hmm. Now we're getting somewhere,' she replied through gritted teeth.

Ulvi was momentarily distracted by two figures appearing out of the woods. One in a hurry, the other being dragged along. They were screeching and shouting, in Portuguese.

Miguel had a woman by the hair. Her long blonde ponytail was wound round his hand, the other, grasping the waistband of her very tight white jeans.

Nisba noticed red thong knickers underneath, showing as pink, through the material.

Miguel presented his trophy.

Portuguese Tart.

She wrestled round and spat at him.

Ulvi did not react to his wife's predicament, turning away from her, back to Igor.

The A-Team couldn't guarantee she would be leverage but had nothing to lose. This didn't change anything.

The woman began to shriek with outrage, which still did not invoke any further response from her husband.

'Give me my fucking money, or I'll kill your whore freak,' Ulvi enunciated, walking up to Igor, almost touching him, immediately sensing his loss of impact. He became diminutive, as Igor towered over him.

Igor raised his hand showing his span, all ten inches of it, holding it towards Ulvi's throat. He didn't need to offer any warning, or explanation of what he could be capable of.

Ulvi stepped back suddenly, turning to his two heavies.

Igor took Nisba into his arms to protect her, turning his back on Ulvi and the two men.

'If not her…then…let's see now…' Ulvi signalled to his heavy to point the gun at Miguel, who was still gripping the squirming woman.

A look of shock and panic crossed Miguel's face. He braced himself. Despite the warnings from his teammates, he hadn't been prepared for this. His prey was shouting expletives, still flailing her arms, her hands now formed into fists, attempting to make contact. Miguel was conflicted. Should he be an equal scumbag to Ulvi and use her as a shield – position her in the firing line? But maybe this wouldn't deter Ulvi, he thought, facing the possibility this could be the last thing he would ever do.

As soon as the young heavy had lifted his arm and taken aim, there was shouting from the other man – screaming at him; terrified.

Ulvi spun round.

'What the…what the fuck is the matter with you?'

He then spotted the red laser sight, set on the younger man's forehead.

Ulvi's other heavy, much older and unfit looking, dropped his weapon and held his hands up momentarily. He then ran, stumbling on the shingle, almost falling over, as he hurtled back towards the woods.

'Fucking coward,' screamed Ulvi after him. 'Ha!' He turned back towards his prey. 'Do you think I'm going to fall for that trick? It worked well on you though, didn't it?' mocked Ulvi, waving at Igor. 'The little laser light. I had a lot of fun with that,' he laughed.

Igor had turned back to face Ulvi, releasing Nisba from his embrace. Igor raised his eyebrows and placed his hands on his hips. Igor seemed to have increased in size, presence, and menace. He had rolled up his sleeves.

The tattoo did not go unnoticed by Ulvi's remaining companion, who now appeared to be losing his nerve, fearing what forces they might be up against. The hand holding the gun, now dangled by his side, jittering. He was considering his options.

Ulvi stomped up to the young man.

'Give me that,' he snarled, snatching the gun out of his hand, swinging it in the direction of Igor.

There was a muffled crack and whipping, whistling sound. A shot.

It echoed across the lake.

Ulvi fell backwards, the gun dropping out of his hand. He landed hard on the shingle.

Igor heard a sharp cry as Nisba crumpled in his arms, sinking into a heap onto the ground at his feet.

Ulvi stirred. Groaning, winded for a moment, he clutched his wrist, attempting to scramble back up.

Raj came running over. He placed his foot on Ulvi's chest, forcing him back down.

There was a mournful wail coming from Igor, who was now kneeling on the ground, clutching Nisba's lifeless body to his chest. Her head had flopped back. Face, white, blood dripping from her earlobe, into her hair.

'Nemaye. Nemaye. No, No!' They had come so far, so close.

Despair, guilt, grief. The burden. It was too heavy. This was not a reality he could accept.

He could not live with it.

He would not live with it.

With Nisba's body, still held tightly under one arm, he scrabbled and stretched to reach for the revolver a couple of feet away. His fingers were fully extended, stretching until he could almost, very nearly touch it. With another heave of his body, he finally had a purchase on the handle, turning the gun on himself.

His head was then suddenly full of screaming, screeching, shouting and shingle scattering.

He found himself on his back – in pain, with Raj's knees on either side of his chest, his wrists pinned down onto the sharp stones above his head.

Igor, breathless and bewildered looked to his right, hearing Yuri's boots crunching their way towards him.

Raj sat back onto Igor's stomach, swearing to himself, emptying the revolver of its bullets, which bounced and rolled off Igor's chest. Raj then slid off him, gasping with relief, taking a moment on the ground to recover.

Yuri bent down to Igor.

'Sorry about that mate,' he quipped, in Ukrainian. 'She was half a centimetre too far over.'

Igor's brain had not quite made sense of the previous few seconds. Whilst still processing it, his body scrambled up to kill him, his hands reaching out for Yuri's neck.

Yuri laughed.

'Oh, come on Max. I didn't mean to scare you,' he exclaimed, stepping backward and gripping Igor's wrists to take the pressure off his throat. 'Give her a slap and she'll be fine. I only clipped her.'

Igor's face froze in horror, looking at his hands and what they were about to do.

He dropped to his knees, placing a finger on the pulse in Nisba's neck. He croaked and patted her face repeatedly.

Shazmina grabbed hold of Nisba's feet, raising them above the level of her head.

'She faints,' Shazmina whispered to Yuri, who had begun to look worried.

Igor looked desperate. 'And she's pregnant.'

Yuri along with Vlod, who had now appeared out from the trees, showed dismay and joy in turn.

Then there came a little voice from the ground.

Igor scrambled astride Nisba on the ground, peering into her face.

'It's me – Igor,' he whispered.

'Prince Igor,' she whispered back, reaching up to his face.

'Yes, that's right…that's me.'

***

'Bloody typical,' said Nisba, brushing the dirt from her sleeves. 'What did I miss?'

There was a distant moan and wail of police sirens.

She scrunched across the shingle, supported by Igor, toward Raj and the others, who were all looking down, regarding Ulvi. He lay squirming on the ground, breathing heavily through his nose, his top lip curling back.

Igor stepped forward to take a look, barely recognising him. A stranger. Hideous.

'Ha! Don't you want to know why?' Ulvi asked, smirking.

Igor didn't move. His face didn't move.

'It was so fucking easy! There for the taking. Fucking rich people. You didn't even notice! And what a soft target your sister was.' He laughed, enjoying his mirth. 'For all those brains! Pathetic. Women just love to hear bullshit, don't they?'

Igor winced. His nostrils flared. He would not be goaded and held his hands back to prevent any reaction from his friends.

Disappointed by the lack of response, Ulvi continued.

'Why?...' Ulvi sneered, shaking off Vlod's grip, as he tried to sit up. 'Why couldn't you just fucking die, like you were supposed to? It was perfect. A fucking war. And you hellbent on signing up,' he spluttered, staring at Igor.

Igor blinked and took a step back, as if he had been pushed.

Nisba hurled herself in front of him and stood up on her tiptoes slapping her hands over his ears. 'Don't listen to him, Igor. Don't listen!'

'..You should have been killed like all those others…but you had to survive and ruin…fucking Everything.'

'Stop him,' shrieked Nisba.

Before she'd finished her words, Vlod had grabbed Ulvi, holding him in a headlock, his free hand covering Ulvi's nose and mouth.

Ulvi began to scrabble the shingle with his feet, clawing at Vlod's arm. His face was beginning to bulge and panic as the oxygen slowly depleted. Vlod looked about him, unmoved. No facial expression.

The group looked on, watching Ulvi convulsing, wondering if Vlod would let go, knowing that he probably wouldn't.

Igor reached down, laying a huge hand on Vlod's slight shoulder.

'That's enough.'

Vlod dropped his load, which hit the pebbles.

Ulvi remained quiet, nursing his neck and the back of his head.

'Huh. You're never more than two metres away from a rat,' said Raj giving Ulvi's foot a kick. 'Isn't that right Nisba?' He turned, giving her a crooked smile. She gave him a weak one in return, still recovering from Ulvi's tirade.

'I'm sorry, Raj.'

'Listen...I was a dick. We're way past that now though, aren't we?'

'We most certainly are.' Nisba nodded, vigorously, then winced as she touched her left ear. The cartilage had been nicked by Yuri's bullet and was now starting to throb. Her hand and neck were sticky with congealing blood.

Then she remembered her hair.

'Oh,' she said sadly, lightly touching her chopped locks.

'I fix it, for you,' said a voice next to her in English, with a strong Uzbek accent.

Nisba looked up in surprise at Rustam, who was assessing her. She blinked several times. He laughed at her reaction.

Igor touched her arm.

'Rustam was a professional hairdresser. Then he retrained – as a nurse. He's Lev Shulkin's carer.'

Nisba's mouth dropped open.

'I only learned that this morning.' Igor looked down at his shoes, ashamed, humbled, and regretful.

Nisba wiped her forehead. Things were just not how they appeared to be. She'd got so many things wrong, feeling the need to punish herself.

She felt a sudden and strong urge to lie down and curl up into ball. The faint felt like it had drained all the blood from her body. Her eye sockets ached and her head felt thick and heavy.

'Dr Saparov has just arrived,' called Raj, waving his phone. He beckoned Nisba.

At that moment, six policemen strode out from the darkness of the woods, accompanied by Ben Shulkin, who was doing his best to keep up. They included the two officers from the Parkent police station.

Ben shuffled up to Raj.

'I got them all out,' Ben whispered. 'And I have plenty of incriminating footage from legitimate devices.'

Raj nodded discreetly.

'I recommend that you...none of you play it back...any of it.' Ben looked at him earnestly. 'It will take a while to get it all out of my head.'

Ben grasped Raj's arm for a second. Raj then watched Ben limp slowly away, back toward the policemen.

Raj swallowed hard. He would save his feelings for later. His part of the plan had been fulfilled; to execute it without leaving a trace of criminal activity. There would be no proof of illegal surveillance within the winery.

Igor was entitled to have cameras all around his private property, including the lake.

There was no proof of any shots having been fired by any member of the A-Team.

Yuri had retrieved the shell casing and the bullet. They would find no trace of a sniper rifle, if indeed the police even considered it a line of enquiry.

The only evidence would be that of the revolvers in Ulvi's and his associates possession. Yuri had pre-empted Ulvi discharging his weapon by grazing his wrist.

Yuri hadn't missed. Contrary to what Hollywood would have you believe, he had said to the group the night before, it is not possible to safely fire a gun out of a man's hand to prevent them from shooting someone. His tactic was to minimally wound, if he had to, diverting any potential threat. He considered his mission a successful one, albeit with a minor unplanned, but non-fatal consequence.

***

It was 10.15 pm by the time the police left. They had been there nine hours.

There would be a necessity for the A-Team members to provide further information in the coming days, but Nisba had to provide her full statement there and then, as her visa required her to leave the country within the next twenty four hours.

She was confined to the bedroom, away from the others to be interviewed by two officers, accompanied by Doctor Saparov who insisted on checking her over first.

The wallchart had been pulled down that morning and bundled away, down the back of the log store, to be retrieved for future reference, if necessary, or burned.

The line was, they were dealing internally with the theft of their payroll fund, following company policy. They were considering the step of reporting it to the police on Monday but were set upon, at the event. All true, Raj had said.

Igor's firearms, although licensed and legally held, had been relegated to a safe, in one of the outbuildings.

After giving her statement, Nisba perched on the edge of the sofa, sipping camomile tea. She was so far beyond tired; her eyes were fixed in a stare and her heart was still pounding. Her stomach was rumbling, having had no food since the previous day, but the idea of eating anything made her feel sick.

Dr Saparov had given Igor some Lorazepam to help him relax and deal with the ensuing drama of the police tramping around his house and bombarding him and his friends with questions.

Dr Saparov was in a state of fury, with everyone. He spent some time muttering under his breath. Igor caught some of the words.

'Irresponsible. Crazy. Lunatics…'

Dr Saparov had given unequivocal instructions to the police, owing to Igor's PTSD, to postpone taking his statement and avoid putting him through prolonged questioning, until the following day.

Igor lay on the sofa behind Nisba, logging on to his laptop.

Despite needing rest and recuperation, he was still the CEO of a winery. He hadn't addressed any of his emails for two days.

'Ahh.'

Everyone looked up. He'd got everyone's attention.

'My visa for the UK– it's been approved.'

Nisba stood up gawping, clutching her chest.

Igor clambered off the sofa. They flung their arms around each other, hugging, jumping up and down, laughing like two small children.

Raj and Miguel exchanged glances. They were happy for their friend, their boss, but they were conflicted.

Uzbekistan had never been Raj's forever home. Unaccustomed to putting down roots, he had moved from country to country, project to project every two or three years. He'd been unsure how long he would be there and what would cause him to move on.

The time had come.

Igor's friendship was unconditional, he realised. His debt had never been called in, but he had felt compelled to pay it back in some way.

He was now free of this self-imposed burden. His friendship, now on equal terms, was better, more honest and deeper.

The future, which he'd never dared to contemplate before, was something he was now looking forward to; excited about even.

Raj looked across at Shazmina, his heart rate spiking.

He had been upset, overcome with regret, when he learned that she'd been into him since her first day at the winery, two years ago. So much lost time, he thought sadly, her having assumed she would be nothing to him. Ironic, he thought. For him, it had been a foregone conclusion, that he would be nothing to her, so never even bothered to look. Shame.

Raj shook his head.

He'd made a decision about a couple of things that afternoon. He'd given up the F-word and alcohol. He wished to clean up his act, to be worthy of such a f-amazing woman.

Raj stood up. There were things he needed to say to her. Properly. Now. She looked up, following him with her eyes. He leaned down and whispered, to ask her if she would like to join him outside.

Miguel was unsure what the future held.

If he was Igor, he'd stay in the UK to bring up his family, but what direction was the winery going to take? Would he even have a job? One thing was certain, he was not ready to go back to Angola. He had no one to go back to. Nothing, except bad memories.

He wondered what it could be, that would keep him in Uzbekistan, without Igor.

***

'Shall we join Raj and Shazmina, in the garden?' asked Igor, turning to Nisba. 'I need some air.'

Nisba nodded, making a move across the kitchen. The others began to pull out their chairs to follow, as she led the way to the open back door.

Nisba stopped abruptly in the doorway, placing a hand on each side of the doorframe, causing a pile-up in the small space of the utility room, behind her.

'Umm. Let's give them a minute,' she said, looking back over her shoulder. She turned to usher the group back into the kitchen.

'There is gonna be some Big Lovin' at Raj's tonight,' said Yuri in a loud whisper.

There was some gentle laughter.

It wasn't like that.

She'd spotted Raj – seated, Shazmina standing. He had his arms wrapped tightly around her waist; his face buried in her chest. Her head rested on his, as she stroked his neck, holding him equally tightly.

They were crying. Proper crying, trying to say things to each other.

This show of vulnerability on Raj's part was for Shazmina and Shazmina alone.

Nisba would officially unsee it. Never speak of it.

It was hard not to think about, not react to.

Nisba felt a lump form in her throat.

Something very special had occurred between the two of them today.

***

The group picked up where they had left off, taking their seats at the table, resuming their conversation and game of Patience.

Nisba was wondering about Mila and knew Igor was thinking the same thing. Unfortunately, circumstances meant that he could not be with her or warn her. So, she was unprepared, when the police had come knocking, to deliver the news, that her husband had been arrested and was in police custody. The arrest was made, based on the suspicion of conspiracy to defraud. It transpired that Ulvi – not his real name, was also wanted in three other countries for similar offences, including a murder investigation in Angola.

Sultan Bekov, the former site manager had been found, bound and gagged in the basement of his home, for attempting to resist coercion into using the winery funds and providing sensitive information for Ulvi. He had been threatened into purchasing the equipment that had led to him being fired by Raj. It was this equipment that had monitored Shazmina's system access. Sultan was not voluntarily complicit, unlike his half-brother, Dav.

They had also arrested six Nephews, as well as Barefoot Man and Portuguese Tart.

Shazmina had been anxious about an assault charge. Her behaviour could in no way be construed as self-defence, she'd said. Raj had reassured her that it would be a colossal irony if terrorists felt it expedient to press charges for being smacked around the head with a plank and being relieved of their shoes and socks. It would go away. She wasn't to worry about it.

Dav Uzmanov had not returned from Vietnam. Untraceable.

They were not sure what happened to Irina – or the money.

***

Nisba had commenced her self-punishment.

She was supposed to see things other people couldn't, so considered herself a failure, especially when it dawned on her, that Misha had told them who it was. Misha had tried so hard to tell them, but they had ignored her.

Misha could see Ulvi for what he was and she had died for it.

Nisba cried for some minutes over this. It would take time to come to terms with.

The other thing gnawing at her, was the landslide. It had also crossed Igor's mind, the possibility, that it had not been entirely a natural disaster.

Igor had noticed that one of Ulvi's gunmen at the lake wore a fleece with a mining company logo embroidered on the pocket.

Igor cast his mind back thirty days, trying to recall the sounds, the sights – it had all happened so fast. Could it have been an explosion, or the aftershock of a tremor?

They decided to opt for Act of God. It was more romantic.

Igor played back the conversation with Ulvi, the one by the pool. How different the meaning was now, to everything Ulvi had said.

In the meantime, Zeinab had texted to inform Igor that she had to report to the police station in the morning but was keen to come over to the house that night to see everyone. She had a bad case of *FOMO*. It would be her first outing without her wheelchair.

The ensuing silence from Mila was making Igor nervous. He should call. Enquire. She hadn't called or texted as expected.

He began to think about going to the house when the lights came on outside.

She was at the door.

Out of habit, they had kept it locked. Raj peered through the glass, turned the key and swung it open.

Miguel shot up out of his chair.

The air was still. Silent. Except for the ting, ting, ting of the kitchen tap splashing off a saucepan in the sink.

Mila surveyed the group for a second and caught Miguel's eye, showing a flash of recognition and surprise. He sat back down. Amazed, bewildered. Guilty. For some of the thoughts he'd had about his best friend's sister.

She was his sister!

He held his head in his hands in shame.

Igor sat up.

Mila seemed different. Looked different, he thought.

Igor slowly arose and walked over to her, not knowing what to say.

They stood facing each other for several seconds and then hugged. Tight and long.

The others began to slowly file quietly out, toward the back door, to sit outside.

Nisba attempted the same, but they had disengaged from their embrace. Mila caught her trying to leave.

'Don't go Nisba,' Mila said, holding out her hand. 'Please,' she called to the others. 'None of you leave on my account.'

There was a hiatus, shuffling and bumping into each other, as the team members returned to their seats. They were quite a large group now, with the addition of Saparov and Ben. Raj and Shazmina had rejoined them on Mila's arrival.

'The children?' Igor whispered to Mila with wonder.

She held up a finger, smiled and walked back outside.

They waited.

'You can come in now,' they heard Mila call out, then slam the car door. She spoke in her perfect Oxford English.

Aziz and Alina were in their pyjamas. Cautiously, they edged through the doorway, using their mother as cover.

The quiet was suddenly broken.

'Miguel! There's Miguel,' shouted Aziz, in English, pointing at the same time as Alina called out; 'Mummy! Mummy! That's the man the bad people hurt.'

Aziz ran over to Miguel. Aziz had mastered the high five game. Alina grabbed Miguel round the legs.

'You saved him,' she gasped.

Miguel was rather enjoying this hero's welcome and the surprised but joyful reaction from the group.

Igor stood, one hand on his hip, the other rubbing the back of his head, eyebrows raised.

Miguel knelt down to respond to Alina. 'No…it wasn't me, in the end. This very brave woman,' he turned to Shazmina, 'she saved him.'

Alina was very impressed, particularly by Shazmina's hair.

'Was it because you love him?' Alina asked her, gravely.

Shazmina froze, her mouth open. There was laughter around the room. Shazmina blushed, defeated for a moment.

Alina had got her answer and looked like she was going to burst.

'We are team, friends…so we take care of each other,' responded Shazmina, looking around at the group members, who nodded in agreement.

Raj grinned. Good recovery, he thought, as Alina scrambled up onto his knee.

She examined the cut on his cheek and proceeded to prod it.

'Does that hurt?'

He laughed, taking her hand away, giving it a little squeeze.

***

There was a lull in the drama and noise as Mila took a seat at the big table. The only sound now came from the snug. Miguel was sitting on the floor, sprawled on beanbags with one child under each arm, quietly reading.

Once Mila was seated and facing them, no one knew quite how to behave. The group looked on, apprehensive, feeling bad for her.

'No pity please,' she commanded holding up her hand. She jutted out her chin and breathed in hard.

Raj poured her a glass of grape juice. Mila gave him a brief but grateful smile and then suddenly grasped the tumbler of brandy to her left and proceeded to knock it back. She shuddered as it hit home, banging the glass back down onto the table.

The group stared at her.

She laughed, sweeping her hair back. Her cheeks were pink, eyes sparkling.

'Thank you,' she said suddenly. 'Thank you for what you have done.'

There was a confused silence.

Nisba wasn't sure for a second if Mila was being sarcastic.

Igor broke the silence.

'I'm sorry Mila. That he's...'

'Gone?' Mila raised her eyebrows. Angry and laughing at the same time. 'Good!'

'But...the children?' attempted Igor, quietly.

'They hate him!'

There was a little gasp and then all heads slowly turned in the direction of the snug, watching the two little children, enthralled by their storyteller.

Nisba caught Igor's eye. His crows' feet started to crease. They both had the same thought.

But they love Miguel.

'And I hate him – whoever he was,' Mila added, through gritted teeth.

Her audience was stunned.

A wave of nausea crept over Nisba. She swallowed hard, to clamp down on the rush of saliva at the thought of what Mila's life may have really been like.

'So,' Mila continued. 'You've all done me, Alina and Aziz, a big favour.'

She picked up the tumbler and waved it around looking at the anxious faces.

'Would you like a top up, Mila?' asked Raj.

'Yes please,' she replied, without hesitation. Then Mila seemed unsure, examining the gold liquid, pushing the glass back and forth with her thumbs and middle fingers.

'You have all achieved something quite extraordinary,' she stated with a little smile. '...with your unique combination of skills.' Mila traced her finger around the cut glass pattern of the tumbler for a moment.

They group around her began to reanimate and with relief, breathe as normal.

Igor remained motionless, processing the uncharacteristic behaviour and his sister's words.

She was not bereft, heartbroken, or despairing, he thought.

And then he began to slowly remember what she was really like. Before. Before she'd met Ulvi. Igor began to nod and smile.

Yes. This was more like Mila. Understanding, kind and – fun. He would ask her.

'And how...how are you *feeling*...?'

'Fucking angry!'

They all laughed. Briefly.

'I have been… harsh, judgemental,' she continued, looking down at the glass, heaving her shoulders from a deep sigh. 'I was also afraid of your difficulties, Igor. I am sorry that I didn't talk to you about it and that I wasn't…available. I am very grateful to Raj and Yevgeny for looking out for you – taking care of you. I should have done a better job of that, otherwise…none of this...' She shook her head in disbelief. 'I don't know why we were unable to talk. You know, communicate...it's so important!'

Igor opened his mouth to speak, unsure where to begin. What to say. How to say it. He could tell that Mila hadn't finished. There was more she wanted to say, so he breathed in deeply and listened. She seemed uninhibited by the group of more or less strangers around her.

'You show me every day, that it is truly possible to start over. Build a new life – from nothing. And be brave, continuing to fight, despite the overwhelming burden you carry. I worry that you think I don't approve of you…your relationship, being so…whirlwind.' She waved a hand at Nisba, smiling at her. Her eyes then returned to Igor. 'But I admire you so very much for that.'

Mila swallowed hard.

She would let her defences down, all the way.

'I see hope and a future Igor, thanks to you. This is not going to break me. Us.' She waved a hand in the direction of her children.

She gave a little smile and examined the ceiling for several seconds, then turned to Nisba again.

'I never thought it possible to love a man so much, to do what you have done; so, I will remain optimistic.' The corner of her mouth turned up a little. She fought a smile.

'The challenges you face…I had no idea. I've learned a great deal from you, from you both. From what I've learned about all of you from Zeinab.' Mila waved her glass at the group again and then ran her other hand through her hair.

'I realise how important it is, to be kind. I will teach my children to always be kind. You just never know what people are living with, do you?'

Nisba's bottom lip started to wobble.

Mila looked up and examined the faces of each team member.

'And you are all so brave. The friendship you have…how hard you've worked together and what you risked, helping Igor…it's truly remarkable.'

Mila continued but changed to a brighter tone and looked toward the snug again.

'They're better off without him you know. He never wanted them. He had no interest in them whatsoever and when he did, he was belittling and cruel. Look at what he did to Alina's beautiful long hair; to spite her.' She shook her head, her eyebrows furrowing. 'I'm not worried though. They are clearly not short of positive role-models.' She grinned, acknowledging the room again.

Igor wiped tears from his eyes.

Nisba had started to feel overwhelmed by emotion. She was trying to control it, calm things down but then she suddenly had a thought. A bad thought.

'The house!' Nisba clapped her hand over her mouth. She'd forgotten her training for a moment, unable to stop the blurt.

She felt that she had to continue now with an explanation. 'He'll have sold the house.' Her hand was suppressing the beating of her heart and the accompanying adrenaline rush.

Mila turned calmly to Nisba.

'You are a very clever woman, Nisba...but then, so am I.' She grinned sheepishly, giving a little shrug. 'Well...' Mila looked down at her hands. 'Sometimes...not always.' She trailed off, looking wistful. 'I put some things in place to prevent that. I just didn't do enough...soon enough. I'll recoup as much of the losses as I can, Igor. I'll see to that.'

'But Nisba,' she resumed, more cheerfully, holding her hand up, disallowing Igor any chance to respond. 'You must rest and eliminate stress from your life. I did warn you...' She smiled pointing at Igor. 'But you seem to know what you're taking on.'

'Well Mila, I honestly think that works both ways,' replied Nisba. 'As you pointed out, I do have some stuff and I'm also a bit of a fuck-up.'

'You're not a fuck-up,' said Igor, in a loud whisper. 'You're just a bit...fucked up, that's all.'

He turned and gave Nisba a noisy kiss. The group laughed.

'But, we know we have to deal with it, properly. Take responsibility for it, and we are,' said Nisba. 'It's important – so we don't pass it on.'

At that moment, the outside lights flashed on. A vehicle scrunched up in front of the house.

There was a pause. And then they remembered. The danger was gone.

Zeinab limped very slowly in on crutches through the front door. The group cheered and chairs scraped the floor as the team stood up to greet her.

'You really have to do something about your driveway, Mr M. Anyone would think you didn't want visitors. I had to pay the taxi driver extra!'

She hobbled over toward the table, but Raj had leapt out of the office chair and wheeled it over.

'Thanks, Raj.'

He slowly trundled her to the table.

'Wow, Zeinab. We're so happy you could be here.' Nisba squeezed her hand.

'Well…Elias doesn't know I'm out.' She winked at Nisba. 'He's on a project for a couple of days with his new job.' Zeinab began to shift in her seat, fiddling with the levers. 'This is a great chair. I had one, just like this, in my office.'

Raj ruffled the back of his hair.

'In fact, it's so wonderful to have everyone here, in one room,' called out Nisba. 'I wonder,' she said, sounding a little more subdued, 'if this will ever happen again…all of us together, like this?'

She then suddenly felt the weight of impending Goodbyes.

'I think this calls for an A-Team group photo,' shouted Raj. 'C'mon Miguel, Alina, Aziz.' He clapped his hands a couple of times. 'Let's try and get ourselves organised quickly, otherwise it's going to be a f-riot.' He began to turn chairs outwards in front of the table. 'C'mon, hurry up people, because…Ben and Rustam have to get back.'

Ben had just received a call from the carer covering for Rustam. It wouldn't be long. His dad had rallied briefly but was now sinking fast.

Yuri, Vlod, Ben and Shazmina took their seats, sitting cross-legged on the table. Mila placed Alina on her knee, Zeinab, Dr Saparov and Miguel, (Aziz on his knee) were seated on the dining chairs. Igor and Rustam lay down on the floor at their feet, propped up on their elbows, with Nisba seated between them, one arm around each of their shoulders.

Raj had pulled out the armchair from the snug and balanced his camera on it. There were three attempts using the shutter release on timer.

The first: Raj, a blur, dashing back to his position next to Shazmina. The second, in position, but everyone with their eyes closed, and the third – no-one smiling, having suffered many minutes of smile fatigue.

One hundredth of a second caught all thirteen A-Team members for posterity, appearing fed up, like they didn't want to be there. Not at all capturing the mood of the moment.

Two Years Later

Tuesday 2nd February 2025

He sat at the farmhouse table, his back to the window facing into the bright wide-open space.

Igor loved coming back to Uzbekistan to the Prikat house for the holidays, enjoying the extensive work done on it for his rapidly growing family.

He'd refurbished the interior, repurposed rooms and had raised the roof, like he had always wanted. Yuri and Vlod spent six months with them to help.

They extended out the back and side, creating additional living quarters from the tumble-down outbuildings. The walls in the garden were restored, surrounding beautiful gardens with fruit trees. There was even a gate.

They used all the space. They needed it. For The A-Team Reunion. They were preparing for what would be their second.

Igor sat back in his chair, stretching his arms, reflecting. While he continued to work on his guilt and trauma, he was able to enjoy the deep sense of contentment he felt about how much his life had changed.

His phone, sitting on the table in front of him, suddenly lit up and began to buzz. He answered it, smiling.

'Hey, Zeinab, how's it going?'

'I apologise for intruding on your holiday, Mr M.' There was a pause. '…But you'll never guess what…'

The End

Glossary

ADHD: Attention Deficit Hyperactivity Disorder is marked by an ongoing pattern of inattention and/or hyperactivity-impulsivity that interferes with functioning or development. National Institute of Mental Health www.nimh.nih.gov

Baruch ata Adonai: Transliteration from Hebrew. Blessing (Judaism). Blessed are you our lord our g*d, king of the universe…'[who has commanded us to light the sabbath candles]

Challa: a special bread of Ashkenazi Jewish origin, usually braided and typically eaten on ceremonial occasions such as Shabbat and major Jewish festivals

Cheder: school for Jewish children where Hebrew and religious knowledge are taught

Chervona Ruta: a popular Ukrainian song written by Volodymyr Ivasyuk in 1968 and performed by many singers. It is named after a mythological flower, the Chervona Ruta, which if found turning a red colour by a young girl, was meant to bring happiness in love.

Dyadya: Transliteration from Ukrainian - uncle

Doppi: a small traditional Uzbek hat worn by Muslim men

EBITDA: Acronym - Earnings before interest, taxes, depreciation and amortization

FOMO: Acronym – Fear of Missing Out

Gajo: Angolan Portuguese slang – guy

G'mar Chatimah Tovah: Hebrew - A good final sealing is the traditional Hebrew greeting said before (and on) Yom Kippur, the holiest day of the Jewish year and the culmination of the High Holiday season.

G'mar Tov: is also said but often the reply to the above, translates as 'a good seal.' Those observing the holiday believe that the book of life, which determines an individual's fate for the coming year, opens on Rosh Hashanah, and is sealed at the end of Yom Kippur.

HUS: Haemolytic Uremic Syndrome, a rare but serious disease that affects the kidneys and blood clotting often a complication of diarrhoea based infections, most frequently caused by E. coli

Ippodrom: Uzbek. Shopping centre

Kippah: a skull cap worn by orthodox Jewish men and worn by non-orthodox Jewish men whilst attending Synagogue and Jewish festivities. Sometimes also worn by women in progressive/reform Synagogues

Maghrebi: the term commonly applied to Algerian, Moroccan, and Libyan Jews. These communities have shared histories such as their Arabic-speaking background and expulsion from Arab and Muslim countries in the mid-20th century

Matzo Balls: a traditional Jewish small dumpling made from seasoned matzo meal. This is bound together with egg and chicken fat. Usual served in chicken soup.

Non Kabob: a Central Asian variation of Kebab. A dish of grilled meat often served on skewers

Pau grande: Angolan Portuguese slang - big dick

Randall and Hopkirk (Deceased): 1969. A British private detective television series

Salaam alaikum: Arabic. Peace be unto you

Salom: Uzbek, informal – hello

Samsa: *Central Asian Samosa*

Shabbat Shalom: Hebrew - Sabbath Peace

Wa Alaikum assalam: Arabic. And peace be unto you [also]

Yom Kippur: Day of Atonement is the holiest day of the year in Judaism. It occurs annually on the 10th of Tishrei (seventh month of the Hebrew calendar), corresponding to a date in late September or early October.

References

1) **The First Time Ever I Saw Your Face:** 1957 folk song written by British political singer-songwriter Ewan MacColl and covered by several artists thereafter.

2) **Swallows and Amazons:** Novel. 1930 by Arthur Ransome.

3) **Pirates of the Caribbean** - The Curse of the Black Pearl. Film. 2003. Directed by Gore Verbinski.

4) **Die Hard:** Film. 1988. Director John McTiernan.

5) **Wizard of Oz.** Film. 1939. Director Victor Fleming.

Acknowledgements

With thanks to:
Eleanor Doyle, Dr D. Keogh, Dr J. Keogh-Bennett, Galina Ratcliffe, Naiyla Khaled, Paul B Cohen, Sara Smith, Helen Conway, Domingos Mucuanha, Sharon Garner, Jo Bunker, Ella Mayfield and Fiona Brewin.

www.ingramcontent.com/pod-product-compliance
Ingram Content Group UK Ltd.
Pitfield, Milton Keynes, MK11 3LW, UK
UKHW020817230425
5580UKWH00023B/878